VA-VA-VOOM

RED-HOT LESBIAN EROTICA

EDITED BY ASTRID FOX

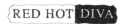

First published 2004 by Red Hot Diva Books,
an imprint of Millivres Prowler Limited,
part of the Millivres Prowler Group,
Unit M, Spectrum House, 32–34 Gordon House Road,
London NW5 1LP UK

www.divamag.co.uk
www.divamailorder.com

'Angelica' by Astrid Fox is taken from her collection *The Fox Tales* (Red Hot Diva, 2002), reproduced by kind permission of Millivres Prowler Ltd.
'E:volution' by Sunny Dermott was originally published in the *Fiction Firm* short-story collection (ed. Jake Arnott) for Cumbria County Council in 2002.
'In and Out of Time' by Shameem Kabir was originally published in a longer form as the title story in *In and Out of Time* (ed. Patricia Duncker) for Onlywomen Press in 1990 and is reproduced here by kind permission of Lilian Mohin.
'Sound Check' by Scarlett French first appeared in *Best Lesbian Erotica 2005* (ed. Tristan Taormino), published by Cleis Press in November 2004.

A CIP catalogue record for this book is available from the British Library

ISBN 1-873741-95-2

Printed and bound in Finland by WS Bookwell

Distributed in the UK and Europe by Airlift Book Company,
8 The Arena, Mollison Avenue,
Enfield, Middlesex EN3 7NJ
Telephone: 020 8804 0400
Distributed in North America by Consortium,
1045 Westgate Drive, St Paul, MN 55114-1065
Telephone: 1 800 283 3572
Distributed in Australia by Bulldog Books,
PO Box 300, Beaconsfield, NSW 2014

Introduction

Like Alice's Wonderland biscuits, I always think anthology introductions should come labelled: DON'T READ ME FIRST. Reading a synopsis or a *précis* first is like glueing your nose to a TV guide, sniffing out summaries so as to watch films or programmes after you're already well acquainted with the plots. I tend to read short-story collections consecutively (I suspect I buck the norm). I like themes to materialise slowly as I read tale after tale, and guess at the editor's intentions. For orderly readers like me, an introduction gives too much away. For disorderly readers (probably much more fun!), the editor's sequencing is lost anyway, which allows the reader to seek out their own themes or chaos – and an intro is equally pointless.

So why is this an introduction and not an afterword? Restrictions of format and house style. Please consider it an afterword.

DON'T READ ME FIRST.

For disobedient souls and those who've already ingested the contents, let me now tell you a bit more about these saucy and very interesting pieces.

The first half-dozen or so stories, with a couple of exceptions, are raw and immediate. This type of writing style, in the context of literary fiction, is often described as gritty but, when it comes to sex writing, is more likely to be considered "pornographic" than "erotic". I like the old adage that "erotica is the rich man's pornography", and therefore I am taking the liberty of jettisoning the whole tired porn/erotica argument because I feel the distinction is frequently an issue of class. I also suspect that this distinction is often due to the fact that "gritty" stories such as these are written in the first person (as if distance to a reader makes a piece more classy – "Hey, it's not me doing it, it's someone else – therefore it's okay!").

In this edgy and brave category, please find Fiona Zedde's moody, lovely and still snappy "Fast", Wynona B. Verr's wisecracking "Eat the Beat", Charlotte Cooper's hot and fantastical "Jerk", and the post-modern porn story "Tongue Deep" (by Linda Innes), a tale whose tongue is deep in many things, including cheek.

There are two additional works near the beginning of the book that have a rough, street feel: Louise Carolin's "Calendar Girls" and Kathi Kosmider's "Svetlana". In both of these pieces there is also a sense of reminscence, of afterthought if not quite nostalgia. Both beautifully written, they lead us evocatively into three strong and moving stories about memory and desire: "Don't Slip Away" by Helen Sandler, "Lamaze" by Monica Trasandes and Rachel Kramer Bussel's "Memories". There is both sorrow and sensuality in these works: I do not feel that the two are mutually exclusive. Another notable piece, found far later in the this collection, is the wistful, open-ended excerpt from a piece by Shameem Kabir entitled "In and Out of Time".

Like life, the past comes first in this collection, and then the future (Kabir's contribution excepted). Do you remember the first time? What follows remembrance are four works that examine newness, freshness, beginnings: "Labour", a poem by Rita Das on Love's (and Lovemaking's) birthing process, "The Ride" by Elena Moya Pereira, "Clean Slate" by Yvonne Dale and "The Path" by Helen Taylor. Even though many of the characters in these pieces start out jaded, they end up hopeful. (Note: for non-cynical diehard romantics, there are heart-stoppingly gorgeous pieces about long-term love sprinkled throughout this book – "Come and Join the Dance" by Fiona Cooper, "Cuvée Opulence" by Cherry Smyth, "Sound Check" by Scarlett French and "My Forever Girl" by Crin Claxton – and equally moving what-could-be-love sex stories such as "Cecily and the Boy" by Winsome Lindsay and "Front-Page Girl" by Tanya Dolan.)

Indeed, the heroine of "The Path" starts out in cloudy claustrophobia and fantasises nature all around her, an optimistic-despite-itself story which segues into two pagan (no other word is appropriate) pieces: my own "Angelica" and the imaginative "Moon Wood" by Julie Travis. Frances Gapper's tale of adolescent longing,

"Wanting It", reflects this same sense of rivers and forest, space and sky, and is followed by another brief piece, short yet filling (in every sense): "Kneading" by Ginger Allen.

Our wings thus spread, the whole world opening up, we really take to the sky and stars with three stunning tales that could all be published easily as fine SF stories in their own right, but are probably a bit too juicy for your average non-porn SF editor: "Venus as a Boy" by Ape McCabe, "Pac-Girl" by Robyn Vinten and "Dream of Shadow, Shadow of Love" by Larry Tritten.

Then we get down to earth and down-and-dirty with three charming and sexy sport stories: "Coach Morley" by Isabel Lazar, "Fantasy Football by Sophie Neon-Blanc and the paintball fantasy (yes, you read it here first!) "Combat" by Eli Donald.

Paintball, angels, memory, romance and carbohydrates aside, what about just good sex – no fantasia, no love (yet), just raunchy hot fucking? You'll find it here, too. Check out the supersexy and wickedly kinky "A Piece of Her Night" by Rosie Lugosi, the artist's model fantasy "Anonymous" by Bethia Rayne, one-night-stander (but so much more) "Blushing" by Kate Wildblood, clubbers' delight "E:volution" by Sunny Dermott and the funny, extremely horny "Low-cut" by Clare Sudbery (for hot-but-bad sex, sample "A Slice of Melon" by V.G. Lee).

Yes, we've got it all. Now go read the stories. You're naughty girls, every one of you.

Astrid Fox
November, 2004

For Adiza, Chris, Crin, Deni, Emma, Kimmo, Martin, Nele and Simone,
for helping bring the other VVV to fruition

Contents

Acknowledgements	ii
Introduction	v
Fast by Fiona Zedde	1
Eat the Beat by Wynona B. Verr	9
Jerk by Charlotte Cooper	16
Calendar Girls by Louise Carolin	21
Tongue Deep by Linda Innes	29
Come and Join the Dance by Fiona Cooper	34
Svetlana by Kathi Kosmider	43
Don't Slip Away by Helen Sandler	48
Lamaze by Monica Trasandes	60
Memories by Rachel Kramer Bussel	73
Labour, 16th June 2004 by Rita Das	79
The Ride by Elena Moya Pereira	81
Clean Slate by Yvonne Dale	90
The Path by Helen Taylor	100
Angelica by Astrid Fox	113
Moon Wood by Julie Travis	120
Wanting It by Frances Gapper	127
Kneading by Ginger Allen	129
In and Out of Time by Shameem Kabir	132
Pac-Girl by Robyn Vinten	149
Venus as a Boy by Ape McCabe	158
Dream of Shadow, Shadow of Love by Larry Tritten	174
Coach Morley by Isabel Lazar	183
Fantasy Football by Sophie Neon-Blanc	193
Combat by Eli Donald	204
A Piece of Her Night by Rosie Lugosi	209
Cuvée Opulence by Cherry Smyth	216
My Forever Girl by Crin Claxton	223
Sound Check by Scarlett French	231
Cecily and the Boy by Winsome Lindsay	237
Anonymous by Bethia Rayne	249

A Slice of Melon by V.G. Lee   259
E:volution by Sunny Dermott   269
Blushing by Kate Wildblood   280
Front-Page Girl by Tanya Dolan   286
Low-cut by Clare Sudbery   304
Contributors   313

Fast
Fiona Zedde

Bridgette Peoples thought that, when death came, it would be quick – the slam of steel and metal, brakes screaming, burnt rubber steaming on the pavement, a searing fire. But she was wrong.

Jette drove her cars fast and liked her women even faster. She loved it when they curled into her body on hairpin turns, trembling in fear at the quick downshift and the feral snarl on her lips. She didn't believe in a speed limit.

"Slow down, Jette," her date squeaked from the passenger seat. The girl's long brown legs were taut against the floor, as if searching for the brakes to stop the 1968 Shelby GT 350 Mustang convertible herself. Still, her breath came quickly and her nipples were hard against the thin cotton shirt.

"It's all right, honey." Jette called them 'honey' because she always forgot their names. "I know what I'm doing."

The speedometer inched up to ninety-five and the girl's legs widened. Jette grinned. It was almost time. Wind pounded into the open convertible from all sides. When a soft whimper of fear leaked from the girl's mouth, the car reached one hundred. The coastline beyond the Mustang was a blur of trees, electric sky and blue-green water. Jette abruptly dropped into fourth gear. Then third. In a whirlwind of gravel and sand, she stopped the car. Suddenly it was just her and the honey. The growl of the Mustang's engine and the girl's rapid breath kicked her pulse into overdrive. Jette could smell the girl.

"I'm sorry I scared you." She wasn't. Jette went for her, climbing over to the passenger seat. The girl met her halfway, lips parted, wet, and ready, her hands already sliding under Jette's leather jacket. Long legs opened to receive and Jette's fingers slipped quickly between them, past the barrier of shorts and panties to bury themselves in paradise. With her other hand, she shoved the seat back, giving herself more room to move. The girl squirmed, gasped, panted as Jette tongued her nipples through the white cloth, bathing the straining flesh beneath. The windows fogged. Jette's clit throbbed harder with every gasp the girl released, with each pull of the girl's wetness on her fingers. The honey's bare thighs trembled. Her hips bucked in the sweat-slick leather seats and her naked foot slid against the foggy windshield in quick, staccato squeaks.

"Let it go, honey," Jette hissed.

The girl flung her head back and howled at the sun. Twenty minutes later, Jette dropped her off and sped away in a blur of blue.

A week later, Jette was back at the same overlook, only this time she was alone. Just her and the sea. The pounding surf below echoed the unfamiliar quiet in her blood. She hadn't been able to sleep that night. Something in a waking dream had brought her back up there to brood under a sky that was on fire with the last colors of the sunset. The wind flung her thick black hair before her eyes like a veil. A full moon already hovered, pale and ripe, ready to take its place among the stars.

Beneath the sounds of the wind and surf, Jette heard footsteps. She turned and her breath stopped. To say that the woman, her sudden companion on this stretch of lonely road, was pretty would have been an insult. She had the round, soft face of innocence, but her mouth was a dark slash of color, like drying blood, against her mocha skin. Jette drew in a deep breath just to make sure that she could. She acknowledged the woman's slow smile with one of her own. The stranger was all softness and warm breeze in a blue dress the color of the Mustang and the sky. Her dress was loose, but the wind molded it to her body, giving Jette an unrestricted view of full breasts with their crown of wide nipples, the gentle round of belly and honey thick thighs framing the delicate V of her womanhood. But this was no mere honey. She was like silk unfolding on a breeze, a teasing whisper of sound and graceful motion.

Jette's world narrowed to the vision walking toward her. Sunset, full moon, and not another soul in sight. She licked her lips. What a treat this was. She expected the woman to go straight for the car, to ooh and ahh over the butter-soft leather interior, the sleek classic lines, maybe beg her to put the top down so they could watch the sunset from the Mustang's cozy interior. But she walked past the car, smiling.

"You must get a lot of pussy with this car."

Jette smiled. "I do all right."

"Hm. I bet you do." Still watching Jette, the woman walked back to the Mustang and leaned back against the hood of the Mustang. She closed her eyes. The breeze ruffled her dress, lifting it away from her dimpled knees. "I'm Luna."

Below them, sunset-colored waves flung themselves at the cliffs. The moist spray flicked against Jette's face, wetting her mouth and cheeks.

"So, Bridgette, have you ever been... taken?" Luna asked without opening her eyes.

Jette looked closely at the woman. She hadn't been called that name in a long time, and certainly never by someone she'd just met. "Do I know you?"

"No, but you will." Luna opened one amber-flecked eye. "Are you going to answer my question?"

For a moment, Jette was tempted to tell her to fuck off. But a stronger part of her wanted to know where this conversation was going. "No. I've never been fucked. And I don't want to be." She frowned, not quite sure that she wanted to answer any more personal questions from this stranger, although she herself had asked that question of many strange women – just before making a home inside their bodies for her fingers or tongue.

"The old saying is true, you know," Luna murmured. Her gaze was lazy, but watchful. "You never know what you're missing until you try it."

"Usually I'd agree with you. But not in this instance. Not when it's about me getting fucked."

"So you're going to stick with what you know? Fucking girls in your fast car then peeling out at 110 miles just to get back to your lonely little apartment?" Luna propped herself up on her elbows and watched Jette with amused eyes. "Doesn't sound like much fun to me."

"Then you obviously haven't tried it." Jette grinned.

"I've experienced something like it." The woman bared her own teeth. "You feed on their fear and turn it into lust. You're no better than a leech, or a vampire." Luna didn't sound judgmental. Simply like she was stating a fact.

Suddenly uneasy, Jette shrugged and turned around to squint into the darkening distance. She didn't see anything wrong with what she did with these women as long as both of them got off and nobody got hurt. She turned back to face Luna. But the woman was gone.

"Damn!"

The faint outline of her body, drawn in mist and steam, lingered on the hood of the Mustang. Jette leaned back against the car and tilted her head at the horizon. The colors of the setting sun had lost their appeal. Instead, a vision of Luna, soft and full, burned brightly in her mind's eye like the afterimage of a too-bright flame.

Jette was dropping off one of her latest thrills when she spotted Luna, full-hipped and gorgeous in a pale dress. In the midst of the hectic, early-Saturday-evening foot and street traffic, she strolled, swinging her ass and the tiny nothing of a bag that seemed attached to her fingers by air alone. No one shoved her, no one pushed against her. She floated. Jette quickly parked the Mustang and caught up with the woman. Luna turned. She seemed not at all surprised to see her.

"Was she any good?" She gestured behind them to the girl Jette had just left behind.

"Well, *I* was. So we had a good time."

Luna chuckled. Her laugh was a delicate ripple that floated along Jette's skin. "I'm sure she'll be back for more," she said.

"Maybe, but I won't be there. I never perform the same trick twice."

"Cold little bitch, aren't you?"

"Not in the least. I'm hot. All the time." Jette's eyes ran over Luna's body, lingering on its bold curves and the dip and rise of what she quickly realized was an amazing ass. "Especially when you're around."

Luna's laughter was slightly mocking. "You look good, Bridgette. But you're not quite as good as you think you are. Don't try to handle me like one of your girls, because you won't be able to."

"I wouldn't dream of it," Jette said, though she did. Intensely. After she'd met Luna for the first time, her nights had been filled with visions of the voluptuous woman. Hot dreams of heavy breasts and excited hips, Luna calling her name, gasping that she'd never had it so good. But even as Luna had moved like a puppet through Jette's fantasies, the small woman's dark eyes had glowed feral in the bedroom light, her lips parted over savage, sharp teeth.

Her eyes flickered over Luna's body again only to encounter a dark, knowing look.

"Know what you're asking for, Bridgette. Isn't that what you always tell your little girls? Know that you'll never be the same afterwards. Know and accept." They stopped in the midst of the crowd. People flowed past, barely stopping to acknowledge them on the crowded sidewalk. Everyone was high on the goodwill of a Friday night, no more work for another two days, and possibilities pranced around in high heels and tight shirts. Why worry about something so insignificant as an amorous couple standing in the middle of the crowded sidewalk?

Luna pressed an open palm to Jette's belly, inciting a riot of tiny butterflies under the skin. "Think of me the next time you fuck one of your girls. Wonder what it would be like to let someone else drive for a change." The fingers started to move, stroking the flesh under Jette's jacket. "The one thing you wouldn't have to wonder about is how it would feel." Nails scraped the suddenly sensitive skin and Jette felt her pussy perk up and begin to salivate. "I would be very good to you." Luna drew back from the other woman and began to walk forward again through the crowd. "But let me know what you think about my offer," she threw over her shoulder.

What offer? Jette wondered, still drowning in the sudden and immediate arousal spiraling under her skin and the river rushing beyond control between her thighs.

"I want you, Bridgette. When you're ready for me. *If* you're ready for me. I'll come." And without seeming to, her steps picked up speed until she soon disappeared altogether.

Jette wasn't pleased. She tried to follow the woman, but quickly realized that was an impossibility. She had been dismissed. After a half-hearted attempt to pick up someone else on the strip, she headed back home.

Jette couldn't concentrate. Luna was the throbbing engine that drove her obsessive visits to the cliffs and to downtown Long Beach, hoping to catch a glimpse of her again. Other women, no matter how tasty, couldn't take the power of her memory away. When Jette's fingers found them wet and wanting, it was Luna's mocking face that she saw. When the women's mouths touched her throbbing pussy, Jette heard Luna's low, taunting voice.

She almost gave up on finding Luna — but she didn't have to. Luna found her first.

"Hey, sugar." The voice came from her passenger seat, along with the light scent of night-blooming jasmine.

Jette was so relieved that she didn't bother to ask Luna how she had got into the locked and alarmed car. "Where do you want to go?"

"Down to the beach." Luna's teeth glinted in the darkness. "Near the cliffs."

They cruised down the boulevard, top down despite the rain-heavy, gray clouds that floated above their heads. At the beach, Jette nosed the car past a high gate and down to a ramp leading to the water. Waves crawled up the beach, lapping at the Mustang's tires.

Luna touched Jette's thigh. "I hear you've been looking for me."

"And you wanted to be found?"

"More or less." Luna's smile turned playful. "So now that you've found me, what are you going to do?"

Jette wasn't used to all this talking. The other woman's bright smile intimidated her, started a shiver of fear in her belly that she'd never known before. It felt good.

"Let's go for a walk." Jette opened the car door.

They made it as far as the hood of the Mustang before it started to rain. They stopped and stood under the cool shower, watching each other. Silver droplets caught in Luna's eyelashes and traced the full curve of her mouth.

"What do you want, Adrenaline Girl?"

"You tell me," Jette said. "Aren't you the one who's sure that she knows what I want and how I want it?"

Luna chuckled again and stepped closer. Jette's skin tingled in anticipation. Her world slowed, tilted until the warm hood of the Mustang was under her back. She closed her eyes. Rain danced against her mouth, streamed down her face and into her hair.

Luna moved over her, shielding her from the rain. "I have exactly what you want right here."

She tasted like a well-aged Merlot, wet and soft, with a touch of oak and cardamom. Rain blinded Jette again as Luna moved away. She felt a hungry mouth nuzzling her throat, the delightful slide of the woman's tongue on her skin.

The pain. It blossomed gently under the hothouse mouth. Jette gasped and swallowed rain, eyes fluttering, blinking quickly under the steady drops. It felt like she was losing her virginity again. Pleasure slowly obliterated the pain. Jette's hands hooked in Luna's hair, holding her against her throat, pressing the greedy mouth into her skin. Her body was wet from the inside out, spreading and softening under Luna's hands.

Deft fingers floated over Jette's belly, down to the zipper of her slacks. Luna opened her body, slid inside its welcoming heat. Her pussy clenched and sucked the fingers deeper. That's when Jette felt it, a vibration like the roaring of the Mustang as it slid into third gear. Jette's body trembled under the soft hand, then shook, then shuddered before finally coming to rest.

Luna slowly pulled away. "Now," she said. "What can you do for me?" Her eyes glowed like headlights through the rain.

"I thought I already did it?" Jette touched her own throat, felt the rawness there. Her voice trembled. She knew exactly what had just happened. The part that most concerned her was that she'd let someone else do the driving. She said as much to her new lover.

Luna laughed, husky and low. "You *are* worth keeping."

Jette once thought that death would come quickly. But now she knew better. Death was languorous and sweet, perfuming the air with the scent of blood and woman and jasmine. She came at night, lingering over Jette's throat and thighs with a hunter's patience, drinking her fill. Slow.

Eat the Beat
Wynona B. Verr

I said "Hi, darlin'," to Deedee, the club's owner, at the door, experiencing the usual frisson of pleasure at the feel of her smooth, warm skin as I slipped my arm around her waist, a waist exposed between her signature tiger-print harem top and hipster pants combination. A quick smooch, an exchange of pleasantries – "Watching tonight?" "What else?" (with a smirk) – and I moved into the bar, checked out who was in and moseyed up the stairs, calling "Wotcha!" to Maggie behind the upstairs bar over the low hubbub of early punters – no one there I wanted to talk to. I moved into the playroom to catch the first scene of the night.

Yep, it was as expected – Emma and Pip shagging on the table as I came into the red-lit room. First time of seeing, it had been a blast. There I'd been, little greenie up from the Kentish sticks, shaking a bit in anticipation of what I might see, hoping that at some point in the evening some kind regular, on a break from her own scene or after fresh meat and smelling virgin pussy, would take pity on a poor singleton and shag her dry in a quiet corner. It hadn't happened. No one, not a single mucky minge-lover had made a move on me, peeling back the flaps of my rubber skirt (for which I'd paid a hundred and friggin' fifty pounds in *Sh!* that very day) to reveal the knickerless snatch on offer, like an oyster, fresh up from the Kent coast that morning.

Then I had been saved from geeky, new-girl-in-a-rubber-frock embarrassment by Em and Pip, who'd come in from the bar and just got down to it. Pip had lain back on the table, Em had put on a rubber glove, lubed up from a small tube she pulled out of a fanny pack on her hip and had begun working Pip, who opened up like a pro.

I'd just stood there, tongue mentally hanging out – my mouth must have been hanging open for real, 'cos there was dribble on my chin when Pip began grunting and moaning. I wiped it away in new-girl embarrassment as she shrieked "I'm coming!" loudly enough to be heard on Kennington Lane, let alone in the rest of the club. And *I* was embarrassed!

When they'd finished, Pip smiled up at Em, grabbed her head and bit her ear before locking them both into a languorous, post-pounding clinch. I'd nearly applauded – is that what you did in a sex club? Did you throw money, or offer to buy the exhausted shaggers a drink? Hell, what did I know? Yep, their 'spike-haired butch does doe-eyed femme before your very eyes' routine was a gusher first time of seeing – I thought I'd died and gone to Lesbos.

Well, that was then. Now, looking into the blank faces of early birds, just beginning to curl at the edges from expectancy into disappointment, it looked like it was turning, for them, into another, same-old-same-old Friday night – same scene-weary faces, same excitement junkies waiting for someone to do something they considered outrageous so they could get their fix.

Me, I love the various sounds and tones of the night, like a piece of music: opening chords, intro, verse, chorus, verse, hook key change building to money-note climax and... post-chordal ciggie. The anticipation of the moment when you feel each mood slide up a notch. Well, the band had just tuned up, Pip's "Aaaaaaagh" being the guide note from which they all took their first tones, and I waited for the night to get going – that key-change was mine – breath held for the first kerrang.

The Twins were here. *Kerrang*. A & B – I'd never reckoned much of their routine, so had never bothered to learn their names. A & B stands for Arsehole and Buttplug, the Beavis and Butthead of bedroom SM – that's not the hard stuff, just the kind of titillating extra you might throw in to spice up the once-a-week screw. A & B like to think they're so cool, but they're a couple of tossers. They always dress the same, like clones, same dyed-black hair, pale make-up, heavy eyeliner, short black rubber skirts.

They're always handcuffed together and A always starts the set by swinging B around – fuck anyone else; out the way, suckers – grabbing a candle from the windowsill over Em and Pip's table and laying B on the padded bench that's always set off to one side, against the wall. With a theatrical flourish, making sure as many people as can be bothered to are watching, she drips hot wax on B, varying the moments between drips so that she surprises A, who hisses in *faux*-pain. Big yawn. It would take a pneumatic drill to get through that hide – it's obvious from the scars and weals on B's skin that these two party hard at home, really hard. These are flea-bites to B.

They then go onto the wheel, a wooden, four-spoked giant, with straps on each of the struts for wrists and ankles, and foot rests and hand holds by which the sub gets onto the equipment. The whole shebang is mounted on a pivot on the wall so that it turns freely, a foot off the floor. It looks impressive, but B doesn't feel the intermittent whacks A metes out with a riding crop – it's set in a bracket on the wall beside the 'Wheel of Pain' for this purpose. The culmination of their 'act' is when A gets B down off the wheel and hugs her. Ahhh. Even bigger yawn.

So, like all good intros, the Twins introduce the novice to an approximation of the themes of the evening; a build-up to pain, the whirl of disorientation, not knowing when or where the 'punishment' may come from, and a happy resolution, when absolution is given to the good girl who takes her licks. And if you believed that that was all there was to SM, you'd be as sorry as Beavis and Butthead.

Verse. She always arrives – just arrives. One minute the tall-backed, metal chair under the mezzanine bed platform is empty, the next she's sitting in it. She comes in the late/early hours and sits in the chair, watching and waiting for one girl. Always the same girl. Again, I've never asked the girl her name, but she's not in the same league at all as A & B. She's medium height, lithe and sinewy like a willow switch, but at the same time solid muscle and sculpted. Edible.

I'd never think of asking Madame her name. She's Madame. Say the word "Madame"; say it quickly, clipping the vowels, and you see the classic, fetish mag image, don't you? Wasp-waisted, hard-faced bitch in killer heels, arms protected in gloves, whip in hand, in tight, tight rubber. Rubber is silky, tactile. It allows the wearer to create the illusion of contact, but inside the second skin, inside you don't feel a thing. You are contained, enclosed, locked away where no one can touch you, deprived, kept to yourself and alone.

Say "Madame" slowly; linger over the "m", caress it, compress your lips and let it vibrate across them, through the chambers in your head, and she becomes another creature altogether. She's "mouth" and "moist" and "motherfucker".

And she knows it. Madame knows, because she chooses to wear a black, long-sleeved dress that reaches down and smoothes her to just below her knees – like the kind my mother used to wear – underneath the tight basque, the badge of her office. Velvet gloves. On the surface, she's basque and business and brisk, yes, but underneath she's managed and manipulating and mean and midnight. And makes me wet just by sitting there.

Whoever else comes up to her, she always shakes her head – she always waits for the sinewy, solid girl. When the girl walks from the upstairs bar into the playroom, there's a moment of eye contact and the room suddenly crackles. Whatever else may have happened before this – and there are always scenes of one sort or another going on other than those I've mentioned – this is the real moment when the night comes alive. My skin prickles as I look at them, looking at each other, energised, silently bargaining and setting the boundaries for their scene, if you can call what they do a mere scene.

Madame gets up. There's a look on her face – always the same – and it's not a smile and not a smirk, not a look of expectation or relish; it's what an intake of breath would look like if you could see it. She begins to throb from inside. I can see it. She gestures – keeping eye contact with the girl – to what looks like a vaulting horse, set back from the centre of the room, and the girl turns and walks in front of her to the rounded end of the equipment and leans on it. There are chairs arranged around the room and I sit in the one nearest to them, tucking my short rubber skirt beneath me – it's starting to get slippery. I cross my legs; the skirt is short.

Madame has a small case with her. She puts it on the floor beside the horse and snaps open the catches. She opens it up and reaches inside. The girl never looks at what Madame chooses; it's always different. Sometimes it's the leather paddle, smooth on one side and with a raised, rougher surface on the other. Or it might be the short leather cat, which stings like fuck.

The girl is always dressed the same: a woollen top like a vest, aerated, see-through, showing the ripple of her muscled shoulders underneath, her fit, firm body, slim waist curving out to surprisingly fleshy buttocks for such a taut figure; ripped denim shorts, which she bends down and take off to reveal a thong, hidden underneath, which cuts up her crack and delineates the clean curve of her buttocks. They flex and stretch as she leans over the horse, wobbling slightly and she adjusts herself, spreading her legs a little wider to balance, arms folded under herself across her breasts, not in protection, but hugging the moment to her – I know.

I'm breathing more deeply now, and my lips are dry; a pulse begins to beat in my head and my hand is shaking a little where it rests on my knee. I know it, the tenseness she feels, the anticipation of the first flick of the whip.

Madame bends and slowly brings out the thick, many-stranded latex lash, running it through her fingers, caressing and smoothing it down, soothing it in preparation. As she stands, she catches my eye. Her eyes flicker down to my exposed crotch; my clit twitches. There's a ghost of a smile, a minute lift of an eyebrow. She turns back to the girl and stands for a moment in front of the blank canvas of the body - and our eyes run over it, observing the contours, appraising it, licking it, she and I.

She leans in and whispers, but so I can hear: "Stretch". The girl reaches up to the nearest handle on the horse and opens her legs wider still, legs stretched out behind her, arse firm and taut now.

Madame begins slowly to caress the girl's body, running her hand languorously up her back, then following suit with the lash, letting the silken, fluid strands slide gently down over the arse cheeks. The girl sighs in pleasure at the sensation and angles her arse up to meet the following hand that smoothes down and around, warm, soft, and begins gently to pat the hard, peach-like flesh being offered up. She works into a rhythm, by turns patting and caressing, lulling us both into a warm place of remembered sensation. Who's been a good girl, then? Who deserves a hug, then? Who does Mummy love?

No more caressing. Madame takes off her gloves. The patting gets harder, the slaps audible. My arse twitches, tensing as the girl's tenses, growing hot with the heat of rubber and moistness and sympathetic feeling. Madame begins to slowly swish the latex lashes against the warm cheeks, flicking underarm to catch the softer skin underneath, between arse and leg-top. The girl hisses softly. Chorus.

My arms are folded in front of me now. I squeeze my right nipple gently, feeling the nipple ring against the fabric of my shirt, pulling at it; the nipple begins to swell under my thumb and finger; I pinch it awake, watching the arse before me growing pinker, the girl beginning to move under the gentle lash, my tweaking throbbing in time with each stroke.

Madame takes a step back, and begins to swing overarm, criss-crossing the whip in front of her, placing each down-stroke precisely: left buttock, right buttock, left buttock, right buttock, the same firm speed, working the arse, warming it up, bringing it alive. The girl is beginning to moan for real now, groaning in pleasure as the stinging beats shake her perfect, fuckable fanny, writhing into the stinging. Madame is getting into it: she is beginning to breathe more deeply, the slightest tinge of red touching her cheeks as she works, the rhythm of strokes changing. Her arm tenses – she grabs the lashes in the other hand, bunches them and brings them down hard, and leaning in as the girl cries out. "Who's been a bad girl?"

The girl groans.

"What did you say?" The lash comes down again, raising an angry red mark on the left buttock.

"I have…" Again, the lash. "I have, Madame."

Madame steps away, slowing (*verse*) the pace and pain level to the soft-soft-left-right again. My hand slips down under the flap of my skirt to my wet cunt, fingers moving in and dragging moistness up to my pulsating, shouting clit. My finger circles the hardening nub, flicking it up, down, running the finger back down to the juice, up to circle and stroke, other hand pinching hard at the throbbing, tingling nipples, fully erect, out for fun and bruising.

Bruising. The girl's arse is very red now. Madame (key change) goes quickly to her case and brings out a cane, flexes it, then runs it across the girl's cheeks, before bringing it hard down across the enflamed buttocks. The swish of the cane through air and whack of wood meeting flesh, the cry of pain, pushes two fingers into my running cunt, hard, hard, harder, in time with the swish/crack/cry. My nipple cries as I dig my nail into it, pulling at the ring so that it nearly comes out, puffing and hissing in pain, thrusting fingers in faster and faster. Yes, Mummy, I'll be a good girl. Beat me, Mummy, smack my bottom. I'll be a good girl for Mummy, I will, Mummy. Smack me, Mummy, hurt me Mummy.

The girl is crying with each stroke, tears running down her cheeks, jumping as the cane bites into raised, wealed flesh. "Yes, Madame, yes, Madame, I'll be good, Madame. Yes... yes... yes... Yes!" I shudder in coming – she shudders suddenly: "Ape, ape..."

Madame stops, breathing deeply. She lowers the cane and steps back, face cool in the red light of the room. Calmly, she reaches into the open case for a cloth and wipes sweat and a few small traces of blood from the cane and replaces them both, closing the case with a snap. She goes to the girl, sliding her gloves on once more, and gently strokes, soothing the girl's arse. The girl pushes herself up from the horse and Madame takes her in her arms, rocking her gently and rubbing her back, holding her for a long while.

I look down so no one can see – not even me – if I'm crying or not. *Hold me, Mummy; love me, Mummy.*

Jerk
Charlotte Cooper

Owen Wilson, the blond actor with the crooked nose, stands before me. He is dressed in his *Royal Tenenbaums* cowboy drag. His shirt is loose and his right hand slides down his belly and into his pants. I'm saying pants instead of trousers because at this point I feel compelled, mysteriously, to use American idioms. There's a snaggle of hair poking out between his fingers. His pants are unbuttoned and now both of his hands are creeping in, getting ready to hook out whatever it is that he's got down there.

Owen towers above me. He drawls: "Get ready, girl" in a voice so impossibly sexy that I'm suddenly aware of my tight breathing and I secretly hope I don't have an asthma attack. His golden skin gleams and his muscles are firm and plump. He smiles a cockeyed smile that suggests a secret in-joke between us. His hair is looking very good indeed. I'm wondering what he'll smell like up close, what his skin will feel like next to mine, about the weight of him lying on top of me.

Suddenly the door explodes, there's splintered wood and shards of glass everywhere and Keanu Reeves bursts into the room. He's sweating, as though he's been running for miles.

"Leave her alone, dude!" he half-yells, half-screams at Owen. Keanu points at me and shouts triumphantly: "The bitch is mine!" Owen steps back and kind of evaporates, although I know that I can call him back whenever I want and he'll be there.

Keanu kneels down beside me and takes my hand in his. He apologises for using such harsh language. He doesn't know that I don't mind, that in fact I rather like it. He gazes at me with his big brown eyes. Oh God, I can't believe how perfect his eyebrows look, all groomed and angular.

Keanu says: "Charlotte, I've never told this to a soul. I was afraid that it would damage my career as a Hollywood heartthrob but now I need to come clean and I think you should be the first to know. The thing is, I've always fancied chubby, dykey women. Chicks like you, in fact. I've read all your books, all the stories and articles you've written. That's not all – I've been reading your website, www.CharlotteCooper.net, I read every single page of it every day and I can't believe how cool and smart and witty you are. I love you, Charlotte. You're my ideal woman and I want to give you all of my money so that you can buy yourself a swimming pool, and then I'm going to fuck you until you beg me to stop."

Stop. Stop it. Stop. It.

This isn't going to work, it's all wrong. These guys wouldn't pick me in a million years. I feel embarrassed by them. I wouldn't know what to do with all that gloss. Their buffed-up gym-bodies make me cringe, I can't begin to imagine having sex with someone like that, the whole six-pack thing is ludicrous, I hate buying into that body fascist shit. Everything about this is just stupid, I need to scale it back a bit.

Okay, how about this… Juliette Lewis is looking predatory, wearing nothing but a pair of black leather short shorts and a skinny little bra. She's bending over backwards in front of me, hair trailing on the bar room floor, all upside down doing a crabwalk. I'm here with Peaches, who's standing behind me resting her chin on my shoulder, holding my tits in her hands. Peaches calls out to Juliette to shake her ass a little bit for us. I'd do this myself but my English accent makes the word "ass" sound affected. I can feel Peaches' dick pressing into my own ass, straining somewhat, like it wants some action. Peaches' breath smells sweet, she's chewing at my neck, getting as close as she can to me. Meanwhile, Juliette is doing one of her spectacular writhing dances in front of us. She's got a gun wedged down the front of her pants and she pulls it out and sucks on the barrel. She keeps her eye on me the whole time. She cocks the pistol and winks. My heart's beating way too fast and before I know it there's Michael Moore striding in, finger wagging, going: "Shame on you, Charlotte. Guns are bad news and you know it. Stop this decadence at once." The needle skids across the record, the film burns against the hot projector bulb.

Shitdamnfuckinghell, I lost it again. Maybe I need to try and keep it real. But real's a drag since the only people aside from my honeys that flirt with me are the sleazy old guys that whisper "Hello, beautiful, nice big girl" at me on the street as I walk past. Um, maybe not this time.

I need someone else, someone hot for the right reasons, someone really real. What about B...? No, she's a pain in real life. What about J...? I saw her today. Nah, Kay would kill me if she knew about her. There's always I... Ha ha, no way! Only joking. Okay, so I'm thinking of R... she's good, she'll do.

Where are we? We're on a nice, big, white, fluffy cloud. We're up in the air. The sky is blue, the sun is soft and gooey on the horizon. We're standing together, no, we're lying, arms and legs all twisted up in each other. R... is kissing my face and humping me. She's naked as the day she was born. I'm running my hands all over her, up her back, pushing my fingers in her mouth, watching her throw her head back as she sucks on my fingers. Everything is clean and fresh. Oh, maybe a little bit too fresh. This whole thing reeks of vanilla – I need to crank up the dirt a little more.

So we're not on a cloud. We're in a ratty old motel room and we're making the bed cry out for mercy underneath us. Neither of us does drugs but, just for the sleaze factor, let's just say that we've jacked each other up with a tasty speedball and thrown our works across the room all devil-may-care fuck-the-world. The broken television skips back and forth between channels, now some crazed televangelist shit, now a shopping show, now the news, now a hair-metal rock video. Bzzt bzzt bzzzt, it crackles and pops. The cops are outside. I still can't shake these Americanisms but there's no time to start worrying about that.

Sixty per cent of R...'s body is covered with tattoos, including bluebirds, flaming 8-balls and a long list of the ladies she's loved and lost entwined with roses down her thigh. She's wearing big pants (stop laughing, I like them on her). Her tits are huge. No, they're not, they're small. I'm sucking on them like I'm trying to suck out her soul, or her heart or something and she's groaning and shaking, letting me know how good it feels.

She's undoing my jeans and grabbing at me. Her hand snakes its way into my knickers and I'm wet for her. She orders me to open my legs wider for her so I strain and push and open them as wide as they will go, just so she'll have no excuses not to treat me right.

Outside, shots ricochet around the car park, there are sirens blaring. R... bites the skin around my neck and shoulders, it's gentle but it hurts because her teeth are so sharp. Her eyes are luminous and deep, we're on fire. Christ, it's so hot, our sweat is condensing on the walls and the speedball makes everything come alive, shapes are edged with neon flares, lights zip in my peripheral vision.

She's pulling off my knickers, ripping them off, actually. She gets her face down there and eats me out. It feels like velvet, feels luxurious and I bend and flex against her tongue. I move as though my spine is made of rubber. She's opening me up, getting me ready and I'm lying there like a queen waiting to be serviced.

Yeah, this is more like it, keep going.

R... rears back, like a panther ready to spring and now she's got a dick, she's stroking it and it's big and hard and I can't tell if she's a boy or a girl but I know where that thing is heading. She dives into me in one smooth clear movement. Her cock slides in and I feel it all the way through me, big and wild, so tight. She fucks me so fast, pumping it, hammering it home. It's tearing the life out of me, I can barely keep up, I'm holding tight like a rodeo rider on a bucking bronco. I'm a mess of sweat and goo and cunt juice and, yes, tears too. I want to shit and piss with excitement and because this is a fantasy I can do that. I can let go with everything I have and my shit turns to flowers and my piss evaporates into perfumed steam in the heat of that room.

We're both screaming. Veins protrude at R...'s temples and along her forearms. I've wrapped my arms and legs around her so tightly that I'm locking her into me. And now new protruberances grow from our bodies. I have extra pairs of arms with fingers ending in claws that scratch R...'s back making holy white weals. R... grows whips where angels have wings. She beats and thrashes me as she fucks me. The whiptails cut into my skin and leave trails of red poetry.

I think I'm getting there.

As the room whirls around us we find ourselves in the vortex, where everything is still. R... peels herself off me, then another R... climbs off me, and another, and another until there are five or six R...s standing and staring at each other, dusting themselves down. It's so quiet that you can hear the sound of their hands patting at themselves and straightening their clothes. I soon realise that I can make clones of myself too, it's easy, I only have to imagine it. Before long there's a mini-army of me facing the R...s.

I shout: "Go! Go! Go!" and we leap together, fusing somehow, arms reaching out to pull the stragglers in with the rest of us. We form a giant sticky ball of bodies, like the rubber band ball you make to pass the time at work. We're completely intertwined in a tangle of naked limbs. Bodies sprout new cocks, flesh gives way, forming new cunts. Everything is hard and willing and open and ready. Tongues lick and kiss and suck, hair glistens and muscles stretch. I look up and four R...s gaze back at me with hungry eyes. My cunts are wet and begging for more, my cocks are tight and desperate. And so it begins, I'm fucking and being fucked. I can feel every movement, every stroke of the flesh, every single thrust and withdrawal. I'm bigger than myself, I'm part of R... too, and she is within me. We move as one, our clits are bursting with desire, with electricity and pleasure. Every breath, every pulse feels like the most satisfying feeling I've ever had. We're fucking and oozing together, all one thing, and spinning round, moving urgently, speeding it up. I catch pornographic snapshots of one, two, three pussies jammed full of cock, ten, eleven, twelve fists disappearing up wide and wet cunts. We're moving faster, there's nothing stopping us, and I roll back my eyes in my head and breathe it all in.

Don't stop.

Now there's nothing around us any more, no motel, no bed, we're no longer even human. We've turned into a huge fucking dragster grinding up the track at 300 miles per hour. We are the stink of nitro exploding through an engine. We are the roar of jet engines blasting. Stars burn in the sky around us, like smears of brightness. We are pure speed and we're laughing and loving it.

I think that'll do it, yes, that'll work.

Calendar Girls
Louise Carolin

I just woke up one morning in sunshine and it was all over: I didn't feel too bad. Everyone's got a talent for something and mine's for beginning again.

It was eight months since Deborah dumped me and about time my nose stopped bleeding at the thought of her and her dumbitch new girlfriend and their cute matching coke habits. Deborah finished with me because she didn't want to come home from New York. I asked her why and she said cocaine cost less there. She dropped me for cheap gear. It was nearly enough to put me off drugs, never mind women.

Another duff English summer was getting underway and I'd just blown twenty on a leg wax to encourage it, wondering why I was bothering since nobody was going near my gams, apart from the girl at the salon.

'You've got lovely soft skin,' Bettina told me, stroking my legs. For a straight girl, I suppose she gets to caress more female thighs than most, but as a lesbian I have to observe mine aren't particularly soft. I'm not about to tell her that I'm queer. I'm incognito in this waxy world of girls, but there's something about the way they touch your skin that almost feels like sex.

'There now, torture's nearly over,' soothed Bettina, as she yanked away another strip of epidermis, inching closer to my bikini line with her manicured fingers. I gritted my teeth, sweating it out.

Miss June turned up for our blind date two hours late and right on time. No one with such a narrow face and crooked teeth has ever looked so good to me.

We were set up by some mutual friends over a dinner in May. They were disgustingly in love and it was putting me off my food but my appetite returned when one of them mentioned their

American friend's forthcoming visit. 'You'll love Sacha,' her pals enthused, holding hands across the table. 'She's from San Francisco. She's really cute.'

I knew they didn't mean like Kylie because I'd already told them how I only go for girls who look like navvies, and spilled the totally embarrassing tale of Irma, the German I picked up in October when I was still numb from the heart down after Deborah sacked me. I took Irma for a butch because at six foot two with a soft suedehead and no visible tits, she looked like a geezer. How wrong I was. Her sexual skills were nonexistent, and she flinched right out of bed when I offered to suck her cock. Apparently in Berlin they all look like that. I've never been there. How was I meant to know?

But back to Miss June... We met in a West End bar that our friends had selected for the introductions because there was a pool table. I don't play pool and neither did Sacha but it gave our mates something to do while we asked each other stupid questions and tried to be cool. After half an hour they took off, feigning tiredness, which left me and Sasha to our own devices.

I was pretty gone on Sacha's Yankee accent, but it was her gentlemanly wiles that really revved me up. The way she let me go first through every door (dropping her eyes to my arse each time) was foreplay enough and, though we hadn't even kissed, by the time we reached my flat I was practically surfing a wave of my own secretions.

So why did I have to get my records out? I'm sure Sacha didn't know. I could tell she wasn't into vintage ska, but once I'd started I somehow couldn't stop. It was like being sixteen again and paralysed with lust. All I could do was splack another dusty 45 on the turntable, yakking like an anorak and trembling with nerves. Eventually she stretched, cleared her throat and drawled, 'Hey... do you wanna get next to me?' I was so terrified I couldn't even look her in the eye, but I angled my neck coyly in her direction and luckily she took the hint and fell on it with her crooked teeth and soft, soft mouth.

Deborah had a secret crush on Belinda Carlisle. Well, secret from everyone else, but I knew. She often said she liked me because I had red hair, like Belinda. 'But I've got a skinhead,' I observed. (I had, in those days.) 'Don't ever shave your cunt,' she told me, going down. One great thing about Deborah, she gave terrific head. I just never was sure who to. Sacha didn't do anything like that without latex. In fact, she didn't do anything much without latex. We were actually on the bed and my clothes were coming off really fast when she suddenly reared up and requested a rubber glove. Apart from the Marigolds in the kitchen sink, I didn't have any. 'You English chicks,' she said. 'None of you practise safe sex, do ya?' I had to agree. I didn't know anyone who thought of safe sex, except as a set of petty restrictions imposed on a girlfriend one thought likely to stray.

'I've never had sex with a man and I've never used needles,' I told her, hopefully. 'I don't think I'm positive. Are you?'

Sacha looked outraged. 'It's not polite to ask,' she hissed, appalled by my lack of etiquette. Then she relented a little and admitted she was not. The small matter of our shared HIV status was not, however, enough to persuade her to break the rules. I was mortified, the prospect of my first decent shag in eight months receding before my eyes.

'Don't worry,' she reassured me. 'There's plenty of things we can do.'

This was a barefaced lie. Sacha's prohibitions were simple: no genital contact without rubber. Any behaviour that compromised her sensitivities was met with a swift grab of my wrists (not unpleasant in itself) and a sharp intake of breath, followed by a short lecture. I soon tired of my efforts to catch her out. Eventually we were reduced to lying face-to-face, exchanging filthy whispers. She certainly had the gift of the gab. Then she noticed me dreamily grinding my crotch into hers.

'You don't think *cotton* is a barrier, do ya?' she exclaimed, jerking away. I stared down at our underpants: her white Calvins and my slinky pink La Perla. Cotton, maybe not, but surely satin? Sacha threw me off and retreated to her side of the bed where she set up a safe-sex safe-space and went to sleep, while I lay on my back staring discontentedly at the Artex on my ceiling.

At seven a.m. Sacha got up, kissed me five times fast on the face and left. I got up at nine and noticed that she'd snagged my new, sheer mesh bra with her crooked teeth.

I met Miss July at a soirée I attended for the sole purpose of schmoozing people I thought might get me work. It was miles away from where I live and I had a raging hangover from the night before. Everyone knew everyone but me, and the only people with jobs to spare were really, really drunk. I was about to leave when Sarah walked in and I changed my mind. She wasn't my usual type, not mean enough, too nerdy, but there was something about the set of her shoulders I liked. I started getting ideas right away.

Afterwards, she told me she never thought a glamorous girl like moi would go for someone like her. To be honest, I noticed her clothes were a bit strange but I didn't care. I knew *I* looked hot. My jeans fit just right and my fuschia bra-straps kept falling off my fake-tanned shoulders. I'd painted my nails Pepto-Bismol pink and put on my best red mouth. I looked like the sort of girl who puts out and it was a good look. It would've been wasted if I hadn't got laid.

It took me a frustrating half hour to weasel my way into her little clique, one failed conversational gambit after another, becoming more brazen with every plastic tumbler of cheap wine, then a half hour longer to snag her attention for real. I felt like the poster-child for How To Pick Up Girls. I was an operator, grooming her ego, flattering and flirting and laughing at her jokes. I knew it was starting to work when she offered me an unfeasibly tiny space on the sofa next to her. I could have sat in her lap but I made like a lady and declined, perching myself on a nearby chair and fixing her with an attentive gaze.

The party rolled on around us but our participation in it was increasingly perfunctory. Every hour or so I'd make another visit to the bathroom and practise mouthing, 'You can take me home if you like', into the mirror, like a mantra. Eventually I returned from one of these sorties to find her gone. Twisting around, I noticed her standing on her own in the hallway and wondered vaguely why. Perhaps she didn't like me after all. A moment later she walked back in and whispered loudly, 'I've been trying to beckon you into the hall, but you seem to be ignoring me.'

I followed her out of the room. 'What are we going to do about this?' she asked me. It was my moment.

'You can take me home, if you like,' I barked abruptly.

'But I've got a girlfriend,' she objected. I remembered that I knew that but I really didn't care.

'Listen, I only want a shag,' I said. 'I'm not a marriage-wrecker.' That was all it took. She grabbed me and kissed off all my Perfect Silent Red up against the magnolia woodchip. Then we left the party and skulked back to hers where she disconnected the phone and fucked me stupid all night.

The next day she asked me for my number and said we should have an affair. She rang that evening to say her girlfriend was livid and she couldn't see me again. She was apologetic and exhausted. Her girlfriend had been round and broken things. They'd spent all afternoon patching it up, while I was at work, staring out of the window and counting everything we'd done to each other, a litany of sex. After we hung up she called back to remind me never to ring her number. I put down the phone and muttered, 'Have a wank for me, stupid.'

Miss August was a man. I must be the only dyke who's ever gone all the way to that lez mecca San Francisco and fucked a bloke, an English bloke at that. We met in a straight bar I went to for the music, on my own. It was midnight when I got there, like Cinderella backwards. I didn't know it was a pick-up joint, but it only took two seconds to sink in. Lone males circled like coyotes while a giddy group of women flounced and shimmied on the tiny dance floor. I'd been hoping for a nice anonymous dance in a dark corner. No such luck. Half a dozen sharky eyes regarded me as I waited for my drink, trying to look like I belonged. I needed some protection and there it was, behind the decks: English Dave. His name was on the flyer, but I didn't give a toss 'til then. When he dropped out of the DJ booth and approached the bar, I was ready with my line.

'Hi. I was wondering... might you be English Dave?'

He was taken aback, but perhaps it was my unexpected Estuary accent. 'Er, that would be me,' he said, recovering himself. 'And who are you?'

'Oh… I'm English Louise,' I smirked, getting a second taste of scotch from earlier. I was already loaded from the dyke club I'd been in before, so when we sat down at the bar I sipped water for a while. Much later, my heterosexual sister insisted that an invitation to sit is always a prelude to sex, but I didn't have that down at the time. It was easy to make him laugh, and our conversation seemed to fill some nostalgic yearning in his exile heart. I decided not to tell him I was queer. I switched to beer.

I was all dollared up for a taxi to the East Bay, where my borrowed flat and travel-mate were waiting, but I'd never caught a cab so late in the city before. The music winding up reminded Dave he had to make a move and I was still sitting by the bar when he came back and said, 'So how are you getting home?'

A voice that sounded like my own emerged from nowhere. 'With you, if you've got a sofa I can sleep on.' Dave goggled at me dumbly for a second or two. 'Yeah, sure. If you don't mind waiting, I'll go get the car.' I still didn't know if I wanted to fuck him. I decided to play it by ear.

Back at his place it quickly became evident that he was doing the same. 'What do you fancy?' he asked me. 'Tea, coffee, lemon-flavoured vodka?' I plumped for the vodka, watching his face. He grinned.

We sat on his sofa and listened to CDs. It was like Miss June in reverse, except I was enjoying the tunes. Neither of us seemed ready to make a move but each time Dave came back from the stereo he sat down a bit closer, until our limbs were starting to overlap and my heart was thumping in my chest. It was time for someone to commit but my inner slapper was on strike and Dave's had plainly been strangled at birth. The idea had taken hold that if I met his eye he'd know I was gay and it would all be off. But now I knew I wanted him, at least. 'I've put the moves on many girls,' I thought. 'He isn't going to lunge, so I'll have to take control.'

When he got up to putz with the CDs again, I sucked up the rest of my vodka double-quick and grabbed him from behind, disabling him. 'Are we going to sit here all night?' I snarled into his ear. He leaned back into me, relieved. 'Let's go to bed.'

His bedroom was vast and empty besides a turntable, and boxes and boxes of 45s. He threw himself across his bed and I threw myself on top of him, wondering how this was going to go. It went okay. We pulled each other's clothes off, just like girls. Dave closed his mouth around my pierced left nipple and sucked, pulling gently on the little steel ring. 'Have you met one of those before?' I asked him, sure he hadn't. He seemed like such a nice boy. I was right. 'No,' he answered, looking up through his lashes at my face. I was curious and touched: 'Is it freaky?'

'No,' he said. 'I like it.' There was something about the way he let the word 'like' roll off his tongue that I liked too. I kissed him and his tongue filled up my mouth, pushed all thought out my head. He slid down my stomach, removing my pants and burrowing his bristly face into my cunt. I shivered away as soon as was polite. It wasn't that it wasn't nice (although it wasn't, very), but it wasn't what I'd come for. I cleared my throat quickly. 'Um, we haven't discussed safe sex,' I said, thinking of Sacha, who happened to live nearby. Dave looked anxious. 'I think I've got a condom somewhere...' He rummaged and found it and then put it on. I felt like a kid in a biology lesson. It was so weird. His cock looked okay. I had no idea what to make of it. Was it big? Small? Deborah's black silicone prick was a good 8 inches and thick, but all dykes are size queens when they're shopping for dick. We fucked and it didn't feel so different from hers. Dave had good rhythm. I went off into that dazed, dopey state where you're not thinking about anything but the thing in your hole. It was good. Then it went wrong.

'You're not really enjoying this,' said Dave.

'Eh? What?' I was stymied. I wasn't enjoying it? I was enjoying it fine 'til he decided I wasn't. My runaway yap struck again. 'You think I don't like to fuck?' I whispered, getting down in his face with my eyes shut, brushing my tits across his chest. 'I like to fuck. I like to fuck girls because I like fucking cock. Do you know what I mean? Girls stay hard forever.' On I went. It was like an incantation, a filthy prayer, I didn't know where it was coming from but it was the truth. There was a strange withering sensation

27

in my cunt. I opened my eyes. 'What's going on?' Dave rolled me off. 'I'm sorry,' he said. 'Um, loss of confidence.' He didn't seem cross or embarrassed, so I felt it was okay.

I kissed him five times fast to show there were no hard feelings on my side, either, and we turned our backs to sleep.

Next morning, I lit out of there like Kelly Holmes, cold light of day smudging the mascara into panda circles round my eyes. We hugged goodbye and Dave said, 'Thank you. It was fun,' but it didn't sound as real as, 'No, I like it,' only hours before. On the doorstep I turned hard left towards the steep hill of 24th Street and almost ran into a cute little dyke with a bag of tools and a flannel jacket. We looked each other up and down a moment and moved on. 'Where were you last night?' I muttered under my breath, but I didn't really mean it.

The sunny city spread out before me like a sharp, sweet dream. It was still early and I wondered if my friend back in our borrowed flat had even missed me yet. Perhaps I'd tell her about Dave. Perhaps I wouldn't. Suddenly I was rushing with power and a kind of brilliant, feral excitement. I tipped my head back and laughed a proper laugh, at me, and Dave, and Sarah and her wife, and Sacha, and Irma, and Deborah and her new girlfriend and every good joke I'd ever wrung from all the fucking misery and bad sex. Below, in my knickers, my cunt clenched hard, a fleshy secret wink, and I whispered down to her, 'Baby, it's you and me.'

It was. And it is.

Tongue Deep
Linda Innes

'Listen,' I said, and hooked my knee over Zoe's thigh: '"I plunge my tongue deep into dark, secret places, where you sheathe and enfold me, quivering. Let us savour this moment, I think, but my mouth is full and it's rude to speak. I withdraw slowly, for an instant. My chin is running with your sweet, milky juices. Instead of diving deeper, I bury the tip of my tongue in the line of your wiry hair, tracing the edge of your plump skin till you tip your mound desperately towards me, reaching, yearning, your heels digging for purchase, knees trembling with tension. Lickingly, I tease the folds and creases of your glistening cunt, escaping tiny moans from your throat. You clasp your feet into my back, spurring me on, grabbing my hair like a mane, wanting to ride my face, bareback, upside down. You are all gravitational pull and I am falling for you in a big way, losing myself in you, plunging headlong, drowning, out of control."'

I stopped, put the book face-down on the duvet over my chest and waited for Zoe's reaction. Nothing. I looked across at her face, nestled by the pillow, where she lay staring at the ceiling.

She glanced at me, 'What?'

'Well, what do you think?'

'It's shit,' she said simply, giving me a twisted grin.

I was shocked. 'Doesn't it do anything for you?'

'Duh... No-o!' She laughed, her face screwed up into an incredulous expression, which made her cuter than ever. A naughty pixie, eyes twinkling, eyebrows askance, her short hair ruffled like a small boy's. Gorgeous. Even when she was taking the piss.

And has it come to this? The years on the pull, the nights on the town, the girl in every port? When the twinkling eye, the slick chat, the one-night-stand was all enough, all I wanted. This is what it's come to. This is it, then, being in deep, so far, so hard, it hurts. This is what love is. Life is. This.

'So what does it for you, then?' I asked, rising to the challenge.

'You!' She kissed my arm.

I waved the book in the air, one finger holding my place, while the pages flapped, 'Come on, there must have been something in it you liked?'

'Cunt.'

'Cunt yourself.'

'I liked where it said "Cunt". And that's about it.' Zoe returned to her psychology textbook.

I frowned. I'd been reading this lesbian anthology of erotic stories for ten minutes, and already felt the familiar throb of my clit, swelling with lust. I wanted to share the experience, but Zoe was already back to studying psychopaths – not good foreplay, in my experience. I swung my leg further over hers, pressing my heel nearer her favourite word, feeling the tickle of her pubes.

'I'll carry on,' I said, clearing my throat.

'If you must,' murmured Zoe, turning a page of her text.

'"I pull back, only thinking of you. If I take time, take pleasure, I can make it better, longer, deeper, stronger... "'

'Like bog roll.'

I ignored her, '"My fingertip skims your silky inner thigh. 'Tickles,' you breathe. My brain takes several seconds to recognise this as a word, let alone its meaning. Your first word since we began, inarticulate in speech, our language something more than words, more than five senses..."'

'It's just bloody words...' Zoe's petulant voice broke in again, 'It's too bloody literary!'

'Okay! Okay!' I skipped a paragraph and cut to the chase: '"I clamber up the bed to smooth your rounded belly, to the soft cup of your breast. I squeeze, feel the skin tighten, your nipple hardens. My clitoris ticks an alarm, beneath, a convulsion of opening, closing. Your hand reaches for me, grabs my breast, mirroring my touch, pinching and rolling my stiff nipple, the direct line to my clit, which echoes with its own rippling twitch. My mouth finds your nipple and sucks, till your legs roll open again, and my fingers circle your clit, hard as an oiled bean, the button that turns you on, switches up the volume, increases the heat, the intensity."'

'Oiled bean? Oiled *bean*?!' Zoe's exclamation was so high-pitched, my ears almost bled.

'Ah, forget it!' I gave up, unfurling my leg from hers and reading to myself. It had been several months since we made love and I was hoping that an erotic story would get her in the mood. Somehow, we didn't seem to have time for one another, what with Zoe's job and degree course, and my work, too. Tomorrow, I'd try the massage oil.

Disappointed, I flicked through to the next story, and skimmed the words.

Zoe thrust her chin on my shoulder, 'What's the scenario?'

'Scenario? Isn't that a bit too bloody literary?'

'I meant it literally.'

'Leather dykes at a gay bar.'

'Yeah. And?'

'No words.'

'Cool. Not literary, then.'

'Just shagging in the toilet.'

'My favourite!' Zoe grinned, kissed my ear, and rolled back to her book.

I read on. The main character, May, a brawny leather bulldagger, had voluptuous Dinah pinned against the cubicle wall, and was ripping her blouse undone. May buried her broad face into Dinah's cleavage and licked the salty sweat from her straining breasts before peeling down the black lace cups and exposing both heavy tits, nipples hard as hat pegs, catching on the lace as May tugged down the bra. Dinah was groaning, her breath heavy, her panting quick and shallow.

I felt Zoe's hand clasp the top of my thigh.

May took both of Dinah's huge tits in her hands and squeezed them, then sucked hard at one nipple. Dinah took a deep intake of breath. Her panties were already damp when May reached down, and wriggled one finger into the drenched crotch.

Zoe's hand stroked me tentatively, but when I made no move to resist or encourage, her touch became more confident. Her hand brushed across my leg, feeling the soft hairs, electrified, goose-pimpling my skin across to my inner thigh.

May's teeth tugged at one nipple, pulling, teasing, as she wrenched down the black panties and grasped Dinah's aching cunt, already slick with come.

Zoe slipped the duvet down to my feet and dipped down to my belly. She circled my navel with a fingertip, then her tongue, and one hand gently prised my thighs apart. Her tongue traced a trail down my belly that caught the chill air, and my breath.

Dinah propped one foot on the toilet seat, widening her dripping hole, eager for May to fuck her. May slipped three fingers easily inside Dinah's hot wetness till she groaned, feeling her tightness strained as May rammed in her fist up to the hilt.

Zoe gently parted my pubic hair and held open my lips. My clit responded to her hot breath, hardening in anticipation. She licked once, teasingly, and I gasped, barely able to hold onto the book and focus on the words.

May punched in and out of Dinah's hot cunt, Dinah yelling in rhythm to the powerful fist-fucking she was getting, shaking the Formica walls of the cubicle and making her big breasts shudder with the force of May's thrusts.

Zoe pushed her tongue under the hood of my clit and began the rapid licking she knew made me melt. I closed my eyes and rested the book on my stomach, my finger still lodged inside, afraid to lose my place.

Then Zoe pushed one upturned finger inside me, which I gripped, desperate. She kept her tongue circling around my clit, while her finger rubbed the hard ribbed beak of my G-spot. Up and down, firm and good, joined by more fingers, countless, and my clit unable to bear it, bursting. In and out she thrust, while somewhere, vaguely in the back of my mind, May fucked Dinah hard and squeezed her tits tightly, and I was being brought to the edge. Fucking. Dinah's wobbling tits, swaying with the force of May's fisting, and Zoe's fast, hard, thrusting made me come in a great wet gush, and I cried out, and cried so hard, with happiness and tears and vulnerability, because I felt whole and wanted, yet open and fragile.

A series of powerful spasms grasped Zoe's fingers so tight that she couldn't remove them. She left them quiet, inside me, while I sobbed, and she lay across me, so close, trying to get inside my skin, to let me know I wasn't alone.

She left her fingers inside, because she knew I would be bereft without them, deep inside me. She left them there until she felt the convulsions and the slow, deep ticking subside, with my tears.

It goes beyond what you know and where you feel safe. It's knowing no boundaries, or recognising that boundaries merely stop you. Acknowledge them, but leap over them. They are there to separate you. There was no separation here, now.

Zoe gradually pulled her hand out of me, with a torrent of juices pouring out in its wake. I came slowly back to consciousness, smacking my lips, swallowing and blinking as if emerging from a deep sleep.

'Did I make you miss the climax?' Zoe smiled.

I didn't comprehend, until I followed her nod and gaze. I held up my near-paralysed hand, still clutching the redundant erotic anthology, my index finger a crushed bookmark, red and creased, but still holding its place.

'I don't think I need this now,' I murmured, 'Thank you.'

'My pleasure.'

Come and Join the Dance
Fiona Cooper

I guess twinkle-toed Fred A. Snail and Ginger Slowcoach have been hoofing it up all night under the moonlight again, for there are silver footprints on the basement step in a pattern like an illustration from an old *'How to...'* Ballroom Dancing paperback. A sparkling twin trail of slime curves around a daisy and into a dark crack in the concrete. I grin like a woman crazed – oh Daisy! – and walk down the street, picturing Fred and Ginger juicing away in damp soil, soft curls of grey green flesh sliding together in molluscular ecstasy.

Let's do it!

On second thoughts, snails are hermaphrodites and they don't need *nobody* to float their boat. They probably do it anyway, just like we all do, awake or asleep, alone or together, mesmerised by the irresistible flood of desire. Maybe it was the daisy drove them into their Palais Glide under the starlight just the way you drive me crazy dawn to dusk to dawn, oh my starry-eyed Daisy! The very thought of you puts me into overdrive, eyes alight like a woman possessed, desire surging from so deep within, every orifice a seismic eruption on the California fault line – even my navel could outgush every geyser in Yellowstone Park. Oh Daisy, look at me now, squeaky clean in every pore, here I am in brand-new lace and silk wet and hot as cling film under my jeans, sticky as any night of hermaphrodite desire, every step an electric shock of anticipation.

Today I'm meeting you.

Daisy, Daisy, give me your answer, do!

I soft-shoe shuffle to the café first. Order a macchiato and Americano, as usual, one to shock me awake and get me buzzing, the other to shmooze me into the day. Sit at one of the pavement tables, feeling like a tourist in my own town.

And this is our café, where we played me and Mrs Jones for years until that day when we were playing no more. And every day became a holiday then, a holiday of loving you.

I have company: two long-legged flying creatures locked together on the peeling wood, tiny gossamer wings shuddering a rainbow of insect passion as they jitterbug towards the slice of blue sky above the High Street. I've just downed my macchiato when a peacock-breasted pigeon starts coming on all Barry White in the gutter, waddling and wheedling, pouting and touting his charms to a lady pigeon who's playing hard to get with a half baguette she's found discarded by the drain. One step, two step, he's belly dancing on her tail and she never stops tossing crumbs for the whole ten seconds of their brief *affaire.*

Met this smashin' bird down by the car tyres, 'cor she was a goer!

The macchiato sends a thousand volts tingling through me and every cell of my body is mad scientist alive. I look at my hands and there's an incandescent blue glow around them. These are my hands.

Well, they were my hands, but now they belong to you. And have done from the moment we first touched.

I am fascinated by my hands as the sun slides up over the all night café and rent-by-the-hour rooms over the street. Sheer daylight adds dazzle to the blue smoke around my fingers. My whole being shimmers into my fingertips and… *I am yours.*

If my hands were a relief map, my fingertips would be a range of impossibly steep mountain peaks. My fingertips thrill as they hover just above your beautiful skin, divining your pleasure. Touching you takes me to heights I've never even known how to dream of. And every tight whorled line there has explored you, mind blown like the first seafarer must have been setting out across untracked oceans and finding that the world has no edge – it goes round and round under the sun and you don't fall off.

When first I touched the curve of your chin and cheek, there was nothing else in the world, only my fingertips and your skin and our eyes shining like fireflies – *oh yes!* We hadn't got a map, there were no signposts, just you, just me, just our fingertips yearning to follow the wordless lights in our eyes, sparking like the birth of a star a zillion light years away. We were confounded and dumbfounded – a pair of stumbling fools who'd happened upon each other. All we knew was we had to be together, no matter where or when, call it love, we were swung into a new dimension and nothing we already knew was a damn bit of use. No words could express it, no reason could halt it, just you, just me. Just us. We hardly know how to breathe for every breath is so heady. Love is our telescope, more powerful than Hubble and in love we fly to a galaxy no one has seen before.

I'm half crazy, all for the love of you!

It amazed the first European explorers that the world we know is round and oh, Daisy, there isn't a straight line in your whole body. Your neck curves into your chin, and I want to tattoo purple flowers of passion there with my lips and teeth. Wanted so much to bite you, and then came the day we could. And my teeth grazed your skin until the blood rushed there and your lovely mouth bit into me and all with no pain. We flaunted our love bites like tattoos all summer and someone said 'you'd think you were teenagers', and we laughed because we know that being in love means you never grow old.

Oh god, how we are in love!

I love to crouch over you, leaning on knees and hands and make my tongue go huge and soft and spread hot saliva deep from the guts of me right up to your earlobes starting at the smooth dip at the base of your throat. Only my tongue touching you, licking you long and loving like a cow licks her newborn calf. Tasting your skin, salt sweet. I let the tip of my nose rub into the smooth contour of your shoulder, rising from the white waves of our bed like an undiscovered sun-kissed island. I press my nose against your arm so all I can breathe is you, your perfume is sunrise caressing wild herbs in a dew-soaked meadow, and our desire is the mist burning into the morning heat.

My second Americano tangos through my veins, a train on a familiar journey, no leaves on the line and no points failure. And still the blue mist wisps around my hands, and you are there, Daisy, always at my fingertips.

I put the warm rim of the cup to my lips and feel your lips on mine for the first time again, the tip of my tongue hesitant - yours too – and then so sure, tasting the first wetness of your beautiful mouth, pushing against your exquisite teeth, lapping your tongue like a thing alive, sucking your lower lip between mine, grazing your upper lip between my teeth, our noses breathing the same air, our eyes gone nova.

When I first slid the white buttons of your shirt from their blue-stitched button-holes, you lying on your side, I became a pilgrim, totally devoted to you. Seven silken veils in a Hollywood sheik's harem could not have been more tantalising than the curve of your breast in white lace. My fingers slid white lace from your breasts and my hand pulsed over your nipple, your soft pink skin twinkling stardust and drawing the pad of my thumb to you like a magnet. Our heartbeat became one.

My mouth filled with a juice so heady my head was spinning at the taste and I drank at your breast, both hands cupped around your flesh, swallowing you like the sand sucks at the foamy head of a wave. I was beached on your wonderful body, your toes stroking the arch of my foot, your magic hands on my shoulders, head buried in your breast, cheek floating over your flesh, then your other breast buried in my mouth, sweeping my head from side to side like a swimmer, moving my lips from you only for nanoseconds to seize a mouthful of air.

Everything a first – my god, Daisy, how do you do what you do to me? – I don't care, just keep doing it. It's as if no one ever had ribs before you, or flesh to cover them, the palms of my hands read your ribs and your navel clasps me like a baby sucking milk. And I never had skin before now, I swear, for your hand on my side and smoothing my hip turns me into uncharted oceans, and where we touch I feel alive as never before. Your fingers wander into the small of my back and my spine is a chain of islands in a turquoise sea. You stroke my back and I am swept by a typhoon, shuddering and helpless, I can only lie in your arms, stroke you as you stroke me, hold you close in this hurricane that blows us way off the scale.

We kiss as divers starved of oxygen, and somewhere my hand

fetches up against your belly, thumb hooked in your navel, fingers hypnotised into a bolero of sheer desire, straying into your hair. I feel your thighs spread apart and your hair fills my hand, my middle fingertip drags down along the incandescent heat of you, shuddering as your flesh gives way to me and oh my god Daisy – worlds collide! – and my fingertip is swimming in the Holy Grail of your desire and need and longing and love for me.

For me. For you.

For us.

I slide down your body, and part your lips with my tongue just like when I kissed your mouth. You taste of wild mushrooms, lychees, sea air, salt water, you smell of all these things and more – my nostrils remember a forest floor, fresh-cut pine, the ozone tang on a midnight beach in an electric storm, and I drink you, gorge on you, starved of you and I never knew what was missing. I am clamped to you until the waves crash and the trees blow away like matchwood, and the wild goats stampede through the trees and the sweetest sound I've never heard before fills my ears – it is you coming to me, my love, my Daisy, it is me coming to you.

There's no going back now or ever and we know it.

And then I am back at this pavement café table, every cell of my body is radar and my phone flashes electric blue and it's you at the push of a button.

'I'm at the end of the street,' you say, 'Don't turn round, I want to look at you waiting for me until I get there.'

I can feel you walking towards me, hear your heels on the pavement and your breathing through the phone, and then your lips are on my neck and I stand to hold you, knock over the chair, the coffee. Daisy, you are wrapped in rainbows and you sweep me off my feet and we shimmer together from head to toe.

'I need to make love with you,' you say.

You always read my mind, not that there's much written there apart from loving you.

'And I want some coffee,' you say, sitting down.

And I say yes and yes and your eyes undress me, and mine X-ray you as you spoon froth into your mouth and lick your lips deliberately slowly, my cat who is the cream of all pussies.

'You've done it again,' I say.

'What's that?' you say, making baby-girl, big blue eyes at me.

'You're even more beautiful than ever,' I say – and it's true. 'And you've just made me have a public orgasm.'

I can see the way your fingers tremble, and I know that rosy pulse in your neck so I just keep staring.

'Ditto,' you say. 'My god, let's go to bed.'

Somehow we walk along the pavement, your breast against my arm, somehow, we lindy-hop down the basement steps without falling, one of us makes magic with a key, and Open Sesame!

We are in our flat, the one we thought we'd never have, the one we live and love in. I don't know why I always dress so carefully, or why we put on new lace and silk and satin next to our skin as it's only ever there for ten seconds as we strip each other as if we'd nearly drowned and our clothes were wet and we were freezing. And now and today even more so – hey, yesterday even more so, tomorrow even more – I love you, Daisy, and your breasts are glorious unfettered from your sensible work bra.

Now we can take our time, my Daisy belle, time to stop and smell the roses. I bury my face between your thighs and my body is an electric eel. Time to stop and stare. We have a spotlight on the floor and I flick it on, all the better to see you with, my darling love. In that tangle of gold and brown hair there is silver too and I stroke the wet fronds aside, leaning my head back to look at the rose deep between your fabulous thighs where my hands pirouette, improvising a new rhythm to love you with.

The skin of your fabulous sex is the palest pink gold, glistening in the spotlight and I dab you with my tongue so you quiver and push towards me. My fingers glow ultraviolet as I part your inner lips and the deep pink flesh leading inside you shines like mother o' pearl, a wave of desire welling from you and spreading over my fingers as I watch your heartbeat pulse in the deep scarlet folds of you. One finger trembles there and I see and feel you open for me, as I move round and round and you open wider, the way sea anemones do in a rising tide.

It is irresistible to move two fingers inside you and feel you tug at my hand. Your quick fingers move in my hair and you say *darling darling darling* like a mantra. You swallow three fingers, then four, and I feel you inside me, the way we do, what you feel I feel, and my passion is a twin to yours.

I am your pilgrim, my Daisy, and my other hand moves towards you, slides inside you palm to palm, and I am praying to you, head bowed, the waters of love pouring from my throat onto this sacred hidden shrine. I worship you, my woman, and my thumbs dance a slow waltz on you, drawing the baby pink core of you from it,s snug folds of flesh, and I pray to you for you are heaven.

Oh god my darling

You draw me deep inside you, swallow all the knuckles of one hand, and my other hand floats along your skin to clasp your breast. You want me deeper and deeper and I feel my middle fingertip clasped by the incredible softness and wire strength of the neck of your womb. I drive deep inside you and let the tip of my tongue go fine and hard oscillating on the taut tip of you. Your nipple grows between my thumb and finger and my palm holds the priceless weight of your breast. My hand is locked inside you, your thighs crash against my breasts, my tongue has become you, and I throw my head back to see you, to see you.

And liquid ecstasy gushes between my fingers, and my love, my lover, my Daisy, we are beatified and you are pouring all over my hand, my face, and you taste like water in the desert, water from a deep, green well. My ears roar with the fragrance of you – waterfalls deep in a wood, steaming glühwein when the air is freezing, salt lassi curbing the burn of ginger and tamarind – my nostrils snuffle into you.

You pull at my hair and say, 'Hold me in your arms.'

I wrap myself round you, rocking you in a wetland of sweat and your delicious thighs wrap round me then collapse.

Where do you take me oh darling where do you take me?

I kiss your neck your lips your eyes your hair and you smile as if it was Christmas. You force your eyes open and there is a universe there, stars, comets, meteors – our eyes make cosmic fireworks in our basement bed. In our love.

'I got no bones,' you say, and your arms flop on my back.

Oh my boneless woman, my Daisy, my lover, my soul made new. I kneel and look at you. At the golden feather between your thighs, the shadows sculpting your body, I lie beside you, shifting your breast so it rests on mine.

'I'm in love with you, Daisy,' I say, all serious to your unresisting lips seeking mine.

'Ditto,' you say and your laughter starts at your navel and ripples through you and you spring on me, throw me down and growl into my neck.

'You're mine all mine and that's forever.'

You must have stolen all my bones, oh Daisy, as your mouth seizes my nipple and a forest fire roars along my thighs. I have no spine but my back is a carnival dragon swaying through fireworks, your eyes are gold, and now your elbows throw my thighs wide and your smooth shoulders pin down my thighs.

Where do you take me, Daisy? Where do we go?

The ceiling is a meteor shower as your tongue strokes me, and my navel, my neck, my ribs, my toes – every part of my skin – is a psychedelic sunrise on some planet light years away as your touch rockets me into eternity. My mouth gasps for air, my ears are fizzing with sheer delight and for all your shoulders hold me down, I am suddenly floating weightless in a different galaxy.

'Hold me, Daisy, I am yours and that's forever and I am you and you are me and we are one.'

'This is the best bit about night shift,' you say, pushing pillows round my molten body, cradling my mind blown head on your shoulder. We are curled together soft as snails with a sheet as our shell. You tilt my chin and prod my eyelids open. I just can't do a thing, Daisy. I'm not asleep, my darling, just loving you.

'I love sleeping with you,' we say together.

'And when we wake up,' you say, 'we'll go snogging down by the water. And eat. And then go back to bed.'

'So bossy,' I say to your breast.

And we sleep and sometime I wake, still in your arms, your nipple still in my mouth. I am hungry for you and slip along your sleeping body and start to smooch your hair, feel you waking as I start to taste you, feel you coming to me with a hot salt gush.

Sleeping with you, waking with you, living with you, loving you.

We can get up and shower and dress, knowing we'll be back in our bed later.

We shimmy down the street hand in hand always.

'How's your story?' you ask. 'Baby, have you finished it?'

'Don't know how,' I say, 'You got any ideas?'

You look at me and smile and your mouth finds my ear.

'What about *"They lived happily ever after?"*' you whisper, your breath and your wet tongue make me weak at the knees. 'I like that one best.'

You lean back and look at me, your lovely eyebrows are question marks.

'Me too,' I say.

'Yes,' you say, 'they made love all the time and they lived happily ever after – because we do.'

My god – we do!

And here comes that grin again and even in the street where the crowds are so thick you have to sashay or be shoved, our feet take us on a cakewalk conga through clusters of parrot-headed punks with wings all tattoos and studded black leather, we limbo-dance around clean-skinned Americans in designer bondage pants, your hand always in mine, and we eagle-walk the path to the canal, where a man in African dress is leathering a wild lambada out of twin drums.

Svetlana
Kathi Kosmider

There is nothing to this. This is nothing. Just as easy as I could say fuck it. The moment was nothing.

This was something that I came to find one weekend. Something that only a fuck could secure. A quick fuck that leaves you with a great deal of security. A sense of security about the power of nothing. How great the nothingness of everything can be. That's cool. That's an epiphany.

It all felt like an Ionesco play, sometime in 1955. I was nowhere and everywhere. While in nowhere, I watch the lady walking with no legs trying to inch her way to the Housing Office to get her housing paid for the month. Who will carry her up the stairs, I wonder? Next to her, this guy just grooves out on the tunes that his CD player is blasting, ignoring even himself. He doesn't give a fuck about Ms Legless. Meanwhile, the bus breaks down and the conductor is playing John Lee Hooker on his harmonica right off Graham Road and it's cold, baby. It's a fucking frozen tundra night. I guess you could say we're all crawling. We're all going nowhere.

My sense of space and time are now suspended in a hologram. And a crawl. A slow, green, caterpillar crawl.

Every single iota of energy was taken from me a while back. I had been moving too fast, trying to find some sort of fusion and fission of grabbing. Grabbing something fast while losing speed and energy.

I had nothing to give to anyone. No stamina for endurance. Nothing for myself, either. I was the empty carcass you see out there from time to time. An outline after the crime scene. I was beautifully simple. So, so sweetly simple.

Will you take me in? It's Paris, it's October and I am spinning out. Like a geranium waiting for the buzz to drink from it. I am no bee but I am dancing for you. Dancing to the beat of some 1985 house-beat that I used to dance to. I'm old now. Well, so much fucking older than your little sister who is standing right in front of me making sure I feel the nothingness of life as purely as I can with her little finger finding its way into my mouth. Fuck that shit.

I got no time to trust her to do the right thing. What's she gonna give me if I feed her for the next few hours in my flat? What a bitch this chick is. She knows it all already. I guess even by the time you're eight, you already know it all. But this one, she moves around me like some chick in *The Big Sleep*, you know when Bogart walks in the door and Lauren Bacall's sister just walks in this circle cruising the guy up and down.

But we're not *film noir*-ing it. That's in my dream. That's in my data bank of memories. Now I only have this flat where the girl dressed in jeans from Jordache and a STUPID CUNT-logo T-shirt stands in front of me, moving into me and ruling against the wall. The peeling, chipping minty wall that I love, that I could lick, and she is dancing against it. She is you. Pelvis is moving against your little-girl pelvis and you must be only 16. You are the sister of the girl I'm supposed to be staying with for the weekend. I don't know, but we end up like this. The wall holds me against you, holding me against the circumference of the fucked-up world that spins around me tonight as I cop a feel for a cop of that shit that'll do me such good.

Look at how my pelvis fits just so. Right there. Look how gorgeous that is. The cut of my bone carves so nicely into the groove of your groin. I always love to look. I look. Most hate that. Look, little girl. She is not looking, but her body is falling into the mint, while I watch her dancing against the void of this fuck that she is in.

Aw, such, such good for me tonight, yeah.

I yours for now. Stupid Russian girlie. What the fuck is your name again?

I keep thinking it should be Svetlana. Yeah, Jerrie. Okay, Jerrie. I'm fucking you, Jerrie. Ooh, do you feel it? Yeah. *Jerrrrie*. Sounds like I'm giving her all the lyrics to these old schoolhouse tunes I remember. That's always a good thing to fall back on when you draw the blank, when you're just a carcass, when the spillage doesn't happen as often as you like it to.

Is this what you want me to say? There is always a script with these chicks, isn't there? Trying to figure out the magic word that makes it all click for each chick is like playing Scrabble, but under compressed time restraints.

I elongate her name. She wants that. She wants me to do that, so okay, I'll do that. Rocking her name with a lull of my lips and my strain to cop from her skin. Is that okay with you? Is that good enough for you, *Jerriiee*?...

You fuck me, you say my name and fuck me.

She is now demanding. Give her what she wants, faster. The faster I get my prize. I mime the words that make her body kick. I'm Ms Marcel Marceau of the fuck-moment. I know how to jack-off an illusion.

Now is better than forever, remember that, Jerrie. Forever is shit. Now is the bomb. She's one of these chicks that will use the 'fuck me forever' line. Any sentence with the word forever is poison and also a superstition of mine. Something really fucked up will happen to this girl. You can feel it.

This girl goes quick and pushes me away. I laugh at how it is. She doesn't want anything but the push of me. Like the weight of a truck-driver, you need that force. Just like she loves her needles. Quick and a short pull. A little shove there. How quick it is. She's sweet, 'cause she doesn't give a shit. Just a quick feel. A little ripple down her spine, so she has a sense of something. Something is better than nothing. Even I know that much these days. But then nothing becomes us both. Suits us.

She gets the shit and we freebase and smooth it into our skins so we stink sweet like some moisturiser for the ladies in Harvey Nicks. Like a spa we're in; we're sweating in this stuff, steaming off our nothing. Yeah, it's like all the nothing at the same time. Over and over again. I know I'm not making sense. I didn't start these words wanting to make sense. I look. I always look while it's happening. The smoke when it comes out of me, into her. Blowing something so sweet is part of my nothing-nature. Part of me to remember Ms

No Legs by and to try to put it in the camera of my brain.

I'm just a fuckin' speck in the peel of her wall, minty and tart. I begin to peel a little of the wall off, while smoothing out my shirt that she's lifted up, little-girl hand and fingers inspecting what I've got hidden inside this leather bra that keeps me tied in. I hate my tits, so I like to strap them down with cool bras that keep me compact. But this chick plays a tune on my nipple, open-mouth laugh held in suspension as she closes her eyes and feels me. *I feel like she's in The Andromeda Strain.* Like she's caught something lethal while she checks out the feel of my nips.

For now she just keeps one forefinger tapping. Like the tap to her syringe. Tap, tap, tap. Baby, nothing's gonna come out of them, so let's move it on, okay.

We're going past Lola Foods now to get some biscuits. We're in Stamford Hill now near Stoke Newington, near the cemetery. Somehow Jerrie ended up coming back to London with me. She had this need to find the Ladytron and Chicks On Speed CD. I guess she couldn't get it in Paris. She began obsessing. I could see she was manic just in the way she tapped my nipples. She's already onto this guy I pointed out to her. She could show him some tricks, because I'm all tricked out. I've moved her on pretty quick. It's all part of the shit I'm on.

Yeah, *Jerrrrieee*… If I remember your name through the Eurotunnel and the silly stuff you gave me, maybe, just maybe, I'll keep on remembering your name. If I don't lose this wrap of gum with the scribbled name and address of someone like you on it.

I see myself at the National Film Theatre four weeks later with a coffee in the huge epic window facing the Thames and I pull out the paper and draw a blank. The girl, the name and the face. Nothing matches. Between Jerrie is the night. Between Jerrie is the nose and the breathing and the shot that keeps me coming up to myself and facing the night time. I can't keep on watching the night unless I'm copping. I cop to see the black. And baby, I am black 'cause black is beautiful. Especially these days in the October light.

Say my name, baby, she says to me.

Fuck, what *is* her name? I ask myself.

I'm a blank again. Not Jerrie, not Sarah, not anything. But I will say 'baby' one more time. And elongate the word. They like that 'cause they think you mean it. Say it like you mean it.

'Okay, baby, yeah; I want you, baby, and you feel so good. Baby just feels so good.'

Now gimmee the works and let me go. Get the fuck outta here. Nothing ever felt good against my skin. One person maybe, but that person is nothing. Always was, 'cause maybe it felt too good to be nothing. But, you know, it's part of it now and forever.

It goes like this. Always like this.

Something into nothing. Or was that nothing is always something?

Just call this nothing that we're in. Validate our void and you'll see the next thousand years in our eyes. We're the ones secure in our plans and priorities. For now, it's trying to get the fucking moths out of my cashmere sweaters. Eating and sucking away at the strands. While I get on Eurostar again to find the sister of a girl I'm supposed to stay with and hope I can cop a feel of the stuff of her that will sit in the palm of my hand, just like so. Those are the plans and the priorities.

Lady gets on train with me, passing out from a panic attack. She has a sweet sense of fear all over her face. It's almost addictive to smell this off someone. I help her. She's someone who stares out of the pass-out moment, eyes rolling out of her head. She seems to be going where I try to go each time, just not quite getting there. Except she seems to be doing it better. These are our plans. Going to nowhere slow and sweet. There is nothing to it. That easy. That fast.

Don't Slip Away
Helen Sandler

Being a lesbian is big news. The government, the press and the college rugby club all hate lesbians; and Sam comes out to everyone, all the time. She comes out to an elderly friend of her tutor at a sherry party in the white house that is the English Department. In front of French windows giving onto neat lawns, she says I'M A LESBIAN. It seems like she's shouting when the word erupts into a roomful of straight people with such force. She is the source of the force, the epicentre, the lesbicentre, the vagicentre. LOOK, I'M ONE!

The guest asks if she has a girlfriend.

Her wise second-year mentor, Ben, prescribes the university-wide Gaysoc. He dresses her in his new red and white paisley shirt from Camden Market and sends her off into the bright evening, promising it will be good for her. But just going into town is stressful. When she gets to Bloomsbury, there are students striding up the street in pairs and groups, past colleges with more definitive names, like University College London or the Institute of Education, and imposing frontages that offer few clues as to which is which. She is late and close to a panic attack when she spots a queue for a cashpoint outside a corner building and above it a small sign saying ULU. This is the University of London Union, known as Yooloo, where Ben once brought her to a disco. She shows her student card at the door, finds the room number on a list and nervously takes the lift to the fourth floor.

About twenty men in jeans and shirts are sitting in a circle. A few wear glasses and one has a worn Frankie Says T-shirt. There is only one other woman. Sam sits in an empty seat across from her and glances at her compelling face: dark-blue eyes, naturally red lips, black curly hair to her shoulders. She looks like someone in an advert for holidays to Dublin. Sam is buzzing, sweating and sparkling at her first-ever gay meeting and she is going to speak to this woman as soon as the men stop talking about coming out.

So far she knows two things from the following list:

This is Anna.

Anna is fresh and new and twenty-two.

Wherever Anna goes, people stare. Her beauty is a liability.

Anna has long fingers.

Anna's hair gets in your face.

Anna's voice is a smooth, deep, knowing BBC English with a tang of the Estuary.

Anna has thick dark pubic hair.

Anna spends her evenings marking essays.

Anna's kisses are wet.

Kissing Anna during sex is like drinking white water.

Going down on Anna is like being blasted over the head with white light.

Going to the pub with Anna is like being made to wait.

Anna is every one of the twenty women Sam will ever get to fuck.

Previously:

The dick of a boy called Pete Pankhurst in Sam's vagina. They agreed to lose their virginities on New Year's Eve at their friends' flat. (More accurately, two flats: Neil's, where they were having the party, and Di's upstairs, where they were having the sex.) Sam had to ask Pete if he had put it in yet. This did not endear her to heterosexual sex and probably did him permanent psychological harm.

The dick of a boy called Baz in her hand while they sat on the couch waiting for Neil and Di to bring out the spag bol and Lambrusco.

The fingers of a boy called Hugh in her vagina on his bed on a summer afternoon before he got up and said it was time to go outside.

The dick of above-named Baz in her mouth and she has no idea how he persuaded her to bend to his fly at the door of their friends' flat but his fat red member was better in her mouth where she couldn't see it than in her hand where she could. She only kept it there for a few seconds. It would be years before it occurred to her that the point of a 21-year-old electrician going out with a 16-year-old girl in a private-school uniform was to get her to do any small thing and then go and reconsider it in the comfort of his own home.

The lap of a girl from school called Becca who encouraged her to share her chair at a party at their friends' flat (as above). Becca was a cool fully formed woman who had been sent to live with her aunt in Manchester (drugs, crime, poverty, violence, racism, riots) to get away from the bad crowd she had fallen in with in Oxford (spires, courtyards, punting). Becca glanced across at her boyfriend, the brilliant actor and heroin addict, took a bottle of poppers from Pete and smiled with her face so close to Sam that she thought they would kiss but Becca was just pressing the bottle to Sam's nostril till Sam's heart exploded.

The dick of a man called Taff thrusting between her thighs when she refused to let him put it inside her on the basis that she had her period and anyway she had only asked him back to her room in the hall of residence because he had nowhere to spend the night so why was she now on the floor under 15 stone of drunken male, trusting only his disgust at menstrual blood to stop him going further?

The fingers of above-named Pete in her pants, bringing her close to climax on the floor of her family's living room before her dad came down to see why he hadn't gone home yet.

The laugh of a girl called Lila not only in the school theatre where they were rehearsing their scene alone but also on the radio two nights a week in a running skit on the Timmy Mallett Show on Piccadilly.

A painted male angel is falling in all his glory from the ceiling. A warm breeze blows through the open door. Red Stripe is half-price, there are actual lesbians everywhere you look, and Anna's leg has just touched Sam's under the table. A surge goes to her toes in their

DM boots and to the ends of every short hair on her head. Her fingers as they reach for her beer are shaking.

A helper at the Gaysoc meeting told them about the weekly women's night here and they agreed to go together, for moral support. All week Sam has been sure it isn't a date.

She doesn't move her leg and neither does Anna.

"So, I'm finally getting some feedback on my teaching practice," says Anna.

"Oh yes. What's it like at the Institute?" asks Sam. There is no way she can exactly match the previous line of dialogue because she is highly distracted. For the first time in her eighteen years, she might get to make love to someone she truly desires.

It is urgent. She takes Anna's hand. Anna Anna Anna. She looks at her and sees that she's not looking back, it's all unclear, it's not quite... is it right? She moves her fingers across Anna's palm and sees her feeling it, feels her feeling it; their legs press against each other and Sam is filled with courage and moves her own knee to fit between Anna's thighs. She is burning, her face is burning. Christ.

Anna is expressionless. This is not going to happen in the way it happens with a boy. Sam has to be the boy. She gets up. "Let's go for a walk."

They go out of the pub, cross the road and walk through the children's play area, where twelve-year-olds are drinking from cans, down to the canal. Sam's heart feels like she's glugged a pot of coffee. Her breathing is too shallow and she's staring too hard at Anna. This could still go wrong. This may already have gone wrong. And then Anna smiles.

Sam has kissed a lot of boys and thinks she knows about kissing but when Anna's lips meet hers, there is more to them. There is more give in them and they seem to carry on into her mouth and Sam's mouth is inside Anna's mouth or the other way round, their mouths are wet and merging and the only hard thing is teeth. Anna has a squashy squeezy wet mouth and she apparently wants Sam. She wants her so much that she is coming back to the hall of residence.

*

These things are not yet clear:

Anna is more experienced with men and less experienced with inner torment.

Anna doesn't want anyone thinking she might be masculine like Sam.

Anna has to pick up a kitten from her parents' house a hundred miles away next weekend and Sam is the one who sits in the back of the car with it.

Anna is not going to tell anyone she is with Sam.

The noticeboard is covered in the previous occupant's rendering in marker pen of Fred Flintstone buggering a dinosaur. Why hasn't Sam covered it up? It looks disgusting. Why would a beautiful intelligent grownup teacher want to have sex in this room? The intimacy they gained on the bench by the canal has been lost again on the journey home and now Sam can easily imagine the potential slipping out of the evening: Anna yawning and saying casually that she should be going.

But Anna is in the toilet down the corridor and there are still ways to prevent that outcome. The narrow bed is up against the wall, under an overhanging cupboard, where Sam pushes it each morning to make enough space to walk across the room. Now she leans down to pull it out and something bangs against her skull from the inside: the lead ball that has built up in her head over the past two hours, the pressure. She puts on the kettle and the new Communards tape, takes off the quilt made out of pieces of her childhood. 'You Are My World' sings forth in Jimmy Somerville's high voice, full of parties and buds in spring.

The door swings open and there is Anna, rolling her eyes. "Nice bathroom."

"Oh God. It's horrible, isn't it? Someone stole my jeans out of there last week!" Keep talking. "Most of the halls here are really beautiful old buildings, but this is a new one."

"It looks like they haven't finished building it."

"No," says Sam, "they ran out of money so they didn't bother plastering the walls."

"Hmmm." Anna narrows her eyes and gives a lazy smile. "Got anything to drink?" It doesn't sound like she means tea. She crosses the small space to sit on the edge of the bed – the only seat available. Sam has to stand on it to get the whisky from the cupboard. She glances down at Anna who is looking at the Flintstone noticeboard with mild interest.

To distract her, Sam says, "The cleaner told me the girl next door keeps a gerbil in her cupboard."

In the short silence that greets this remark, Jimmy goes to bed with a prayer that Lover Man will make love to him. Sam sinks down with the bottle in one hand and a glass in the other, crosses her legs to steady herself, hands the glass to Anna and fills it to the top with Scotch. "Let's share it."

Like a cat making friends, Anna gives a slow blink and a relaxed "Mm". She drinks languorously and passes the glass to Sam, allowing their hands to touch for a second. It is as if she planned all along – while Sam was expecting a platonic drink in their first gay pub – to end up here in this cell. And now that she's here, she has switched into the mode she would use with a man. The kiss by the canal seems long ago, with a different Anna.

Sam takes a swig from the glass. The whisky burns down her tubes and opens them up for air. The beat of the music presses her onwards. 'Don't Slip Away'. Is there any doubt what will happen next? Possibly, probably, yes, anything.

She gives back the glass and watches the other woman drink from it, then uncrosses her legs and puts it on the floor. It's like being in a lesbian film on Channel 4: two women in a room alone on a bed. Then Sam does what would happen next: she strokes Anna's arm.

"I really like you," she says, heart pounding, pressing her left leg against Anna's right.

Anna moves her head suddenly, stares intensely at Sam and says, "Kiss me, then."

Their noses slide against each other as if they are nothing but polished bone and their lips feel for each other as if they have never kissed before, because this is the start of making love to a woman for the first time and as they press their mouths together, Sam feels the thrill of it, the fear and dread and strange right wrongness of it. She is so full of want but she can't get to what she wants. Their hands are on each other's backs and their mouths are locked together, tongues exploring and both of them involuntarily moaning from the power of the kiss and what it promises.

Then Anna's hands are on her waist. Where Sam doesn't dare to reach under Anna's blouse, Anna is pulling at Sam's shirt while she kisses her, her hands moving up inside it to stroke Sam's breasts. Sam gasps and pulls her mouth from Anna's. "Oh my God." She flops down on the bed.

"Shit. Anna, lie down... I can't." She starts to laugh.

"What?"

"I don't know, I'm... Isn't it weird?"

"Yes."

Then she wishes she hadn't said anything because doubt comes into Anna's face. "Shall we stop?"

"No! Please, no. I really want to do this. With you."

"Yeah, but..."

"Lie down. Anna! Lie down with me."

And she does. The song is about getting an angel. And then they are on each other, passionate but still unsure, a combination that Sam hasn't known for years, since the first time she sat in the cupboard at the youth club with Ray Hand and kissed him till his long thin tongue was right in the back of her throat and his namesakes were inside her bra. Sam doesn't wear a bra any more. Anna opens Sam's striped shirt and the air cools her breasts and frightens her. Anna is stroking Sam's breast. Anna is.

Sam slips a hand under Anna's blouse and up, wanting to do the same to her. She strokes her breast and cups it. It is a bit bigger than her hand and held tight by a bra made from smooth material. While she is guessing, immobile, Anna takes control and unbuttons her own blouse, looking at Sam with disbelief. "I don't know what we're doing," she says.

"What do you mean?"

She raises her eyebrows.

"What?" asks Sam.

"Don't you feel the same?"

"I feel…"

She is pushing her hand inside Anna's bra to avoid having to undo it but Anna reaches round and releases the clasp, saying, "Don't you feel like we shouldn't be doing this?"

"No." Sam stills her by taking her in her arms. Their breasts press together but the bra is still in the way. "I feel like we should."

Then Sam is wrapping and coiling Anna's curls round her fingers as she pushes her tongue deep into Anna's mouth, sucking on her, pulling her out of her resistance. Where is the flirt who blinked at her ten minutes ago? What is it they are both afraid of? Just this and what comes next?

They kiss until they can't breathe. Sam inches her mouth round to kiss Anna's cheek, soft and smooth, then her neck, her shoulder, pressing Anna's warm body into hers. Anna's skin is pale and she doesn't have much flesh on her but she is softer than any boy. Each kiss traces smooth skin and under it, sinew and bone. Sam doesn't know anyone who looks like her and has nothing to compare this to in real life but she is easing off Anna's blouse and bra. Her naked breasts are curved and beautiful. Sam kisses one and Anna's moan shoots through her. Their legs wrap closer, thighs pressing into crotches, hips starting to move.

Anna makes a sound and raises her mouth to meet Sam's. They are joined so tight, they're merging. But the challenge of Anna's black trousers lies ahead.

Sam says, "I want to…"

"Mm."

Without thinking, her knee is jammed between Anna's legs, her mouth back on her breast, sucking at the nipple and then at the whole soft mound of it, with the other one in her hand for later, precious, and both in a place where a man only has a chest.

"You're so soft," she says, looking up.

"So are you."

*

It does not occur to either of them to say:

> I need it, you bitch.
> Fuck me.
> Oh, you know what I like.
> You're so big and hard.
> Who are you thinking of?
> I've had an HIV test.
> I'm seeing that other girl on Wednesday.
> Eat me out.
> Put your fist in me.
> You want that, don't you?
> Take it.
> I used to inject.
> I love your dick.
> Hurt me.

Sam wants all of her at once. She unzips Anna's trousers and eases a hand inside, gasping at her own audacity and the feel of a woman's pants under her fingers. She half expects to be told to stop or wait but there is just a gasp from Anna as Sam slips a finger under the waistband of those plain black briefs. She slips it out again and runs it over Anna's belly but regrets the backwards move and slides back in there, two fingers running down across smooth skin to thick hair. She bends her head to look, rolls Anna's knickers down with her thumb and brushes her fingers through the curly hair.

Anna is nothing but breath. Sam has to get those trousers off. She wrenches at them and Anna comes back to life to help her, shoving them down her legs and kicking them aside, not looking at her. Sam needs to see her face before she goes any further. She does a push-up and looks Anna in the eye, kisses her gently and deliberately and is reassured by Anna's tongue pressing urgently into her mouth.

Go.

"I don't know…" murmurs Anna.

Stop. "What?"

"I don't know what to do."

"Neither do I." But even as she says it, she is guessing what to do, stroking slowly down to where the bush of hair starts to feel damp, kissing Anna's neck as her fingers glide through that hair to more wetness, blindly feeling for a way in. Anna cries out and Sam is pushing between or through... There is a moment when she thinks she will have to give up. Then her finger slides into place through the slippery entrance to this mysterious other woman with her own vagina, like but not like Sam's. Now they both cry out. She didn't know it would be like this. Her fingers are in Anna and they are moaning into each other's mouths.

Sam pushes two fingers further inside Anna and starts to move them in and out, back and forth, slowly exploring, wishing the chorus about forbidden fruit wasn't belting quite so loud out of the cassette player. Anna is narrower than Sam inside. Her juices are slippery and her hips are moving slightly. Sam is still wearing jeans. She doesn't know if that's all right or not. She wishes she could feel Anna's legs against her own but it's too late.

Anna's breasts pillow hers. She drops her head and sucks. That part is strange. The vagina part is beautiful but the breast part is more unfamiliar – she has put her fingers inside herself many times but she has never sucked her own breast.

"I think you've done this before," says Anna, who seems to have composed herself and started deliberating.

She moves her head for long enough to say, "I haven't." Then she thinks of other places to put her mouth and moves down Anna's body. She wants to lick her but doesn't know if she can do it at the same time as moving her fingers in her. First she has to find the way. The smell is sweet musk, channelled from between Anna's legs to Sam's nose. She lowers her head and licks just above her own fingers, up and down, trying to make it seem like she's exploring rather than unsure. Anna moans. Sam makes longer licks, moves to the right a little and finds something that could be the clitoris. She pushes her tongue harder against it and Anna's hips jolt.

Oh God. She has her fingers in a woman and her tongue on her too. That would be enough in itself but it's not just any woman, not someone she threw herself at to have an experience; no, it's Anna, who is amazing.

Anna's hand drops to the back of Sam's head and strokes her hair like a pet. She's moaning in time with Sam's movements and it's the only sound in the room – the tape has finished and the other noises are from other rooms, voices in the corridor, a radio upstairs, someone outside talking to a friend. No one knows what is going on in this room. The perverted things they've been debating in Parliament are going on in this room.

Anna is close to climax. Sam is pushing her fingers in and out and licking at that small swollen bud because she guesses it's the right thing to do. And it's appreciated. She feels two hands tightening on her head and focuses her movements. Her face is trapped; it's hard to breathe and it's uncomfortable, hair scratching against her nose and mouth. She wonders if she's got it right, but moans are escaping from the back of her throat: first Anna moans, then Sam, then Anna.

They are both quiet but intense in their sounds and Sam lets herself be the sound and the smells and the rich, tangy taste. She pushes her fingers in deeper and feels Anna tighten round them. Now they are moving together, faster and faster, Anna gasping and moaning and giving in to it, moving her hips up and down as her hands drop from Sam's head to press into the mattress. She moans louder, more like speaking, more high pitched, and then slumps, her insides still gripping Sam's fingers in quick pulses.

It seems like she has had an orgasm but Sam has never been with anyone else when they had an orgasm except Pete and Taff and they weren't like this. She wants to keep going. She remembers when she first started masturbating, years ago, how she wanted to find out what was beyond the orgasm and she kept going even when it felt bad and sometimes there was another surge that shook her harder still. But she doesn't think Anna wants her to keep going. She leaves her fingers inside her and licks her once. Anna's hips ride up from the bed again.

Then there's a sigh and a hand on her cheek. Sam slowly pulls her fingers out. They are separate.

She wipes her hand across her face and moves up Anna's body. Those big blue eyes are wide open and Sam kisses her, soft lips merging into each other. She has done it. She has made love to a woman and done it right.

She lies on top of Anna until she can't ignore the pounding in her own body, gets off the bed to pull off her jeans and lies back down, uncertain of her reception. Anna kisses her like an apology and moves her hand down between their bodies to Sam's cotton pants. She slips her fingers under the waistband. That's when Sam shudders and whimpers, knowing that Anna will do some or all of what has been done to her.

Next day, Sam stops on her way from the Middle English seminar to the library and steadies herself against a tree because her head just jerked and her legs just gave at the knee as Anna's fingers sliding into her cunt came back to her like a visit from an angel, like a ghost of Anna that wants to fuck her on the lawn.

By the time the House of Commons has approved Clause 28 of the Local Government Bill, Anna has qualified as a teacher and is back with an old boyfriend. She's not a lesbian after all.

Eighteen years later, when they bump into her in a dyke bar, Sam's partner says, "She's pretty."

"Yeah. I remember she had this kitten..." She stops.

"And?"

"Never mind," says Sam. "It's probably dead by now."

Lamaze
Monica Trasandes

Claire is floating, naked, in the middle of her pool on a humid night in the middle of August. I am holding her. Seven months pregnant, with a belly covered in freckles, she looks like a lily pad from some undiscovered planet. Her hair, which is dark brown, curly and long, floats all around her head and makes me think of a Spanish poem about a dead gypsy lying on her rooftop under a big, white moon. I watch Claire's eyelids – closed but flickering lightly, trying to stay shut.

I move her around a little, the way one plays 'boat' with a child, although we don't move much because, even in water, a pregnant woman is a heavy thing. Claire smiles.

"Am I too much?" she says, her eyes still shut.

"No," I say and, as if to prove it, kneel lower and put my face against the hardness of her belly. I press my forehead against the side of her stomach – a hard wall of flesh – and wonder if the baby, on the other side of the wall, is also pressing his forehead against the very same spot. Like two people on different sides of a dark window, will we suddenly see one another? The thought frightens me a little and I stop doing it.

Claire lifts her head from the water. "Want some watermelon?" she asks.

"Sure."

I carry her to the steps, which takes so long, it feels as if we are moving in slow motion. Climbing out of the pool, she holds on to the railing tight, not for show, like most people. She waddles to the lawnchair where she discarded her clothes and tries, in vain, to reach for the dress lying there. No use.

"Oh, whatever," she says and goes inside.

I put my arms out and shut my eyes tight and push out onto

the middle of the pool somewhere. Even I don't know where I've ended up.

Across the patio and inside the house, the refrigerator door squeaks ever so slightly and I hear the scraping of the fruit crisper as Claire pulls it open. She's forgotten that the watermelon is sitting on the counter.

Sometimes, when I think of Claire and me and Lolly, the boy due to arrive in a couple of months, I feel as if our lives will resemble one of those television commercials where the parents rub lotion on their child and on one another, the type of commercial where the lighting is done in such a way that the people look like peaches, their skin gold and fuzzy and with narration done by someone – preferably with an English accent – whose voice crackles with love. That's some of the time. Most of the time, I feel as if we are, and will always be, three very separate entities with no hope of real connection.

I've known Claire for a very long time – twenty years to be exact – although we didn't really communicate for about five of those years, the five in which she met and married Dave Wexler, Peace Corps dropout, successful hat manufacturer, dimple-chinned coward.

I don't hate him because he's her husband. Let's get that theory out of the way immediately. Actually, I don't hate Dave at all. When we happen to overlap, we chat amiably. He knows I'm more than a friend, I know he's less than a husband, but really we have no reason to dislike one another. Dave's not in love with Claire any more and I think he sees me as the kindly nanny who is caring for this person he married, the one he doesn't have the guts to divorce.

He's not entirely to blame. She's afraid, too. They're both afraid and so am I. Imagine how Lolly must feel.

This weekend is supposed to be different. None of that is supposed to matter. Dave has gone to New York to buy wooden hat blocks, so Claire planned this weekend for us. She thinks of it as a chance to do all the things we never get to do – make love for hours, cook in her kitchen, swim, take walks... Crowning our weekend of domesticity will be the ultimate matrimonial act – on Sunday we are to attend a lamaze class.

I think lamaze is a good idea. In fact, I've been having dreams that the baby will want to come out early and Claire, not having had a single class, won't know what to do. In my dream, instead of pushing, Claire starts crying. No one can get her to stop and finally the baby gives up and just falls asleep – forever. She needs to be in a lamaze class, but I'm not sure I do.

I once wanted to float away with her, go to a place where our lives could start over, together. We even talked about it, about all of the places everybody else has been talking about for the last ten years. "Costa Rica," we would say, "let's go to Costa Rica." No, it's full of expatriates now. "Spain?" No, the Spanish are too arrogant. "What about Portugal?" we would say. We didn't know much about Portugal, except for stories told by a friend about a castle on a hill with lakes filled with black swans. So that's where the fantasy always ended – with Portugal, which, because of our ignorance, seemed a safe, sweet haven.

I'm not sure what Claire's fantasies with Dave consisted of. She's never talked about them, but, come on, they are married, after all. Maybe they dreamt of buying a house in the Pacific Northwest, where Dave could fish every day after work, or maybe they thought about moving to Montana or Idaho. I don't know about her other fantasies, but I do know that she went nowhere, that she was stuck in Santa Monica, in a loveless marriage and a nearly loveless extramarital affair, which I think is why Claire rebelled.

Frustrated with her inability to change her life for herself, Claire decided to let nature do the work and she got pregnant.

Claire comes back out of the house with a big salad bowl filled with watermelon. It's very pink and, for a minute, looks like flesh.

"That looks like meat," I say to her. "Like beef."

"Have some," she says. "I put lime and salt on it."

Claire is the editor of *Entrée*, a food magazine, so everything she puts into her mouth is different from the way most people have it. Her water sometimes has a sprig of mint in it, or a slice of grapefruit, sometimes just plain old lemon. I like this about her. She doesn't dress herself very expressively. On her person, she favors silk shirts and tailored pants or a nice dress worn with a single string of pearls, but her food is always decked out. Ever since going to Mexico last year, she's taken to putting salt and lime juice on fruit, which does indeed taste wonderful.

She pulls a lawnchair toward the pool with one hand, still holding the bowl of watermelon with the other.

I was once very, very much in love with her. In fact, I remember being seventeen and floating in my own pool, late at night, after my parents had gone to sleep, staring at the stars and at the fat, squat palm trees my father had planted too close to the pool, and wishing she would love me. That hunger for Claire, so strong and seemingly impossible, still hurts my heart. I doubt I'll ever want anything so much.

She and I did everything together in high school – debate team, tennis doubles partners. On weekends, we would drive ourselves to the beach and lie under a blanket reading J.D. Salinger aloud and drinking red wine, which made us feel so womanly, though we hadn't a clue. We pronounced it Merlott (as in house on a lot or the wife of).

Her parents liked to visit family in Los Angeles and Claire and I, on the pretext of having to study, would stay all alone in the big, sprawling house, which was draughty and slightly dingy but also had two pianos and shelves full of books and a whole wet bar – nothing like my own home, where the three books we owned were on the coffee table, one atop the other with a dried rose crowning the achievement.

Claire's father was an accountant, her mother a real estate agent and, although I now know they were just middle class, to me they seemed rich, upstanding, landed.

When Claire's parents went away, we did, indeed, spend all of Saturday studying, usually on her bed or together on the couch, but, always, by seven, the books were put away and each of us retired to a bathroom where we bathed and dressed for dinner – Italian food, delivered – which made us feel terrifically grown up. And we never ordered pizza, always fettuccini alfredo or linguini with clams. We went through a Chinese period after watching a

Woody Allen movie, but that faded fast and we soon returned to linguini.

We always ate in the dining room and drank Merlot, then retreated to the living room where we read aloud to one another or played the piano. It was actually Claire who taught me to play the piano, spending hours patiently moving my fingers onto the right key or just listening as I labored through a song, note by painful note.

On those weekends alone, we always fell asleep, on the couch or on her bed, always hugging.

We were aware of what we had and even named it – synchronicity, after the name of our favorite album by The Police. Sting, the band's leader, was also our man, the object of our affections, the impossible heartthrob who made it safe to be in love with each other. "Synchronicity," we would sigh and fall asleep like a happy old couple, together fifty years.

And then, about a month before we were to leave for college, after having spent every day together, savoring every second of every hour, I got the flu and she had to spend four days without me. On the third day, when the doctor said I would no longer be contagious, she came over with orange popsicles and a Police fanzine.

"Hi sweetie," she said. That's what Claire called me then. She unwrapped the popsicles, pulled out the magazine and climbed into bed with me. With my mother god knows where in the house, Claire and I sat in that bed, holding the popsicles away from the bed so they wouldn't melt and kissing one another with the kind of ferocity that only a young heart could endure.

That was us then, before we parted for four years of undergraduate studies, two of graduate school (three for me). Then she married and moved to Los Angeles, where she started at *Entrée* as a temp. I came out of the closet and became a reporter at a small paper, before landing a job as an education reporter in Los Angeles, where we met again, completely by chance, in the bathroom of a Bullocks department store during a three-day sale. If it were not for the sale, and a line out the door, she might never have stepped out of the stall and seen me standing there, staring at my shoes.

We had dinner together that evening, and brunch the next day with Dave. By the second evening, that which had been interrupted by college and schoolgirl attempts to live our mother's lives was set in motion again.

"Don't you want more melon," she says, as I tread water in the deep end, which is not very deep, only seven feet.

"How's Lolly?" I ask her.

Ever since the sonogram, we've known it's a boy. Dave's father, the first person to weigh in with an opinion, wants to name him Lyle. Dave has no opinion on the matter. Claire and her entire family are set on Jordan, which to me might as well be Lexus or Rolodex. It's so yuppy it makes me physically ill. I've stayed out of the formal name contest but have given the child my very own nickname – Lolly. I don't care if he is christened Lyle Bonaparte Jordan III, to me he's Lolly.

"He's in a meditative place," she says. "He's meditating, or sleeping. He kicked today, at the gas station."

"The fumes."

"You think," she says, as if I've just predicted he'll be born deformed.

"He likes them. He's destined to drive a Harley and spend way too much time hanging out at the Chevron, cruising girls in short skirts, just like his mom."

Claire throws me a nice condescending smile. That is part of the problem, of course, that she would never admit to looking at a woman in a short skirt, or a long skirt, or any woman anywhere.

"Dave says he's going to be a doctor," she says, revenge for the short skirt comment.

"I guess Lolly will figure it out for himself," I offer and close my eyes and float away again – my revenge.

I swim underneath the water for a long time. It's so quiet and wonderful inside her swimming pool. They have a black bottom, which I've convinced myself looks and feels like the bottom of a river. I swim around pretending to be in a Jacques Cousteau documentary. I'm the world's best diver. I'm it. I'm the only one they call when they need this sort of job done – whatever job it is that I do. I'm so famous and have been for such a long time that I can't imagine what it feels like not to be indispensable. And I'm also out of air.

As I emerge, Claire kicks water at me.

"You were under a long time," she says.

"Big lungs."

Claire and I go into the house and take showers then go to bed and drift off to sleep holding hands.

The next day, we get up early. It's Friday but I have the day off because I've been working late all week, covering school board meetings. The Los Angeles Unified School District is having a huge crisis over a group of white, middle-class parents who single-handedly took over a school, saying that they are going to bring it "back to basics".

Nothing is likely to happen today, but, just in case, I have my beeper, laptop and cell phone. This story, which has caught the attention of the national media, means I've made it, that I'm playing with the big boys and girls chasing page one superstars: serial killers, crooked politicians and stealing CEOs. But, even better, the main character of my stories – the angry tax payer who just isn't going to take it anymore – is a real hero, known for his or her courage, not infamy. He's the newest page-one superstar.

I'm not exactly proud of what I do – telling the people's story. The people, in my opinion, are currently a rather undereducated, over-empowered bunch, but what can I do? I wanted to be a reporter, I studied to be one and here I am now, loaded down with gadgets and constantly on call, which only reminds me of the cruelty of life, making us yearn for something forever, only to pull the plug on desire just as the object of affection walks through the door.

Claire has to prepare the cover of her magazine for the next issue before she can take any time off. She's gotten a well-known fashion photographer, Juan Mali, to do a shoot featuring dark green vegetables, red fruits – cranberries, if she can find fresh ones, definitely pomegranates – and fall-colored foods like pumpkin soufflé and squash soup. She's going in to work to try it out and see how things look. I am to do the food shopping for us, for the weekend. She's very excited about cooking.

Dave, who is a vegetarian, rarely lets Claire cook his food. She can cook whatever she wants for herself, but all of his food comes from some sort of vegan service. Every year, a new product is extracted from his diet. Last year, it was butter, because of its fat and so forth, now he's talking about outlawing wheat, because it allegedly sticks to your colon.

"That would be too much," Claire says when she talks about it. Personally, I think it's his brilliant way of pushing her to leave the marriage.

In addition to butter, I am to buy all sorts of spices for Claire's homemade Cajun blackening mix, as well as red potatoes, white corn (open each stalk and make sure the teeth are small and lined up straight because they're the sweetest), cilantro (small-leafed, not large), mangos (firm or it'll be too sweet), strawberries, whipping cream (heavy), pancake mix, syrup (all maple), swordfish and a whole lot of other very specific items. Sometimes I can understand why Dave pulled completely out of any culinary arrangements with a woman who is a food specialist.

It takes me forever to finishing shopping, probably because I waited until the afternoon and ended up in a huge glut of Santa Monica servants trying to buy all the firm mangos. In the salad dressing section, I even witness one maid, holding a cell phone to her ear, reading the ingredients of the honey mustard dressing to her boss, I presume.

"It doesn't say how much fat," the young woman with dark skin and stooped shoulders whispers into the phone, obviously not accustomed to calling people from the middle of grocery stores. She looks as if she is talking to a beau from her parents' room.

Moments like this make me certain of what I need to do: say goodbye to Claire, say goodbye to the newspaper, fly to Costa Rica, and start an English-language newspaper for all of the expatriates living there. *Yank No More*, it could be called, or *Bye, Bye American Pie*.

I fantasise about leaving during the entire time spent at the check-out line and then on the drive back to Claire's house.

When Claire comes home, I'm lying on a lawnchair reading a movie magazine.

She pulls a chair up to me and sets down a bottle of wine and hands me a glass which she fills, smiling all the while, feeling pretty proud of herself. Claire loves wine. The fact that she can't drink has been the worst part of pregnancy. Like people on diets who force those around them to eat, Claire forces myself, Dave and all of her friends to drink up and consume her share of wine, which is significant. Perhaps I've not had sympathy pregnancy, but I have gained weight right along with her, from all that Chilean Merlots and Australian Shirazes she's plied me with.

"Thanks for shopping," she says, still smiling. I can't echo her mood, so I focus on the wine, which tastes good going down the back of my throat. By the third sip, it feels like courage.

Claire is leaning in, as if she wants me to kiss her, but all I can do is put my hand on her leg.

"I've got the vegetables," she says and I know what she means. She came up with a good mix, good colors for the cover. "Did they call from work? Anything happening?"

"No. Everyone's taking the weekend off."

"Good," she says, then out of the blue, Claire pulls up her dress to expose her belly. She's tried to put on sexy purple briefs but the effect is not quite right and she looks as if she's wrapped a thin necktie around herself. "I'm happy," she says.

"Nice underwear," I say and it comes out sounding sarcastic, mean.

Claire looks at me for a long time as if I just hit it, the limit, the place at which cynicism and unhappiness are so prevalent, so thick and heavy, like a bad smell hanging in the air, they will no longer be ignored.

"What's the matter?" she says and throws her hand on mine, a somewhat affectionate, but also punitive gesture, since the heavy silver ring she wears raps my knuckle as her hand falls on mine.

My throat closes up. Why is the truth so frightening?

"You're a married lady," I tell Claire and the candor takes even me by surprise.

"That's right," she says. "Should I be otherwise?"

This scares the hell out of me. She's never directly asked if I want her to divorce Dave.

"What do you want?"

"Well," she says and looks at me honestly, not thinking about anything, I can tell, just looking at my face. "I want to be happy," she says and picks up my hand and holds it in hers. "What do you want?"

My hand feels good inside hers, warm, protected. When we were girls, we held hands often and even took a picture once of our fingers entwined, so enamored were we of the idea of us, together.

"I don't know," I say. "I guess that's my problem. I don't know what I want any more. I just don't know, Claire."

She nods a few times and stops looking at me. I can tell she's reworking my words in her mind, attaching their appropriate meaning. I'm 32 and she's 33. In a lifetime of boyfriends and girlfriends, we have both had more than one person say "I don't know what I want," and we have both understood what it meant.

I don't dare do anything but look at the pool. Claire takes the glass of wine and finishes it, then goes inside and lies on the couch. She stays there for an hour or more, while I sit by the pool. Later, we talk just enough to decide we don't feel like cooking. Instead, we open an avocado and spread the bright green meat on rosemary bread, which Claire seasons with a combination of cayenne and salt. By ten, we're in bed – together but as far away as two people could ever be.

At about two, maybe three, Claire sits up in bed, which awakens me.

"The cayenne," she says and rubs the area under her belly, where she must imagine her old stomach to be. "I don't feel so well and it's so fucking hot," she says. She's talking the way people do when they're only half-conscious.

"Okay, okay, lie back down. I'll get you water."

"Yeah, yes, please, water." She lies back down, still rubbing her stomach.

As I reach the kitchen, I hear a television somewhere in the distance. Her neighborhood is usually quiet and peaceful.

Neighbors here don't watch television until all hours, like in my neighborhood. Or if they do, they're watching civilised things without laugh tracks.

Not tonight. Even the mineral water is noisy, the bubbles crackling and popping in the glass. The kitchen is as light as if in daytime. I lean toward the window – a full moon. No wonder someone is watching television.

While Claire drinks her water, I go into the bathroom and find, below the sink, something to surprise her, a spray bottle, which I fill with cool tap water.

"It's hot," she says, lying down again, her eyes closed.

"I know." I spray her legs first, so it won't be such a shock, then her arms, and a little on her face. Finally, I hit her belly.

"It's raining, Lolly," I say and that makes her smile.

"Thank you," she says and turns to the side. It's easier on her body that way.

Claire rearranges the cadre of pillows with which she sleeps, the ones behind her for back support, the ones between her legs to help her hips, and, finally, the one she hugs like a teddy bear. Within seconds, her breathing is steady and she's asleep again.

I can't sleep so I toss and turn for a few minutes thinking that eventually I will slip back into unconsciousness. Maybe a walk and a glass of wine will help. I pour myself a glass and decide to go sit beside the pool, but my nightgown is upstairs, so I go into the laundry room. Towels are stacked atop the dryer. They look like hotel towels and I can tell that Wilomena, the Wexler's maid, has ironed them again. Claire has told her countless times not to iron towels but Willi is convinced that tiny bugs fly into them, bugs that only a hot iron can chase away.

I take two towels and wrap one around my hips and the other around my shoulders, like a spa guest. The beeper sits in the middle of the fruit bowl on one of the counters. I mustn't forget it.

The thought takes away my breath and I rush outside.

I don't want to think about this, but I can't help it. As I sit and put my feet in the water, my mind begins an inventory of all the little things I've either left or loaned her, things I should remember to take with me – white shirt, black dress I wore to her friend's party, the earrings from Mexico she gave me, the Spanish poetry books, now out of print, my signed Borges collection...

When I was 16 and 17 and 18, Claire's love was all I wanted. I wanted it with all of my heart. I don't know that I can say the same about anything since.

My parents would go to bed at about 11:30 or midnight and I would walk out onto the patio and up the little gray walkway leading up the incline, to the pool. Even at night, the sidewalk was warm, holding on to some of the day's sunshine. It was hot in El Cajon, where we lived, and, even at night, the temperature rarely dropped below 70 degrees. I'd float for a while, thinking of nothing, just getting used to the water, staring up at that big, dark blue sky, then I'd start chanting "please please please" over and over again, in my mind, talking to that moon and whoever lived in the sky.

At first, it didn't seem right, asking God for help in this matter. But then I realised that I'd known God for a long time and had been going to him with all my problems since long before I even knew what sex was, let alone realised I was in love with another girl. He was the first one I went to when I fell in love with Claire, asking that it not be so. Then, finally, when I gave up because it was so, I would spend hours praying, asking over and over, for Claire to feel the same way, sometimes putting so much feeling into it, my jaw would ache from biting down and concentrating. Other times, it seemed impossible and the hurt so great, I'd find myself crying, tears rolling off my face and into my chlorinated lake. I wanted it so very much.

And now it's come true and I don't want it.

How can that be? If dreams that come true fail to satisfy, then what hope can we have? Poor Lolly.

I wonder if Claire and I will become friends again in time for me to meet Lolly as a baby, or at least a little boy. They say it takes twice as many years as you were together to get over one another. At that rate, Lolly will be shaving by the time I'm able to meet him.

I hope that's not true because I have a feeling about this child, the sort of feeling you have before you've met someone with whom you know you'll hit it off. I feel sorry for him, that's true. I think he'll be wedged painfully between two parents who don't love each other any more. But more than anything, I have a feeling I know him. Sometimes I'll be standing at an art store or at a record store and I'll see something – purple paint, say, or a Sonny Rollins CD and I'll have a feeling that Lolly would like it. It's not something I love necessarily – I can take or leave Sonny Rollins – but I've got myself convinced that Lolly will love his music. Don't ask me why.

I lie back on the concrete and kick water up at the moon – fucking moon. Whoever was watching television, has finally shut the thing off and is giving up to sleep. I should too.

My parents have been together for 32 years, exactly nine months more than I have been in this world. They adore each other. Sometimes I look at them and I wonder how they manage that kind of love.

There must be a tiny moment in time – a fraction of a second, maybe a minute, or maybe a half hour – in which you are so perfectly in sync that the feeling holds you together forever. I think every couple in love has that. If they're lucky, they recognise the moment, and hold on to it for dear life, if they don't, they let other things matter more and soon it evaporates.

Claire and I, our moment is not in the future. If indeed we had such an opportunity, it came and went long ago, perhaps one day at the beach while reading about Frannie and Zoe, or while playing the piano for one another, or maybe on that hot day sitting so close together with pictures of Sting on our laps and orange popsicles melting all around us.

Memories
Rachel Kramer Bussel

Ultimately, all you have left of her are memories, but they are the kind that linger on, that stick around and even when you want to picture someone else, all you see is her. In an instant, you can transport yourself from your messy room, your messy life, back to when the world looked so much brighter with her by your side. As much as you'd like to forget her, as much as you desperately need to forget her, to move on and exorcise her completely from your memory, she is still there, her memory so strong she may as well be talking to you, a hardy ghost who shows no signs of receding. You have no idea how to get rid of these unwanted memories, more powerful than anything happening in the present, so instead you indulge them.

Memory #1: You slam her up against the wall, hard. She is wearing the blindfold covered in glitter, looking like some kind of space-age kinky alien, the contrast with her pale skin so alluring you want her even more, unable to see, trusting you with everything. Her hands are high above her head, her legs slightly spread, and you pause there for just a moment and appreciate her stance. You know exactly what she wants: for you to fuck her, hard, for you to slam her entire body against the wall, for you to spank her outstretched ass so hard she will feel it for days. But it also says something else, something even hotter and more profound. It says she will do whatever you want her to, will let you make the decisions, will let you dictate how long and hard and deep she gets fucked. Oh, she tries to pretend like she is in control, tries to get away with things like moving her arms down ever so slightly, with whimpering indications that she wants more — the bigger dildo, the knife digging into her back, the wall just a little bit closer to her face, her control surrendered that much more — but you both like it best when you defy her, deliberately give her what she doesn't think she wants, even if only for the sake of contradicting her. You give her instructions — get your hands back up, stay still, be quiet — and the words have so much power, they exist like a third person in the room.

Memory #2: She lies on top of you on the bed, your bodies pressed together in every conceivable way. You shove your fingers into her, pushing with all your might and she pushes back against you. Then you pull out, knowing she wants more. Back to the future, your new lover, utterly unaccustomed to such practices, asks you, "Why does it feel good to spank someone?" You have to pause and think. That was never what you wanted before her, never something even remotely on your agenda. And then one day she was on top of you, naked and curvy and infinitely beguiling, the same body as always and yet it felt different in some compelling, daring way. Your hand found its way there, to that small, rounded ass, and you couldn't stop yourself from palming its beautiful, perfectly formed curves, squeezing and groping, and then wanting more. The words trembled on your lips, so uncertain despite five months of being intimate with her. She is likely to say yes, but there is still that chance of the terrible two-letter word that would kill your dream and ruin it all, but you take a chance anyway. "Can I spank you?"

You don't know that those four words are about to unleash the most delicious part of your relationship, about to unfurl the inner kink in both of you, and when she says yes, you do so, tentatively, searchingly, awkwardly. But within minutes, it's like you've been doing it forever. She takes to it like a fish to water, her small, slightly fleshy ass, the most padded part of her thin body, quickly turning red and making her squirm. You're amazed you never thought of or wanted this sooner, because you love the way your hand tingles after it connects with her ass, the way you can almost feel her wetness radiating out from her cunt as you spank her, the way the smacks seem to vibrate throughout her body, the way you get to control her just that much more, the way it makes her want you to choke her, hold her down, sit on her.

Memory #3: The tiptoeing around has finally stopped, the unspoken questions about seeing other people, about the other girl, the ones you've pushed from your mind because they are too painful, too raw, have surfaced and pushed past your qualms. With this honesty comes new-found rewards: you have decided to commit to each other, even though the idea of only one girl, one lover, no room for anyone else, is scary. It has taken you this long to admit that you don't want anyone else, that the freedom you've been seeking for so long has been replaced with the kind of love that feels so prophetic and whole, so fierce and strong that there is hardly room for anyone else in your heart. You talk and cry and cry and talk and when it's all done you take her in your arms, in your bed, the bed built for one but somehow managing to accommodate two.

You splay her out in front of you in the cramped space, and somehow it seems to expand, to make room for your bodies. She does the same, welcoming you into her, and you press your fingers inside her like you'll never get the chance to again. You lean down and lick her clit while your fingers reach as far in as they will go and she clutches the sheets and grits her teeth and cries out your name. Her nub is so hard yet tender, responding to every flicker and stroke, and like some magical game each movement of your tongue draws your hand in further until without even trying your entire hand is inside her, lubed solely with her desire. You worry that you will hurt her, she is so small and you still haven't gotten over the notion that small means fragile, but instead, as your fist probes places inside her you've only imagined, she again asks for more, that eternal erotic refrain. You push further, hitting skin and bone and you have tears in your eyes because you don't know exactly what this means except that it's heavenly. You go slowly even though she is asking for it harder, deeper, lost in her own whirl of pleasure and you push and push and fill her until you are sure you will both break. But you don't; instead of shattering you come alive as she pulses beneath you, and though you don't know why, this seems like the most beautiful act ever invented. You ease out gently, regretting not using lube, caution, patience, but with her it's so hard to remember to be responsible. You pull her close to you when you're done and tuck her into your arms, clutching her because now there is even more to safeguard, even more ways your heart has opened for her, and you don't ever want to close it back up.

Memory #4: There you are out and about in your summertime playground, the East Village. On Avenue A, walking home after a day made long and beautiful by hours of fucking in a friend's sublet apartment, you finally break to get some food. Too impatient to wait for the slowest waitresses at one café, you head to another favorite, and you eat feta cheese while teasing her under the table, and over it, telling her that you're ready for her again; it really doesn't take much for either of you to get back in the mood, as it rarely leaves. You see her shift and squirm, pick at her salad, and know that she is ready for you too, full but hungry again. It's like that with the two of you, or it was, an insatiable need for more and more and more. You finally leave and you can't help but touch her, your arm going innocently enough around her waist, but then you want more, and it slips lower, cupping her ass under her skirt, hoping your hand doesn't show to those who might be walking behind you, but not really caring.

Soon walking is just a pretext, a way to keep moving as your fingers nimbly sink down until they creep along the crack of her ass and then stroke the tight wetness you find there, hidden and yet plain as this glorious day to you. You are only a block away from the apartment but that block is now much too long to possibly wait for that glorious, greedy pussy and you push two fingers into her, making her walk to keep up, neither of you talking. You're sure someone watching must notice something amiss, that your arm around her is not quite so innocently placed, but with her it doesn't matter, it never matters. An eternity passes and then you are in the doorway to the apartment. She fumbles for the keys while you try, but fail, to be patient. Once the door swings open, she is all yours. You slam her skinny body up against the wall, barely giving you time to close the door before she is pressed flat, her skirt and panties down on the ground, your fingers slamming into her from underneath. You pull her up by the roots of her hair as your fingers find her wetness over and over, feel the ways her cunt's contours are different standing up from lying down, but still so familiar. You lick her neck, then bite it and hold her up as she tries to sink to the ground. You're messy and sweaty, dirty animals who can't wait for niceties like beds and sheets and manners.

You've passed some wall between you, passed that "what do you want me to do?" stage until you know exactly where you're supposed to be, and you slam her into the wall until she literally can't stand it any more and sinks to the ground, tousled and liquid, but still ready for more. You push three fingers into her slick pussy, then fumble for the lube and add four, the slick, slippery entrance begging you to overtake her. She looks at you with pure longing, the distillation of a whole day's, a whole lifetime's, worth of fucking bottled up into those watery blue eyes, on the verge of decadent tears before she grabs your wrist and shoves you into her; now it's you who has no choice. For a small girl she's surprisingly strong, but you want to be the strongest and reach for her hand with your free one, twisting your wrist to press up high against her g-spot, stroking and seeking until you hit pussy pay-dirt, the place that makes her moan and arch and beg and scream and makes you want to stay there forever. Your clothes and belongings strewn about all over, you fuck with the energy of the possessed, for that is what you are at this moment.

Your entire body is alive with the force of wanting to fuck her, needing to have her, to place some indelible mark on her delicate skin, to make her love you forever. You kiss her, her mouth hot, melting beneath you as you crawl over her, burrow into her. A long while later you retire to the bed, to the comfort of pillows and sheets and electrical outlets. To cuddling against each other, to more mundane pursuits, lazy hands drawling across skin, small fingers pinching nipples until they want to burst, hands seeking heat beneath the darkness of night, the afterglow staying with you for hours.

Memory #5: Your are on the plane, your first real trip together, alone, cross-country. You're giddy with excitement and the chance to spend four days all to yourselves. You feel a special giddiness as you think of what you've planned for her, a kind of pride that she is your student and will do whatever you say. For starters, you fasten a glittery purple collar around her neck in the airport bathroom, surely one of only a few, if not the first, to have used this restroom for just such a purpose. In an instant, she has changed, transported, mutated in the most profound way. She is Yours, and as you lead her toward the gate, wondering whether the metal ring will set off the detector, you make sure everyone knows it, tugging on it strategically to make her pussy contract just so. For the rest of the trip, the collar sits around her neck, even in sleep, and it gleams in the California sun like it belongs there, like she was born with it, regal and elegant and beautiful. It became an intrinsic part of her the moment you fastened it, so that you can't remember what she looked like without it. You don't realize at the time that what seems like a lark, a fun, shiny toy to hold onto while you fuck her, to play games with as you lead her around the room, will mean so much to you. You don't realize then that every time she whips it out of her bag and presents it to you to fasten, so slyly, cunningly, unexpectedly obedient, your heart will melt just that little bit more. You don't realize that sometimes it will be enough just to watch her, naked save for this symbol of love, power, respect. You don't realize how much your heart will break when she takes it off for the last time.

Sometimes it seems like these stories happened to someone else. You see them in your mind like a beloved kinky movie, pressing rewind on the best parts and skipping over the rest. She is forever there, your willing servant, her eyes closed in ecstasy as you fuck her on the floor, against the wall, on the plane, on her bed, holding her by the scruff of her neck or the roots of her hair, pinning her down with your hands and your heart. You have to stop, pause, regroup, recollect, fast forward far, far ahead to the place where you each exist in separate universes, baring your bodies and souls for new lovers who never seem to quite get you to that same place. You wish they were someone else's memories, movie stills, fantasies, dreams, anything but reality. Instead, they live on, permanent pesky reminders, and you're not sure ultimately whether you'd prefer them to stay or go. Fortunately, or unfortunately, you don't have much choice.

Labour, 16th June 2004
Rita Das

I am prised open
My legs
Are forced apart
Into a natural
But self-conscious
Position.

Sweat comes
With each sustained
Almighty
Crush of pain.

In between
No
Rest
But rush
Of nausea,
Sour vomit.

Long.
Hard.
This labour

Of unpredictable
Love

Of coming

Is the world safe
Enough?

For my bairn
Who has never
Seen daylight
But has grown and
Laughed
Inside of me

Are you
And I
Brave enough

For the
Tearing of labia,
The mess of shit
And wet,
Sleeplessness
Through nights
And nights?

Are either of us
Brave enough,
My darling,
For the raw
Sight
Of ripping
Precious flesh,
And flood
Of
Red Red
Blood?

The Ride
Elena Moya Pereira

Sophia walked into the Vespa Lounge on a hot summer Friday night thinking, as usual, that she'd be home a couple of hours later. She had become used to a non-eventful single life, with no romance, no sparkle, almost no hopes of meeting anybody new. She had accepted a lifestyle where her job as a restaurant owner and manager in central London consumed all her energy and time, filling her bank account well enough to pay the mortgage of her three-storey home in Camden. Sex was a mechanical action two nights a week and on Sunday mornings, helped by the high-power vibrators she would get during her annual visits to the *Sh!* Store. It was now two years since she'd split up with her ex.

"Hello, Sophia!" somebody shouted, as she walked into the bar's upstairs room with her three friends.

Who's that? Sophia thought. She didn't have her glasses on. She could see, however, a tall woman in her thirties with long dark hair tied up in a ponytail looking at her and smiling. Sophia turned back to see if the woman was trying to get somebody else's attention.

"You, you! Sophia! You don't recognize me outside work?" the woman said.

"Maite!" Sophia gave her a big smile. "What are you doing here?"

"What do you mean 'what am I doing here'? How about you?" Then the woman kissed Sophia on the cheek.

"Oh my God," Sophia looked at Maite from head to toe. "I always suspected you were a lesbian! Er, well, are you?"

"I am bi, really, but yes, have been with women for a while now," the woman replied. "I always thought *you* were a dyke."

Sophia smiled and at the same time Anne, one of her friends, brought her the gin and tonic she had asked for.

"Meet Maite, Anne – we bump into each other at finance conferences all the time, but we can never talk because she's always in such a rush, or I'm in meetings all the time, and now she's here."

"Ah, good, nice meeting you. Let me give this beer to Rachel." Anne walked away, obviously conscious of Sophia's excitement. She'd seen her friend sitting bored in the Vespa Lounge and First Out almost every Friday night for at least a year and wasn't going to stand in the middle of the first conversation where Sophia's eyes sparkled.

Sophia and Maite talked about work, life and being a lesbian in London for at least half an hour. The bar was filling up; people were queuing for the pool table; the smoke and the loud music made conversation more and more difficult. The two had to get closer to be able to hear each other. Their second gin and tonic made the closeness easier.

"So, tell me about you now – are you seeing anybody?" Maite asked.

Sophia grasped her head. "Not, not really, I had a girlfriend for about a couple of years, but that ended two years ago, so nope, single," she said, looking down.

Maite put one arm around Sophia, touching her shoulder for a few seconds, approaching her head to hers. "Oh, I am sure you'll be all right – you're very nice."

Sophia moved her body slightly towards the other side. She wasn't ready to get close to somebody only after a half an hour's conversation. Time had taught her to be cautious, defensive. She took one step backwards.

"Of course I'll be all right. I'm all right now," she said in a tone that had lost the easiness of the past thirty minutes. "Why shouldn't I be all right? Because I don't have a girlfriend?"

"Well, I mean, of course, I know it's great being single, and I know you're doing very well at the restaurant, but... and pardon me, I don't want to be indiscreet," Maite got closer to Sophia and whispered, "what about sex, isn't it a bit hard to cope without it?"

How rude was that! Sophia moved slightly backwards. "Who said I'm not getting any sex? Being single, one can always get by. You know what I mean."

"Of course, of course," Maite said, drinking more of her gin and tonic. "I do it all the time as well. It can be very good. But that's, say, more of an orgasm. I mean sex, like long, hours-lasting sex." Maite drank a bit more gin and tonic, slowly releasing her lipstick-covered lips from the straw, smiling to Sophia. "You know, cuddles, caresses, kisses, touch – feeling somebody. You know what I mean."

"Yes, of course I know what you mean." Sophia felt she could actually talk to Maite. She wasn't too embarrassed, because she didn't know her that well on a social level, but well enough professionally to trust her. Maite was an intelligent woman. Sophia felt safe with her.

"I miss that, of course." She looked straight into Maite's eyes. "I miss my back being kissed, actually," she continued, smiling. "Martha, my ex, kissed my back in a way nobody had done before. She was just perfect: she would start at the bottom of the spine, and she would kiss, very softly, gently, all the way up, to the neck. Sometimes it took an age to get all the way up to the head. I don't know how she could do it so slowly. My whole body would have goosebumps; the tension was unbearable at some moments; sometimes I had to ask her to stop, because it was too much. I've never seen anything like that. Miss that a lot. All I have now is a full-body massage once a month. Sad, but that's as close as it gets."

"Oh dear," Maite said extending her arm on Sophia's back, rubbing her shoulders, then the middle of the back, going to the loins, and all the way up again, following the spine. Sophia felt the relief. Maite's hands were soft and warm. She could still feel them, even if they were over her tight top. She felt relief after a long week's hard work. She took a deep breath.

"That's very nice, thanks very much," Sophia said, lowering her shoulders, taking a deep breath. "Can I get you a drink?" she offered.

"Yeah, gin and tonic, please." Maite smiled.

I can't do this, I can't do this with her, thought Sophia. I don't even know if she's single, I don't want to ask. Her hand felt lovely on my back. "Hello!" Sophia called in vain to the waitress, who ignored her at the bar. This was turning into a nice night.

Sophia felt Maite's hands on her waist and turned immediately to her.

"Maybe I could give you a hand, I know them well here. Otherwise it always takes ages," Maite said, lifting her arm, making a sign to one of the eighteen-year-old waitresses, who seemed to be trying for a record in slowness.

"Gin and tonic?" Maite asked Sophia, who nodded. "Two GTs, please."

They got them half a minute later.

"You're very good at the bar," Sophia said, pushing her long black hair behind her ear, smiling and softly putting her lips on the straw, drinking about a quarter of the gin and tonic in one go.

"Well, long story there," Maite said raising an eyebrow.

Sophia smiled. "Which one?"

"The short blonde, the one at the till."

"Not too bad," Sophia responded.

"The best is hidden. Absolutely phenomenal breasts. Couldn't get enough of them, would have been playing with them forever. Having my face in between those breasts is one of the best things I've done in my life," Maite said, taking a gulp of her gin and tonic immediately afterwards.

"So you like breasts, eh?" Sophia smiled, breathing faster, deeper, feeling how her own breasts were moving with each breath. She was proud of them. They were each the size of an orange, and she always wore Harvey Nichols underwear. Even if she hadn't had an audience for them in two years, she still liked to wear £150 knickers and bras. She looked at Maite's breasts, but couldn't see much, as they were hidden under a straight, power-suit black jacket. She felt sexy in her tight white top.

"Yes, I do. Who doesn't, really?" Maite smiled. "I like touching them and having them touched, all over. That really gets me going."

The two women looked at each other, now in *that* sort of way.

Can I do this? Can I do this tonight? Sophia thought. With her? After all those times we've met at conferences. We could have been doing this, and we were just working. She's kind of sexy, isn't she? Nice face.

Maite looked around, slightly following the rhythm of the loud music, putting her glasses on her head.

Cool eyes, very green, like a cat, very sexy, Sophia thought.

Maite finished her drink and moved towards Sophia.

"I am afraid I have to go now," she said, putting her glasses back on, leaving her drink on the bar.

Oh damn it, what had she done? Maybe Maite had spotted that Sophia was beginning to want her. Damn it, damn it. "Of course, it's getting quite late and very loud in here, isn't it?" Sophia said, trying to hide her disappointment. She was sure Maite was going home to her girlfriend. Sophia looked at her watch. "I guess I should go home as well."

"Are you taking the tube? You're on the Northern Line, right?" Maite asked.

"Yes, in Camden. Whereabouts are you?" Sophia asked, resigned.

"I'm also on the Northern line, need to change at Euston for the Victoria line. Should we go together, then?"

"Yep. Let me say good bye to my friends, hope they don't mind me going, but I am actually feeling very tired. Will be back in a minute."

"Okay, I'll go to the loo, I'll be right back here," Maite said.

"Cool," Sophia said.

Mind the gap, stand clear of the doors, stand clear of the doors, the automated, impersonal tube voice said.

The doors closed and the train, at 11:50 p.m. started leaving Tottenham Court Road station. Everybody sitting moved with the wagon, slightly backwards, forwards, backwards, forwards. Feels good, Sophia thought.

Maite, sitting next to her, whispered to her ear, "My ex used to kiss my back as well. It was fantastic, and I also miss it."

"Yes. Very nice, relaxing, and quite hot," Sophia whispered back.

"Yeah," Maite said in an extremely soft tone.

Sophia leaned slightly towards Maite, even when they weren't talking.

"You know what?" Maite said after a few seconds.

"What?"

"I'm not wearing anything under my coat."

Sophia opened her eyes wide. She looked at Maite. She stared at her thin, summer coat, all done up except for the last button on the neck. She couldn't tell whether Maite *was* wearing anything under the coat, which had long sleeves and reached her knees. She noticed her bag was substantially bigger than when they were at the bar.

"Where's your suit?"

"In the bag."

Sophia looked at the bag again. Then whispered, "Nothing at all?"

"Nothing."

Sophia looked to either side of her. One drunk singing, a couple sleeping, a woman reading, dressed as if she was just out of the opera, and some American tourists discussing loudly how to get to their hotel. Nobody seemed to be looking at them.

The next station is Goodge Street, the voice said, Goodge Street.

Sophia didn't say or do anything. As the train slowed down, she saw Maite's naked body inside the pale green coat. She imagined big breasts underneath – or perhaps they were small, she couldn't tell. She imagined Maite's tummy, probably flat, muscular. *No knickers, either? Oh my God.*

"Like, absolutely nothing under your coat?" she whispered.

"Nothing."

Mind the gap. This is Goodge Street. Mind the gap. Five seconds went by. Please stand clear of the doors.

The train started moving again. Sophia could see Maite's legs, and what was in between, in her mind. *Short hair, I am sure. How would it feel? Was she, was she, was she wet? Now?*

Maite moved towards Sophia: "You don't want to check it for yourself? There's a reward if you do. But you have to check it before we get into Euston, otherwise I'll just change trains and go home."

Sophia felt immediately very hot. She could imagine her hand under Maite's coat. Her heart started beating faster and faster. She looked hurriedly at the map. Euston. Where were they? Only two stops! Warren Street and Euston!

"It's only two stops," she murmured.

"It's only two places that you need to check, I would say," was the answer.

Sophia looked around. The drunk had stopped singing and started sleeping, joining the couple, who were now hugging each other. The opera woman seemed in limbo. The American tourists were now even louder – which was good, as they would get all the attention, Sophia thought.

She extended one arm towards the coat, without knowing what to do, and quickly brought it back. *How am I going to do this?* She looked around. Nobody had noticed.

"Do you know what time is it, my dear? I lost my watch," she said aloud, extending her arm to reach Maite's wrist, to find she didn't have a watch, but giving her enough time to make sure that the black jacket's sleeves weren't there.

She could still be wearing her underwear.

A few seconds went by.

"Nice necklace," Sophia said, turning towards her friend again, touching the silver collar that, fortunately, she had on. She touched the stone, slowly, and moved her palm lower, towards Maite's upper chest. The shivery hand moved back to the necklace while she looked around the carriage. The woman of the couple had woken up. Sophia froze. But the woman wasn't looking. The hand moved lower, almost to the top of where the bra should have been. Another quick gaze around the wagon. The hand moved quickly towards the right breast and, yes, there was nothing in there. Just Maite's erect nipples, and soft and round and what felt like gorgeous breasts. Sophia couldn't leave them; she touched the nipple, playing with her thumb on it, noticing how it became harder and harder.

"Where are we?" the woman of the couple said.

Sophia dropped her hand to her knees. She closed her eyes, taking a deep breath. She didn't know if the woman had caught her.

This was like being a 15-year old. She couldn't believe she was doing this. She pressed her eyes even more. She could still feel Maite's breasts on her fingers, which were moving, very slightly, on her knee, as if they were still touching the erect nipples. She took another deep breath, opened her eyes and looked at Maite, who winked, smiling.

The next station is Warren Street, the voice said. Warren Street, please change here for Victoria Line trains.

How was she going to check the knickers? It was absolutely impossible.

The train stopped, the doors opened. For some reason Sophia would never understand, at 11:58 p.m., on a Friday night, about a dozen people got into the train at Warren Street. What were all these people doing here? They must have all come from the same party.

The new people occupied all the empty seats and some had to stand up, blocking Sophia's sights of the opera woman, the couple and the drunk. Now everybody was looking at everybody. Maite and Sophia smiled at each other.

The next station is Euston, change here for the Victoria Line and railway networks, the voice said.

Maite uncrossed her legs, moved slightly towards Sophia, and crossed her own right leg on top of the left one, towards her friend. Maite touched, gently, her right knee.

Sophia was looking. She fantasized about her hand feeling Maite's legs. They were long, strong, thin, very sexy legs. She wanted her hand to go all over them, from toe to top. She needed to get there. She wanted it. She wanted this woman. She imagined what it would be like to be between her legs, licking Maite all over. She wanted to taste the flavor, she imagined she would be wet, very wet, almost as much as herself at the moment. Her hands started to sweat.

She had to think, not sweat. It had to be now. How?

"It's the next train station that we have to get off, isn't it?" Sophia suddenly said to Maite, who looked surprised.

"Yes," she replied, more as a question than as an answer.

"Okay, let's go then."

Sophia stood up and walked towards the doors. Maite followed her, intrigued. Sophia pushed Maite facing the door and stood right behind her. With her left arm invisible to people as her own body blocked the view, she reached the front of the coat, undid the penultimate button and inserted her hand inside.

It felt warm. Slowly, she touched the skin, then the hair, very little, very short, nice. It was becoming warmer. The hand moved lower and touched more skin, very nice, then a bit lower, a bit more of an effort extending the arm, until she reached Maite's lips. Yes. She touched them to make sure she was in the right place. She was, one and two, there, naked for her. Very warm, very wet. She touched them with her palm, then with two fingers, up and down. Then with one. Up and down. They were very open, very soft. She touched the middle, up and down, then beyond, entering Maite, who made a slight sound. Her eyes were closed. The finger reached her deep inside and stayed there for a few seconds, until the train stopped. The doors were about to open and people were waiting on the platform to enter. The finger, full of white, left the coat as the doors opened.

The two women stayed immobile for a few seconds, both breathing very deeply. The doors closed, the train continued.

This is a Northern Line train to High Barnet, next station is Mornington Crescent.

Clean Slate
Yvonne Dale

'You know what I'd really like?'

Sara's voice over the telephone is husky with yearning. Even though we have yet to meet face to face she already seems to be reaching out to a deep barely articulated need within me.

'What?' Mellowed by red wine – but still alert with desire – I am predisposed to expect a sexual invitation. And to hope for one. My breath quickens in nervous anticipation.

'I'd like to start again with a clean slate. Just walk away from everything and leave all the baggage behind. Forget all about the past.'

'Sounds good to me,' I reply with meaning. After all, I have some baggage of my own I would like to put down.

'Okay,' she said. 'Let's make a pact. We won't talk about the past or even what's happening now. We'll meet in a pub neither of us has ever visited. We won't even swap addresses or tell each other what job we do. It'll just be us as we are.'

'All right.' I agree, feeling reckless and daring. 'You choose the time and the place and I'll be there.'

As we make our arrangements to meet, it fleetingly occurs to me that Sara might have even bigger skeletons in her cupboard than I have in mine. The most likely scenario is that she is with someone and wants a bit on the side. That is fine by me. I am not sure whether I am ready for full-on monogamy myself.

The truth is that I do not know what I want right now. I have decided that I may as well have some fun while I work it out. The likelihood of Sara turning out to be a possessive stalker is pretty low. She rather gives me the impression that she can take me or leave me. This makes me want to please her all the more.

Sara chooses the pub randomly from the Yellow Pages. It is two bus rides away, but I do not dare complain. She is calling the shots and I am more than happy to let her. I have no intention of losing the opportunity of this meeting by quibbling over the venue. Sara takes my compliance for granted and I do not want to incur her displeasure.

That night I have trouble remaining seated on my journey to meet Sara. I am smiling to myself stupidly and the other passengers must think I am a nutcase. The bus empties as we go deeper into the countryside. I am the only one to get off at the last stop outside the pub.

I stand and watch the bus trundle away. Whatever happens I am stuck here for a while. The next (and last) bus back to civilisation is not due for two hours. It is not the cold night air alone that causes me to shiver.

A gust of wind makes the pub sign creak in protest. I can just make out the picture on the board. A hollow-eyed skull stares back at me over pale crossbones. The lettering has faded away almost to nothing. I couldn't read it in this light if I did not already know what the letters spelt out. The Skull and Crossbones. An unusual name for a pub.

Suddenly a cloud crosses the moon and sucks the light away turning the night even darker. It occurs to me that I have not told anyone where I am going.

Music throbs in the air. Watery light spills over the car park from the tiny windows of the building. It makes the splashing rain sparkle. Each drop is an insubstantial, ephemeral diamond.

Feeling nervous, I thread my way through the puddles towards the thickly glazed door. There is no turning back now. Sara's dulcet tones have hypnotised me like a mermaid tempting a sailor to a watery death. I think of her deep sensual voice and I couldn't turn back if I wanted to.

Two men, unsteady with drink, stumble out past me as I enter the hot smoky atmosphere.

I scan the crowded bar, wondering why such an isolated place is so busy on a cold Sunday night. There is no clichéd meeting of eyes. In fact, there is no one who looks as if she is waiting for me. Of course, I am early. I doubt Sara is the kind to wait around for anyone. It is I who must do the waiting.

Everyone is paired up or part of a group. I feel quite alone – a fish out of water. It is quite some time since I have been in a straight bar and my usual swaggering seems somehow inappropriate here. For a second, I almost wish I were back outside.

I buy myself a pint and stand at the bar where I watch the doors in anticipation of Sara's arrival. Butterflies dance in my guts each time the door swings inwards. Self-consciousness prompts me to drink too quickly. Soon I have nearly finished my second pint.

It appears I have been stood up. I feel relief and disappointment in equal measure.

Then the back of my neck prickles. A spooky sensation tells me that someone other than the curious locals is studying me. I turn around and come face to face with her.

'Hi,' she says. 'I watched you from the car.'

Sara's voice displays the confidence of a woman used to getting exactly what she wants. Her green cat eyes sparkle with mischief. She flicks sleek black hair from her face and languidly extends a hand.

I take her small cool hand in mine to find her grip both brief and firm. She is groomed and fresh. A woman in control. I categorise her immediately as a dominant femme. Quite a rarity, in my experience. I assume that her company must be in demand. She is probably used to discarding anyone who bores or irritates her without qualms. All I can hope for is to sustain her interest for a while.

Her eyes linger slowly and frankly over my face and body. Her composure makes me feel awkward, clumsy, and hopeful. I already know that I want her, but will she feel the same way about me? Instinct tells me this woman will not spare my feelings if she chooses to reject me. She is not the sort to waste her time letting a girl down gently.

An irrational need for Sara's approval hits me like a fist in the stomach. I burn with humiliation at my weakness. When I speak, my voice is husky from too many cigarettes and lack of use. A tremor betrays my nervousness.

'How did you know it was me?' I ask shakily when I find my tongue.

'I just did. Anyway, your body language gave you away.'

Sara's smile is almost a smirk. She is enjoying my discomfort.

'Oh.' It is the only reply I can think of as I look into emerald eyes that shine a little too intensely. With desire perhaps? Or madness? In my experience one usually leads to the other.

The inadequacy of my conversation highlights my blundering idiocy. I begin to wonder if I am out of my depth.

'Shall we get a drink?' She laughs at my hesitation and I get the uncomfortable feeling she can read my thoughts.

I nod. A gang of giggling girls spills in behind us and squeeze themselves among the throng at the bar. Their laughter is fuelled with Bacardi Breezers and hopes unspoiled by experience. They do not look old enough to be served, let alone go out in such scanty clothes. Sara looks them over and seems to dismiss them as unworthy of further attention. I hope I am not about to be dismissed in the same way.

As we are pushed together by the crowd, my hip touches hers. I feel the small metal buckle of a thin leather strap press against me through the material of her skirt. She has come out ready to play.

My attention is immediately and hotly focused on her. All I can think of is what she is wearing under her skirt. I am soaking with arousal and, judging by the look that she gives me, she knows it.

Sara orders our drinks without asking me what I want and we jostle our way through to a recently vacated table. An old heavy metal track crashes out of the speakers. For a moment, I am transported back to the eighties. A time I remember fondly because it was before my life spiralled out of control. Before I picked up the baggage I am leaving aside for tonight.

Everything about Sara is deliberately, consciously sensual. From her silky black hair to her painted toenails. She reminds me of a lithe cat and I begin to feel uncomfortably like a mouse. Nevertheless, I want to slide my fingers over and into her cunt. My

Yvonne Dale

own is dripping so much my pants are soaked through.

'I think we'll go for a drive now,' she states.

I nod and almost choke on my drink. Nodding seems to be all I am capable of tonight. I am like a nodding dog. It is fortunate that Sara is taking control. All my chat-up lines have escaped me, evaporated into the air in the face of this sexy stranger.

We leave our drinks half finished and I follow her out to her car. I am so caught up in watching the confident wiggle of her bottom that I strike my foot on a large stone and stumble noisily. Sara does not look over her shoulder to check that I am okay. I feel certain she is smiling to herself.

Sara's large black car bleeps and flashes in response to her remote. Even her car is obedient. I scramble after her and climb into the passenger seat. Without speaking she starts the engine. I have no idea where we are going and this sends another *frisson* of nervous excitement through my body.

As Sara drives, I examine her face. The tilt of her chin suggests a confidence bordering on arrogance.

She drives assuredly with one hand resting idly on the steering wheel. We glide along quiet, unlit lanes. I wonder if she really chose our meeting place randomly. Despite the darkness, she obviously knows exactly where she is.

The stereo plays something classical. I recognise the music but I cannot name it. It reminds me of something Hannibal Lecter would play. The thought sends a shiver down my spine.

Sara pulls over, allowing a car travelling towards us to pass. As we wait she lets her legs loll invitingly apart. Seeing me looking she pulls her thin skirt up as high as it will go in the confines of the car. Just far enough to expose the tops of her black lacy stockings.

The invitation is obvious. I tentatively place my hand on her supple thigh and feel a shudder reverberate through her whole body. Suddenly she slaps my hand away sharply.

'Did I say you could touch me?' she challenges.

'No.' I am aware of the delicious stinging sensation on my hand. My knuckles tingle from her slap and I dare not meet her eyes. She has let me know that I have stepped out of my place and I am more turned on than ever. Sara's confident rebuke promises further delightful discipline later. The anticipation sends waves of horniness all over my body. My nipples and my clit are hard and erect.

Sara reaches over and turns my face to hers. After the slap, I automatically flinch but her grip holds me still. I cast my eyes down away from hers.

'Look at me,' she commands.

I look up into her eyes. Her hand grips my face harder and I do not resist. Strong fingers dig into my chin and I imagine them sliding over my wetness.

'Good girl. I hope you're going to remember who's in control here.'

I nod, aware of little else but the electric touch of her hand upon my cheek and half-hoping for another slap.

'Good.' She says and withdraws her hand.

Immediately I want her hand caressing my face again. I long for her touch, but would not presume to demand it.

We resume our journey until Sara turns into a tiny isolated car park set into the forest. The car crunches over gravel and its headlights sweep across trees and a National Trust sign.

She parks the car, releases her seatbelt and clambers across the gears to sit astride me. I am pinned against the seat as she pushes her warm soft body into mine. Her skin smells of salt and perfume. I wish I could bottle her scent and take it home with me. Instead, I shut my eyes and make do with breathing her in greedily.

She begins to grind her pelvis over mine, riding me to her own rhythm. I meet her thrust for thrust, hotly aroused by her expression of bliss and her quickening breath.

It is not long before her sighs deepen into moans of abandoned pleasure. I smile to think that she has temporarily lost control of herself with me. Knowing that I am having this effect on a woman who has been so composed until now is powerfully erotic. The urge to slip my fingers over and into her little cunt becomes more urgent than ever.

I watch her as we move together. Her eyes are closed and her lips parted as she is transported to another place. I reach out and pull her face to mine, but she throws her head back away from me and pushes herself against me harder and faster until I begin to moan myself. My moans of frustration and desire get louder. I desperately want her inside me. Want her to fill me up and fuck me hard.

I slide my hands up past her stocking tops over her smooth thighs. A rush of pleasure and relief floods through me. She is allowing me to touch her and the thought that she might want to punish me for it later only intensifies my arousal. I grab the leather straps fastened around her hips and pull her roughly and desperately over me. We are both too far gone to bother with the struggle of undressing fully. Unusually, I can feel myself near to coming without anything inside me. I stretch my legs wider. Each thrust mingles pleasure and pain with sharp bruising intensity.

She grabs my short hair as a long deep cry escapes her. Her grip tightens as shuddering spasms take over her body.

When she finally collapses limply into my arms, she seems suddenly soft and vulnerable. I hold her close and stroke her hair until her breathing steadies. The disappointment that I have not come yet is overwhelming. I am desperately afraid that I will be cast aside unsatisfied.

A car screeches to a halt behind us shattering the night time quiet. I hear two doors open and slam shut.

I feel suddenly uneasy but Sara seems relaxed.

Two sets of footsteps crunch on the gravel and I wait for whoever it is to walk by. Instead, they stop and someone pulls open the passenger door. The car is automatically lit inside.

I try to wriggle out from under Sara, but she pushes me back into the seat.

'It's okay,' she says firmly.

The outline of two dark figures fills the doorway.

I think that Sara really ought to cover herself up. Her blouse is only half buttoned and I can see her breasts threatening to tumble out of her crimson Wonderbra.

Sara speaks with familiarity to the couple.

'I've got us another one,' she says.

They exchange knowing smiles.

Sara slides from my lap and climbs out of the car. She stands in the rain smoothing her skirt before buttoning her blouse.

'Get out of the car, love,' the larger woman of the couple instructs.

I obey.

My knees almost buckle when I stand and I am obliged to steady myself on the car. I am in the middle of nowhere on a dark night with three strangers. It crosses my mind that this is no ordinary scene. Anything could happen. Fear ought to dampen my arousal but instead it only sharpens my excitement.

'Turn round and put your hands up on the car.' The big woman barks out with authority. I wonder if she is a police officer. Am I about to be arrested for lewd behaviour?

The woman kicks my legs roughly apart from behind and searches me like a professional. Except she lingers a little longer than necessary as she pats my arse. She finishes by giving it a squeeze.

'She's all yours.' The woman addresses her companion and moves away. I can feel her eyes burning into me.

The second woman steps up behind me. She circles my waist with her hands, unbuckles my belt and slides it out. My breathing has become fast and shuddering. The woman roughly pulls my jeans down, exposing my arse. I break out in goosebumps all over as the cold air hits my bare cheeks.

Everything about this scene is practised and smooth. Sara and her companions know exactly what they are doing. This makes me feel oddly safe. I am happy to hand over control of my body to them. More than happy. I am turned on and eager to submit to anything if it pleases Sara. Leaning against the car I am exposed, vulnerable, and horny as fuck.

'I think you know what's coming honey,' Sara drawls throatily. 'And I know you're gonna like it. I can tell.'

When I feel the thwack of what I think is my own belt against my skin, I realise that I have been holding my breath. I exhale and then gasp as the first lash of leather is followed by another and then another. My arse burns and tingles, but I do not get a chance to appreciate it before the belt slaps against my buttocks again. I feel the hot red welts left behind and know I will be tender for days. The rush is unbelievable. I push my cunt against the cold metal of the car craving relief.

Out of the corner of my eye I notice Sara watching me and smiling. She has regained her composure remarkably quickly. I want her inside me so much it hurts.

The whipping stops just when I think the pain is becoming too much. I feel gentle caressing strokes travel down my smarting buttocks. Fingers brush the outside tops of my thighs and wander teasingly towards and away from my cunt. Then lips and a wet darting tongue do the same, but I need something much harder and more intense than a tongue. I am squirming with desire.

'That's enough of that for now,' Sara says, and takes the woman's place behind me.

She leans forward to whisper huskily in my ear. 'I know what you want, baby.'

Sara pushes the heavy rubber of her large strap-on playfully around my cunt. I lift my arse in anticipation but she pulls away.

I groan in frustration. Surely she will fuck me soon. I can hardly bear to be teased for a second longer.

'You have to ask me nicely for it.'

'Please,' I moan, ridiculously grateful for her instruction and desperate to give her what she wants.

'That's good, but I expect you to tell me exactly what you want and then I'll decide whether or not I'm going to give it to you. And speak up so we can all hear you.' Sara teases me mercilessly.

'I want your big dick inside me,' I beg loudly, panicking at the thought of not having her. Surely she will not deny me now.

She pushes herself into me suddenly and quickly, slamming me hard against the car. At last she is filling me up and stretching me as wide as I can go with my trousers round my ankles. I push my arse up against her, wanting to take as much of her as I can.

Sara rams herself rhythmically into me. Pain and pleasure mingle, exquisitely. I feel myself coming too quickly and cry out in anguish, wanting this to last forever.

When I do come, it is long, intense and shuddering. The best ever. Sara pulls out and I sink to the floor, too weak to stand.

I am surprised and pleased that Sara helps me to my feet and pulls my jeans back up for me. She guides me back into the car and I hear the two women return to their car without a word before driving off.

Sara takes my face gently this time and kisses me long and hard. She starts the engine and drives me back to the pub car park.

'I'll give you a call,' she says, before speeding away and leaving me alone.

I hope she does. Yet I cannot help wondering just what is in that past Sara seemed so eager to forget about. There is something bad and dangerous about her. What happened to her to leave her with such an intense need for control? Was it the usual broken heart or something darker? And on what side of the law were those two nameless women?

We cannot really put our baggage down; all we can do is create increasingly sophisticated elaborations of our pain and pleasure – and how out of control is that? My brain tells me to stay away. My throbbing cunt urges otherwise.

Half of me wants to find out more. The other half is scared to death of what I might discover, about myself as well as Sara and her playmates.

After all, there is no such thing as a clean slate.

The Path
Helen Taylor

The sun disappeared behind a cloud. The warmth that had been bathing her skin vanished into thin grey light so suddenly that she opened her eyes. Out of the window she saw clouds piling against each other over the moors and they looked as if they might soon turn into rain. Chris swung her legs off the windowsill.

Well, rain would make a change. Not. She massaged her calves, which had started to shoot with pins and needles. Bloody Yorkshire weather. Nothing but rain for the past two months. Although she had to admit there had been a variety. January had brought fine rain that had blown across the valleys in grey swarms of water, soaked you to the core. She had been involved in excavating a shallow grave on an isolated stretch of moor during January. It had held the body of a girl who had disappeared before Christmas, and the police probably wouldn't have found it if a dog-walker hadn't stumbled across the patch of disturbed earth on New Year's day. It hadn't been the greatest way to start the year. Her New Year had involved sitting at home with her cat Freddy Krueger (her ex's idea of a joke, but it had stuck), drinking red wine and waiting for the season of good will to pass.

A couple of weeks ago she had arrested the girl's step-father when forensics matched DNA found on the girl's clothes. It had been a good result but, as Chris looked at the growing clouds, she could still picture the wet mud and the grave slowly filling with water as the rain came. She rubbed her eyes. Even the weather was sticking in her head today.

February had brought three weeks of rain that she had thought didn't exist outside the Australian rainforest. Thick heavy drops of it that made going outside like being underwater, but this stuff was colder. So cold that it was almost frozen, but still wet enough to get inside even the most impressive Goretex number. The guys at the station had described it as stair-rods. Rain like stair-rods. Chris had never heard it described like that, but she knew what they meant, and she liked it. It was one of those Yorkshireisms that came from the ability to laugh in the face of adversity. The sheer practicality of the phrase made her smile. She imagined years ago an old weather-beaten farmer staring out at the rain. His wife had told him to go and feed the cows. He shouted back at her, "I'm not going out there in that; it's like bloody stair-rods." So she chased him out of the house with a broom.

It was a stair-rod day that had led to her first meeting with Dawn at 2.30 on Monday afternoon three weeks before. Chris was taking a day off and, after a slow morning of tea, bagels and newspapers, she decided to go to the gym. At 35, she was finally having to put some effort into keeping in shape. The weather wasn't too bad when she set off; it had been drizzling and the air was foggy but, by the time she was halfway into town, the heavens opened and the sky turned a deep mottled purple. Chris slowed down as she approached a corner where there was a zebra crossing and, as she drew closer, she noticed that the flashing orange lights were out. She slowed down. A set of headlights approached her fast from behind, Chris braked harder to avoid a trio of school-age kids on the crossing, and her car slid to a stop just before the white lines. There was a screech of brakes and a soft bump as the car behind nudged her back bumper. Fuming, she flew out of the car, ready to confront the arsehole who had just run into her, and was taken aback to be faced with an equally fuming woman in a suit. They both did a double-take, neither of them having imagined that they might be faced with another dyke.

"You fucking moron, how fast were you driving? Too bloody fast! There were kids on that crossing; you could've killed them." Chris pushed the soaking hair off her forehead in a gesture which she realised later she'd thought might look attractive. She despaired of herself. The woman folded her arms. Her short dark hair was rapidly plastering itself to her head, and she had the most intense eyes Chris had ever seen.

"You just braked out of nowhere," the woman said angrily. "I didn't see the crossing – how could I, in this rain?"

Chris opened her mouth, shut it and opened it in disbelief. "Just because you've got an expensive car doesn't mean you get to own the bloody road." She glared at the silver Merc that was touching the back of her bumper. She looked quickly back at the woman, whose attention had snapped to her face, and Chris realised that the other woman had been looking at her chest, which was now soaking wet in her white T-shirt. The woman flushed and Chris glowered at her. The dark-haired woman reached into her suit pocket and pulled out a card, then took a pen from another pocket and wrote on the back.

"Here, that's my business card, and my insurers are on the back." Then she looked at Chris's M-reg Mondeo with contempt. "I can't imagine that it would cost that much to fix, and I can't see that I've done any damage to it anyway."

Chris reached into her pocket, and pulled out her own card, swapping it with the one the woman had thrust at her. "That's *my* card, and the DI is Detective Inspector. If there is the slightest scratch on my car, you'll be the first to know."

The other woman looked at the card for a moment, then turned and got back into her car, reversed it sharply and disappeared into the falling rain with a squeal of tyres. And that was that, or it should have been.

She put her feet up on the windowsill. She checked her phone. No messages. She stretched her arms out behind her head. Her boss wouldn't be back for a while, and what did they call this now, power napping? She imagined, though, that most people who power-napped didn't spend twenty minutes fixated on a woman they didn't like. She knew even before she closed her eyes who she would see. Dawn. Her face, the colour of her skin, the turn of her mouth – everything about her, clear as day. It annoyed Chris to be at the mercy of such a persistent obsession, and she momentarily frowned before she relaxed. Anyone watching her might have thought she had a toothache that didn't hurt quite enough for her to go to the dentist. She couldn't say how it had happened. It just had. One minute she hadn't liked the woman – in fact, she considered her to be pretty unpleasant – and she certainly hadn't thought her attractive. Then the next moment she still hadn't liked her, but she couldn't stop thinking about her. Without Chris noticing, this bloody woman had sneaked in and welded herself into her head. There was no escape; she just wouldn't go away, although Chris was trying hard to keep her locked into the realms of fantasy and not let her cross over into reality. That would be too dangerous.

She was tired, but then she was always tired lately. Maybe it was early menopause and hey, that was something to really look forward to. It wasn't the job – the job was fine. It was everything else. Sometimes she found herself fantasising about escaping. Doing something exciting, finding the thing inside her that was missing. Fantasy had become her great escape. Over the last eight months, she'd imagined affairs with hundreds of women. Most for a couple of weeks until she'd got bored, but at least they had been safe. Fantasy women made of thousands of little dots on a television screen, or untouchable straight women – an addiction that Chris happily cultivated. But this time it was different. This time the lines were blurred, and the woman was made of flesh and bone. She was real.

Being in the police force didn't help. She worked long, stupid hours. She knew her fantasy women would cope with all these problems. Chris could see Dawn's face as if she was standing in front of her. Her dark hair, her eyes the colour of earth were burned in her mind. How did I let her get in like this?

She decided to call it a day and drive home. The rain was already starting to spot on her windscreen as she left the station. As soon as she started to drive, her mind wandered back to Dawn Andrews, Sales Executive for Omega Dyes and Colourants UK, or so her business card said. Dawn, Dawn, Dawn. Did she have a girlfriend? Where did she live? What was she like in bed? Chris made a strangling sound and shook her head, gripping the steering wheel so tightly that her knuckles were white.

She turned on the car stereo and tried to think about food. What was in the freezer for dinner? She realised too late that this probably wasn't a good idea. Boil-in-the-bag fish, lasagne-for-one ready in five minutes in the microwave. A bottle of wine.

Lasagne for fucking one. She made a mental note to go shopping at the weekend and buy some vegetables. She wondered if Dawn cooked, or maybe she was too busy. Maybe she had enough money to eat out every night, rich bitch probably did. She most likely didn't even own an oven. Chris flipped through the CD changer until she found a Fleetwood Mac CD and Stevie Nicks' voice filled the car.

Dawn, Dawn, Dawn. Chris knew that she lived locally. It didn't take a detective to work that out. The company she worked for was based in Halifax, and she'd seen her the previous week in the only gay bar in Bradford. The gay scene wasn't something that Chris had much to do with, but sometimes she dipped a toe in the water. Last week, after an appalling day at work, she had decided to pop into Blue Jack's on the way home, Blue Jack's being a gay pub on the outskirts of the city. She had spent most of her day being squashed in a car with another detective watching a mobile phone shop that was suspected of being a drugs cover. Nothing happened all day, except that Chris's feet had frozen, and the DC had proved himself to be one of the most obnoxious people Chris had ever had to share a car with. He also had bad breath and, she suspected, a severe allergy to water.

When she went to the pub, she'd only meant to stop in, have a half and pick up the gay papers, but as soon as she sat down at the bar, she knew that she was going to be there for a while. The place fitted her mood and she didn't want to leave. One pint turned into four, and slowly the tension that had been building in her all day began to fall away. The kitsch statues, the gold sequinned curtains, the stained red carpet, the half-light of the bar, everything soothed her. None of it mattered; none of it meant anything. She was staring at a print of a naked angel when she felt someone's eyes on her. The sensation was so intense that she almost flinched. She scanned the room, and her eyes fell on a woman sitting with two others in the corner of the bar. Yes, the woman's eyes were fixed on her and met Chris's for a second before looking away. It was the woman who had run into the back of her two weeks before.

Until this point, Chris hadn't thought about the woman once. She had disappeared from her thoughts as quickly as she'd sped into the rain, but one look across the bar and Chris felt like someone had plugged her into the national grid. Her chest was tight, her stomach did a somersault and her face was burning. It wasn't long until she felt the eyes on her again. She hadn't appreciated how attractive the woman was, probably in her late 30s, could even have been 40. Her skin was pale, even more so against her coal-black hair. Could it be dyed? She was handsome, but it was her eyes that made Chris's mouth go dry. As she watched, the woman looked across the bar again. Chris smiled at her and the woman almost smiled back, but then seemed to think better of it and turned away, leaving her with a view of her back. From that moment, Chris was smitten. The woman was arrogant, abrasive and rude. As soon as Chris had rolled out of the taxi and into her house, she had dug out the woman's business card. Dawn Andrews. Now at least she had a name. Chris studied her handwriting on the back of the card for a long time, trying to decipher her personality from the arcs and squiggles. Eventually she gave up, but went to bed with Dawn Andrews' face burned deep into her mind. Now, a week later, the infatuation was worse. She had a serious issue with whoever had first said, "Out of sight, out of mind." As far as Chris was concerned, out of sight was like a black hole inside her that was filled with only one thing. To get Dawn out of her mind, someone would have had to lift the top of her head and fill it with concrete, or cut it off altogether.

It was nearly dark when she pulled into her drive. She crunched across the gravel to her front door and opened it. The house was freezing again. The timer on the boiler had been on the blink for weeks, and Chris hadn't got round to getting it fixed. She called out to Freddy, but he was nowhere to be found. Chris didn't blame him – he'd probably gone next door – where the central heating worked.

After the lukewarm lasagne and two glasses of wine, she ran a bath. She took a trashy novel into the water, and hoped the steam would soothe her brain into obedience. No more fantasies about anyone real. Dawn. She dropped the paperback on the bathroom floor in disgust and shut her eyes.

The fantasy starts when her phone rings. She picks it up and looks at the screen. There's a name on it, Dawn. Her name's come up on screen because Chris keyed it into the phone a week before, when she wasn't entertaining the full-on burning obsession she has now. It was just an ember at that point.

She answers it and a voice says, "Hi, is that Chris?"

And she says, "Yes. Who is this?" Even though she knows.

"It's Dawn, Dawn Andrews. I don't know if you remember me; I ran into your car," she says, "a couple of weeks ago." And her voice is nervous and unsure and full of something that Chris wants to grab hold of and touch and undress and kiss.

"I remember," she says. "What do you want?"

"I just wanted to apologise, really; I was rude and, well, I wondered if maybe I could take you out for a drink to say sorry."

And Chris says, 'Maybe. Maybe that might be okay. When?"

And the voice on the other end of the phone lightens. "What are you doing now?"

And Chris is out on the moor. "Working," she says.

And the voice says, "Where are you – maybe I could meet you for lunch?"

"Up on Brackenbank Moor," Chris says, and she is on the moor in the bright sunshine that's full of clear blue sky, and she's tramping across a hillside covered in thick bracken and big clumps of heather because there's no path, and suddenly she misses her footing and plunges into a bog. "Fuck, I've just gone ankle-deep in a bog," she says, and on the other end of the phone Dawn laughs and, even though her foot's piss-wet through and black with peat, she is tingling and hot and happy like a kid.

"*How* have you fallen in a bog?"

"There's no path up here."

"Can I come up there and see you?" she asks. "It's a beautiful day, and I really need to talk to you."

"Sure, why not, I'd like to see you," Chris says, and as the words come out she knows the path she is taking is right and wrong all at the same time. She has no idea where it will lead, but she can't help herself, and for once she feels brave and for once she doesn't care.

"You would? Great, I'll meet you up there in ten."

"Fifteen – let me dry my foot out."

But the phone is dead, and is burning a hole in her hand. What has she done? There's no going back now. The inevitable is coming, the first touch, the look, the look in her eye.

Hidden in the bracken, Chris finds a path that weaves across the moor, leading her towards the woman who has seared herself in her head. She sees her car in the first parking lot and she can see her inside. A dark figure on the driver's side. Chris's chest contracts, her legs are light, all the blood in her body rushes to a two-by-two-inch square that burns between her legs. Dawn sees her and gets out of the car. She is all that Chris remembers. She must be having a day off because she's wearing a heavy green jumper and jeans, with a white top that sticks out above her jumper, and hangs down below. Everything's she's got on is too big. She's smiling, her dark eyes watching Chris, and she's waving.

"Hi," she shouts.

Chris gets close enough to her to talk, and suddenly doesn't know what to say. Dawn is looking at her foot, which is black and dripping water onto the ground. "You really did fall into a bog."

"Did you think I made it up?"

"No, but I thought you might have exaggerated."

Their eyes meet, and hold, and the silence is immense. Chris opens her mouth and nothing comes out, then she says, "Why would I exaggerate falling in a bog?" It's all she can think of.

"Oh, you know, some people might do."

She looks amused, and Chris still doesn't know what to say. Everything she can think of sounds stupid, so she studies her foot, then says, "Why did you want to see me?"

Dawn shrugs. "I don't know, it's strange. The last few days have been strange, since I saw you in the pub." She stops and looks uncomfortable. Chris doesn't help her out, so she fidgets with a loose strand of her jumper, runs her hand through her hair and finally says, "Oh fuck, look, I just want, I can't get my head straight, you keep getting in it." She looks at Chris for a reaction.

Chris sat up in the bath, and ran in some scalding-hot water. She couldn't decide what to do next – she could play hard to get, stand back and make her squirm. Pretend she didn't like her, tear a strip off her for having a shit attitude, tell her to sling her hook. She swished her feet about in the water to make it bubble. Or she could encourage her, give her an opening, give the woman a chance. She settled back in the water. She decided to take option two.

"Shall we go and sit in the car?" Chris asks. "It's cold out here." Dawn shrugs, but they move back towards her car. They get in and sit, watching the clouds through the windscreen. It's windy, and the white shapes are thin and strung out across the sky, their shadows chasing after them across the moor. The sun is hot through the windscreen on their skin.

"It's beautiful, isn't it?" Dawn raises her chin at the view, and Chris looks at her. They are as close as they have ever been. "I'm sorry about your car." She seems so vulnerable, so close, different from the times Chris has seen her before.

"Why did you ignore me in the pub?" Chris asks, and Dawn looks away, out of the windscreen, to the moors in the distance.

"I don't know – I guess I didn't like what I was feeling. I didn't expect to see you there, and I didn't expect to feel like I did." She looks back at Chris, her dark eyes impossible to read.

"How was that?"

"Like this." She fixes Chris with her eyes, and stays silent.

They look at each other, and then Chris lifts her hand and touches Dawn's face with her fingertips. Dawn closes her eyes, and Chris traces the gentle lines, deep at the side of her mouth. She touches her lips, her eyes; she sees her face with her hands. Dawn reaches up, and takes Chris's hands in her own. She holds them tight and looks at Chris. Times stops, everything stops. Dawn's breath is short, shallow, and she reaches forward very slowly, really slowly, so their lips just brush, almost nothing, but the sensation is like fire, then pulls away. Chris can't free her hands, and she wants to hold her tight, run her hands up the back of her neck and kiss her hard, possess her, taste her whole mouth, but Dawn holds back.

"Wait," she says quietly, and brushes Chris's lips again with her own. Chris opens her mouth slightly, and Dawn bites her bottom lip, rolls her tongue along it and then kisses her harder. She lets go of Chris's hands and slips one arm around her waist, the other on the back of her neck, and twists across the seats so she is straddling her, kissing her hard on the mouth. Chris runs her hands, now free, up inside the back of the green jumper, up inside the huge white top. Her hands are cold, and she feels Dawn tremble and sigh, and tense and relax. She moves her hands onto Dawn's stomach, forcing them up over her small breasts, rolling her nipples between her finger and thumb. Dawn groans and she starts to move her body against her, grinding her cunt against her leg. Her tongue is deep inside Chris's mouth; she tastes warm and slightly metallic. She smells of paint and earth. Chris pulls her hands out from the jumper, and puts them on the other woman's face, one on each side, and pulls her away. She is panting.

"Can we go back to your house?"

Dawn nods, slowing her body down, and Chris runs her hands around her back. Dawn rolls off her, and they drive to Dawn's house. They don't say anything.

It's a big house. There is a large kitchen to one side that Chris sees for a few seconds before Dawn shuts the door. Dawn takes her by the hand and leads her along the hallway through a big glass door at the end, into a large room with a high ceiling. The windows are tall, and hung with thick curtains. Weak sunlight seeps through the dusty glass, throwing great golden shafts of light through the heavy air, shining in strips off the wooden floorboards. The room darkens as a cloud passes over and there is a gentle click of water against the glass as the rain comes. The cloud passes and the room is bright again. In the centre of the room is a huge sofa covered with a thick, grey woollen blanket. Dawn leads her to it, and pulls her down next to her, smiling softly. Her face glows in the watery sunlight.

"I don't know where this is going," she says. "I've never felt anything like this before."

Chris leans her head against the back of the sofa. "Neither have I."

"I suppose we should just see what happens." The air in the room is warm, and there are birds singing outside.

"I suppose it doesn't have to mean anything, go anywhere, you know?"

Dawn looks at her. "No," she says, "I suppose it doesn't."

Their words hang in the air. The momentum has slowed, and Chris can feel that, even though they have just sworn allegiance to the God of No Commitment, this is going to mean something. It has to; everything always does, even when it doesn't.

They look at each other. Dawn shifts on the sofa. "Stand up," she says. It's not an order, or a request; it just seems right. Chris stands up. Dawn leans back in the sofa, stretching out her legs. She speaks quietly. "Take your clothes off."

Chris hesitates, but Dawn puts her hands behind her head and grins at her, so she pulls her top over her head, and drops her top to the floor. She pulls off her T-shirt and drops that, too. Dawn runs her eyes appreciatively over Chris's body, resting on her breasts as Chris unclasps her bra and drops it on top of her other clothes. Then she unbuttons her jeans slowly. She enjoys the sensation of being watched, admired. She pulls her jeans off roughly and then removes her knickers, so she is naked. Her whole body is burning.

"Come here." Dawn holds out her hand and Chris comes towards her. Her skin is tingling without even being touched. She stands in front of Dawn, and she can feel the other woman's breath on her. Dawn leans forward, and slides both hands round the backs of her legs, pulling her forward. She runs her tongue from Chris's belly-button slowly down, and slides her hand between Chris's legs so that Chris lets out a long sigh. Then Dawn pulls her hand back and slides two fingers together back between her legs and deep inside her. Chris groans and Dawn catches her round the waist and pulls her to the sofa, keeping her fingers inside her. She kisses her on the mouth, climbing on top of her, pressing her legs apart with her own and fucking her hard with her hand. Chris moans underneath her, and Dawn starts to rub her clit at the same time as she's fucking her. Chris groans louder, her body rising against Dawn's.

"I'm going to come," she gasps. "Slow down, I'm going to come."

But instead Dawn pushes her down harder into the sofa and forces her legs wider with her own, and fucks her deeper and harder, and her body spasms and bucks as she comes, and comes, and comes, and her body begins to slow and warmth spreads through her veins like whisky. Dawn's arms are around her and she curls against her. Dawn is kissing her face softly, kissing her eyes, her mouth, stroking her hair, holding her tight. Her arms are strong, holding her safe, wrapping her away from the outside, safe from the outside, warm and satisfied and for the moment not aching inside.

The bathwater had gone cold and Chris's feet had shrivelled. The windows in the bathroom were wet with steam and were dripping long lines of moisture down the glass. Chris pulled herself out of the water, and away from thoughts she kept sinking into like a fine bath, like a deep bog, like quicksand. This was the fantasy that, given the chance, given one little chance, might just be. She stepped out of the water and, as her feet touched the floor, her mobile rang. The phone that she had been looking at all day, the phone that she had willed to ring, the phone that had burned a hole in her pocket for a week, rang. It vibrated on the floor as she stared at it. She picked it up and read the screen.

Oh fuck. The screen said DAWN, because she had keyed her number into her phone the night after the pub. Mouth dry, heart beating fast, she answered. "Hello."

"Hi, is that Chris?"

And she said, "Yes. Who is this?" Even though she knew.

"It's Dawn, Dawn Andrews. I don't know if you remember me; I ran into your car," she said, "a couple of weeks ago." And her voice was nervous and unsure and full of something that Chris knew she wanted to grab hold of and touch and undress and kiss.

"Where are you?" she asked, and Chris sighed.

"Up shit creek," she said and braced herself for the ride.

Angelica
Astrid Fox

The glen had many trees with leaves that glowed. That's right, amongst the waxy greenery was phosphorescence; one leaf in three pulsed with the soft light of 1950s clocks.

The nun knelt there below the trees. Her eyes were closed, so she didn't see the lightning bugs that bobbed up and down amongst the already glowing foliage; didn't see that everything was rinsed with a tender green light except for her in her dark dress, dark stockings and brown leather shoes. Her order did not insist on habits, anyway; they were thought unmodern.

It was a special place where she knelt, but no longer a holy place. In the second decade of the previous century, three children had claimed that the Virgin had appeared to them here and, for a year or so, this little glen had been a place of pilgrimage, until the children, one by one, had admitted that they were lying, and no one came here any more, mainly out of embarrassment.

An altar that had been placed here during that long-ago first year of excitement was still present, though, and it was here at the foot of four stone steps that led up to the former shrine where the nun knelt and prayed. She knelt the difficult way, straight up from the bend of her knees, rather than resting back on her haunches.

It was not just the leaves and the insects that emitted light in the glen, for she had lit a series of tea lights, which framed the shrine and the steps. When the light was uneven behind her closed lids, she attributed this unsteadiness to these small candles, for they were notorious flickerers. The truth was, however, that it was the fireflies buzzing by silently within inches of her face.

These airborne insects were refugees from a genetic modifying lab some four or five miles away, and because of the harshness of their captivity they had been taught to fly quietly.

What did the nun pray for?

Here is how her prayer went, or rather how her prayer dissolved back into pondering thought, as prayers so often do:

Dear God, dear Virgin or whoever you might be,

Excuse me if I insult you by that address, but if I weren't honest about my doubts in your existence then you'd surely know. Yesterday Celia and I were discovered by Mary. It was just a kiss, and not our first, but it was such a sweet kiss, too, and in my heart I know that something so good and right can never be a sin. I know you know this as well. But Mary reported it, and Celia told Mother Wilgefortis that it was I who had initiated it. Celia took all that purity and sensuality, God, and she soiled it with denial. I am trying to forgive her, but I feel rage, not only that I will be disciplined for Particular Friendships, but rage at someone who only yesterday made me feel happiness, the soar of real emotion, God, the real true light of your Son and my Lord. No matter what happens, I will not deny this as Celia did, and no matter what pattern of frail and flawed human repercussions follow, I will continue to believe that you are truth, and light, and love.

This was where the prayer portion of her mind stopped, because then she knelt there on the hard stone and kept thinking of what Mother Superior had shouted at her about Noah's Ark and the pairings of opposites; and she also kept thinking, though, that such pairings would only be matched like bookends if the gender was the same instead of differing; and therefore Mother Superior had got it all wrong after all, particularly since Mother Wilgefortis always said 'Like attracts like,' over and over again like a blasted litany. Even if she were asked to move to a different order, the nun decided she wouldn't care.

And her eyes flipped open then from sheer anger, and she felt it in her chest, but she had come to this quiet place for peace, after all, not wrath. She could still hear Mother Wilgefortis in her head: 'Adam and Eve, not Anna and Eve; Noah's Ark, not Gay Day in the Park,' and she could hear her own voice arguing back, 'But Mother, you also say "like attracts like".'

The lightning bugs were everywhere. She gasped just once and then held out a hand to touch one and it landed on her index finger like a butterfly, though she had never heard of lightning bugs doing anything as social as that. Perhaps they were some new variety. For that matter, she had never heard of lightning bugs in this area of the country, either.

Above her, the trees swayed slightly with the wind and she saw how their very leaves glowed, one leaf in three. It was like the lights at Christmas, but here it was not ornamentation but the actual leaves of the tree that shone, rather like those fiberoptic plastic plants she had once seen in a store window.

Oh, it was quite lovely. Then she looked down at herself and saw that her finger was turning white with light where the lightning bug had landed, and the glow was working its way inward to her whole body, finger then back of hand then wrist then three-quarters of her arm glowing now, the prettiest infection she had ever seen. She did not feel especially surprised. It had been a long day, and the fantastical does not shock a tired mind as it does a well-rested one. Instead, she watched with pleasure until her entire arm was glowing, and then her neck, and then she felt heat rush to her face and she knew it must be glowing, too. The white light slid down her other arm, and down her breasts and ribcage and abdomen and groin, and the whole sensation made her feel warm and tight and full of love. The wave of light reached the tip of her toes and stopped, and left her flesh illuminated like the small plastic statues they used to sell of the Virgin in the 1970s, statues which glowed green-white and faded with the hours of darkness to mere muted plastic by dawn, when you didn't need the Virgin watching over you any more.

She looked up. Yes, she felt warm and fat and tight, like she had drunk a huge mug of glow-in-the-dark cocoa, or the same way she had felt on all parts of her skin after she and Celia had kissed the first time two weeks ago, right after morning prayers.

'Adam and Eve, not Anna and Eve. Noah's Ark, not Gay Day in the Park.'

'But Mother, you also say "like attracts like".'

She stretched out her hands and they shimmered like the tree leaves, and the lightning bugs moved with her in a little dance, and she felt she was travelling with them as they swirled silently around her head; as if she and the bugs were working together in the magic of shine, though their species were different.

She took all her clothes off then. How could she not? It felt right, there in the little green glen with the moon shining, and the trees glowing ghostly, and the insects, and the tea lights; and she laughed with delight when she saw how smooth the glow was from her breasts and how the tight muscles of her bare arms glittered with movement. And her bottom; she turned around to see it, too, and it glowed perfectly there, a fine sheen to it that made her haunches look quite attractive, in her opinion. She hoped only that it would not rain, for then she would get cold.

While she was checking out the shine off her bottom, someone coughed near the altar.

She took her time turning around, not feeling particularly frightened because if she could glow like this then, if it was someone dangerous like a rapist or a murderer, okay, she would just kick her heels together and fly up out of reach. Why not? If she had already started glowing, well, anything could happen now.

But there was an angel coughing there, sitting down casually on the altar. 'I've got a bit of a hack,' she explained. 'My homeopath said phosphorus would work, but it hasn't helped me out yet.'

Yes. It was a 'she'. Despite the fact that the nun had always been taught that angels were sexless, gender-free. She didn't remember who had told her that, however. It wasn't like angels were mentioned by name all that often in the Bible, anyhow, only twice, Gabriel and Michael, and two and a half times, she reckoned, if you were allowed to count Lucifer.

'Then again, I really haven't been taking the phosphorus at regular intervals,' the angel admitted to the nun.

Like the nun before her, the angel also got to her feet and stretched. Her frame was sleek and androgynous, but it was irrefutably female. She had high small breasts and since she stood immodestly, with feet apart while she stretched and yawned, you could even see a bit of luminescent labia peeping out from between her thighs. Also, the angel had pubic hair. And when this heavenly messenger – who in general radiated white – spread her arms out, her wings shook, and the nun saw that each feather was a different shade and each glowed as if lit from a lamp underneath: apricot, rose, bright blue, darkest black that still shone, blood-red, green, peach, orange, yellow, violet and, of course, all the metallics like silver and bronze and gold, that goes without saying.

The nun remembered reading that white was all colours together, so maybe this whiteness was more concentrated in the angel's flesh, as it were, and more diffused in the feathered wings where the white light burst out into rainbows. The nun had that warm tight feeling again, looking at the angel.

'If you want to kiss me, feel free,' said the angel. 'I'm sure you'd enjoy it.'

The nun was only a trifle embarrassed that the angel could read minds. At the same time it was exhilarating, because it was being made quite clear that such desires were nothing at all to be ashamed of.

Five fireflies landed on the nun's arm in a line, blending into her own naked glow in the shiny green glen, and they travelled along for the ride when she joined the angel atop the altar and put her fingers up, uncertainly, to stroke the angel's feathers.

The angel's whole body rippled with pleasure. 'Do that again,' she told the nun. The nun caressed a soft avocado-coloured feather then, and watched the angel's face crease into ecstasy as she did so. It was quite extraordinary and it filled the nun with a kind of pride.

'My name is Margaret,' said the nun, shyly. 'What's yours?'

'It's Angelica, of course.' The angel seemed a bit snippy that the nun hadn't guessed. 'Nothing daft like Angela. I hate that name.'

'Oh, I completely agree,' said the nun happily, 'I've always disliked the name Angela. But Angelica is a lovely, lovely name. Quite different,' she added, stroking the angel's other wing with a bit more confidence and enjoying the rapture that passed over the angel's features as she did so.

The nun now realised that there were flowers dotted in between the trees around the glen, *Herba angelica*, an aromatic umbelliferous plant. It seemed exactly right, in the circumstances. If she were ever to bake a cake for the angel, it suddenly occurred to her, she would decorate the frosting with candied stalks of angelica, as well.

The angel smiled at her, tenderly, and wrapped her long arms round the nun, pulling them close together. There was a tingling feeling where their crotches met, and their breasts matched the nipples of the other quite perfectly, and the nun felt that warmth now from her feet to her groin to her areolas to the back of her neck and then out to her fingers clasped round the angel's trim waist. And then the angel folded her wings round the nun, and pressed her closer as they stood there on the altar, and put her lips to the nun's lips.

The kiss was wonderful. It felt just perfect. It made the nun think of Jesus and love and all that was right with the world. The angel's tongue in her mouth had the purity of desire, and the nun began to tremble, clasped there in those huge wings and by the angel's arms around her waist, and then she began to kiss back as well. She shifted her own hands so she could run them up and down the angel's body, which was a delight beyond compare. The angel's glowing skin was smooth like a living flower petal, and just the feel of the angel made the nun go wet between her legs.

Which turned out to be a good thing, because the angel was releasing her and urging her down, down, to lie with her on the overgrown grass of the top stone step, and the angel was kissing the nun between her legs, and the nun felt such stabs of clear need that she shifted position so that her face too was at the angel's thighs. And when the nun licked at her there, the angel was certainly not sexless; she was the best things of sex that have ever been named, and her nectar there tasted like water, but such sweet water, and the nun wondered whether the wetness would leave glowing traces all over her face.

But also, the nun was enjoying the angel's persistent licking on her own sex, a steady rhythm that changed for the nun from shivers of pleasure that concentrated themselves at the nun's hole and little bud and then grew to the whole area below her waist. Between her legs she was soaked with the sap of desire, and then the beat of pleasure overtook her just as the glow had worked itself from her finger along the rest of her flesh, and she bucked and tried to move her sex more rapidly against the regular licking of the angel's heavenly tongue. She could feel just the slightest tickle of the angel's wings on her back, and this made her even more desirous. And all the while she ran the flat of her own tongue back from hole to bud across the angel's sex, which had turned from white to glowing red with need, and the rapture grew greater and greater. The nun jerked her hips forward again and again towards the point of the angel's tongue, trying to prolong the final ripples of pleasure, bitter yet candied, that made her itch for one more wave, one more crest of tingly bliss.

When her head came out of the clouds, though she was as wet as anything and the angel's tongue was still spinning pleasure on her sex in the aftermath, she kept up her own part of the bargain, as it were. She licked the angel into an orgasm on the stone step, so that the angel at last went all purple, then blue, then ebony, then fuschia with pleasure and cried out silver tears and laughed and sang out the most beautiful rendition of Violetta's *Follie!* aria the nun had ever heard.

Above them, the trees glowed with appreciation.

The angel rose to her feet and, though she was still shaky herself, she chivalrously helped the nun up as well, and wrapped arms and wings around her as she had before, and kissed her for a long, long time.

'Forget Celia,' the angel told the nun, 'forget Mother Wilgefortis. Forget them all. You know yourself what feels right.'

'Okay.' The nun's response was so speedy that she grinned, at herself.

The angel kissed her on the nose and the nun barely had time to wonder whether she'd get freckles there before the angel stretched out one hand, and the nun grasped it hard, for she had a thing about heights, and they both rose above the discredited shrine, like Superman and Lois Lane, the nun thought, that's really great, and a chain of intrepid fireflies followed them up into the clouds as well, for light after all attracts light.

Moon Wood
Julie Travis

Moon Wood was beautiful that day.

Moon Wood was always beautiful, but on that day it had felt special from the moment I arrived. I usually came here in the mornings, sometimes early enough to see the dawn break, to sit on fallen leaves and other debris and see the trees, smudged by the darkness, come into focus. There were squirrels to feed and birds I'd never seen before, singing their songs or just curious about their uninvited guest. It was here I would come if I felt unsettled or sad, if the harshness of the world was tearing down my defences. Here I could heal and gather my strength.

Paths criss-crossed the wood, some wide enough for prams and wheelchairs, some making their way down the more gentle slopes to the picnic areas and the river that cut the wood in two. Smaller trails, marked by coloured rings on wooden posts, darted off at intervals, and roughly beaten tracks showed where people had made their own routes. Never afraid of walking alone in the wood, I was nevertheless cautious when I first began to explore, but it wasn't long before I felt hemmed in by the people I saw on my walks, even though they were often few and far between, so one day, when I was sure I was alone, I stepped off the path. The way ahead was undisturbed, uncharted territory but I sensed that it was safe, so I made my way among the bushes and was soon swallowed up by the trees. This was real solitude; I could not see my way back to the path, and no one on the path could see me. I found a trickle of a stream, enough to cool my feet on a warm day, and followed it. Moss-covered stones made rudimentary bridges, and ferns covered the water completely in some parts, but I found the stream again and made my way to a small, grassy clearing.

This became my place. I could read here in peace, write letters or sometimes sleep off illness. As my confidence grew, I would sunbathe topless, the grass comfortable enough to lie on. Eventually I sunbathed naked. In this place it was the natural thing to do. I never heard another human voice, or the bark of a dog, or the sound of children playing. This was my place and before long I would shed my clothes the moment I entered the clearing. Inevitably, a new pastime came to me and often I would lie on the grass and masturbate, the sun warming my inner thighs as I stroked myself. Sometimes, when I felt especially needy, I'd take my dildo with me to the clearing and stand, face up to the glorious sky, legs slightly bent, and fuck myself into a near stupor. Sated, I would then curl up on the grass and doze until the wetness on my thighs had dried.

I didn't know what it was that made Moon Wood feel so different, so inviting, that day. Perhaps I just needed to be there; I had some things on my mind and wanted a place to think. As I approached, I noticed how very quiet it appeared – no cars were parked by the entrance; no one was walking on the paths. It was as if the area had been closed to everyone except me.

The smell of pine and water filled the air as I stepped off the main path. I had already discarded my shoes and I expected the walk to be a little painful, but the broken branches, twigs and stones were softer and warmer than usual underfoot. Once I reached the clearing, I tried to think, to make some order of the things whirling around in my head, but the longer I sat, the less I could concentrate. I stood up and walked around, hoping that it would settle me down, but it made no difference. Down between my legs, a pulse began, throbbing like a heartbeat.

Now I knew what I needed. If I satisfied myself, my thoughts would be calmer, more considered. As I undressed, I realised how uncomfortable I was here now unless I was naked. The clearing had some debris in it, which I placed out of harm's way. A large branch had fallen across one end. Instead of moving it, I decided to make use of it; lying on the grass, I placed my legs on the branch so my hips were slightly raised. I passed my hand over my breasts, but I was too impatient for foreplay, so after a cursory tweak and squeeze of my nipples I began to give my clit the attention it so obviously needed.

Masturbation is a very physical thing for me. I can thrash around, curse, talk as if I am possessed, and once I begin it is almost impossible for me to stop until I've reached a guttural – often yelled – orgasm. Often, I liked to spread myself wide open, but this time I began with my legs closed, the pressure on my clit adding to the pleasure. By the time I threw my legs apart and dipped my fingers inside, I could feel myself building up to an amazing climax.

But then I felt eyes on me. Someone was watching, of that I had no doubt. Angry that someone had found my place, was taking pleasure from my sexual act, I managed to pull my hand away from my cunt. Twisting around, I looked for the culprit. No one was in sight.

"Please, carry on," said a voice. "Don't stop on my account."

The voice was undeniably female, but it was strange, bubbling sound, like the stream that had first bought me there. I sat up, but still could see no one.

"Who are you? Where are you?"

"I'm right in front of you."

I looked ahead. For a moment it seemed as if the world was melting. The sight made me feel dizzy, but I took a deep breath, shook my head and looked again. Something was pulling itself away, forming from the essence of the wood. Its shape settled and a figure was soon recognisable: a woman, made from all the things that surrounded me. Her hair was long strands of reed and grass, her limbs were thick branches, her body was earth. On her large, sagging breasts fresh, open daisies took the place of nipples.

Now complete, the wood-woman walked towards me. She stepped easily over the branch that my legs still rested upon and sat down on it.

"I've watched you here before," she said, in that watery voice. "But today, your need seems so great that I wanted to be a part of it. So, if you will, carry on."

I stared at her, a thousand questions forming and then disappearing. After all, at this moment, what did it matter who she was or where she had come from? I lay back down and reached between my legs. It was still hot and wet there, and my clit reared up at the return of my touch. I'd never masturbated for anyone before. It had always been about me, my own pleasure, but now I would be doing it for the two of us. It was an exciting prospect. As I stroked myself my gaze went from my body to her face; went from my breasts rippling as I moved to the curves of her stomach and thighs. Her legs were not open enough for me to see her cunt, so I fantasised over what it would look like, how wet it might be. The clearing became a stage, the sunshine a spotlight, and I rose to the performance. I wanted to give it my all, to leave my audience of one happy – but perhaps still wanting more. In between my grunts, I could hear her gasping, and it made me determined to please her. I came with a cry that sounded almost aggressive, my body jerking and twitching.

When it was over, I closed my eyes, enjoying the sweat on my brow and under my breasts. As my breathing began to even out, I thought about the wood-woman, the fantasy that had made me come so hard. I didn't think I had it in me to conjure up such a thing.

Then I heard twigs snapping beside me and found that it hadn't been a fantasy after all. I opened my eyes as the wood-woman lay down beside me. She propped her head up on one hand and congratulated me. "That was very sexy. Thank you."

She bent over and kissed me. Her earthen face was cool, her lips soft and mossy. Her tongue slithered into my mouth with a life of its own. She kissed my neck and then focused her attention on my breasts. As she massaged them with her mouth, I reached down and brushed through her tangle of hair. She eased herself on top of me and began rubbing her body against mine, flesh against mud and wood and flora, creating a wonderful friction. My strength was returning and so I wrapped my arms around her, drawing my nails down her back and over her wide buttocks. She sat back on top of me, straddling me now, and I pulled myself up and licked the petals of her nipples. Her rough wooden hands gripped my head for a minute, but she pulled away suddenly, squatted and swung her hips in order for my face to meet her cunt.

She was dark and wet down there, as soft as any woman I've ever had, but the scent of wild flowers, mingled with the unmistakable smell of her juices was a heady combination. For a while I didn't move, content to leave my face buried almost inside her, but she did not let me stay that way for long.

"Lick me. I want to come over your face." Her voice now swept around the clearing, waving the branches of the trees like a breeze. I held her tight around the tops of her legs and began, kissing and nuzzling all over her cunt, enjoying the wetness on my face until I found my lips resting against her clit. It was hard, a small, hot stone amongst the earth. I used my tongue to trace its shape and then licked, gently at first then a little harder, but always persistent, wanting to reassure her that I had no intention of stopping.

We rocked back and forth, her strong arms holding me tight, her body becoming tenser as the orgasm built up inside her. She held back as long as she could but, at last, her body became rigid and I knew it was time. She bellowed like an animal and it was as if a river had burst its banks, splashing over my face and down, dripping across my chest and dribbling into my ears. When her body finally relaxed, I put my arms around her and kissed her stomach, wanting to be in her arms for a while, but the wood-woman had no interest in stopping just yet. She picked me up and carried me into the nearest line of trees and lay me, face down, over a tree trunk. Her long, twig-like fingers scratched their way down my back, but they were far sharper than my close-cut nails and my skin gave way under them. The pain was equally awful and sensual. I cried out and gripped the trunk, the thick bark providing a strong handhold. Blood began to ooze out of the wounds and I giggled, light-headed. My cunt felt like a yawning hole. I begged her to fuck me.

"All in good time, sweetheart." And her fingers carried on doing their work. She tore the skin all over my back, up and down my arms and shoulders, and then reached around me to cup my breasts in her rough hands. She massaged them again, tenderly this time, giving me relief from the pain, before squeezing my nipples hard enough to make me yelp.

"Now you get fucked. Spread yourself wide and relax and I'll fill you completely."

I had no thought of not complying. I pushed my knees as far apart as they would go and lowered my head towards the ground to show my complete submission. With one hand coiled around the back of my neck, she began to play with the outside of my cunt. The sharpness of her fingers worried me slightly, but I trusted her not to tear me apart inside – after all, such a creature would surely know the delicacy of a woman's body – and I was not mistaken. I heard a scrabbling sound – and grew aware that she was tying me to the tree trunk with lengths of ivy. I strained against my bonds to test them and, to my delight, they were solid.

And so the fucking began.

She'd softened her fingers so they were warm and flexible. Two, three went inside me, beginning a slow and deep rhythm. She teased me, as all lovers tease. "You want more? You can take more than this, can't you, my girl?" she asked.

"Yes! Yes! As much as you can give. Fist me, *please*."

Four fingers went inside and then five. Without missing a beat she put her whole hand in my cunt.

"Okay," she said, and pushed herself right in.

I may have pissed myself at that point, but I really can't remember. It didn't matter. Deeper and deeper she went, slowly increasing her rhythm, gasping with pleasure every time I screamed and came. My cunt muscles squeezed against her hand, but she was stronger. The only part of my body that could move was my hips, and, deep as she was, I pushed against her to make her go even further inside me. I was as greedy and selfish as I'd ever been but she was equal to it, the noises she made proving she was getting as much from it as I was.

At some point it had to end, and long after I was past knowing how long she'd been fisting me or where I was, she eased off and eventually stopped. She stayed inside me for a while and when I began to focus and be aware of my body – the bark cutting into my stomach, my legs, still wide apart, feeling as if the joints were pulling apart – she drew her arm gently out and freed me from my ivy bonds.

Slowly I made my legs work again, turned over and sat on the ground beside the wood-woman. She gathered me in her arms, the scent of her – trees, flowers, grass and now sweat – comforting me as I shuddered with the intensity of what had happened. The sun was well on its way down and as the light faded, so did she. I closed my eyes, not wanting to see her disappear, and felt her body gradually lose substance. When I was sure she was gone, I dressed and made my way home. It was getting cold.

I've been back to the clearing since then and I haven't seen the wood-woman, but I know she's around. How could she not be? She is, after all, a part of everything there. I can feel her watching me and I can smell her everywhere. I am close to her often, giving myself beautiful orgasms using the leaves and the earth and the flowers. I'm going to Moon Wood again today and I know that when the wind blows through the trees I'll hear her sighing and when the sun shines on me I'll feel her warmth. And when I go home, I'll have the mud from her body smeared over and inside mine.

Wanting It
Frances Gapper

The pond near our house was fed by the Thames. The water came through a tunnel with a barred mouth. Ducks floated between the bars, going in, out. They had ducklings and nested on the island. I wondered, did they get scared in the tunnel? It went under the roads and the houses. A long way. They could have flown instead, but they didn't.

Once I kept blowing my whistle and a woman came running out of a house and told me to stop. Because water carries sound. She was being driven desperate.

Every year the pond was cleaned out, the river turned off somehow. Then you could walk to the island. You could peer into the stinky dark tunnel.

One day while running a stick along the railings, I remembered a dream I'd had the night before. In this dream I was being spanked by my dad. A feeling spread up through me. It came and went, in a rhythm. It got stronger and stronger, till it burst. I wanted that feeling again, now. Now.

In real life my mum was the disciplinarian, never my dad. And being spanked was painful, not enjoyable. And I hadn't been, for ages. I'd been good. So how could I make that feeling happen? My only hope was to have the same dream again.

My best friend Catherine's father walloped her, she'd told me, but what did that mean exactly? I didn't know. Catherine's mother slapped her face, I'd seen that, but things mostly happened in private, behind closed doors. Catherine's father had magazines with pictures of naked ladies. Our comics, the *Beano* and the *Dandy*, had pictures of children being spanked, usually in the last frame of the cartoon. Desperate Dan spanked his niece and nephew, both together over his knee. He laughed, they bawled. The cartoon character grown-ups always laughed while spanking the children. Or anyway the men did. The old women looked cross.

"Mum, please can Catherine stay the night? Oh please, please." "But you've been together all day." But usually my mum allowed us. She rang Catherine's mother. Then in the dark, in our pyjamas, I would tell stories of us being naughty and getting spanked. "Now let's pretend..." Catherine would turn over to oblige me and we lay on our tummies, imagining. But really she liked stories about doing poos in the street, or in the classroom.

Catherine had long dark hair. My mum said long hair is messy, you can grow it when you're older, seventeen or eighteen. Catherine was beautiful. One morning I was saving a seat for her on the school bus. Through the window I saw her, short-haired. A jolt to my heart. She got on the bus. I told her: "I don't love you any more, now you've had your hair cut." She replied: "Then you could never really have loved me in the first place." She went to sit at the back, with another girl.

Now we'd split up, Catherine in revenge took all the little ones. They clung to her in the playground, hung around her, trailed after her. She was their preferred mummy. I cried in the toilets.

The headmaster drew a picture of a slipper on the blackboard in our classroom and wrote beside it, James E. That meant, he was going to give James the slipper. It was to remind himself. I dreamed I was in the headmaster's room and he was smilingly telling me to take down my knickers. And in assembly, my name was read out, the headmaster called me up to the platform, he spanked me in front of the whole school.

But then my dream headmaster turned strangely non-violent. As did my dream father and mother. They no longer seemed eager to hurt and shame me. Frozen, removed, benevolent — I couldn't provoke them into action. I seemed to have forgotten how. Denied the source of pleasure. Good even in my dreams.

Kneading
Ginger Allen

She had just moved to a new sublet a few blocks away from me, just above Delson's Bakery. Her window was open, and I could smell the tempting yeasty carbs, rising from down below. I was trying to control my intake, but it wasn't easy. I was distracted as she was talking to me and showing me her room.

Her bed was about four feet off of the ground. Mid-sentence, she leapt up onto it and lay on her side. When she completed her thought, she curled into a loose fetal position and looked at me. I opened my bag, took out my oil, and walked over to her.

"Do you want to massage me?" she asked.

"If you let me," I responded. I was still deeply in love with — and explosively attracted to — my ex. I knew she would be seeing her girlfriend in a couple of hours, and couldn't help but try to make the most of the limited time we had together.

"Is this the massage oil you mentioned your friend gave you for your birthday?" She was a very active listener, and could always recall incidental details that I hardly remembered sharing.

"Yes. It's lavender." I removed the cap and waved it by her nose.

"Nice, but strong," she said. "Doesn't lavender put you to sleep? I need to have energy for tonight."

"I'm sure you do," I responded, screwing back on the cap. Besides, how would she explain later on to her girlfriend why her entire back smelled like purple flowers? Then again, she had been good about explaining. The night that I shaved her pussy and cut her by accident was noticed, but passed off as something she did to herself unwittingly.

"Would you like to use that one?" she asked, indicating the neutral-smelling lotion on her coffee table.

"Too far away," I said as I pressed into the skin just above her shoulder blades with my bare hands. The smell of hot piping buns wafted into her room from the bakery below, and I was staring longingly at her fine ass.

"Mmm." I could see that her eyes were closed and she was smiling dreamily. And I could feel myself get instantly wet from touching her.

"Lie on your stomach for me," I said. She stretched out and rolled over as I had requested. I circled my thumbs up the nape of her neck and spread my fingers out to massage the base of her scalp. Her breathing deepened, and of course I wanted more.

"Take this off," I said. She slowly sat up with her back facing me and lifted her arms above her head. I slid the tank top off her, setting her breasts free. I pressed myself into her from behind and felt her nipples harden.

"Lie back down, baby," I said, "facing up." She did as I said, and I straddled her. I continued massaging her — her hands, up her arms, onto her shoulders, around the back of her neck. She appeared completely relaxed, except that she was breathing a little harder than before. I bent over her and stroked her soft cheek with mine. She smiled.

"I love the way you make me feel," she said.

"I love touching you," I responded, and I softly kissed her neck, just below her earlobe. When I pulled away to look at her, she returned my gaze, seeming almost innocent. My heart opened and for that moment I imagined that she was mine again, and that we could be together, happy, in love. I closed my eyes and kissed her, forgetting the quite different reality, and reminding myself to savor the moment. She kissed me back, sliding her tongue into my mouth and stroking the back of my neck. I fell right into her.

When she took my hand and guided it to where she was soaking wet, I couldn't control myself and immediately dropped down to take her with my mouth. The taste of her always made me completely high, and she knew it. I wanted to stay there for hours, but there was not enough time. I lapped up everything she gave to me, and slid my finger inside to feel for more. She shuddered and moaned and came on my face and my hand, and

I didn't stop licking her and pressing hard on her G-spot until she told me to stop.

"Don't kiss me, baby," she said gently, anticipating my next move. She would not be able to explain to her girlfriend if she tasted too much like her own pussy, and I understood.

When she got up to go to the bathroom, I looked at the clock and saw that we still had twenty minutes. I had my strap-on in my bag, so I put it on and put my pants on over it.

"I'm so sorry — I have to go in twenty minutes," she said, as I peeked in and saw her washing up over the sink.

"I know," I said, pressing into her from behind until she felt my hardness. I took her wet hands, put them on the sides of the sink, and checked her pussy with my finger, only to find it still dripping wet.

"Is this your fantasy?" she said to me, looking into the bathroom mirror as she was bent over the sink.

"Yes," I said, "I've been needing you like this all week." I pulled the eight-inch dildo out and slid it across her pussy, lubricating it. She submitted and I pushed it inside of her, fucking her hard over the sink and watching us in the mirror.

It was violent, animalistic fucking, and I truly had been needing to do this to her so badly. She took it hard, and moaned loudly. I was so excited that I actually began to come — without any direct stimulation at all — from slamming into her. I grabbed onto her and folded over her, sweating and exhausted. She looked up at me in the mirror with the sexiest look on her face. I knew she had to go, but I couldn't keep my hands off of her. She had to be the one setting the rules, because I was so attracted to her that I could hardly think.

I forgot how it was that we finally left the apartment together. She hugged me and kissed me on the cheek, and as we parted I walked into Delson's alone. I ordered a small American coffee and a hot cross bun. I remember how good it tasted as I broke off a piece, buttered it, and slipped it deliberately into my mouth.

In and Out of Time
Shameem Kabir

London, England. 1984. The room was alive with moving women. Even those seated at tables started to tap and turn in time to the music. Ginnie felt the rhythm of the room taking hold; she swayed to the sounds coming through the speakers, her head tilting to the beat. She was watching Smita on stage, as she started to sing "Blind Date".

> *I'm never sure*
> *what's in store*
> *when I open the door*
> *on a blind date.*

> *Will she be nice*
> *will she like rice*
> *I sit and wait*
> *on a blind date.*

> *Could be great*
> *on a blind date.*

It was important for the band to be good tonight, because Joan of Disc Hits was here. Ginnie had arranged it after frequently sending demos and letters to the company. Finally she had gone round to their offices and had persuaded Joan to come and see them on stage.

> *When she gets here*
> *the stage is set clear*
> *and it's like fate*
> *on a blind date.*

Ginnie was obsessed by the ambition to get a megastar career off the ground. She wanted recognition, at any cost, and she knew the only way to get it was through a major record company deal. That's why she'd been so insistent with Joan, who had at last consented to come and see the Daughters perform.

> *Could be great*
> *on a blind date.*

Ginnie had met Smita on a blind date and had been immediately attracted to her. Perhaps it was her exotic personality that first drew Ginnie to her. She liked her being an anglicised Asian, with bits of both cultures caught in what she thought was an unusual synthesis. She had been charmed by it.

> *Should I charm her*
> *let go my armour*
> *I'm in a state*
> *on a blind date.*

More than anything else, Ginnie was immediately responsive because they both had had unhappy relationships with other partners and were determined not to fall into the same patterns. So although they realised the danger of their date, they were confident they could resist any repetition, and decided, what the hell, to give it a go.

> *The stories we share*
> *take me by surprise*
> *the stories we share*
> *make me realise*
> *the danger of our state*

> *Can be great*
> *on a blind date.*

Smita had made Ginnie laugh in a way she hadn't for a long time. Now, as Smita sang the closing chorus of her song, Ginnie got up to do the next number. She wasn't nervous; she'd stopped counting the hours spent singing. It was a passion with her. She walked through the side aisle, up the corner steps, and was at her microphone in perfect time. The audience applauded as Smita turned to Ginnie, moving her arms in a sweep of welcome. The lights on her dimmed and went gold on Ginnie, who took hold of the microphone and announced "Dream of Gold".

Met you in a dream of gold
that's why I seem so bold
dream of gold, dream of gold.

As Smita sat down at the band's reserved table, she saw how receptive the audience was. There were a lot of fans there that night, regulars who followed the band through the women's circuit. She was aware that many of them felt attracted to Ginnie. She always had that effect; her every gesture was enticing without design. Smita looked up to watch her, desiring her as much as she had three years ago when they met through an ad. She remembered that night. They had made love that same evening. There had been no hesitation on her part, no caution on Ginnie's. They had talked over dinner and wine, their minds meeting on many areas. Above all they wanted to avoid the awfulness of their previous encounters, where they'd either been suffocated or suffocating.

Smita had thought long and hard about her first lesbian relationship. It had ended in such pain and bitterness. It had been Isabel's first lesbian relationship as well. To begin with, they had been deliriously happy, but then her lover started saying how different Smita was, and how it was difficult to be with her.

She said Smita was emotionally too demanding, and Isabel didn't want to make such a commitment. She then started a relationship with another woman, with whom she eventually bought a flat.

Later on, Smita agreed with her friend Naseem that Isabel had been acting out a common pattern. Naseem knew quite a few women whose first lesbian relationships had been disasters. It was difficult when everything was so new and intense, and when issues of autonomy had still to be worked out. Often the woman who had the control in the relationship would walk out on her lover, saying that she didn't want monogamy. She would then go on form a monogamous relationship with a second partner. The two of them would then make the commitment to each other that they'd previously sworn was impossible. But at the time, when this happened with Isabel, Smita only saw the rejection as proof of her not being lovable. She was devastated at being excluded so totally. Eventually she decided that she would build a relationship on another basis, where there would be commitment without claustrophobia, passion without pain. So when she met Ginnie, and they exchanged their respective stories, there had been the shared resolve to avoid repeating the same mistakes. They were too aware of the danger of their date.

You're the danger in my dreams
you're no stranger to my dreams
you're the dancer in my dreams
you're the answer to my dreams.

So give it a chance
to work out right
we can share a dance
we can share a night

Met you in a dream of gold
that's why I seem so bold
dream of gold, dream of gold.

Smita remembered when Ginnie had written the song for her. It had been a breakthrough for Ginnie, who had never written a lyric before, whereas Smita had been writing them for years. She had devised many concept albums because she was sure this was the future for pop/rock. Smita had agreed to go along with Ginnie's suggestion to form a band. She wanted to put her ideas into practice. The song was ending now. She found her way back to the stage, and was at her microphone just in time for "High on You".

> *I'm high on you*
> *high as a kite*
> *I'm flying too*
> *deep in the night*
> *you start to smile*
> *your eyes so bright*
> *and for a while*
> *we feel delight.*

As Ginnie returned to their table, she was conscious of a quickening of her pulse. Must have been all that real coffee she'd drunk. She could do with a cigarette, now, but resisted. It was such an awful habit; she hated being addicted to tobacco. She sat down facing the stage, as Smita sang one of her favourite songs:

> *I'm high on you*
> *high as a lark*
> *your kiss so true*
> *is like a spark*
> *we share a walk*
> *down at the park*
> *and then we talk*
> *deep in the dark.*

They'd been collaborating for nearly three years now, practically all the time they'd known each other. When they first met, Ginnie thought Smita was a jewel among stones. Ginnie liked her way with words; Smita spoke so fluently, so eloquently. Ginnie had been surprised when Smita told her she had a degree in English, but then it made perfect sense. And she spoke so formally. She found that charming too. Smita had once objected to this. She said her speech patterns were part of her cultural heritage, and that it had nothing to do with being quaint. But Ginnie still thought she was funny. And she loved how polite Smita was. Her manners were so perfect; she said "please" and "thank you" on every occasion; she even said "sorry" when she meant pardon. These customs coming from another culture were appealing too.

> *I'm high on you*
> *with eyes of love*
> *I'm high on you*
> *like the skies above*

Their collaboration had begun as a joke, with each taking it in turn to make up alternative lines to well-known songs. Ginnie had really loved the way they had laughed together. And she loved working with Smita, who had taught her many a trick on how to write lyrics. They would spend hours together, writing, practising, composing and performing, and their partnership was a productive one. It had been easy to form the Daughters. The quality of their material made the band popular with lesbian audiences. They were a good working unit. Joan of Disc Hots would just have to see that for herself.

> *I'm high on you*
> *high as a cloud*
> *we know it's true*
> *to feel this proud*
> *both you and I*
> *don't want to crowd*
> *but we're so high*
> *we say it out loud.*

Smita's number was ending as Ginnie went back on stage. She took the microphone and the band started on the opening bars of "Sunshine Dream".

> *I was lost when you found me*
> *I was in waves which drowned me*

but I felt love surround me
when you put your arms around me.

You bring me sunshine like I've never seen
you're my sunshine dream.

It had been electric for them, Smita thought, returning to their table. She let her neck relax, and the music carried her to the memory of those first days. The attraction had been immediate, signalled by their agreement to sleep together. They'd undressed slowly. When they first kissed, Smita felt a thrill of joy.

I could feel your body swaying
I could tell I'd be staying
I could hear your voice saying
you wanted us to see the day in.

Their lips were generous and gentle, demanding with pasion and not pressure. They had started making love slowly. Smita felt in a state of suspension, her hands moving over the curves and contours of Ginnie's body, conscious all the time of the softness of her skin, the scent of her breath on her eyes, her ears, her mouth. She followed the line of her spine downwards, down to where it led to her buttocks, fitting round and warm in each hand. Ginnie pressed Smita's breasts, and her legs crossed into Smita's, interlocking. Their hands were delicate in touch, alighting, stroking, then moving on to some undiscovered part of their anatomy. Ginnie kissed Smita on the nape of her neck, her breath warm.

I never thought a kiss
could do this much
I never felt the flame
quite the same
as with your touch.

Their hands went across their thighs, and then, as they uncrossed their legs, they unfolded themselves to each other, silky hair brushing under their palms. They began to move their bodies in a sway of desire, as they radiated around each other's centre of pleasure. Their fingers travelled up between the lips, exploring the warm liquid joy of passion, finding the core of the clitoris, circular, firm, as they moved to the magic of each other's pleasure. They sensed each other's needs as they fell into the rightness of the rhythm. Smita could feel Ginnie turning under her hand with a response similar to her own, impassioned, urgent, but without frenzy.

When I felt your lips on mine
and we moved together in time
it was like I'd seen a sign
I'd never felt so fine.

Now their arousal took another turn, deeper, in tune. As Ginnie kissed Smita with the edge of a desire neither could control, she made a humming sound at the back of her mouth. The sound moved into her throat, resonated, it became longer and louder as her excitement became extremity. They started on a faster cycle of breathing, their hearts pounding in their breasts with beats of a frantic drum. Ginnie responded to each kiss, each caress, by holding Smita tight, then tighter, pulling her, reaching and responding. They wanted each other: Smita felt a rush. And then, with their fingers in mutual motion, they touched with a passion of fire and flame, meeting, retreating, then meeting together in perfect time. Smita felt release, release in the power of giving and getting pleasure, as they both came, explosively, both in trust and both with surrender. Warmth glowed through them.

You bring me sunshine like I've never seen
you're my sunshine dream.

Then, as they lay together, spent in their exhaustion, their eyes rested on each other, taking in each detail, their heartbeats slowing into another, quieter rhythm.

As Smita returned on stage, Ginnie touched her shoulder, and there was still a thrill in her caress. Smita reached the microphone and began singing "Don't Do Me Wrong".

> *Don't do me wrong*
> *like I've been done*
> *don't do me wrong.*

When Ginnie returned to the table she wasn't really listening to Smita's song. She was still feeling high on her own voice. When she sang, she sang with power and passion. After all, it was a performance; she believed in giving her best. Now, as she glanced around the tables, she knew that a lot of women were looking at her. She loved that; she loved the sense of power that this adulation gave her. She was ambitious for fame; she could be a major star. Why not? She was attractive; her voice was brilliant; she was charming. She loved being in the public eye, and enjoyed knowing that a lot of these women were fantasising about her. She was looking good tonight and was glad she'd chosen her special black outfit. She looked around again and saw Sarah at the bar. Strange how it still happened, that same shock of recognition, ever since their first encounter, meant to be casual, yet growing to more than either had ever anticipated. Ginnie liked Sarah's laughter, her wit, her detachment. She wondered if Smita would be upset that Sarah was there that night, but it was a public place, after all.

> *You've got me reeling for you*
> *where will it lead*
> *I've got a feeling for you*
> *more than need.*

When Smita expressed her intense love for Ginnie, it felt good to be the subject of such passion. But it worried her too. There was no doubt about it, Smita was intense. Her emotional attachment felt similar to what Ginnie had previously gone through with Mia. The familiarity between them had led to Mia's dependence on her. The more Ginnie had resisted, the more Mia's clinging became something of a complex. Smita, however, claimed she really did enjoy getting on with her life separately from Ginnie, as long as when they were together it was good between them.

> *Together we're good*
> *we can shine*
> *fire and wood*
> *water and wine*
> *don't leave me stranded*
> *on the line*
> *I couldn't stand it*
> *another time.*

Smita was perfectly cool about Ginnie's wish to be non-monogamous, and didn't try to change it. If anything, it was Ginnie who had felt bad in the beginning, when she first slept with Sarah. Though Smita said she could take it, Ginnie still felt a terrible responsibility.

> *Don't do me wrong*
> *like I've been done*
> *don't do me wrong.*

Ginnie couldn't understand herself sometimes. She was trapped by her own guilt rather than by any possessiveness on Smita's part. It aggravated her that she had the freedom to do what she wanted and yet felt in the wrong. And this was without being able to blame Smita for making accusations. She almost wished Smita *would* accuse her of betrayal, of inconsistency, anything, just so she had something more definite to go on than this vague weight of guilt she carried. As she went up on stage to do her last number for the first half, she decided she would spend the interval with Sarah. Smita would just have to put up with it. Ginnie certainly wasn't going to go through the guilt she'd felt when she first wrote the song she was going to sing next, "My Mistake".

You said you'd go
but you didn't show
that night at the bar
I was feeling lost
and I paid the cost
by going too far.

I'm sorry, love, my mistake.

Now, as Smita went back to the table, some friends came over to join her. The interval was coming up and she could have a drink. She was looking forward to talking to Ginnie – they had so much to say and so little time spent alone together.

I saw a friend
at the corner end
and decided there
I'd have a fling
I'd really swing
coz I didn't care.

I'm sorry, love, my mistake.

When Ginnie had first slept with Sarah, Smita had tried to be understanding; she knew from experience not to be a guilt-tripper. It was all right as long as Ginnie still loved her. Of course it was hurtful when Ginnie started to sleep with Sarah more than just casually, but Smita still refused to let it become an issue. Without knowing it, Ginnie seemed to be pushing Smita to become possessive, so she could then confirm her suspicions that Smita was just as demanding as Mia had been. But Smita really did try. Sure, she wanted the same things as before – monogamy, sharing a flat, things like that – but there was no way this was an issue with them. She had learned her lesson too well to insist on such points.

Know it's my fault
not calling a halt
I didn't think
went right ahead
went over and said
let's have a drink.

Now you mistrust me
now you distrust me.

It was true Smita felt a sense of failure because Ginnie was obviously in need of more than she could bring to her, but she didn't resent Sarah the way Ginnie suspected. But then Ginnie's state of suspicion began to affect the quality of their time together. She kept looking for signs that Smita was being demanding. Of course Smita couldn't deny her dependence on Ginnie. Sometimes she'd get scared by it, but it was a part of her life she accepted without question; it was there and she had to live with it. What she tried to do was express her dependence with a minimum of demands. The trouble was that Ginnie insisted on making an equation between being dependent and being demanding; she couldn't separate the two. Her own sense of guilt made her feel that Smita was being manipulative.

We left soon after
I liked her laughter
and that was that
it was so crazy
was feeling hazy
back at her flat.

I'm sorry, love, my mistake.

Now Ginnie came off stage for the interval and Smita was disappointed to see her go over to the bar. Suddenly, Sarah stood out. They kissed hello. Sarah said something to her and Ginnie laughed, locking into her arm. Smita looked away. She was relieved when the interval ended, and she went on stage with the energy of a fighter who can't or won't accept being beaten. She sang "Afraid" as if she was short on time.

> *When I first met you*
> *some time ago*
> *I had to get you*
> *to also know*
> *I wouldn't let*
> *just walk away*
> *and I bet you*
> *wanted to stay.*

> *But I'm afraid what we've made will be betrayed.*

As Smita began the second half of their set, Ginnie was glad there's been no scene about Sarah. Of course Smita wouldn't have made one. But if she had insisted on talking to Ginnie in the interval then things might have got heavy. Ginnie felt ready for a bit of drama. Anyway, they would have plenty to say when they met Joan at 11 o'clock. Meanwhile, she was excited. There was no doubt about it; her feelings for Sarah were as potent, as powerful as they had always been. Sarah was looking as striking as ever tonight, in the height of fashion as usual. She desired her with none of the complexities of he relationship with Smita. It was safer because they were similar in ways that Smita and she were not. Sometimes Smita's difference made Ginnie long for the stability of sameness she got with Sarah. And, even though she denied it, Smita could be difficult. Her love was too intense; it frightened Ginnie.

Cos I need more
than you give at times
and I ignore
the danger signs
I cling and claw
you meet my need
but I feel at war
nothing's guaranteed.

And I'm afraid what we've made will be betrayed.

Ginne felt a great guilt at letting Smita down, which she could not confront because Smita was being so understanding. Though Ginnie blamed herself, she felt compelled to sleep with Sarah. It was a way out from what she felt was a rut in her relationship. They just didn't laugh together as much as before. It was all very well saying things were okay, but they weren't. Ginnie did not consider race as a factor in their relationship, so that wasn't the reason for the tension between them. They were both middle-class, so that didn't explain it either. But she agreed that there was an inequality in their relationship. It was the inequality of emotional dependence, a devotion, which had become less pleasing. Smita said she knew that Ginnie was the loved and she was the lover, but that she didn't want this to create a power imbalance between them. The possibility of this seemed to frighten Smita more than anything else.

Our affair
has me scared
and though we've dared
to share and care
I'm still scared.

Ginnie was fed up with this tension she carried. She felt she had to force things to a conclusion. Smita had once had the nerve to suggest that Ginnie really did want monogamy. That was why she felt guilty at sleeping with both her and Sarah. Ginnie thought this was nonsense; she didn't need Smita to tell her her own mind. Ginnie was sure that setting up home was the last thing she wanted. She believed in change, and monogamy seemed mediocre to her. Ginnie liked to think that she was more radical. And to prove it she was going home with Sarah tonight. She knew Smita wanted to talk to her, but she would just have to wait.

> *And how we feel*
> *and who we are*
> *has made us heal*
> *we've got this far*
> *so let's not steal*
> *what we can't take*
> *let's just seal*
> *what we can make.*

As Smita ended her song and came off stage, she really was scared. She could see the danger signs but she preferred not to analyse them. They were less painful as unformed thoughts. But tonight, she saw pieces fitting in ways she'd avoided before. Now she knew Ginnie was heading for a confrontation. As Ginnie started singing "Heading for a Fall", Smita could feel her blood beating furiously.

> *The moment has come*
> *for us to confront*
> *we may feel numb*
> *from what we want*
> *but we can't stall*
> *when we're heading*
> *heading for a fall.*

Smita desperately wanted Ginnie to know how much she still wanted her. If only they could talk things through. But Ginnie was never there. The little time they had together would be spent in extremes of either fighting or making love, with no middle ground.

Smita had been prepared to go along with the situation Ginnie had set up for them. But when her attempts to be reasonable only alienated Ginnie, she really didn't know what to do. She was trying to keep them together, but maybe Ginnie didn't want her any more. At the thought of this, Smita's heart missed a beat.

The anger you feel
is really pain
and so the wheel
turns round again
please don't be rash
when we're heading
heading for a crash.

Smita could take Sarah's importance to Ginnie. In fact, though it hurt, she accepted this importance as eclipsing her own. But she was so frightened at losing Ginnie that the pain of it made her accept Ginnie's terms. They were together in a team, and it didn't matter that it was mostly around work, as long as they still shared some intimacy. Smita enjoyed the fixed routine of their arrangements to meet; they gave her a stability, and she believed in what they'd created together. She wanted it to last.

What we've built
shouldn't get destroyed
I'll hurt with guilt
you'll feel in a void
but we'll survive
when we're heading
heading for a dive.

Ginnie had also enjoyed the regularity of their meetings, but in a more prescriptive way. She liked making rules about how often to meet as lovers and, more importantly, she loved the ritual that their work together involved. Performances, even rehearsals, were a delight to her. But she had become emotionally harder, inured, less giving to Smita. She had stayed largely out of habit; she was accustomed to her and, besides, they had invested a lot in their relationship. But now she was less accepting of Smita's love. Sometimes she'd be very dismissive of Smita and had deliberately said things she knew would hurt her. Lately, Smita had not been able to do anything right. Now that Smita was out of her favour, Ginnie had a tendency to explode angrily with her at the slightest reason.

In the beginning it had worked: they had wanted each other, and met each other's want, with what was close to instinct. But now their needs and demands had altered.

Pac-Girl
Robyn Vinten

A pac punk tries to jump me in the alley. I hate that. Just when I am out of tinned tears too. Still, I haven't lasted this long in the job without being handy with my own pac. I flip backwards and slam the punk against the wall with my feet, then watch them drop the ten ms to the floor. It is on the way down that I notice she is a girl. Her old pac suit is filled out in all the wrong places or the right ones. Now my first thought is to leave her there but those alleys aren't nice, even for a pac punk and I'm guessing there is no honour amongst her type. So I nip down and pick her up. She is out cold, I'm not reading anything off her. Don't know if it was my slam or the fall that's done it. I grab her by her pac suit belt and haul her arse into one of the busier roads but out of the way of the cameras. Didn't need everyone knowing what I am up to.

She is starting to come round so I slip her pac off to stop her going anywhere fast.

"What do you want?" I ask. I'm not carrying anything. Just dropped my last disc off and going back for more. Never seen the attraction myself but they're worth a few credits and they keep me off the register.

She peers at me. These punks think I'm an easy target because I'm small. Why my mother couldn't have picked a taller donor I've no idea. Though knowing my mother it was probably a loaner rather than a donor. She had a thing for touching. I don't even want to think about it. Anyway, I'm stronger than I look and I'm a tele. I know what they're going to do before they know it themselves.

It's my pac she is after. Hers is bust. I run my hand over it, a rusted-out fuel line, dodgy wiring and a boaster out of the arc. Nothing that can't be fixed. These punks are too stupid to think of repairing anything. I feel despair coming off her, hopelessness, uselessness seeping out of her head. It is horrible; I need to turn it off.

"Come on." I chuck her pac back at her. "I can fix it," I say.

She looks suspicious. They always do when you offer them something. Guess they're not used to it, not for nothing.

"I can't pay you," she says, her voice is a bit of a surprise. Sweet and husky.

"No shit." I laugh. "Thought you were a credit queen."

Her mind is racing, she believes I can fix the pac but she doesn't trust me. I catch flashes of the past. Everyone wanting something and taking it. One image is so strong it makes me take a step back. Hands wanting to touch, reaching out. Fingers grasping, pulling, stroking. And her wanting it, loving it, needing it. Thinking it is the best thing.

"I don't want anything," I say. "I'll just fix it so you don't try and jump me again. I like that alley, takes a quarter off my time." I'm talking too much but then she is thinking too much.

"Come on," I say again and grab her in one arm and take off. I don't like being this close to her, touching her but there's at least two layers of pac suit between my skin and her's. I try not to think about it, her skin that is. I concentrate on flying. A kick and a quick blast and I'm up 10 and I'll be heading home. She is scared but not terrified. She has travelled this way before because she knows to hang on to my belt and wrap one leg around mine. I mic work and tell them I'm through for the day. I cut them off before they start complaining. Let them fire me, there are loads of other firms out there that would take me.

Home isn't far away and it isn't all that either, I know. But it is dry and warm and no one has managed to break in yet. I leave her on the roof while I release the locks and the drop through the trap door. I land and shrugged my pac off.

"Jump," I say.

She thinks about it hard for a moment and then steps into the hole. She is scared but she still does it, I am proud of her. Guess she figures it is scarier on the roof than it will be in here with me.

She isn't exactly impressed. Doesn't help that I only just catch her. And if I was here for the first time I wouldn't immediately see its charms either. Not with the work bench and all the parts and tools everywhere. Never was the tidiest.

I lock the trap door again. Don't want unexpected visitors. I set some water boiling on my sola stove. I haven't had a guest for... well, for never. There's a chair somewhere. I have to dump a whole load of stuff on the floor before I find it. She sits on it, when I push it towards her. I want to get on and fix the pac. Get her out. It's not exactly comfortable with her looking at me, watching everything I do. Thinking her thoughts as though I can't read them.

"I'm a tele." I tell her, just in case she is going to think anything she doesn't want me to know.

"I'm an empath," she says, again that sweet voice.

"Then you know I'm not going to hurt you," I say.

"I know that you think you're not going to hurt me," she says.

I don't quite follow so I shrug. Whatever.

I start stripping her pac. I forget about the water boiling. She gets up and turns it off, finds some mugs among the junk and even the cha. Makes it just how I like it, not too strong with lots of sweeties. She hands it to me.

"How'd you do that?" I ask.

She shrugs. "How'd you do that?" She points at the pac now in bits on the bench. I shrug. She smiles and I feel warm all the way through.

She leaves me to it. Finds my bed and curls up in it. I know she feels safe now and for some reason this makes me feel good.

I get on with the pac. I have a fuel line from an old pac that is just about the right size. I solder the loose wires, replace a couple. I add a few modifications of my own to give it a bit more grunt. A girl out there by herself needs all the power she can get out of her pac. It's late when I finish. I wipe my hands on my arse and realise I still have my pac suit on. I strip it off so I'm just in my underwear and wash my hands and face in the water left on the sola stove. It's cold.

I turn around and she is there watching me. She is naked. Completely, utterly naked. Standing by the bed, her hair a bit messed up, her skin smooth and shiny. I have the strangest urge. One that horrifies me as much as it draws me in. I want to touch her. I can't tell if it's coming from her or from me, this urge, but it is really, really strong.

I put my hands behind my back. "I've fixed your pac," I say.

"Are you coming to bed?" she asks, her voice steamy now.

I can almost feel her skin under my fingers. Feel the softness of it, the smoothness, the firmness. The pull towards her is so strong I have to hold on to the bench to stop myself reaching out to her. I cannot believe I am feeling like this. I have never wanted to touch anyone before. I have never wanted to do anything as much as this before. I thought the discs were bad enough, people touching, I thought the saps who paid through the nose to watch them were sad enough. But the people in the discs, I thought they were mad, sick, dangerous even and here I am barely able to stop myself touching this girl, this pac punk, this... I look away.

"You can go now," I say. My voice sounds choked, sounds broken.

"I don't have to," she says. She knows what she is doing to me and she is enjoying it. She makes me look at her. Her eyes are huge, warm pools of liquid wonderfulness. Her lips are red and wet. Her neck is long and graceful. Her... I can't look any lower. I feel sick with wanting to touch her, taste her, feel her, have her touch me, have her... I can't believe the things I want her to do to me. I'm scared, all these new feelings, they're scaring the shit out of me and she knows it. She is smiling. I feel her excitement at knowing she is making me feel all these things and I feel excited too. She can do that, she is an empath.

"Please," she says, taking a step towards me, her lips hardly moving. She reaches out one hand to touch my face. I try to step back only I can't because the bench is right behind me. I feel her fingers on my cheek. Her bare flesh on mine, the lightest touch but I pull away as if I've been burned. I am breathing hard, like I've been running fast though I haven't moved at all. I can't move.

She brushes the backs of her fingers across my lips and it's all I can do to stop myself opening my mouth and sucking those fingers in. She takes another step closer. I hold on to the bench tight, feel my nails dig into the plastic of it. Her hand brushes past my ear and down to my shoulder. The bits I've seen on the discs, the touching thing. The look on their faces, like it was the best thing, the only thing. I couldn't understand that. The last person who wanted to touch me was my mother but she was just weird like that. I have never wanted to touch anyone before, before now. Now with this pac punk touching my shoulder, barely touching it. Standing so close I can feel her breath on my cheek, I think my body is about to explode.

"Can I kiss you?" she asks, her lips already nearly touching mine. She says the words aloud but in her head she is already there, her tongue on mine, her hands touching me, finding their way under my vest, into my shorts.

"No," I say. It comes out louder than it should. I push past her, my hand on her arm. Moving her out of my way, out of my face. My hand is shaking, it can feel the warmth of her skin, it can feel the softness of her. It wants to feel more, my hand, my traitorous hand. I head for the bed, I want to be under the sheets, away from her. Out of reach and sight and smell of her.

She follows me. I can feel her behind me, I can feel her thoughts as jumbled and tangled as mine. The wanting, the fear. I feel her hand on my shoulder, her lips on my neck.

"I know what you want," she whispers in my ear. And I am melting into her, under her hands, her tongue. All the fight drained out of me.

Her hand is under my vest, touching my skin, stroking it, teasing it. She is kissing my neck. I am liquid, the heat of her turning me to gas. Steam, floating away. I will be gone forever, nothing more than a mist over the room, a hazy the sun will burn away. But even as I think this, know it, I want it more than anything else in the world. Though it doesn't matter whether I want it or not. This is going to happen. I have no choices left but to let her do what she wants, what she knows I want.

She turns me around and kisses me on the lips. I kiss her back; I can't not. I feel her feel my desire for her and she reflects it back to me mixed with her own desire. It bounces backwards and forwards between us, gathering momentum as we kiss and touch, stroke and lick. Arms and legs entwining, drawing us closer and closer together until I cannot tell what is her and what is me. I don't know even who is thinking what, our minds are locked as intimately as our bodies. I can feel everything that she feels and she feels great.

Every sense of mine is filled with her. My eyes looking into hers, her satin skin under my finger. The hot, spicy smell of her, the little groans she is making. The taste of her under my tongue and the echoing resonance of her thoughts in my head. My thoughts, our thoughts. I know where she wants to be touched because it's where I want to be touched. I can feel the simple lust of her, her naked desire. Her delight in my body, my breasts, arms, legs, toes, skin, all of it, as I am overcome with the beauty of all of her.

Like a whirlwind, our matching, growing desire whips us up. Catches us up and spins us together, centrifugal forces pushing us closer and closer. Faster and faster until I cannot see, cannot breath, cannot think.

And then we come. Like two metals melting into each other. Copper and zinc making iron. Making a stronger, better thing. It only lasts a moment but in that moment I feel incredible, invincible, perfect. It is the best thing, the very best thing. Then it's gone, not suddenly but it seeps away and as it goes I go with it, drawn into sleep with the pac punk in my arms. Two separate beings again.

When I wake she is gone. So is her pac and mine and half the tools off the bench. I'm not surprised. Disappointed, yes, but only a little. It's just how things are. I can get another pac and most of the tools are replaceable. She has't blown the locks on the door and I'm still alive. It could have been a lot worse. On the bench where my pac was is a disc. A tiny, shiny thing. No bigger than my thumb nail. Small enough to fix into the seam of a pac suit, big enough to store several libraries' worth of information. She has left it and my putor. I insert it and press start. I'm not sure what I will see, what I want to see. What I see first is her face up close. I don't usually watch discs; I can't tell what the people in them are thinking and I hate that. I can't see what she's thinking. Her face pulls away and she is in a room a bit like mine, on a bed like mine. There is someone in the background a little like me, washing at a bench.

I stop the disc. I don't understand. Well, I do understand but I don't see how she could have done it, not without me noticing. I should have been able to sense what she was up to, I'm a tele. But then she is an empath, they can do things to your mind. I start the disc again. She walks away to the person washing. It's hard to think of it as me, on the disc it could be anyone. They, I, look okay from the back. Small, tight in my underwear. Busy, hunched over the bench, tense.

I, the me on the disc, turn. She's in the way at first but then she steps to one side and I see my face. Eyes huge, staring at her, her naked body like I've never seen one before and I realise I never have, not in person. She moves towards me, tries to kiss me. I push past her, closer to the camera. I'm in full view now, full frontal. She's behind me, kissing my neck. There's no sound but I can see she is whispering in my ear. My mouth falls open, lips fat, eyes glazed like I'm on a bender, like the people I see on the other discs.

I stop the disc, pause it. Hold the image, her hand under my vest, me leaning back into her. It's beautiful, her and me. If it wasn't me there on the screen I would say I was beautiful. I want her, that woman in the picture, that me. Without being able to read her mind I know exactly what she wants. And I want the other woman too, the pac punk. I want her to be kissing me now, again. I want her lips on my neck, her tongue in my ear, her hand on my breast. I want that all again.

I play the disc on. I see my vest come off. I see hands stroking skin. I see bodies glistening with sweat. I catch glimpses of faces distorted with emotion. The pain, the pleasure, the concentration, the longing and the having. And I want to be there again. I want to feel those things again.

As I watch it feels like it is all being played in fast motion. I want to slow it down, see each and every moment, every image separately. I feel dizzy with the speed of it, with the memory of it. Then suddenly there's that look on our faces that I've seen on other discs. Heads thrown back, I can see her face better than mine. It's the best-thing look.

It lasts for a moment, only a moment and then it is gone. Our bodies separate, lie spent, exhausted on the bed. And I'm exhausted again having watched it. I want to curl up on the sheets as the disc me is doing. Innocent as a baby. For a long time nothing happens, we just lie there. I am asleep, she seems to be too. After the frenzy of movement the stillness is bliss. Then I see her stir, the punk. She carefully untangles herself from my arms. She disappears from view for a moment and then is back. Face huge in front of the camera.

"Call me." I see her mouth move. I understand her without hearing the words or being able to read her thoughts. As she takes the camera down I see a flash of something, red on white and then it's dark, The disc whines in the putor and then stops and there is only static.

I put my head in my hands. Thoughts are racing around inside my head, feelings fighting it out. Humiliation is doing quite well, anger is ricocheting off the walls, off the scales. Despair is there too. Exhilaration is struggling but something is making a strong late run. It is something I have never felt before, it comes from my body not my mind. It is settled deep inside me and has set up a vibration that is reaching out to every part of me. It is silencing the clamour that is going on in my head. It is lust and it lets me know that I will see her again.

I look around the room. The flash of red on white in the disc. The white is the mirror over the bed, the red is her number written in the colour of her lips. Looking at the number, my face reflected behind it, I realise that all the things I felt from her, all the emotions I was reading, were really mine. My feelings reflected back off the smooth, shiny surface of her empathy. It was a trap of sorts but one I would walk into again even knowing that. One I will walk into again and soon, I hope.

And the disc, I don't know if that is the original or one copy of many now out there being delivered to sad bastards sitting alone in their vacuum-sealed apartments. My breath catches as I think about other people seeing it. I look at my face in the mirror and it's glowing with an excitement I have never felt before.

I turn back to the putor. I play the disc again in slow motion. It is beautiful, like a dance. I dial the number on the mirror. I realise I don't know her name.

"Hello." Her sweet, soft voice answers.

"Hello," I say, suddenly shy.

"I was hoping you'd call."

Across the space between us I can't feel her, I can't tell if she's happy to hear from me or not. I have to trust her words and I know you can't do that. I feel half blind, half deaf, only half alive.

"You like the disc?"

I nod, then remember she can't see me. "Yes," I say.

"Good," she says. She sounds like she is smiling, wants to laugh. "Want to make another one?"

I close my eyes. I feel like I'm standing at the edge of a great height and don't know what is below me. I remember her stepping off the roof into my place.

Venus as a Boy
Ape McCabe

She observed herself coming, an amazing sensation in zero-G, and a hell of a blast when you first experience it. With nothing to push against except your own hand, or the other new applicant for the 15,000-Mile-High Club, your body has only itself for reference. Body jerks are disorientating; expressions like 'come' and 'pulsate' only have relevance when there's not only a point of origin to come from, but a there for the come to go, as it were. Limbs, flesh can only truly pulsate when it can feel it has something solid against which to do so. If there's nothing physical for your shudders to impact upon, or for your lust-rush to go except back into itself, then your body is disappointed. It has influenced and affected nothing else by its release. However, the company had thought that one through. The shoulder and ankle straps that anchored her to the moulded couch just a foot below her (self-adjusting) kept the body level and steady, while allowing the limbs and torso plenty of freedom for however much or little movement the passenger enjoyed during sex.

Out of the large picture portal to her left, she watched the red and brown hues of Australia pass slowly by, far below. Small, white clouds curled and whorled around the southern tip of New South Wales, the barren interior blank and empty except for red blotches which showed where the sun had beaten and burnished the land into a bronzed god. The stratosphere glowed faint neon-blue; such a thin, fragile barrier against the cold black of space. It looks like one small pinprick would burst it and expel all the little ants on the surface out into the vast void, choking and dead. She always felt philosophical afterwards. *Jeez, lighten up. Save the navel-gazing for the article.*

Besides, there was someone to thank this time. The Personal Flight Attendant straightened up, smiling and wiping its mouth on a tissue. There was no one else in the Couch Suite at this time, so it hadn't been programmed for discretion. Mic gazed into jade-green eyes too perfect to be human. Jade Cream, No 52. Amazing what you remember from past relationships. Having had a robo engineer for a flat mate for a few months had taught her a lot about how to spot a *homo sapiens* sapiens from a *robo sapiens sapiens*, a useful trick if you were after a skin lay in a bar. She ran her eyes admiringly over the blonde synthetic bob (Corn, No. 18), and a large-breasted torso tapering to curved hips under the short-skirted, green Lycra uniform. All as specified on her pre-flight form, all exactly to taste and sure to get her relaxed into the proper mood. Very nice.

'How was that for you, Ms Mic Peters? I hope my tongue technique was within the specifications as stated on your pre-flight form.' It went through the motions of tasting her come, every movement exact, perfectly executed. Jeez, she thought, you'd never know if you didn't know what to look for, and if you were anti-robo, you'd be pissed.

'Mmm. You taste a little salty – can I suggest you take the fruit and salad option for lunch, with a light mango sauce and sucrose juice of your choice? We have cherry, blackcurrant, papaya, *kum*...quat –'

'Yeah. Thanks for the... the... tongue was great... thanks. Could I get a Pepsi with lunch, please?'

'Mm.' The symmetrical smile faded a little, and an imitation of a frown gently furrowed the brow. 'Artificial sucrose is not recommended, Ms Mic Peters, but –' the PFA paused suddenly, the jade darkening to malachite, head flicking for a fraction of a second to one side, as if listening to or receiving silent orders '– as you are a special guest of Sexpression Holidays, whatever you require will be our pleasure to provide.' The smile returned smartly, like a sun appearing suddenly from the dark side of a planet, its corona lighting up the outer rim surface like liquid plasma.

It paused again. 'The Chief Steward has just informed me that we will be going into Deep Space for our flight to the Sexpress Yourself resort, Sexpression Holiday's most popular destination, a little earlier than scheduled, due to reports of imminent solar wind activity. I am afraid we must get you back to your seat straight away for an early lunch.'

'You know –' Mic watched as the PFA turned and, metallic suction pads on its kitten heels keeping it grounded in the buoyant atmosphere of the Suite, crossed to the wall control panel, buttocks swaying like a synthetic peach, the buttons bleeping as its fingers, moving fast, tapped out the gravity restoration sequence '– I'm going to really enjoy this holiday.' Slowly, the gravity returned to optimum earth conditions, and she came to rest gently.

The PFA swayed back over, its pneumatic breasts nearly bursting from the restrictive uniform. 'Let me help you.' It smiled, its eyes glowing, translucent, neon, and ran its hands – such soft mano-skin on the palms – down her naked body to the ankle straps, pulling apart the Velcro, and easing them off. Every movement was sensual, smooth, measured, programmed. It slipped the restraints off her shoulders, and, as she wiggled her feet, swinging them over the side of the couch, and shook her hands to get them used once more to earth grav, it brought her a soft, fluffy cotton robe – blue to match the colour of her own eyes (real) and blonde hair. She sighed and slid into its warmth, relishing the sensation of comfort and post-orgasm lassitude. They've sold me, she thought, following the smile, pendulous butt and sinuous sashay of PFA 14 down the short, narrow corridor back to her recliner in the open cabin. If it was this good here, what must it be like there?

There weren't many passengers on the flight, a sign of the waning excitement and interest in Sexpression Holidays. It had been such an amazing and welcome idea when the company first engineered and built its free-floating resort stations, outside the rule and jurisdiction of any government and therefore unrestricted in the services it could offer. The off-world body-pleasure holidays were mega-popular with the sexually frightened inhabitants of earth; other known races of the Andromeda galaxy found the research had been extensive, and their rituals and peccadilloes were catered for, too. However, what with the combination of earth's high viral load problem easing in recent years, thanks to new discoveries in treatments, the puritanical faction in EarthGov growing stronger and more popular – *Earth for Earthers! Stay on-world! Don't let Otherworld immigrants take our jobs!* – and straight Earthers being encouraged to stay on the planet and boost the home tourist economy, Sexpression had found themselves with fewer and fewer hetero human guests. For gay humans, the liberal atmosphere Sexpression resorts offered was a relief from the increasing hatred and pressures on earth. Many were now seeking jobs with Sexpression to escape the heightened danger of exposure and its consequences – having to take the treatment and go straight.

Anyway, not wanting the expense of having to melt down and redesign their pleasure *robo sapiens*, Sexpression went the cheaper route; they offered Mic, a travel journalist for the highly popular World Today Online, a free holiday. They'd pull out the stops – whatever she wanted, she could have. She'd have a great time and they'd get their free advertising, her face beamed into every home, apartment, office, computer, pond, slime puddle, gas cloud and head in Andromeda, extolling the virtues and glories of the Sexpress Yourself Holiday resort. And PFA 14 had provided the perfect start. A-plus so far.

The suggested fruit option lunch, reduced in portion due to their imminent jump, was roughage-heavy and taste-lite. Synthetic. Why, when organic foodstuffs lasted well enough in space? Expensive, she guessed. First black mark. Still, the Pepsi was good enough. You can't synth what's already synthed, right?

After half and hour to let the food go down, she was led to the heads to 'clear your bowels – we don't want any discomfort in stasis, Ms Mic Peters', then back to her recliner, helped into the sleep position and strapped in for the two-light-year flight, reduced to just four hours, thanks to plasma drive technology having harnessed the propulsion power of solar winds.

She watched, already beginning to feel sleepy, as the other passengers were settled. There was only one couple, two guys, who'd opted for the naked lunch. They were obviously off to find fresh meat and, like herself, had wasted no time. Their male PFA stood patiently, subservient, as the younger of the two men undid the Velcro at the robo's crotch and freed the flaccid prick. She watched avidly – you didn't see this kind of thing at home any more, thanks to censorship and invasive anti-privacy laws.

Junior sucked and stroked the cock until it stood upright and rigid. The older man watched over his shoulder, eyes glazing, his own engorging prick in his hand, stroking and pulling at it. The PFA's dick twitched as Junior began to flick the tip with his tongue.

'Ah… Mr Jak Uff, Mr Flik Dik –' Mic laughed inwardly at the clumsy pseudonyms '– the Captain informs me we shall be making the jump in five minutes. I must settle you and go to my regeneration booth…'

'Oh, come on, PFA 2. Just a quick, pre-flight snack. Please.'

'Certainly, Mr Flik Dik.' The robo's buttocks suddenly jerked twice and it shot its load over the surprised Flik's face. The delighted Jak ejaculated explosively over his partner's back in response.

'Aaaargh. Honey, did you have to do that?! I gotta lie down.'

'Please do not worry, Mr Flik Dik. I shall clean you off.' The attendant readjusted itself, went off, smiling its perfect smile, and came back with a towel and two colour-co-ordinated wraps. As it towelled off Flik's back, Jak licked the come off his friend's face.

'Mmm. Delicious. Rum-flavoured. What a guy! An attendant, prostitute *and* bartender all in one. Every living space should have one. That was great, darling. Aren't these people great?'

'Yeah, but it was over too fucking soon.' Flik pouted at him, obviously the prissy, sulking baby to Jak's sugar daddy.

'That's what you always say, angel. Don't worry, we'll find you plenty more.' The older man leant in, kissing him roughly on the lips, then settled down, pulling the younger man into his arms.

She rolled over, amused, from the scene, and scoped the fifth passenger. The fifth and last passenger, draped elegantly in an open, golden velvet robe, was a she/him – some called them shims – with soft, full, pouting lips, pale slim face and high cheekbones, shoulder-length, white-blonde almost opalescent hair. An albino. A rarity. Heck, shims were a rarity. They had been almost bred out of the genome. This one was beautiful. She could see a sleekly muscled torso under the robe. She wondered if what they said was true, that most shims opted to keep both male and female genitalia, but maybe that was just wishful thinking. It was clear there were no breasts on this one. What there was was a quiet virility, incongruous with the languid, louche grace of the rest of the picture.

The shim looked up and she saw that the eyes, in-keeping with the hair, were the colour of opals. They caught the phosphorescent light in the cabin and shimmered like the twin moons of Sirus 5, out in the cradle of the galaxy near Canis Major. The shim caught her surprise and smiled. A guarded but warm smile.

She/he extended his/her hand. 'Hi. I'm Ekfor.'

'Hi. Mic.'

'What brings you to Flight No. 8862, and Sexpression Holidays?' Ekfor returned to scanning the holo-magazine shim had been flicking through, but the raised eyebrows said she/he was listening.

'Um, work. Journalist. I've been invited to report on the resort for my webzine.'

'Ha! Which one?'

'World Online.' The elegant, languid expression this engendered said 'impressive'.

'Oh, well. You'll have to be nice if SH are picking up the tab then, won't you?'

'Um, yeah, I guess so. So much for creative integrity, eh? Doesn't sound like you'd give the company a good review.'

'It's okay first time around. Look at all the pretty lights, the funny people! Sex, sex, sex!' The eyes, the patterns in their surface constantly changing and winking, were suddenly lidded. 'But don't let me stop you having a good time. I go there often on business. Jaded, I guess. You enjoy, okay?'

With a quick, dismissive smile, Ekfor turned off the holo-mag and settled down on her/his couch, wrapping and tying the robe close around shimself.

The cabin lights were lowered. PFA 14 leaned over her. 'Good night, Ms Mic Peters. I will wake you in three hours, in time for you to prepare and dress for arrival.' She moved in and kissed Mic full on the lips, the blueberry flavour, one of Mic's choices, tangy on her own. The *robo sapiens* then flicked on the in-couch massager. As the hum and sensation of and excellent massage lulled her to sleep, Mic thought, I wonder why Ekfor didn't have a PFA...

'Thank you for flying with Sexpression Holidays.' PFA 14 stepped back from doing up the zip of Mic's leather-look jacket. 'Your luggage will be delivered directly to your room, No. 852X, Third Level, Inner View, and put away for you by your PBA, who will attend to all your domestic needs while you are at Sexpress Yourself.'

'Yeah, thanks, PFA 14. Catch you on the rebound.'

'You are welcome, Ms Mic Peters. We hope you enjoy your stay at Sexpression Holidays' flagship resort and don't forget –' the already wide smile widened '– Sexpress Yourself!'

'Yeah. Right.' Thankfully, she thought as she made her way through the outer corridor and onto the exit stairs, I shan't have to hear that again.

'Hi there! Welcome, welcome! Sexpress Yourself!' The manager of the resort, in the obligatory Hawaiian shirt of all resorts of any type anywhere in the known galaxy, arms behind her back, stood at the bottom of the steps, accompanied by what must be their PBAs. She reached the deck and was shaken warmly by the hand of – an exact replica, to the last hair follicle and glint in the jade-green eyes, of PFA 14, which stood at the top of the stairs, smiling vacuously. Sheesh – there was nothing like variety, and this was nothing like it.

Ekfor, alone, had already walked away, but turned and, catching her eye, inclined her/his head in goodbye, the finely-cut, silken russet skirt-coat visible on the walkway even among what, even from a cursory glance, she could see was the most eclectic gathering of species in one place in the galaxy. He/she disappeared around the corner.

'Welcome, Ms Mic Peters.' She was brought back to herself. 'I am PBA 14, your personal assistant for the duration of your stay at Sexpress Yourself. Please follow me, and I will take you to your room.'

Jak and Flik, who were on her level, too, walked in front of her, whispering excitedly as they followed their PBA 2 to the glass-fronted turbo lift, enjoying the view of its perfect ass, naked out at the back of pants that left nothing to the imagination of anyone walking behind it.

Mic took in her surroundings, phasing out everything except the interesting bits from the PBA's welcome babble. The resort was amazing. From the arrival deck, the walkway expanded out into a wider thoroughfare, which teemed with life, coming and going in whatever way its species normally did. There were sex tourists from all over the galaxy: Earthers, Martians, Clioans, gaseous coloured clouds from Jupiter, vermiforms from Ganymede and Rigel's rings, liquid beings from the great seas of MK9, which floated by in tanks on hover-platforms, Bootians, Sirians, one-eyed Centaurites – and a dog. Whatever takes your fancy at Sexpress Yourself.

As they walked past the shops and sex booths to their left, they were bombarded with Hypersonic Sound and Vision ads. Passing a small booth, the interior of which was hidden by a silver curtain, the vision of a stylish redhead suddenly popped into her head, like a holy annunciation, the image as clear as the scene in front of her.

"Hi, I'm Casey. It's great to see you here at Sexpress Yourself, Mic Peters. Why not give me a try? I give great head, and am programmed with all the positions from the Kama Sutra database, the Hindi Continent's most ancient and instructive sex manual. I can give you pleasure and make you come like you've never come before." The image winked in what was supposed to be a suggestive manner, and the picture blipped off as quickly as it had popped up.

She walked past the window of a beauty parlour. Guests were reclined everywhere, the attendants buzzing around them like insects, sonic probes darting in and out like stingers, tucking here, stretching there, infusing a pale skin with darker pigment –and in one instance offering just plain moisturisation. Whoa, that was weird.

Another face suddenly flashed up before her eyes:

Hi, Mic Peters, I'm Anglns of Bootes Minor. Why not come in for a massage? I'm programmed with 40 different recognised forms of body manipulation from throughout the Andromeda galaxy – the image smoothed its pale-purple skin with two sets of pliant hands – *and some unrecognised forms you'll never have experienced, but will never forget.* Great. She *had* to try that one – whichever, or all.

Below them, over the balustrade to their right, reaching down to the depth of Minus Twelfth Level, was a lush, verdant forest, full of plants, some familiar, some she'd never seen before. Flitting in and out of the fronds, tendrils, limbs, wafting the petaled scents up to them with their wings, were birds, multi-coloured, with long tails and fluted calls. Heat rose through the domed, plexi-glass covering, which kept the birds in but allowed the oxygen to permeate out and augment the artificial atmosphere of the station.

And above them, like gigantic descendants of the feathered creatures below, were flying billboards, which occasionally darted down from the high, distant ceiling like feeding gannets, to float in front of newcomers and guests with their messages: *All you can ingest in a globular stew at Zilgobart's; Sirian cuisine our speciality, Second Level Esplanade!, Sexpress Yourself!, Toody Angel's for a good time. Truly Heavenly service! Minus Seventh Level, Sexpress Yourself!!, You haven't lived till you've tried Deggy the Bootian. It's a colourful experience!, SEXPRESS YOURSELF!!!*

They reached the turbo lifts on the far side of the central atrium hall, which took them swiftly up to Third Level. Her room, as promised, overlooked the inside of the resort station. She walked over to picture window, and there below her was a perfect vista; the forest and its tiny jewels, the flying billboards, the multitude, each species in which was busying pursuing whatever, to get it to put whatever it had to put into wherever would give its client the greatest pleasure that species had discovered over the millennia of space-time in its own little quadrant of a vast void.

She turned back into the room, and found everything neatly put away and ready for her – including a fully functioning, fully naked, PBA 14.

'Now, Ms Mic Peters,' said the *robo sapiens*, advancing slowly towards her, smiling. 'Let me welcome you properly to Sexpress Yourself.'

Over the next couple of days, she explored the station. Everywhere you went or looked, there were lounges, clubs, bars, pools, oases of one sort or another, and in each of them, at any time of the day or simulated night, there were couples negotiating sex. She came across Jak and Flik. Flik was obviously having a great time, but Jak looked more haggard and depressed each time she saw them.

Five days into her seven-day stay, during which she had been thoroughly fucked, sucked, stroked, licked, pummelled, flicked, whipped, swung, toe-chewed, nipple-slurped and bitten; had been covered in everything from very synthetic cream to chilli jam by the willing and more than able PBA 1; had had a hot date with a Centauri with a neat line in ear sex, and every Casey, Stacey, Tracey (each also a clone of the other, each with the same technique and style), Anglnses, Dot 5.8s, and things with tentacles, she felt like a walking orifice, but had plenty of material for her article. So, she awarded herself a day off from all the research for a spot of retail therapy.

She made her way down in the turbo lift to the Intergalactic Shopping Experience Mall on First Level. As she sauntered past a chemist's booth, she turned to take in the rest of the boulevard and saw, walking swiftly away from her on the other side of the shopping broadwalk, the tall figure of Ekfor. Thank God, a familiar face and one whose owner would have no intention of coaxing her to sit down on it. She started after shim, and saw shim make it to the turbo lifts on the other side and get into the waiting pod.

'Ekfor... hey, EKFOR...'

She ran, but wasn't in time to catch the lift, which went down. She watched it come to a stop on Minus Eleventh Level and Ekfor get out. She waited impatiently for the doors on the adjacent turbo to open. It opened and spewed forth its riders. As she was boarding, she passed an exiting Flik, who was chatting jubilantly to an unknown companion.

'Yeah, I had this beautiful, blue Bootian boy last night. He had a hole in his chest where you stuck your dick, but he didn't have one. I was thinking, fuck, how does he come, and then suddenly he opened his mouth and spewed out rainbow-coloured come. I had him in 3.5 seconds; that's gotta beat the station record. You know, they don't call me Mach 6 at home for nothing.'

His annoying, spoilt little pussy boy's laugh faded as the lift doors shlushed shut. Poor Jak, she thought as she punched the –11 button. No, make that stupid sap. The turbo sank quickly but smoothly to the lower level. She leapt out and looked quickly left and right, catching out of the corner of her eye the flick of a shadow of a figure in a long skirt-coat to her left.

She dashed after the retreating shadow, following around corners, holding back a little so as not to be seen, but keeping the elusive figure always within her radar. The Level was dark, empty, no shops, restaurants, unlike anything else on the station, as if the owners had missed it, somehow. It got darker and more gloomy as she continued. It didn't seem configured like the rest of the station either, where the esplanades and boulevards were oval. It seemed here that she followed the mysterious shadow in a straight line, apart from the occasional corner. Finally, she saw Ekfor at the end of a particularly long corridor, stepping through what appeared to be the wall, but which, as she cautiously, slowly approached, she saw was a hatchway into a small, palely lit bar.

She stepped in through the hatchway, her boots sounding loud on the metallic floor, so different from the manoleum-based flooring of the rest of the resort. The bar was mostly empty, and the customers which occupied the dim recesses and corner tables looked like they didn't want to be seen, shrinking further into the dark to avoid the sweeping gaze of the newcomer.

Ekfor was at the bar, back turned to her, but as the human woman he was talking to across the counter turned and looked at Mic, the shim turned too. His/her face changed from intimate warmth to interested amusement, and he/she left the bar and came over to her.

'Hi Mic. Glad you could make it.'

'I... um... Eh?'

'I heard you call me, and knew I was being followed, so I figured it must be you. No worries. Mimi likes to see new faces, if they're friendly ones. Come on over.'

The shim led her over to the bar, and indicated a stool for her beside her/him. She sat down and glanced back over her shoulder at the room's quietly muttering inhabitants, aware that her having been accepted in by Ekfor was causing interested talk. Ekfor nudged her shoulder.

'Don't mind about them. They rarely see new faces in here from Up Top. No one finds this place accidentally.'

'What is this place? Who are they?'

'Long story. Have a drink first?' She nodded. The shim turned back to the bar woman. 'Mimi?'

'Sure, Ek. Two on the house. What'll it be, honey?'

'What you got?'

Mimi indicated a row of optics behind her. 'Whiskey, brandy, rum, vodka, all syntho, Pepsi, Bobo Scud, Frillian wine...'

'I'll get a rum and Pepsi, please.' Other-world drinks didn't always travel too well, having further to come. She watched the woman as she fixed her rum and Pepsi and a steaming, red Bobo Scud for Ekfor.

Nobody here but us galaforms, Mic thought, and she couldn't say the barwoman fitted that description, though artificial gravity is always kind to the old. The over-stretched skin said mucho face-lifts in earlier days, but not recently. It was a lived-in face, but one for which obviously Mimi couldn't afford repairs. She screwed up her eyes to see as she poured the Pepsi into the beaker, and her hand shook a little as she carefully poured the corrosive Scud into the reinforced tankard. So, no laser treatment, then.

She put the drinks on the counter, her white-blonde hair falling across scrawny shoulders, which were prominent in a strappy, blue dress that revealed more what there wasn't than what there was.

Ekfor turned on her/his stool and clinked the tankard against her beaker. 'Welcome to the real Sexpress Yourself, honey. Come and meet the rest of the happy campers.' She/he got off the stool and led her around the small room, introducing her to the occupants of the tables.

'This is Tidor, here for the third treatment, pre-op. Blue's still deciding whether to be male or female...' They moved around the room, meeting and greeting, the cloaked and wary drinkers eyeing her with mild interest. They were all shims.

'What are they all doing here?' Mic had never seen so many shims in one place at any one time. They usually kept to themselves.

'Those who want them can't get the operations on Earth any more. You know what it's like; being gay is difficult enough, how do you think it is for them? No one will talk to them, employ them, help them. They're completely outcast. They have to get off-world for an operation as soon as hormonally possible. And if they do, it takes time to decide which way they want to go, you know? Time to save up the money, too. This place gives them, if you'll forgive the pun, the space to catch their breath, feel safe for a while, earn some money; being waste disposal crew, many of them. They're also good at passing as *robo sapiens*, and a lot of people, men and women, like what they have to offer in other ways.'

They returned to the bar and sat again.

She was curious. 'What about you?'

'I'm a runner. I bring things up from Earth: treatment drugs, news of loved ones, the name of a surgeon who'll do the op, no questions asked – for an extortionate fee, of course. I prefer it down here, anyway. More true people on Minus Eleventh Level than anywhere else on the station or earth. Living with having no real gender choice is a shit.'

'How do you know you can tell me this, trust me? I'm a journalist, for God's sake'

'I've been watching you closely. Who you've tried out here, where you've gone. When there's a journalist loose, it's always wise for people in our position to keep an eye on them. You've had some males, sure, but you've had mostly women. You're a lesbian; if they found out at World Online, you wouldn't last there two seconds after. I have friends who could make sure your bosses found out.'

Ekfor smiled, a slow, cold smile. Mic felt her gut churn. She looked up swiftly into the opalescent eyes, which despite their owner's threatening words, sparkled mischievously. In spite of herself, she smiled back.

'Shit! Never make an enemy of you, right? Okay, I shan't say anything.' She took a gulp of rum and Pepsi to steady the fluttering in her stomach. Curiosity returned gradually. 'Are you here for the op, or what?'

'No, not me. I like being as I am – in between, both. And I took an overdose of obsidian dust once which saturated my chromosomes, hence the eyes. Anything, medication, transfusion, operation, would kill me.'

'So do you... have you got... both, still?'

Suddenly, all threat in the shim was gone. Ekfor looked her up and down slowly, taking her in, her body under the T-shirt and jeans she had on, her face. A wave of musk, a scent of body warmth came off the tall, lithe figure as it stood up and opened the skirt-coat to reveal the muscular torso she had seen on the shuttle, covered in almost invisible, downy white hair, which stretched down the flanks to a large, flaccid dick.

Ekfor took her hand and, nodding to Mimi, led Mic around behind the counter and through into an even darker back room. As her eyes adjusted gradually to the stygian light, she saw the room was a sleeping room, tiny, barely big enough for the double sleeping mat and one wall unit that filled it.

'Lights, dim,' Ekfor said softly, and turning back to her, she saw the shim's eyes and hair, brightly luminescent, glowing in the semi-dark. A halo for a physical angel, like a being out of the depths of space and myth.

Ek took her hand and, guiding it down to his/her crotch, moved it past the tumescent cock and into – a cunt, fully-formed, moist, warm, outer lips engorging as Mic's hand, unguided now, slid from the slick mouth to the ballsac which hung down in front of it, hiding it from all but the invited, and up to grasp the lower shaft of the growing dick.

Ek gasped as she began stroking, pulling gently, her other hand feeling slowly, languidly, up the chest, through the silky body hair, up the smooth neck and to the soft-skinned face. Just like a girl's. She pulled the shim's face down, licking the full lips with the tip of her tongue, tasting – nothing. Thankfully, no artificial flavour.

She slipped her tongue between the lips into the opening mouth as her hand grasped the stiffening cock and pulled the skin of the glans over the moistening head.

Sinking to her knees, she licked the tip and ran her hand up and down the shaft, wanking the length slowly. With her other hand, she grasped the balls and squeezed gently, before sliding back to the waiting, open cunt.

Ek groaned with the double sensation as she fingered the labia, dipping a finger into the wetness, then coating the lips with the moistness. She slowly slid in between the flaps, and... yes, there was one. Ek groaned louder as she began flicking the little clit; not much of a nub, but clearly big enough to give the shim pleasure.

She came out, and pushed the twitching shim back onto the sleeping mat. She undressed quickly, her own cunt already throbbing and wet, ready for the stiff prick.

'Got any rubbers?'

Ek indicated the wall unit.

Mic found the condoms, opened the little packet – flavourless – and slipped it onto the shim's quivering length. Then, she straddled Ek and, turning her back, got on her knees and lowered herself, inch by inch, onto the prick.

She groaned in her turn, enjoying the feel of the thick cock inside her, as her hand sought the soft, silky cunt. In time with her own thrusts, growing faster and harder, she plunged three fingers into the wide cunt mouth, and stroked the throbbing clit with her moist thumb.

Ek was groaning loudly now, interjecting a gruff, gutteral 'yes' each time she/he bucked upwards to meet her, her/his hands on Mic's hips, pulling her onto the pounding dick. Her hand became slick with juice, and she was able to get a fourth finger and the thumb into the expanding hole. She pushed her hand further and further in, as she plunged down harder and harder onto the pulsating prick.

With her other hand, she found her own clit and, grasping it hard, came loudly and strongly, pulsating around and grasping Ek's cock with her inner muscles. The shim thrust faster and faster, as she pumped and pumped the hot, wet cunt.

'Quick! Get off me! I'm coming.' Ek gasped. Surprised, she slipped the throbbing dick out of herself and watched as the shim whipped off the condom and came. Jizz shot out, an arc of glowing juice slicing through the darkness of the room like the beam of a laser pistol. At the same time, a phosphorescent stream of come splattered out of Ek's cunt. A double ejaculation.

'Wow!' Mic laughed, still throbbing inside from her own orgasm. 'That was amazing.'

'Thanks. A good side effect of the obsidian.' The shim held his/her arms out and Mic slipped into them, resting her head on the come-streaked chest.

'That was worth coming all this way to see,' she said, grinning. 'Who knows, I may just pay to come back for some more some day.'

'Yeah, 'cos you know what they say: once you've had a shim, you get bored with just quim.'

Their laughter reverberated out into the bar, where a number of cloaked figures, smiling brief, knowing smiles, returned to their drinks.

Dream of Shadow, Shadow of Love
Larry Tritten

In a world full of vogue-conscious beauties, Miriam was unique. Her sense of style was the product of a combination of raw instinct and a somewhat quirky taste for the offbeat and the startling. This applied to her ideas of fashion as well as her behaviour and of course made her controversial, no less than provocative, the sort of woman whose image ranged along a spectrum from brat to enchantress depending on whose point of view.

Miriam had grown up in the mountains of North Idaho, a dreamer through high school whose dreams soon enough drew her to Hollywood where she made her living in ways both versatile and capricious, including temp work as a word processor, occasional modelling, a bit of X-rated movie performing (more for the *outré* experience than for the money), and quite a bit of this and that (which included being a writer for a lurid tabloid newspaper, tending bar, and verbally roasting party guests as a party-perker-upper). Like legions of people in Hollywood, she was writing a screenplay (based on her adventures), but unlike most of them hers was a double threat: literate and fascinating.

At home in the fantasyland of Hollywood, Miriam's favourite day of the year was Halloween. It was the one night in the year, she thought, when extraterrestrials might land and mingle with the people and none would be the wiser. It was also that adventurous night when she made every effort to end up with a lover whose identity and appearance were a mystery obscured by his costume.

There were always several Halloween parties to choose from, but on this Halloween Miriam decided to give priority to one being given by her friend Vale, a designer of sunglasses, at her apartment in Westwood. The invitation bore a lipstick print of Vale's voluptuous mouth, two coral pink parentheses, across the features of a new wave witch with a Neopolitan Mohawk. By Halloween morning, Miriam still hadn't decided on a costume. Some people planned theirs weeks in advance, but she was essentially spontaneous and tended to improvise something at the last moment. Even after spending much of the morning at a café on the Strip sipping coffee and watching the Mercedes and Silver Ghosts glide past in the sunlight, she still had no idea what she would wear. It was only when she found herself late in the afternoon back in her apartment that she started to concentrate on it. In the kitchen, over a shot of tequila, she tapped her fingers on the table, deliberating.

Going to her closet, she started to rummage through clothing, touching silk and satin and denim and lace, pondering the possibilities. It wasn't until she glanced at her shadow on the closet door that the idea came to her... she would be a *shadow*. Yes. Perfect! She would wear a black leotard, black nylon stockings, and a black wig to hide her golden hair. She would paint her fingernails black and wear black velvet boots and use stage makeup to darken her face and hands. Only her eyes, blue as cut sapphires, would contrast with the blackness... but she would also wear a black domino mask to subdue their intensity. Excellent.

An hour later, dark as mystery from head to foot, she stood before her mirror in her bedroom. She lifted her hands caressingly up the undercurving of her breasts beneath the jet fabric of the leotard, lightly stroking the sketchy presence of her nipples, then slid them slowly down to the planes of her thighs, bending slightly so she could glide her fingers lower to the curvaceous backs of her calves and down all the way to touch the sooty velvet tops of her boots with her gleaming black fingernails. Looking at herself in the mirror, she stuck out her tongue and its pinkness was startling by contrast. A thought came to her and, grinning, she went into the kitchen and took a licorice whip from a bowl and ate it, chewing it leisurely to juicy bits, then returned to the mirror. Her tongue, as she extended it, gleamed with dark light. And now, primed by her touching, her body began to yearn with sensuality. She touched two fingers to the juncture between her thighs where the fold of her cunt could be felt against the fabric of the leotard. As she did so, her cunt pulse and she savoured the wet heat there, a little shudder tremoring her body.

Patience, Miriam told herself... and then whispered, "Oh, *fuck it...*" Within seconds she was standing ankle-deep in a puddle of black leotard and with the fore and middle fingers of both hands was prying open the slit of her cunt. There was a tiny and all but subliminal peeling sound as the adhesive labia were separated and all at once the tips of all four fingers were touched with wetness. With a small murmur, Miriam looked down to see a sheen of pearly glitter in the vestibule, a fat droplet clinging in tenuous suspension at the very base of her cunt in the manner of one of the last droplets of milk to spill from a carton.

Trick or treat, she thought, biting her lower lip in a straining smile. Yes, *yes...* Miriam moved a forefinger to her clit and began to serenade her nervous system with gentle strokes. The droplet of come fell onto a thigh and she licked her lips in reflex, then slid three fingers up inside herself, very gently, her other forefinger moving to her clit. The musculature enveloped her fingers, her mind filmed over, her cunt becoming radiant, her buttocks begin to circle, finger dabbling her clit as a flow of overwhelming sensation began. Her mind became an art gallery of non-objective paintings, sparks skipping across shimmering blue water, fountains of light erupting, coloured stars imploding, storms of confetti and twisting collops of iridescent light glowing, pulsing. She brought her fingers out of her cunt, saw them ornamented with swirls of come and almost swooned, then impulsively marked her cheeks with the alabastrine stuff, like warpaint, white paths on the black. She closed her eyes and her mind reeled with images of black cats and bats careening, and she was coming, coming, rising into the coming, the other three fingers restored to the interior of her cunt to circle round and round. The orgasm carried her in waves, mounting, cresting, coming, coming, heat of cunt, nerves sparkling, her mind spinning until she was forced, finally, to her knees, still coming, moaning, fading, turning slowly, then sprawling on the floor, the redolent fetor of her marvellous cunt enlivening her nostrils as the residual thrills in her brain and body eased, faded, fading... Miriam licked her delicious fingers in the aftermath, grinning lewdly.

Time to begin Halloween!

When she left her apartment, a full moon as lucid as a chunk of candy shone in the sky. Darkness had blanketed the horizon and was absorbing the last of the sky's twilight lavender. She drove toward Westwood, along Santa Monica Boulevard. At Century City, stopping for a light, she watched a boisterous trio – bandaged mummy, pirate and Bedouin – caper across the street, obviously on their way to revelry, and their merry mood charged her with anticipation. She arrived at Vale's as the last of the light was vanishing. Vale lived in an old-fashioned building of sky-blue stucco. On the second floor her windows were open, an undertone of eerie Halloween music filtering out – Miriam recognised it as the Warhol party sequence music from *Midnight Cowboy*.

Vale met her at the door, a tall slim woman with swarthy Mediterranean beauty, costumed as a toy soldier: she wore blue pants, a red tunic festooned with gold epaulets, her cheeks highlighted with balls of pink greasepaint, a silver shako tilted at an angle in her waves of black hair. They exchanged greetings, a quick mimicry of the obligatory showbiz hug, and Miriam followed Vale inside where the rooms were lit with candles set in carved grimacing pumpkins. A dozen or so guests circulated.

"See if you can recognise anybody," Vale said, and with a touch launched her toward the party. A *haute couture* ghost in an opulent violet satin sheet caught her eye, staring at her intensely through the two eyeholes in the sheet. Was it somebody she knew? Miriam turned away and found herself confronting someone inside a *papier-maché* tree reminiscent of those that threw their apples at Dorothy on the road to Oz. Reaching up with a gnarly hand, the tree plucked a plastic apple from one of its leafy branches, and offered it to Miriam, who took it with a smile.

"Enjoy this, Eve, it's forbidden fruit," the tree said in a male voice.

Carrying the apple held against a thigh, Miriam headed toward a table across the room where someone in a white rabbit suit was pouring a glass of azure punch. She poured herself a glass too and sampled it, giving her head a little shake as the strong alcoholic impact of it jolted her. With her apple and glass of punch, she wandered into another room.

Someone in a policewoman's uniform with a real .38 holstered on her hip passed her. Miriam, who had grown up with guns and done a lot of shooting, including killing dozens of birds and even a bear before deciding that hunting really didn't interest her, wondered if the woman knew how to use the gun. Looking around the room, she noted a fortyish woman incarnated as a Forties teenager in baggy, rolled-up jeans, white blouse, saddle shoes and white socks, Dick Tracy in a butter-yellow suit, and someone in a Penguin costume smoking a Kool, but she didn't see anybody she knew. Of course, it was still early.

She decided to find Vale and get the lowdown on some of the guests, and was on her way when suddenly in the doorway a dark figure loomed ahead, drawing her gaze. Abruptly she was staring at a virtual duplicate of herself – a shadow of her shadow. The woman, exactly her size, also wore black stockings, a black leotard and domino mask, and her face and hands were blackened with greasepaint. She was indistinguishable from Miriam except for her fingernails, which were bright red, and the black satin pumps she wore instead of boots. The blue light of her eyes was so intense and familiar that Miriam took a step backward, alarmed.

"God," she whispered.

"*Oh,*" the woman exclaimed, and she took a step forward so precisely that it was like an inverse replication of Miriam's movement. She stared at Miriam as Miriam stared at her. In that moment, a sense of peculiarity came over Miriam and she suddenly felt the kind of giddy sensation of being on the top of a tall building. The moment seemed to disassociate itself from time, so that she had an impression of reflecting the woman's gaze for an interminable period while the sounds of the party receded into a sort of sub-reality. Then a vivid premonition of sensuality came over her, a surge of strange desire as she stared at the woman.

"*Beautiful,*" whispered the woman, and Miriam saw the black semaphore of her tongue as she spoke.

Then the woman abruptly turned and walked away.

As she disappeared into the kitchen, Miriam moved to follow her as if by reflex. As she entered the kitchen, she saw the woman simultaneously exiting through the back door, and she hurried after her.

A flight of stairs led down to a small lawn and garden that Miriam knew well from occasional afternoons of nude sunbathing. She paused and put her glass and apple on the porch's handrail, then followed the woman down the steps, her heart beating quickly.

At the bottom the woman waited, smiling up at Miriam as she descended.

Now Miriam felt a sense of excitement starting to absorb her, starting a tactile simmering along her arms and legs. She felt a stirring of warmth in the depth of her sex. One hand seemed literally drawn to her crotch and her fingers lingered there, finding the fabric of the leotard flushed with dampness.

"Oh-h," she murmured with burgeoning arousal.

"Oh-h," echoed her facsimile. The shadow came toward her, her face moving toward Miriam's until... their lips met and the woman was taking the pad of Miriam's upper lips softly between her lips and sipping on it, then slipping her tongue fully into Miriam's opening mouth, curling it around Miriam's tongue to conjure it irresistibly into her own mouth. There was a moment of total blankness in Miriam's mind then, followed by a sense of complete commitment as she began to participate in a thirsty exchange of kissing and tonguing until delicious spittle began trickling down their chins.

"Darling," the woman whispered, and with the tip of her tongue painted haloes of saliva around Miriam's heavily breathing mouth, licking the greasepaint off her cheeks, and turning her head to feed in the aperture of an ear. Miriam moved her head swimmingly under the sorcery of the tongue, becoming balmy with desire and yielding fully to the hands now touching her, fingers fanning out over her breasts, slinking down to seek the throbbing presence of her sex.

On the lawn, on her back, Miriam opened her eyes to see her shadow standing over her, taking off her shoes and leotard. She turned half on her side and quickly removed her own leotard, slipping off her boots. They were both naked except for stockings held up by black garters. Miriam's legs were drawn up, her feet firmly on the ground, arms spread. The facsimile put her hands on the inside of Miriam's thighs and parted them until her knees were tilted at angles and her cunt, labia uncloaked, was displayed like a lustrous bloom in the moonlight. Miriam drew her double down into her arms for more kisses, their mouths blending and tongues flowing in concert. She murmured with exhilaration as she felt a finger winnow into her cunt, then forge deeper into the slippery channel, a thumb pressing into the clutch of her asshole.

They began to kiss and embrace each other like possessed houris, writhing about on the lawn. Miriam knew only motion and the exquisite flowing of a powerful sensual continuity that gradually became a mounting flood of orgasmic sensation as both bodies merged and fused, sex to mouth, mouth to sex, both of them finessing little effusions of sweet creamy come from the other's cunt.

And, finally, her cunt exhausted and lips and tongues strained, Miriam opened her eyes and saw what she had somehow known all along. Her lover, drawing back to smile at her, removed her mask and wig to reveal that she was indisputably Miriam herself.

Miriam stared at herself in the soft moonlight. They were identical. Every contour of her body was repeated in the woman's figure – the same slender arms and legs, the exact full roundness of her breasts with thickly peaked nipples in broad, tea-coloured areolas, the pubic thicket so lush with densely massed curls that it extended in twin hedges along both sides of her cunt to the brink of the perineal gorge, and the choppy tangles of wavy honey-coloured hair that tumbled down from her scalp to the curves of her chin.

Miriam closed her eyes again and lay back, feeling the beating of her heart, and waited for... *something*.

"My love," she heard herself whisper in her ear, and she felt her fingers on her body, touching her throat, her breasts, fingers rippling the taut nipples, trailing over her stomach and into the mulled flux of her sex, stroking her arms, legs, the lightly sweated fragrance of her hair as the wig was discarded. And as she caressed herself, she heard herself whispering, "Yes, love... *you*, I came through the mirror for you." It was the sound of her own voice (which a lover had once described as volcanic ash and gold dust), and now she heard the familiar sound of her own laugh, then, "My love, I'm really *you*. Remember the scientist you dated? The biochemist. *Remember?*"

Miriam remembered David, a lover of months ago; it had been one of those brief and failed affairs, just a fragment of the past now.

"David," Miriam's own voice whispered, "needed only *one cell*, just one of your cells, love, to recreate you, to clone you, to make *me* so he could let you go and have you as well."

The words were like veils of moiré through which Miriam glimpsed, waveringly, a spellbinding vista.

"But I love *you*, Miriam..."

Drifting into somnolence with the flow of whispered words, and delicate caresses, Miriam receded into the depths of her mind and body, enclosed by the shadows.

Some time later she opened her eyes and sat up to discover herself alone under a full moon, wearing only her stockings and mask. She stood up and remained motionless for a long while as the odd dream replayed itself in her mind like a film running backward – the ineffable pleasure of the lovemaking, the descent to the backyard, the first sight of her other self at the party. A sound of party activity came from the apartment – music and a mingling of voices and laughter.

Miriam dressed. She was eager to be back inside, to disperse the strange memories with conversation and drink.

Then, as she glanced about for her boots she felt a sudden chill, sensing even before she discovered it that her boots had been replaced with a pair of shiny black satin pumps.

She put the boots on, knowing they would fit perfectly, as they did. Looking at them, she flexed her toes comfortably, admiring the mirrored gloss of the black satin.

"Miriam, what the *hell* are you doing down there?" She heard Vale's voice from the porch. "I thought I saw you leave out front..."

"I –" Miriam began. "I – I'm coming..." She waved at Vale, then started up the steps, wondering, wildly wondering how long it would be before her phone rang at home, how long she would have to wait before she called herself to whisper the words she knew she would hear herself say...

Coach Morley
Isabel Lazar

On the eve of my 34th birthday, I made a vow to myself to put to rest those demons that had been plaguing me since childhood. Well, ok, so I promised my shrink I'd do that, but somewhere inside me I knew she was right. The self-loathing of teenage years, the sexual confusion, the crush I'd had on the Varsity Volleyball coach, ugh. They were all no longer a part of the person I had become and the 'new me' vowed to clear away all the remnants.

Six hours later, figuring there is no better time than the present, I was on a plane back to Chi-town where I'd grown up. Having not survived the red-eye from SF as well as expected, I slept until noon, then dressed and headed out to my old high school. The times I had spent there were torture on my memory banks and I was anxious to start 'replacing the bad memories with the good ones', as Dr Blume would say.

As a kid, I remembered walking down the main drag of the school, past the gym at 2:15 every day. And every day at 2:15, Coach Morley walked out of that gymnasium and strutted her slick butch self down towards me. Every day. And on each of those days, no matter what I was doing, even if I eventually had to double back through the Drivers' Ed entrance to finish my work, every day, rain or shine, I would drop everything, grab some books (for esthetics) and dash down three flights of stairs, push past the throngs of exiting students to emerge winded into the mouth of the hallway at precisely 2:15. There I'd will myself to slow down, saunter even, pretending to be just another weary upperclassman, all just to catch a tiny little glimpse of her.

In our daily ritual, she'd exit the gymnasium, round the corner and make her way steadily towards me. On most days, we'd see each other a good 50 paces away. We'd look up, find our target, then look away again. Up again, watch for a bit, then away. We practiced this ritual all the way down the corridor until, finally within breathing distance, we'd throw one last, lingering, wistful look at one another – exactly at the moment we passed each other – and move on, neither of us looking back.

I never even knew her name until the yearbook came out that year. Locking myself in the bathroom of my house, I devoured the pages one by one until I found her photo and name. She was in the Sports Teams section on page 87: "Varsity Volleyball. Upper row, end: Coach Maureen 'Mo' Morley".

"I'm in love with Mo Morley," I realized that day; then I shut the *Sentinel* and put it away for the next 17 years.

Homophobia ran high in the Reagan 80's and it would follow me like a shadow until I could stand it no longer, making me run hard and fast both towards and away from myself. Eventually it landed me in San Francisco where I found others of my persuasion. Still I never forgot Coach Morley. Her incarnation, her strut, the slow saunter past me every day of my senior year would replay itself over and over in my waking and slumbering dreams. And now here I was again, time warped back into the very place that had tortured me; not really knowing what I was doing here, or even if she still coached brats.

Two hours after lunch, I linger outside the gymnasium in anticipation, nodding pleasantly to confused underclassmen as they hurry past. At 2:15 the bell rings, signalling the end of sessions. I hang back, holding my breath and expecting disappointment. After all, people change. They change their minds, their jobs, even their sex. So why should I expect to find her here after all these years? But then, to my disbelieving eyes, as if on cue, Coach Morley rounds the corner. A little grayer around the edges but still solid. *Damn, she looks good.* I zigzag through the crowd of students to cross directly in front of her and stop. She looks annoyed until her eyes meet mine. I don't move but stand there looking at her, unable to stop grinning. Now she's amused. Does she like what she sees, I wonder?

"Coach Morley. You're still here."

"Excuse me?"

"I say, you're still here." She squints trying to place me. "Jodie Keegan. You don't remember me, do you?" She hesitates and finally I don't hold back. "I had the worst crush on you when I was a student here."

"Excuse me?" Her Midwestern, tight-lipped upbringing (not to mention her job as an educator) wouldn't permit any other response, this I know. So I continue, figuring I have the upper hand.

"'Cept I didn't know it – or, rather, wouldn't admit it, then. I was such a femme at the time." Now she sizes me up like a lover, planting her feet firmly into the ground and crossing her arms.

"And when was that?"

"'87," I shrug and she frowns, disbelieving. Seventeen years is a long time to carry a torch. Is she flattered?

"And now you're married," she says matter-of-factly, looking down at my ring finger.

"Yes." I'm not shy about this any more. Ten years in SF – nothing fazes me. "My wife of 7 years is back at home." Her eyes go wide as she squeezes her jaw.

"But, say, I didn't come here to cause trouble," I say and look her up and down lasciviously... 'cause now, now that I'm married and 'safe,' now I can. "I just came to see some old friends and, uh, put some ol' demons to bed, as it were."

"Was I a demon?" she asks quietly amused. The throngs of students have subsided.

"In a manner of speaking." I let my eyes slide over her broad chest, her tough Midwestern arms and tight jeans. Her legs look like thick stumps in her black Levi's and I can't help but picture them naked with a strap-on bobbing jauntily in between as she heads towards me on the bed. I sigh with regret and shake my head.

"You are fine. Just as fine as I remember. Time has been kind to you. Must be doin' someone, er, something right." Then I look her hard in the eyes... and release her.

"You take care, now." I sidestep around, keeping her eyes on mine, and back away smiling, my gait turning into a skip as I turn and head towards the door.

"Say, Jodie," I hear her call and my heart begins to race. "Would you like to go for coffee or something?" I chuckle to myself then turn to eye her from under my lashes.

"You're gonna make a philanderer out of me yet," I whisper. She looks away towards the wall of windows pensively. Is that a blush I see? God oh mighty, I've made this gorgeous dyke blush on account of lil' ol' me. I have to pinch myself. I walk back the 20 paces it takes to be at eye level with her again and whisper.

"S'when is your next free period?" I feel like an adolescent high school boy getting hot over a cute new girl in homeroom. 'Cept she's the boi and I'm the grrrl, or at least it was that way in HS. Don't know when the tables turned. Guess t'was when I finally grew balls.

"In 55 minutes."

"I'll be waiting out front. I'm drivin' a black Jeep..."

Fifty-seven minutes later we're tearin' down 294 towards O'Hare International. There are closer coffee shops but, uh, none with a bed attached. We don't speak. There is nothing to say. This woman and I couldn't be further apart on the spectrum of life. She's a high school athletics coach. Straight and narrow... well at least narrow. No surprises here, except where they count, and those are expected, even welcomed. Me? I am, as yet, without definition...

We enter the O'Hare Hilton and I stop by the desk to pick up my key, the reservation having been made during 6th period PE.

The elevator ride to the 11th floor is torture. Weary travelers shuffle in and out with their luggage, thankfully too preoccupied to notice that neither of us is even carrying a billfold.

Finally we arrive and squeeze through the crowd to exit. The doors close on the mayhem and we are left alone with our purpose. I find the door, slide in my credit card key and enter the non-smoking, king suite.

She stands just outside the door eyeing me. She'd been following all along so I didn't think to look. Now she stands immobile, waiting for... what?

"Have you changed your mind?" I ask. "It would be ok, you know." *The hell it would,* but I gotta offer.

She looks away, her eyes trailing down the hallway and I forget to breathe while waiting for her reply. In a moment she turns and looks at me as if possessed, a cockeyed grin teasing the corners of her luscious mouth. *That's right, honey. What the fuck? We only go around once in this hellhole we call 'life'. The superintendent ain't here and you're no longer jailbait.* I nod my silent understanding and step aside for her to enter.

She makes a show of looking around the room. I lean against the wall idolizing her. When she doesn't hear me behind her she pivots on her heels and stares me down.

I place my keys gingerly on the bureau and in one clean move yank my shirt over my head. A risky manoeuvre to be sure but I did manage to gain some self-esteem in Cali, enough to know that what I have to offer is not chopped liver. At 34 my breasts are still rock hard and high, I have a six-pack stomach, thanks to 24-Hour Fitness, and a small, tight ass. And something else that she can't readily see. I know how to use my tongue and hands, now. Well.

The chilly Chicago air brings my nipples to attention. She looks directly at them and grins.

"Like what you see?" I ask. The grin fades noticeably.

"I don't remember you this cocky," she says, all military-like.

"Correction. You don't remember me at all," I counter and undo my button flies. Then I stare directly at her crotch, trying to figure out exactly what I'm up against.

"Don't worry, Tiger, I've got what you need," she says and strokes a bulge on the inside of her right thigh that hadn't been there before. I nod in appreciation.

"Well, then. Let's not keep it waiting," I say and dispense with the rest of my clothes.

In two steps she is on top of me, spins me around and flattens me against the wall. She places both feet between my legs and spreads them to shoulder width, providing her with maximum exposure. But instead of touching me she curls her formidable forearm around my waist and bends me over.

"What the –?"

"Don't move," she growls in my ear. With her fingertips she traces from my shoulders down my arms to my hands and fingers, placing her substantial weight on me. And just when I think she's going to take me from behind she twines her fingers in mine and pulls my arms around behind me.

"Open. Says me," she says placing both my hands around my butt cheeks. Then she steps aside to watch.

"You must be kidding," I say and try to stand. Crack! Her big butch arm comes down hard on my exposed flesh. "Yeow!"

"No wonder you never tried out for V-Ball. You should know better than to talk back to your coach." I teeter on the brink of total humiliation, trying in vain to cover my privates. "I'm waiting," comes her guttural command. What the hell, it's better than getting smacked again. I curl my fingers around my ass and pull... Hey, I asked for this, didn't I? At the moment I don't remember anything except the slight ache in my lower back (I'm getting too old for this shit) and the unmistakable feel of blood hitting my clit like the rhythmic sounds of Salsa. If I stand this way any longer, I won't need her at all.

"You're wrong," she whispers. "I remember you quite well, lil' miss I-was-a cheerleader-fine-young-Thang." I grunt out of embarrassment more profound than my position. No self-respecting dyke would ever admit to having been a cheerleader. Ever.

"What can I say? I was looking for validation at a time when I felt pretty crappy." I hear her roll down her zipper and walk over. And in a moment I feel the unmistakable dull pressure of the head of her cock pushing against me.

"And did you get it?" She sinks it.

"Woof," is all I can muster. She pulls me back burying the shaft to the knob and finding her own rhythm.

"Did'ya?" She chants in between strokes, "Huh? Tell me. Tell me, did'ya?"

Did I get that validation? Thank God for the wall, is all I can think.

"Yea, I got it, ugh, or, ugh, rather I'm, ugh, getting it."

"You are at that. Don't you forget it."

"If I knew you were like, ugh, this back then I would have, ugh, come... out sooner."

"Oh, yeah?," she says straining a bit. "That would have made the school paper. Newsflash: Pom-pom and Varsity Coach were caught naked in the showers today. Full story page two."

"Nooo-ah-ah." I shake my head. "That's where you've got it wrong."

"Oh, how's that?" She asks her pace quickening. I can hear her starting to moan. I take advantage of the upper hand and push her off me. Then I turn and give her a good shove that hurls her across the room and onto the bed. A second later I'm on top of her, straddling her cock as her face registers complete shock.

"If we'd'a done it back then, it would'a made the front page," I say, stroking off on her member.

"Fuck you," she flips me on my back in a very impressive wrestling manoeuvre. We grapple like two Sumos in heat. The sheer size of her is imposing but I'm no slouch. She wrestles with brute force but I earned my black belt seven years ago. Using my Chi I shake her loose and lock her arm around her back, the smell of musk and sweat intoxicating me.

"You first," I say and work my free hand between her legs. She jerks and tries to shake me off but I have her off balance in a strategic hold.

"No!" She bucks as my fingers burrow their way deep inside her.

"No what?" I growl in her ear. "Must be a real mindfuck, eh? The femmy cheerleader in the miniskirt is now the Daddy?"

"You? A Daddy?" She begins to laugh hard enough that tears run down her face. This totally fucking breaks my concentration.

"What the fuck is so funny?" I counter. In one smooth motion she somehow flips me off her and gets back on top of me in 0.3 seconds, my knees up, my heels at my ass and my hands there, too. I look like Nadia-fucking-Comaneci doing an upside-down backbend. Worst of all, her menacing little tool is back between my legs and teasing the inside of my ass.

"The day you become Daddy, is the day I become head Cheerleading Coach. And when do ya think that'll be?" she says probing my asshole with her big, fat cock.

"Oh, I don't know. Judging by your sissy-ass way of fucking, could be any minute now." That did it. I knew it would.

She flips me over with lightning speed and lays 10 searing strokes of her hard hand across my ass. I wail in pain and humiliation.

"What's the matter, little girl? More than you bargained for?" She continues to pummel my ass with the severe strength of her big butchly arm. I struggle in vain against the pain, the heat rising all the way to my earlobes. With her strokes controlled and meticulous, she ensures every inch of my backside is covered in the red marks left by her gargantuan hand.

"Had enough?"

"Yes."

"Yes what?"

"Yes, Sir!"

"Yes WHAT?"

"Yes, Coach."

"That-a-girl," she says and releases me. I slide to the floor in a heap. She reaches down and takes a hold of my hand then pulls my limp body along with it raising me to my knees. I follow blindly, my vision coming together on a concentrated view of her cock. I look to her for guidance. She raises her eyebrows and nods her head grinning sarcastically.

"You know what to do. Don't you?" I stare back at her with a blank expression. She can't mean it. "Don't you?" she says more forcefully. My eyes drop back to her cock in disbelief as my head shakes an involuntary 'no'. She puts her hand on the back of my neck and pulls me forward. "I knew you did," she nearly purrs. I close my eyes and open my mouth to her, closing it over the head of her shaft.

Magically I am transported back in time again, this time to the unseemly memory of the back seat of Bobby McCutchen's car. We had gone to see tough Sigourney Weaver in *Aliens* at the Twin Drive-In, but Bobby had a few scary surprises of his own. I swore an oath to myself that very night to never allow myself to get into such a vulnerable position again. The words of that teen-ager now rang through my adult head as if I were saying them out loud, telling me what I had always known – that I was never really confused about what I wanted, just too afraid to face it. I knew for sure I was gay back at that drive-in. Bobby must have suspected *something* when first I bit him then threw up all over him. He never asked me out again. Hmmm? I start to grin, then laugh. This stirs Coach Morley sober and she lifts her head to look at me.

"You find this funny, do you?" she says.

"As a matter of fact, I do. You just solved an age-old riddle for me."

"Oh, yea? Just laying here getting head? Well, I'm happy to oblige. Now care to share your new-found knowledge with the rest of the class?"

"Absolutely. It's simple really. What's the difference between straight cock and butch cock?" She raises her eyebrows.

"I give up. What?"

"Oh, about 15 years of therapy," I chortle, unable to keep a straight face. She looks at me like I'm whacked. I try to clarify but with little success.

"It's amazing, Coach. Some of the lessons you learn in high school, you don't even know you know until you do. You know?"

"Are you feeling well, Jodie?" she says reaching out to feel my forehead. "I think this cock has gone to your head."

"You don't know the half of it," I say, then resume cock sucking in earnest.

Her eyes go wide then roll back into her head. She begins to moan like a child with a fever, her orgasm building. As she watches me through slanted eyes, I work her tool with vigor.

"Damn, damn, damn... oh!" She moans and bucks and moans and comes finally, gasping and screaming and grabbing for me. I hold her tightly as her spasms subside.

Then quietly I offer, "Oh, c'mon. You can't be done yet." I start making my way down her body again.

"No, no! That's, that's good. That's enough now," she pants, pulling at my hair and face. "C'mon. Come up now. Let me... let me fuck you right, now."

"No, no," I say. "Let me," as I release her from her strap-on and slip in on. "After all, one good deed deserves another."

Dr Blume would be so proud.

Fantasy Football
a.k.a Lesbian Footballers' Wives
Sophie Neon-Blanc

By the year 2025, women's football has become the richest sport in England and, for the last six years, has attracted bigger gate receipts than the men's game, which was replaced as the number one sport of the nation by rugby after Alan Curbishley's England team failed to qualify for the World Cup and the England Rugby team won yet another world championship.

The London club Olympic East, who play at the new 50,000 capacity Hackney Marshes Stadium, are currently top of the women's league. The players are mainly lesbian, and their glamorous partners have been fondly nicknamed the Stratford Wives.

JULES

"You can tell how good someone is going to be in bed by the position they play," Jules whispered over her decaffeinated latte.

"Oh, really. So how would a striker fuck, then?" Jane asked.

"Well, their job is to penetrate the defence, get into the box and score."

"Ha ha. That's a bit obvious. So does that mean if you play as a defender, you don't like being penetrated?"

"It depends if you're a good defender or a *faux* defender. If you're serious about keeping the opposition out of your box and keeping a clean sheet, then sure, penetration may be out of the question – but if you're really a midfielder who is standing in for a game or two, well, then, no."

"So tell me about how midfielders are in bed, then. That seems a little less obvious."

"A central midfielder, they like to control things and dictate the scenario, probably a top and very likely into SM. If, however, if they play on the wings, then they prefer hard, fast and spontaneous sex."

Jane laughed. "Remind me to sleep with a winger the next time I date a footballer."

Jules was notorious around the team. She never played football, but had become involved six years ago as the girlfriend of one of the first team star players, the richest woman in football, until an injury cut her career short at the age of 26. Since then Jules had slept with at least twenty other players, that Jane knew of, and was presently living with Anne, the captain, currently the richest woman in the game. So Jane guessed that Jules had picked up enough experience to know what she was talking about.

They'd always been attracted to each other, but Jane never felt like going there, out of loyalty to the team and whoever her latest flame was. Still, now she played for a different team, after being lured away by better wages and a relocation to West London, so her loyalty had shifted. And she'd also missed their flirtations after a year away. Tonight she was feeling like doing something a bit dangerous. Besides, Jane was curious. She used to play in goal, so how was Jules rating her potential? She probed further, knowing something Jules didn't. "What about the keeper, then? Don't tell me – strong wrists, good fists."

"Oh, very funny. No, actually, the keeper has a lot more variety about her performance. She's good at diving, usually has bigger hands, so fisting isn't always required, and she likes to be close to her posts, so enjoys being tied up too."

Well, she'd got some of that right, at least, Jane thought.

"Am I right or am I right?" Jules smiled.

"Jules... there's only one way to find out."

They headed for Jane's E-type Jaguar and drove across to West London. Jules had suggested going back to hers and Anne's place, but Jane lived alone so there was no need. Besides, she always liked having home advantage, and it appeared Jules didn't mind playing away.

They got into the hallway and had barely closed the door when Jules thrust her mouth onto Jane's. They kissed hard and fast, probing with their tongues. Jane edged them down the hallway, padding the wall with her hand for the light switch and pushing the door to the lounge open. As they turned to step into the room, Jules pushed Jane down to floor and deftly began to undo her button-fly jeans. Jane's hands automatically went up to Jules' breasts, but Jules moved them away and Jane let her. Then she removed Jane's jeans and pants in no time at all. Her hands moved between Jane's legs and her index finger teased her clitoris for all of thirty seconds.

Then Jane felt two fingers enter her. "You feel gorgeous inside me – please don't stop." Another finger slipped in. Jules slid in and out of her, biting her top lip and kissing her harder and deeper, as her hand went further inside. Jane could feel herself coming, but held it off for as long as possible, the sweat pouring off her brow and trickling into the side of her mouth. When finally she couldn't stop it from happening, Jane shuddered and cried out, "Oh my fucking god, Jules." She sank to the floor, taking in air like she'd just come up from the ocean after two minutes underwater.

Jane lay mesmerised and speechless for a while. This wasn't at all what she'd expected. For starters, she thought she'd be fucking Jules and would be lucky to get fucked in return. But instead Christmas, her birthday and the FA Cup Final had come all at once. This thought gave her fresh energy and so she moved to her side and then rolled on top of Jules. "Well, that was *so* worth all those years of teasing and flirting. You're a constant surprise to me."

"Jane, I live with the team captain – I rarely get the chance to fuck someone!"

But now came the real challenge – performing to Jules' goalkeeper stereotype. What Jules didn't know was Jane was currently playing in a variety of positions for her new team, and Jules was going to be in for a long and varied night.

ALEX AND LISA

Alex and Lisa had been comparing notes for many years. They met every Wednesday night for dinner and gossip about their latest inter-team conquests, before going off to join the team in their own new café-bar for a post-training drink.

Tonight, Alex was waiting impatiently – Lisa was running a little late and Alex was bursting at the seams to tell Lisa her news. She knew Lisa would love this one.

They were both exes of footballers and had split up from their long-term partners at the same time. They became drinking pals first, helping each other regain confidence again, then, after an end-of-season party, when both had enjoyed some no-strings sex with a couple of new players, they made their comparisons and so this new game began. They met each week to discuss who they'd bedded and, as the weeks went by, they got more daring and more adventurous. It became friendly competition, at the football team's expense.

Last Saturday night, for example, they had been out at the birthday party of Leigh, one of the team's veterans. Lisa had decided to end the night with the team's very butch, very muscular top goal scorer, who'd been keen to keep telling Lisa that her partner was away on business. Lisa saw this as easy prey and obligingly left with her.

Alex by this time had been scanning the room for someone she (or Lisa) hadn't slept with yet. Opportunities had been thin and so she'd figured she might as well leave, until she'd seen someone from the hallway, someone standing in the kitchen drinking a beer.

Margot had joined the team two years ago. She had a boyfriend called Scott, whom few of the team had met. Recently Margot had started to socialise more and Alex had started wondering what it would be like to turn her, but she'd never really wanted to go that far. Until last Saturday night.

"Hi, sorry I'm late. Bloody work, bloody taxi. How the bloody hell are *you*, Alex?"

It was Lisa, bounding over to their table and pecking Alex on the cheek, while playfully ruffling her short, jet-black hair.

"I thought you weren't coming because you were still at it with old Thunder-Thighs-the-Striker," Alex teased back. "You look great, darling. Nice suit. Is it Prada?"

"Nah, it's Versace. Anyway, have I got a story for you –"

"No, let me go first. I've been dying to tell you. You'll never guess who I ended up shagging after the party and through to Sunday morning." Alex was willing Lisa to get it wrong, while Lisa was wondering why Alex always had to jump in with her story first, so she lamely rattled off a few unlikely names.

"Dunno... Kate, Angie, Jo, Sarah?"

"No, you're way off. It was none other than Margot."

Lisa almost choked on her cigarette and turned to a passing waitress and ordered them a bottle of Sauvignon Blanc and a half-bottle of San Pellegrino. "How the fuck did you swing that one, if you pardon the pun?"

"Well, after you and old Stone Butch Cassidy left the party, I was about to give up and go home for a line of coke and some fun with my Jessica Rabbit. I was just getting my coat when she appeared and persuaded me to stay for another drink. Next thing we're dancing to some awful retro techno-shite and she lights two cigarettes and passes me one. As she hands it over, she says, 'I've always wanted to kiss you'. So I tell her to go ahead and she does! We kiss for ages and then she asks herself back to mine. Well, I'm not going to rush her into this, so I say, 'Sure, let me know when you want to leave'. 'Right now' she replies. So we left without saying goodbye.

"As we're walking back to my flat, she stops to kiss me again, probing her tongue deeper into my mouth. Then she quits and grabs my hand and wedges it up her dress and between her legs. 'See how you make me feel. See how I want you,' she says. I tell her we aren't too far from my flat, but she can't wait and leads me into a car park we're passing. We lean against a pillar and kiss, and again she thrusts my hand up her dress, after which I slide my fingers into her wet pants and then inside her. She lets out a small whimper and grabs my hair and pulls my mouth to hers. 'Fuck me harder,' she whispers and so I do, feeling my cunt get wet as her moistness flows down my wrist as she comes, her muscles relaxing, then contracting like a tourniquet, around my hand."

Lisa asked what happened next and Alex continued:

"We went back to mine and had a beer and then she fucked me

on the sofa. I came within minutes of her being inside me. Not bad for a novice! Then we had a few lines of coke each and went down on each other simultaneously. Half way through I stopped us and got a small crystal of coke on the end of my tongue and worked it into her clit. She did the same in return to me, we must have been giving each other head for a good hour. It was the most drawn out intense mutual muff dive, I've ever had. As the coke wore off we started to finger fuck each other, which then turned to fisting each other into the most powerful of climaxes I can remember."

"Wow," gawped Lisa "She sounds insatiable."

"She is. Next we went upstairs and I couldn't believe how hungry she was for more. We had another line and she then asked if I had anything I could penetrate her with. So I put on my harness and went to the bathroom to roll a condom onto the dildo and when I came back into the bedroom, she was climbing on top of it before I had time to reach the bed. While I stood holding her, she worked herself up and down.

"All I had to do was stand there keeping my legs steady, as she slid herself up and down. She was breathing hard as I held her around the waist and started to move her up and down, until I felt my legs were sagging. Then I moved towards the bed and lowered her down onto it and then took over. I thrust into her as far as I could go and she let out a scream, as I moved in and out. Then she started to rotate her hips from side to side as I pushed in and out. She grabbed my arse and pulled me further into her and then we both rotated our hips, as the dildo went in all the way to the harness.

"She kept her grip on me, keeping me right inside her as we both moved to the same rhythm until I started to move in the opposite direction to her movements, thrusting with all the strength that remained in my legs from the balls of my feet, up to my thighs. I felt my cunt growing bigger and wetter as hers did and then she was saying 'don't stop, this is it' and she came, shuddering the full length of her body and I came, too."

"What happened next?" Lisa asked, feeling herself growing wet from hearing this story.

"Then she told me how much she loved her boyfriend and how we could never do this again. Like I cared. Then we went to sleep."

After they ate their meal, Alex ordered another bottle of wine and asked Lisa about her encounter.

"No, I couldn't top that story." Lisa was feeling a little self-conscious, as some diners had overheard parts Alex's story. So she whispered, "Well, let's just say that the woman we all had down for a stone butch fuck-stud likes it best up the *Arsenal*."

After polishing off the wine, Lisa asked Alex if she had any more coke left. Alex did. So they went back to hers.

Alex and Lisa were not seen around the team for a while. A few months later, they reappeared as a couple. Game over.

JANE

Jules was lying on her back on Jane's bed, blindfolded and tied to the wrought-iron headboard. She watched Jane put on her strap-on and smiled – until Jane walked over to her and tied a blindfold around her face. Jules let out an impatient sigh.

Jane decided to make her wait for it and straddled her hips, working from the top down. She kissed Jules' brow, then her lips and moved down to her clavicle, teasing her tongue across the collar-bone. She parted Jules' legs slightly and felt that she was wet and warm, but not ready yet. Finally Jane reached the other woman's navel with her tongue and worked around to Jules' hips before crossing over to her clit, which she licked, sucked and bit teasingly, while Jules groaned, thinking of only one thing, what she wanted inside her.

SUSAN

Susan is the newest addition to the Stratford Wives. Her partner, Abby, has just joined from Fulham for a sizeable fee. Susan is curious to find out what the other footballers' wives have been up to, and Maria gives her some background in the club café-bar while their partners are at the midweek training session.

"So, what happens," asked Susan, "when a footballer's wife is another player? Some would say you have the best of both worlds. You play the game – and get to be a footballer's wife, too."

"For some that isn't enough," Maria replied. "Once we had two players, who had been together five years when they started inviting other players back for threesomes or wife swaps. They even had a key party one night which, oddly enough, backfired – as no one chose their hosts' keys. Six months later, they split up. Got your eyes on anyone else at the club then?"

"Not really, but I wouldn't say no to a rubdown from the team physio."

Maria's eyes lit up. "Groin strain can hamper anyone's performance on the pitch. An over-stretched groin needs special care and attention. She does a private clinic too. Do you do any sports?"

"Karate."

"Perfect – make sure you over-extend your kick next time and then book an appointment for your rubdown."

Susan winced at the thought; she'd rather feign the injury or just ignore the crush. Besides, she was happy with Abby – no need to go looking for sex elsewhere. And anyway, she had always preferred to observe. If the truth were known, Susan was in fact a bit of a voyeur.

Maria continued discussing Amanda the physio. "She's reported to be seeing Maltide, you know."

"What, Matilde the manager?"

For the last two seasons, it had been reported that Matilde Van Dyke, the Dutch boss of Olympic Stratford, had a changeable attitude towards squad selection. In particular, she had a habit of changing her line-ups on whim, not always involving the best of players. In-club rumours circulated, claiming that all she really wanted was to be a footballer's wife – and was exploring this option.

Matilde was married to an ex-Dutch International called Ruud, who had fathered her two children. Although they remained married for the sake of the children, she was best described as a straight woman with a background in European coaching, who was experimenting with English soccer and English women.

Matilde's latest fixation at Olympic was Amanda the physio, whose company was regularly requested at Maltide's country mansion. No one knew whether anything was actually going on, but speculation was rife among the players and especially among the Stratford Wives.

JULES AND JANE AGAIN

Jane was now sucking Jules' toes, as Jules writhed in irritated ecstasy in her restraints and blindfold.

"You bastard, Jane," she muttered under her breath. "Stop that and just fuck me."

"Not yet, Jules."

Jane continued to tease, running her tongue up Jane's legs all the way to her hip bones, where she stopped to titillate further. She then parted Jules' legs and felt her wetness. She entered her fingers, while Jules groaned. Jane withdrew and then lowered her head and worked Jules' clit with her tongue for a good couple of minutes.

"*Now* you're ready," Jane said, and entered her with the dildo.

As she did so, Jules raised her hips and said, "Untie me first. I want to hold you when I come."

TWO MONTHS LATER

The football season had now ended and Olympic East had won all domestic honours and the European Champions' Cup, too. To celebrate, Matilde was throwing an end-of-season party at her home. On the guest list were the players, the coaching and ground staff – and most of the Stratford Wives. *Hello!* magazine had the exclusive photo-call.

Alex and Lisa arrived first as their new-edition orange Austin Allegro pulled up the drive. As the couple got out of the car, Maltide turned to Amanda and said, "Well, Alex certainly looks better for two weeks at the rehab clinic."

Next to arrive, Abby – and Susan, who was wearing an elegant black evening dress and a bright pair of Jimmy Choo heels. "God, how retro," Amanda remarked to Matilde, pointing at the shoes.

As the rest of the guests arrived, they too were snapped by the *Hello!* photographer and quizzed by the reporter.

Then Jules and Anne arrived and Maltide immediately went up to greet her captain (ignoring Jules, who was left to enter the main hall alone). Jules wasn't bothered, as she knew Jane would be along later. She hadn't seen her for a week, due to the close of the football season, and was looking forward to their next private session together.

Once the press had left, the party got into full swing and Maltilde's speech congratulating her team and thanking her staff was met by rapturous applause.

The team were in high spirits and before long the party had split into two groups: the players and coaching staff all hanging out around the pool, and the Stratford Wives in the bar and lounge area.

On her way back to the pool area, Margot approached Alex, who had gone to the bar. "How's it going?"

"Fine, thanks," Alex replied.

"I was wondering if we could maybe meet up for a drink sometime next week?"

"No, sorry. I'm with Lisa and we're exclusive." Alex almost laughed.

Margot left without a word and returned to the teammates and Scott outside.

Lisa approached Alex. "Everything okay?"

"Yeah, she just wanted to know if I fancied a drink next week and I told her no. As we were an item."

They kissed.

Meanwhile, upstairs in some of the guestrooms, some of the women had sloped off to indulge in some off-field activities. Jules and Jane sat drinking a post-passionate bottle of Bollinger and decided to stay put for the night, or until Anne got fed up with the round-the-pool football songs and came looking for Jules.

In Matilde's room, Matilde herself was enjoying the start of some oral massage from Amanda, the physio.

Susan was wandering the upstairs corridors of the house, taking a peek into some of the rooms, when she heard noises. She opened the door slowly and saw Amanda giving Matilde's groin some very special attention. She stood staring for ages until Matilde, sounding quite drunk, said, "Why don't you come in and join us, Susan?"

"No, but I'd like to watch, if that's ok," Susan replied confidently.

Olympic East and the Stratford Wives partied hard into the next day and welcomed the start of the next season, when they'd do it all over again.

Combat
Eli Donald

I stand in front of the cracked mirror on the wall opposite. Just your regular dyke, in an army combat uniform. Oh, I've known a few women who would just love this. But I definitely prefer uniforms on other women... I never look right. I suppose I couldn't really complain about the boots; I could happily take these home with me. They would look great with my jeans.

This was just the thing Paul finds hilariously funny. "Team work," he calls it. "A chance to work together."

I work in a sportswear shop in the local centre and the boss is into team work in a big way. He's decided to send us on a combat session where we are one side and we have to shoot the other side with guns that fire paint and then steal their flag to win. I think they call it paint ball.

I can't see the point in it myself, but he swears by it and I don't really want to argue since we're getting the day away from work. I take one last look in the mirror – god, I'm putting weight on – and leave for the game.

It's raining again, great weather for ducks, but I don't think I fancy the idea of rolling about in it. I won't deny that I'm maybe just a little bit on the butch side – but I do like to stay warm and dry if I can.

We all stand in a line, regular little troopers under the grey Scottish sky. Five of us – Paul of course won't be playing. Teamwork is great as long as he doesn't have to get dirty.

The other team stand to face us... they are from our rival shop. Six big guys. Obviously they have an advantage, five against six; even I know that's not on.

Someone speaks but as usual I don't listen and miss the details. I have the attention span of a gnat.

Oh joy!

They have arranged a sixth member, a big girly girl taking our side... She's tall and skinny, not how I like my women. God, she's wearing nail polish. How the hell is she gonna do this?

Crash... *flash*! There is a storm and it is getting close. Knee-deep in mud on a small farm outside Invergowrie. Just how I really want to spend my time. More thunder. Great, that'll be nice, a big storm to make this so much more cosy.

Off we go, into the mud and probably cow pats as well. Everyone has sorta split up, so we can cover more area. I'm lagging at the back a bit.

Shit, someone's waving at me... must be guys from the other team around. They're waving to get down.

The rain is really starting to muddy this place up now... it's almost liquid and I can hear it under my body as I hit the floor. The mud is really cold.

Splash. The girly girl has just lain beside me. How ironic, she probably thinks she's safe with me, 'coz she thinks I'm a guy.

"Hi!" I look at her, and she speaks again. "The other guys have moved on. Thought I'd lag behind a bit. This isn't really my cup of tea."

No shit, Sherlock!

I smile at her. Should I try to hold a conversation? I look up again, open my mouth to speak... but she covers it with hers.

Her kisses are short but passionate... she must think I'm a guy. Maybe, but who am I to tell her she's playing tonsil hockey with a dyke?

Her mouth is pressing hard against my lips, keeping my head back and not allowing any movement. I can taste her lipstick – I've never kissed a girl with lipstick before; I usually play with butch chicks, so this is a bit of a surprise.

The rain is getting heavier and I can feel it hit my face as she lets her tongue investigates my mouth. The cold mud is running down the back of my neck, making me shiver. She bites my lip a little, reaches down and starts to unhook my trousers.

Her hands are warm but the rain now gaining access to my flesh is cold and causing a little pool to form in my navel. She crooks her head down to my tummy and laps at the pool, her tongue taking small licks at my navel.

God, I'm so horny now.

She has my trousers open and she's pulling at them trying to get them over my hips. I'm desperately pulling at them too trying to help her. God, what am I doing? My head is swimming with lust for this and I've lost all rational thought. "Fuck it."

I sit up and pull them over my hips.

She sits back and stares… oh christ, she must have been expecting a dick. "Naughty girl!"

I stop dead and look at her.

"Imagine not wearing any underwear."

She didn't freak.

She pushes me back, leaving me lying with my trousers at my knees.

God, this is humiliating, but I'm so wet and I want it so much. I can feel every ounce of her weight on top of me. She's so skinny that I could pick her up. She feels so nice. So different to what I'm used to. I reach for her shirt, I want to take those breasts in my hands and squeeze then.

Thump. She grabs my hands and pushes them down to the ground. I lift my head, but she pushes me back with her hard kisses, letting them trail along my chin and down my neck.

I can feel her tiny little teeth nipping at my skin. I wrap my arms around her back and pull her tight against me. She forces them back and bites my neck hard.

I wince at the pain but it doesn't last long… She's got her belt in her hands… what the…

Smack. The pain is intense. I can see the red mark across the front of my thighs… who the hell does she think she is? Smack!

There are tears welling up in my eyes now and the raindrops are burning my legs.

"Don't be stupid!" She has a look in her eyes that scares me. She goes back to kissing my neck and I lay there motionless and dumbfounded.

Her kisses are reaching lower; she's opening my shirt to accommodate them. My breathing is heavy and so is hers. I can see her chest raise and lower. I lean forward wanting to taste more of her kisses. Desperate to chew on her lips again and have her taste mine.

Slap. She hits me hard on the cheek... I just stare open-mouthed. "Big, stupid, dumb butch. Gonna have to teach you how it's done." She sounds angry.

She throws me in the mud again and pulls out her belt... I hold my breath... She doesn't hit me. I wait... but still she doesn't hit me.

She leans over me with her full body weight and takes my hands. She pulls at them, causing me to turn onto my side with my arms still in her hands now behind me.

There are all sorts of things running through me head now. I could easily throw her off and leave her in the mud. I feel pain in my shoulders and arms. What the hell... she has the belt around my upper arms tying them almost together.

She rolls me over so that I'm belly up again – my face must be a picture. I'm scared now, really scared. I wanted this, but now I'm scared. I try to pull my arms from the belt, but can't budge them an inch.

She kneels back, admiring her handiwork. A wide smile appears on her face. "That's better."

Oh god, I'm lying in the mud, in the freezing Scottish rain. It's mid-day in an open field... and anyone could walk by. I'm lying with my combats at my knees exposing myself to the world and she has me tied up... I don't believe I'm allowing this.

Her hand is inside my shirt, tugging at my nipples, my cunt is getting wetter.

God, I want her mouth on me... in me.

I raise my hips, hoping she'll get the hint.

She doesn't... she still sits staring at me.

I'm beginning to feel very vulnerable. What is she waiting for?

She just continues to sit silently in front of me. What does she want from me? She's humiliated me, she's proven herself, what does she want now?

"Ask me!"

I look at her.

"Ask me to fuck you!"

I shake my head in disbelief... what kind of game does she think she is playing?

She stands up and turns to walk away.

"No!"

"Do you have something to say?"

My head is swimming. I don't know what I want... do I want to be fucked bad enough that I would ask this feminine little thing to do it?

"Please –" I feel so ashamed "– please don't leave me here, like this..."

I feel better that I had got it out, got it over with.

"What do you want me to do with you?"

Oh fuck... the little bitch is gonna make me fucking beg.

"Please, I want you to fuck me."

I am so ashamed...

She looks at me, her eyes cold, and then a small smile starts to crack over her lips...

A Piece of Her Night
Rosie Lugosi

Don't listen.

Don't listen when they call us sick. When they spit out deluded, dangerous, perverted, pitiful. Say we are *ugly, shameful, sick*. Oh, and the clincher. The one they save for purse-lipped, hymn-singing, prayerbook-clutching best. That what we do is *abuse*. Don't listen.

Their words; same as those used against us for centuries. Women, witches, queers. Shouted from pulpits, dredged up by the gutter press, whined by politicians with an eye to an election. We won, found our pride. We can do it again. Don't listen. Fight back.

They call it anger. You're not here for my anger, but for my passion.

Oh: your passion. The very thought makes me catch my breath. Run me full of it till I say I've had enough. Oh darling, you give me so much more. Not sweet hearts or flowers. You don't trick me with dime-a-dozen romances where girl meets girl and if they ever do get past the holding-hands stage, they talk about sex like it's *wet flowers,* and *furled petals*. I can read those lies in any bookstore. I want darker stuff to hold in my arms.

You do not have a *cavern of love*. You have a fat wet red cunt and, if I please you just right, you might let me stick my tongue up into you.

I want excitement. Surrender.

Run me full of it till I say I've had enough.

You've a long wait coming.

You know how I hate waiting.

I look at you, across the room. Start at your fingertips, up to your knuckles, then wrist, the smooth inside of your forearm to the crease of skin at your elbow. The roundness of muscle above. Your shoulder. And then. I can't lift my eyes to your face. Not yet. Not until you say.

I wore this dress for you. You've never said you like it; you're not that obvious. But I can tell. The way your hands stay longer at the dip of my waist, the curve of my hip where the fabric pulls tight into shiny creases. Fold me in half. I am your book. You can read me. Open me; wide. I've no secrets from you.

Mistress. Fuck me. I roll them round my tongue: all the words like this I'm not supposed to use. The red flag telling me *No, good girls don't talk like that.* But I've never been able to stick to anyone else's rules. I was always the one ripping opening packets in shops and coming home hours late. I ignored my homework and got sent home for dyeing my hair. I've always pushed it. Answered back. Getting slapped down and being told off was part of it. *Bad girl,* they said. *Naughty.* That's me. Rulebreaker. I'd smile at them to make it worse. To work them up. I always succeeded. Always got what I wanted. I was so bad, I was good at it. I never forgot that excitement, and I've searched for it ever since. And now I've found you. You're as bad as I am. Go on, call me names.

Slut. Bitch. All the words I'm not supposed to use. I love the way your eyelids droop when I speak. You can't help yourself. Like when I grab you by the scruff of your neck: I have to hold you up because your legs go slack at the knee.

Shall I do it to you now?

I watch you stalk around the room, running your fingertips along the back of the button-back leather sofa. Soft, black hide. Your mouth twitches; you know I'm a fool for leather. The creaking of a biker jacket: the sheen on new boots. The animal scent of my gloves, pushed up against your nose. I lounge against the bookcase, watching you make your catlike circuits of the room, slower and slower until you finish up in front of me, your head bowed, as I knew you would. Your eyes are shut tight, waiting for me.

Keep your eyes shut, I say.

Stand still.

Clasp your hands in front of you.

You know I'm here. In your dark space. Can you feel my breath on you? I'm standing so near. Breathing down the side of your face, so close it stirs that wisp of hair sneaking across your cheek. I walk around you. Can you sense me now? I'm standing at your back, speaking to the space between your shoulders.

Don't move. I said, *don't move.*

Your skin tightens into gooseflesh. What are you anticipating? All the things you're dreaming I might do? I can do so much: you know it.

You call me a slut. Bitch. I take it in like breath. It makes me gasp.

I take a few steps more. Do you know where I'm standing now? I said, don't speak. Keep your eyes shut.

I'm dreaming: of all the things we might do. All the things I love. My secrets, the ones you know.

What do you want? As if I didn't know. What have you got to offer me?

I love it when you let me suck your dick. Let me.

No, you say, when I ask.

You stand before me, the ring glinting in the harness over your pubic bone. You always take a long time choosing which cock you're going to wear. Tonight it's the smooth black silicone with the bulge at the tip.

Please.

No, you say, when I beg.

Please. Let me show you what I can do.

Show me then, you tell me.

I take two fingers into my mouth, hold them there rigid as your dick. Though nothing could be quite like that. The smoothness of you. Concentrate. I keep my mouth open, so you can see my tongue. How clever it is, wetting my fingers. Imagine it against your cock, how I'll warm you. I close my lips and push my fingers in, slowly. I don't take my eyes off you. Slide them in, out, till liquid runs over my knuckles.

I pull out my fingers and wipe them across my breasts. I know they're shining; I know how you love wetness. Mouth wetness. Cunt wetness. You're a sucker for it. Your pupils flare and I know I've got you. The way you press your lips together tight. Any minute now.

On your knees. Now.

I fall like a stone. My face is level with your dick. I lick the whole length of you until the silicone glistens. Only when you're dripping do I take you into my mouth, the tip at first, gradually swallowing more and more until my eyes water. You gasp. I'll never tell you that I've heard.

Enough. Stand up.

I'm on my feet, eyes on the floor. You never need to say it twice. You reach your hands round the back of my neck; there's the warm smell of leather, the sting of the steel buckle on the collar. I didn't even see you pick it up. You tighten it round my neck, slip two fingers under it and tug, gently. Enough to make me stumble, not enough to fall. Loop your thumb through the ring dangling at the front, under my chin.

Open your eyes. Now you're mine, aren't you?

Yes, I breathe. The word is tiny, but I can barely squeeze it out between my clamped teeth. I want to shout it, *yes, oh yes, forever*. But there's no time.

Your wrists. Hold them in front of you.

I hold out my hands, chin pressed down. Feel you fasten the cuffs; soft on the inside. I could pull as hard as I wanted, but I couldn't break away from them. *I'm yours*. It's all I can think about.

You turn me round, place one hand between my shoulders and I drop forward obediently over the curved back of the sofa. My dress rides up at the back; I feel air brush the top of my thighs. I chose a dress this short. I am a slut. You know it.

All I can see is cushions, and my cuffed wrists. You're waiting.

I look at the clock. One minute; two. I know this seems like hours for you. I can wait a long time. Listening to you breathe.

I've lost any sense of time passing. Then you tap my ankles with the tip of your crop.

More. Further apart.

You sound angry. But I know it's the deep growl of desire. I'll never tell you that I know this secret too. I move my feet apart, inch by inch. You tap again, once, and I stop. Another minute. At last, your hand on my foot: fastening the right ankle cuff first; then the left, adjusting the chrome bar between the two. I try to squeeze my legs together, feel the impossible resistance of the metal pole that thrusts them apart. Then, your fingernails up the back of my calves, knees, thighs. You take the hem of my dress and lift, slowly, pulling at the tightly stretched fabric until I'm bare-arsed. My buttocks twitch. I hear a rumble in your throat and I don't know if you're laughing.

You know I hate to wait, so you make me do just that. The skin of my butt and thighs shivers and still you pause. I can almost hear you smiling.

I can smell you from where I stand: rich and salty. The only perfume your own musk.

I wish I could hide my desire; that I wasn't so obvious. But I ache with longing and this waiting makes it worse. I can feel liquid smudge the inside of my thigh. You haven't even started. Then the first slap lands on my butt.

My hand snaps into a fist, then flattens out, palm open, straight and true as the wing of a hawk. I let it fall against you. *Slap.* Smack of skin on skin. *Slap.* Flesh blossoms rose pink. *Slap.* One butt cheek, then the other, in turns. Rubbing my hand over you and feeling the warmth as it grows. A small sigh leaks out of your mouth.

'What was that?' I purr, deep at the back of my throat. 'Did I say you could make a sound?'

I can't help myself. I know if I moan, you'll stop. Anything but that. I shake my head from side to side, tiny movements.

'Well then,' I say. 'Maybe you need a stronger reminder. Do you agree?'

This time you nod. I unclip the suede flogger from my belt and drape the tails across the gleaming skin of your buttocks. Watch you writhe under their velvet.

'Did I say you could move?' I bark, and you freeze.

I pause. The sight of you spread out before me makes my heart twist; a line of fire runs direct to my cunt. I swing the flogger, land the first stroke on your right buttock, then the left, back and forth, slow and leisurely to start, building up speed and force, massaging your flesh into letting go. Give it all up. Let it go. Let everything go and I will carry it all. I will drive you there.

The rhythm builds in my head; I hum with exertion, arm muscles singing. Watching your body ignite sparks me to a flame, driving away cold and fear. Opening you up to fire. Wings to carry you.

You are so careful with me. Each blow cares for my body. First, the slow light slaps to warm my buttocks. Blood rises to the surface of my skin and I feel them growing red. I lift my ass higher. I will not shake, I will not stumble. I offer you the greatest feat of balance that I can. I used to wonder if you were asking: *will you fall now?* But now I know you trust me. I'll stand strong for you. Each blow is placed with the precision of an artist; my skin your canvas. I am safe in your hands. All this for me.

I pause, run my hand over your hot skin, lay down the flogger and unclip the paddle from my hip. Rub it across your butt. You push yourself up into it. First, I make quick feathery taps down the inside and back of your thighs, building up speed and pressure. You suck in your breath: swift, small mouthfuls. I build up to loud satisfying smacks of leather against your backside. Your breathing levels out and I know you're flying, cresting a wave of pleasure.

I pause once more, run my fingernails down your spine to bring you back to me. You squirm. Again, I think *cat*, as you arch into my hand.

I lean forward, place my mouth next to your ear.

'And now...'

It's all I need to say.

At once I can sense you awake and attentive. I bite open the condom packet, snap the latex gloves before I put them on, knowing that you can hear. I rest one hand on your glowing rump while I roll the rubber onto my dick. Use my thumbs to open you wide. Run the rubbery head up and down your slit, wetting the very tip of me. You lift your ass as high as you can, silently begging me to enter. I always take my time. I hold myself steady, nudge into you, just the head, watch your thighs loosen. Tease you by holding myself there.

You gasp, don't even know you're doing it. I pull out a little, push in some more, deeper every time. You moan with each stroke of the silicone shaft, as though I am squeezing the sound out of you. I lean over and speak into your ear, very low.

'I'm wearing my biggest cock. It's the only way to fill a slut as greedy as you.'

You release a small whimper, muffled by the cushions, but I miss nothing.

'Did I say you could make a sound?'

You tense up. Good.

I press into you, up to the hilt. Your breath rakes in. I pull out and look down at your wetness glistening along the whole length of me. Concentrate on long slow strokes in and out: my dick pushing you into the sofa, the way I know you love it. I reach my arms around and scissor your nipples between my fingers. Squeeze and release. Squeeze, pull and release. You fight to stay quiet, to stay still. Your body shudders beneath mine.

'That's better,' I growl.

I wait until your shaking has subsided, then I undo the leg spreader and lift it away from your ankles.

'You think you're going to get away with that?' I rumble.

You turn, fall to your knees again before me. I take off the harness, and unzip my leather pants.

'Well?'

You hurry to drag my trousers down to my ankles, hands quivering.

'Worship me', I purr, and you bury your face between my thighs. I tip my chin to the ceiling and watch the shadows dissolve.

Cuvée Opulence
Cherry Smyth

Don't you love the sound of a tight cork being plucked from the neck of a wine bottle? Its history of tree, of earth, heat and toil softens my shoulders, wets the inside of my cheeks, loosens my tongue. It's a sign the worst is over, an aural signal that indolence can begin. Pop! Ahh! Like the feeling a perfect haiku gives – tautness and expansion all at once.

That Friday evening I wrapped a folded serviette round the bottle and poured the wine with a gesture that curved into a smooth upward twist – the only good thing I'd retained from my days and nights of waiting on tables in the Pelican Café.

'*Vino secco*, madam.' I stood to attention, my voice somewhere between servile and supercilious.

The lovely lady sipped and swallowed. I like watching things slip down her throat.

'Perfect,' she said in a clipped tone. 'Do be so kind as to join me.' Androula's attempt to mimic a posh English accent always turns me on. I imagine her working for the UN or the Greek government and being the one who wins back the Elgin Marbles.

I poured my own glass and sat down at our kitchen table. We shared a deliberating pause.

'Sea air,' she said.

She was right. The chilled *Domaine de Rhodes Sauvignon Blanc* evoked rolling down the windows at the first glimpse of the ocean after a long car journey.

'Sea air at dawn,' she went on, 'low tide, the wind from the north when the lavender is in bloom.' My mouth dropped open. She proceeded to pen her rapture on the tasting card that had come with the cut-price box of wine from an offer in the *Sunday Times*. This was our very own wine-tasting evening, a chance to practise our epithets before inviting others to come sail on our wine-dark sea.

The wine fizzed on the tip of my tongue, then tickled the sides with transparent fruitiness. 'Lychee, I would say. After too much black bean sauce.'

'God, it's enough to give you indigestion,' Androula mocked as only she can.

She sipped again and closed her eyes. She looked as though she was dreaming and trying to make the dream last. I hoped I was in it, wished I was the virgin wine passing *adagio* around her tongue. She seemed miles away. Kilometres, even. Will the metric ever infiltrate our distances? Ever since we'd re-watched *Bound*, I sensed Gina Gershon stomping around her fantasies.

'It tastes floral,' she said as she set down her glass.

As I waited for all the gardens of Sissinghurst to be conjured, Tina Modotti's photograph of roses bloomed in my mind. I could see those slightly wasted milk-white petals curling round edges of sepia shadow, packed closely together in the frame. That photo always makes me think of the affair Modotti had with Frida Kahlo and the paintings and photographs it must have influenced. I tasted again. It reminded my mouth of the first chew on a Wrigley's Juicy Fruit, but not because the wine tasted anything like chewing gum. It was more the memory of a freshness that you knew would fade. I used to put the knot of worn-out gum on my finger, let it cool and harden, then chew again on its renewed bite.

I looked at Androula. She was waiting for my response. I knew she'd scoff, so I kept schtum. I tried to love the way she balanced the stem of her glass, her fingers unfurling like a fan and I wanted to tell her about Modotti and Kahlo and Hannah Wilke, who dotted little vulvas shaped from chewing gum all over her naked body. I didn't know why I couldn't. Was our freshness fading? The thought broke into my brain like a burglar. I banished it and locked the windows, hoping the melancholy didn't spill into my eyes.

We'd both been working long hours, with no time or energy for sex for almost three weeks. What would renew our bite? I'd been pretending it didn't matter. But I began to realise that it wasn't just the sex I missed but the way we talk during and after that I cherish too. It makes me dissolve and come together again as a better, more intact human being. There was something missing about being alive – that exchange of spit and tongue and words and skin and looks and sighs and sweat and come. Was this the beginning of the seven-year itch that my beloved would not be the one to scratch? Yet she was everything I wanted – sexy, sassy, stroppy, opinionated and so self-assured. I looked into my glass and tried to contemplate cheerful, undramatic contemplations. I couldn't think of anything to say. From somewhere in my mental record collection slithered a tune and lyrics I could have done without. *'Is that all there is? Is that all there is? If that's all there is, my friend...'.* That nasty little song was creeping in to claim my heart, my tender, ever-hopeful, big gay heart. How could we survive the not-having-a-wedding row, not-having-a-baby blues, only to flounder on passionless pillows?

'Hello?' Androula was searching my face for the woman she'd fallen in love with.

I relaxed my jaw, jostled my shoulders as though I was coming out of a last-of-the-summer-wine reverie that had nothing whatsoever to do with death and dying and us.

'Hi,' I said. I suddenly remembered a teen magazine I used to buy in the seventies called Hi – *People who matter say 'hi'* – how I made myself learn to take on another nationality. I felt more than another nationality now - I was another species.

'We forgot to mention clarity and colour,' Androula pointed to a category on the tasting card. How like her, I thought, to go on with the social game, to keep our keel even and not follow my darkness. I wished I could take her finger in my mouth and suck on it but she seemed intent on serious oenology – she'd explained that morning that it comes from *'oinos'*, the Greek for wine.

A star formed and sparkled through the liquid as she held the glass up to the light. A blonde disk floated on its surface. It made me think of the way sunlight sometimes catches behind the pupil of Androula's eye and shines right through the white as if her beauty has drawn in a single sunray. I rallied a little. I felt something trying to link us, the way changes in light can change your mood.

'Clear as the night sky in Antarctica in summer,' I said, 'and the colour of dew.' I was looking into her eyes, no longer thinking about wine.

Two dimples dented her cheeks as she smiled. She licked her lips. She had no lipstick on and they looked docile and girlish. I love being the one who gets to see her lips bare, unready, touchable. I'm also the one who sees her at night, when she gets up to go to the loo, her T-shirt not quite covering the cheeks of her bum, the plump creased muscles moving freely before me. That was one of the first erotic dreams I recall having, when I was a small child myself. I was on the Strand Road at home, the sandy scuffed road that leads right onto the beach, the tarmac being gradually swallowed up. In the dream, a young girl of about four was walking up the road away from the strand, wearing nothing but a very short dress, her bottom the colour of bleached sand. Later that day, and for days and weeks later, I would re-dream the dream, watching her move away from me, so pluckable, trespassing the line from beach to road, from playing freely to being watched not playing, not realising the rules.

I drank a gulp of wine, forgetting to hesitate for taste. Maybe it's best, I began to tell myself, to just break out the booze, as the song goes, and become a drunken poet like Li Bai, cap lost to the wind, longing among blossoms and the moon.

'And aroma? Aren't you meant to do it first?' Androula swirled the Sauvignon and drew up its scent. I wanted to touch her stubborn, pretty chin. Both attributes had saved me before. Getting to know someone is so sexy that you fail to notice the point when you know too much and must pretend they're strangers to get aroused again. I tried to recall the first touch of her skin, its temperature and smoothness, the rough patch at the centre of her spine which makes her ass seem even fuller and softer, a veritable Rubens' woman. If the devil offered me total erasure, would I lose more by starting afresh with her than I gain from all we've built over the years? All them days, as my uncle said when his wife of fifty years died. All them days. It's what I'd longed for. A wife. A half-a-century-long love.

Androula's nose flared and she smiled. 'It smells angelically unaware, like your breath when you're asleep.'

'Really?' I said, thinking: that's all we do, is sleep. I sniffed feebly. I smelt nothing, like when you can't detect garlic on your own breath, so I lied, my gaze on hers.

'I can smell that time we went to the island of Naxos and – '

'You still remember Naxos?' she glowed.

'Yes, and we stayed... we... oh yes, we stayed in the room overlooking the garden of purple flowers, where we could smell salt and fresh cotton sheets and aubergines baking and petal perfume and where we never had to get up.' The memory made me believe it.

'We don't have to get up now.' Her voice was teasing, happy.

'True,' I said. She leant towards me. I could smell her warm sand and rosemary, her green apples better than any wine.

I kissed her. Our lips were pert at first, then rose and spread. Our tongues met, the wine fused and a thousand tastes exploded on each taste bud. Wild strawberries, French butter, Bazooka Joes, *moules marinières*, gruyère from an organic mountaintop untouched by soiled air...

'Yum,' I murmured through the kiss, my hands finding their place in the sexy little indent between her waist and her hips. My body recognised hers again, the language of touch restored. Relief made my pants bubble. 'That's my baby. You're my *appellation controllée*.'

She laughed and I stood up, pulling her to her feet.

'But we haven't mentioned length and quality,' she joked, setting down her glass.

'I'll show you length and quality, darling heart,' I said, moving my thigh between her legs.

She pushed herself and her two beautiful breasts into me. I was a fat ripe grape at harvest. I saw generations of women from her family, black-haired women of the strong tanned fingers, planting and tying up the vines, tending the grapes, waiting for their ripeness to scent the air. She would become one of them, had plans to plant her own vines outside our front door to make it really home.

We let our tongues savour their wine over and over, savouring each other, marvelling at the richness of spittle and the way it changes quantity and texture the more aroused you become. Then we drove each other down the hall into the bedroom, like trucks down a mountain road, all hard and hungry.

We raced to peel off each other's tops, fell on to the bed in our jeans and began to roll and wrestle like young Mediterranean men on a summer plain. I sat astride her, grabbed both her wrists but she buckled and twisted out of my grip. I love that. I let her be stronger than me. She tossed back her head. She was out of breath. Sweat daubed my chest. I reached to uncup her breasts from her bra and strained up to suck the nipples but she used her thighs to pin me down, turn me the way she wanted. I grasped her long hair in one of my hands and held it off her face and mine. I pulled her forehead to forehead and rubbed as if I was trying to take an imprint of her brow and what lay beneath it. I kissed her eyelids, her eyebrows, ran my tongue along their dark length. She opened her eyes and I sank in.

'You're back, *acushla machree*,' she whispered.

'Yes, precious one, I'm back.'

Then she was kneeling, unhooking her bra. Her breasts seemed to let out a little sigh that only my cunt could hear. She rolled them in her hands as if welcoming them back. Then she tugged off my jeans, her elbows easing apart my legs so that she could lower one breast to my pussy and mash it there, as if trying to enter me, getting it slathered in juice. Then she sat up again, lifted her shining breast up to her mouth and licked it.

'A very good year,' she whispered, her face lowered, eyes raised like Lauren Bacall.

There were brief moaning sounds coming from my throat, urgent commands to coax her to touch me. I rotated my hips like a homing device.

'Oh, there's more?' she cooed. 'How generous of you.'

She started by licking my thighs, teasing round the edges of my labia, then finally she lapped at my clit, making a new wine, our vintage, with a unique flavour that couldn't be bottled.

Funny how later, when we went back to the wine, took it from the fridge, for the last glass, how ordinary it tasted, how flat, how lacking in body, just like any old supermarket plonk in fact.

And the next night we tried the red.

My Forever Girl
Crin Claxton

My Forever Girl is very beautiful. Her hair is long, dark and lean. She can flick it back when she's feeling haughty, come to me with it dripping from the bath and drench me when she's feeling naughty, tie it out of the way when she's getting sporty. Don't know what she uses to make it shine and gleam like a panther in the steam of a rain forest. She would like me to know. Tries to tell me in great detail. But I tell her, "Baby, a butch's mind isn't made for such details."

She has eyes you would swing on ropes over ravines for. Eyes you could get lost in and never want to find your way home. She has long dark eyelashes, black widow spiders that make you not care how dangerous they are. Her lips sit on her mouth the way her thighs sit on her knees. One long invitation. She has a cute and curvy little body. Soft curling shoulders drawing you down to linger on her breasts. Hips designed to pull you closer. And her legs... Her legs sigh and moan when she's lazy, lying out in the sun. They wink at you when they're covered in black stockings. And they whisper your name when she pulls you down to the floor and opens them for you.

My Forever Girl talks to me from her heart. I listen much harder than she thinks I do. She thinks I don't listen because when I come home from work I want to watch 'The Simpsons'. She wants to tell me about her day, every single detail of her day. More details than you could possibly imagine anyone would have in a day. I get up, go to work, do my work. She gets up, goes to work and has conversations with people who tell her their life stories. She bewitches words out of me. Sometimes I get stuck inside myself. She holds me and looks at me till I'm swimming in her affection and softly, slowly the words come, till I'm saying things I never knew I felt. Hearing myself say the strangest things.

My Forever Girl likes to play. Last week we played plumber on an emergency call-out. I was the plumber, she was the emergency call-out. I got into my overalls, grabbed my tool bag and drove over to 'her' (my best mate lent us her flat for the night) house. I rang the bell.

"Yes, who is it?" Her voice came over the intercom.

"Plumber, madam." I spoke into the little box.

"Oh yes. I can see you are."

I looked coolly at her into the tiny camera (my mate's into high tech).

"Come on up."

The door was released. I walked up the stairs, clutching onto my tool bag. I played with the weight of the bag, trying to find the best position to bulge my biceps. Casually you understand, hardly perceptible.

I knocked on the flat door and a second later it slowly opened. She stood before me in a satin robe, and what looked suspiciously like stockings.

"Come in." she breathed, stepping back into the room and beckoning me in.

"I hope you don't mind how I'm dressed," she said. "I was just about to take a bath when I got my plumbing problem."

In stockings?! was my immediate thought. Which I didn't share. After all, I'd just met the woman, and she was a customer. I knew my boss would want me to keep my customers happy.

"Nice muscles, by the way," she threw over her shoulder as she walked in front of me to the bathroom.

"So what seems to be the problem?" I asked, looking round the gleaming, white glass and chrome, and extremely dry bathroom.

"Oh." She looked around too. "A leak, I think."

I smiled at her. "Well, d'you know where the leak is?"

"Um... the bath," she decided. "You're going to have to get down on the floor, undo that thing –" She was pointing dismissively at the bath panel, "– that thing on the side of the bath, and grapple about with the pipes, I think."

I looked at her. "Well, thanks for the advice, madam."

"My pleasure." She smiled her *I know you think you're patronizing me* smile.

I undid the bath panel and sort of looked about a bit with my Maglite. I peered up at the pipes.

"Umm…" I said, as if I was considering the problem very seriously.

"Can you see the problem?" she bent down and put her head very close to mine. I could feel the warmth of her skin and feel the heat of her breath next to my cheek.

"Yes, I think so," I grunted.

She looked at me, holding my gaze, keeping me there until she turned her head swiftly away and dropped me.

"Well, I'll just get my wrench."

"Oh sorry, I thought you said 'wench'." She curled her lips into a smile and winked. "Can I help you with that?" Sticking out her chest.

"Yes, I can imagine you could." I managed.

"Is… this it?" She held up my trusty 6", silver and gleaming in her upturned wrist.

"Yes, thank you." I held out my hand and ducked my head under the bath. I felt her hand on my hand, separating my fingers. Then I felt her lips suck one of my fingers deep up inside her mouth. I hit my head on the bath and still she didn't let go, holding and sucking and thrusting her tongue over and around my finger. Finally, I felt the wrench sliding into my hand and I gripped it. I didn't know whether to carry on trying to find the plumbing problem, so I came out from under the bath and stared at her for a while.

"Why don't you get on with it?" She got up with a flounce. "I'm not paying you to lie around."

I got back under the bath.

"Can I get you anything?" The silkiness had returned to her voice. "A drink perhaps."

"Overproof & Coke please," I suggested.

"Overproof... well... I'm not sure you should drink on duty."

"I'm a plumber, not a policeman, remember."

"Policewoman," she corrected me.

"Whatever," I muttered.

I didn't bother to do anything while she went to get the drinks. Then I got bored and looked at the pipes out of interest. It occurred to me maybe I should have a bit of dirt on me or something and I ran my hands under the bath to get some. There was plenty. Made me think maybe I should hoover under our bath when we got home. It's frightening how much dust there is under there.

"How are you getting on?" She placed my drink beside me.

I came out and took a glug.

"Oh, you've got a little smudge on your cheek. Here, let me." She wiped it off. With the corner of her robe, revealing a healthy slice of thigh.

"Well, aren't you going to use your wrench?" she inquired. "I bet you took a long time picking it out. While some poor, but gorgeous, woman tapped her pretty little foot waiting for you. I can see why, though. It's very... handsome."

I picked up the wrench and tightened up a nut.

"I'm sure that's at the right torque now." I said, not knowing if that had anything to do with plumbing whatsoever.

"Ohh, she said, "it looks tight."

"Nice and tight." I confirmed.

"I think you need to do some very strenuous activity," she suggested.

"Do I?" I worried, thinking there's only so many nuts that don't need to be tightened to play with here.

"Well, you might get very *hot* in your overalls if you did something strenuous."

"Oh." I got it, and decided to feel along the pipes, grunting and play-tightening with my bare hands - which was a lot more strenuous than using a wrench and did bring a sweat out on my forehead, eventually.

"Phew, it's hot under there." I emerged sweaty and now very

dirty and dusty, I washed my hands at the sink.

"My, my," she breathed. "Look at you, what have you been up to under there? Seems to me you've got far too many clothes on."

I swallowed. "Well, these overalls are very warm." And as an afterthought, "They need to be if I have to do a pipe outside... or something."

"Well, let me help you..." She began unbuttoning my overalls, one by one moving further and further down, when she got to my waist she didn't stop until all my fly buttons were down too.

"You want them completely off?" I stuttered as she pulled my bare arms free, slipped the overalls off my shoulders running her hand along my muscles, and started easing them off my hips.

"Completely off," she confirmed. "I really do think you're very, very hot."

Now in my vest and boxers she took a long look at me.

"Oh, you look so much happier now." she said after a while. "And if you're happy, I'm happy."

"I'm happy." I smiled, "But you seem a long way away."

She looked at me, her head to one side. "Well, I was just thinking... Now you've solved my plumbing problem, is there any way I can thank you." And with a single movement opened her robe. She was wearing stockings, a basque and no knickers. I just stared. I think I was in a state of shock. Eventually she helped me out. "If there's any way... *any way* at all," she prompted.

"Well, there is one thing you can do for me."

"Oh yes." She came forward expectantly.

"You could help me try out a new tool I've brought," I suggested. Her eyes widened. "Oh really. What is it? Show me."

I reached into my tool box and brought out a small length of plastic conduit. It's electrical conduit, really, not plumbing – but I didn't think she'd care about that.

"Well, *what* do you do with that?" she arched her eyebrows.

"Shall I show you?"

She looked at me, pouting her lips into a smile. Then she nodded. Slowly.

"Well... it has to be very clean." I showed her it was very clean.

"And then…" playing with the edge of her cunt, opening her very slightly "… then you insert it." Sliding the conduit into her, little by little, moving back and into her again. She reached up for the pipe, pushing herself around it, moving with me while I took her breasts in my mouth one by one, sucking hard on her nipples. She was all over the conduit, her nipples exploding in my mouth and I was trying to stop her coming just so this wouldn't have to stop. And then she did come, despite my best efforts. And the rest of the building must have heard her.

We lay looking up at the ceiling a while. Well, neither of us had really looked at Joy's ceiling before.

"I'm so glad you came to fix my leak," she smiled.

"Is it fixed now, then?" I asked.

"Well," she furrowed her brow, "I'm not sure… It seems to be –" she reached for my boxers "– very wet in here. Maybe there's another leak." Her fingers sliding inside my shorts. "Let me see, I'm sure I can find it. Oh yes. Here it is." Her fingers were inside me and opening me. "I think I can fix it." She played with me, finding me very wet after her incredible performance earlier.

"See what you do to me," I grunted.

"Mmm… nice… and wet. This is definitely the source of the leak. I need to… play about a bit here for a while. I need to… plunge… up a lot and… move in and out… and… I may need to…" pulling me over and on top of her, "…move you about a bit just so… I can get deeper… if I need to… And I need to… this really is a very… big… leak."

And then I don't remember what she said. I just needed to move. Move on her, letting her have me. Have whatever she wanted. I just wanted her. Here and now. This woman, this moment, this fuck. I came splendidly.

My Forever Girl is very inventive. She doesn't believe in a boring sex life. Says lesbian bed-death is a homophobic plot and we should take no notice. She knows how sexy she is. I like that. Of course, it's a fine line between bravado and bragging. My Forever Girl said to me in the first few months we got together: "You can forget it if you think I'll put up with you putting it about everywhere. I'm not interested in playing to your ego."

That took some getting used to. There've been years when my ego's been all I've had. She showed me how tough can be what you do, not what you say.

My Forever Girl holds me when I get scared. I don't admit it a lot but even a big, tuff, confident butch like me gets scared sometimes. When she holds me the years roll away until the child inside me finally feels safe. My Girl's been there in the middle of the night pulling my head down onto her shoulder, kissing my forehead until the nightmare fades into the back of my mind again. She's seen me like that. And she still wants me.

My Forever Girl wants to believe we'll be together for a very long time. But sometimes doubts creep in her head and she's obsessive detective. She opens a casebook and documents evidence against me. My movements are noted. She asks lots of questions. My previous convictions *are* taken into account. When I've had enough I say to her, "Baby, we'll be together forever. No point fighting it." Sex can be scary, but love is the scariest thing of all. I know that. If anyone has the guts for it she does. And so do I.

My Forever Girl makes the sun shine on a dull rainy January day. She is the reason I love for. I love how her body fits into mine, whether dancing, cuddling or making love we fit. I wish for her diamond stars in the blue velvet of a midnight sky. She makes me want to get a legal gig. She is my child's dream of love all grown up and just how I imagined it.

My Forever Girl would have you believe she's cool as a waterfall. But I've seen the look in someone's eye passing her on the street. And I've seen that look from lesbians too. I've seen her dissed for being the gorgeous femme, and I've seen her dissed for being the beautiful black woman she is. I've held her in my arms and let my love swell and grow when she's aching from the pain of it. It was my girl who told me, "When you're really strong you can cry." She likes to Communicate and I'm getting used to it. She says she wants me to grow.

"Baby, I ain't never gonna get taller now," I tell her. And she knows I know what she was really talking about. I want to explore this love and push back the barriers that keep me from her. I used to say, "Baby, I need you." But it was only when I learned I didn't need her, that every day of my life I choose her, it was from that moment I knew she would be my Girl... Forever.

Sound Check
Scarlett French

"And cut," exclaimed my director. "Nice work, Juliet – perfect first take. We'll have a short break before we do the vox pops. Back here in 20 minutes."

George, our sound operator, leaned his boom against a wall and drifted towards the gate for a cigarette, his headphones dangling around his neck. I took a drink from my water bottle and started towards the main dance floor at the other end of the complex. We'd been shooting solid for an hour – intros, outros, pieces to camera, interviews with revellers. I loved being a TV presenter but I needed a break. Presenting for the biggest queer dance party of the year would bring a lot of kudos for me in the community but it was a story I would have preferred to be part of, rather than covering.

My crew were great guys: Dave was director and camera op, a difficult balance at times. George was sound op and purveyor of stylish clothes. Every time I saw him he was impeccably dressed in tartan trousers and black turtlenecks, or in some other offbeat and eclectic combination. Both Dave and George were straight, but they were sensitive to queer issues and didn't do that suppressed cringe common with straight men around gay men. They were both freelancers, but I used them for every story because they were reliable and appropriate and we'd built a good rapport. George had hit on me once and I must confess there was a bit of a spark between us. But it was never going to happen - I wasn't interested in men in that way even if I fantasised about it occasionally. It was one of those erotic thoughts that just wouldn't work in the flesh.

I was feeling pumped, full of adrenalin and the enjoyment of being looked at by hungry eyes as I strode past a seating area full of bull dykes, heading towards the far dance floor to look for my girlfriend. I was wearing a black halter neck and very tight black nylon trousers that went up my crack and rubbed my clit as I walked. I knew they hugged my tight little arse and they shone a little in the light, accentuating its peach-like curves. I felt myself being watched and I relished every step, all the while feeling a building heat in my cunt as I thought about my beautiful girlfriend and felt the rubbing of the trouser seam on my hardening nub.

I reached the dance floor and took the stairs up to the balcony overlooking the DJ. I leaned my elbows on the rail and looked into the pulsating crowd, searching for my girl. It took only a minute. There she was, right in the middle of the floor where she said she'd be, caressed by the music, moving with a deep primal rhythm. My soft butch sexy bitch, grounded and grinding, under the strobing coloured lights.

She was magnificent. I wanted her. I always wanted her. Our hunger for each other hadn't waned since the day we'd met outside a bar in the rain. Outside a bar in the pelting spring rain, waiting for cabs. I keep our meeting story gritty by the detail no soft focus lens could capture – her nipples visibly hard and rosy through her sopping white T-shirt and, minutes later, my eager tongue flickering over them, sucking them into my mouth through the wet cotton. That's what it was like with us; hot, urgent. Always. My mouth watered watching her and I felt my pussy lurching with want, the crotch of my thong saturated.

At that moment she looked up and I caught her eye. I knew she was horny, too. She smiled that languid smile of hers and gestured for me to meet her by the open door. I made my way downstairs to her, grateful for the fresh air from the cooling October night.

"I've got 15 minutes," I said, running my hand down her strong, sweaty back.

"Come with me baby." She grabbed my hand and led me quickly down the dim, club-lit corridor leading to the toilets. A couple of gay boys passed us and cooed, "Love the show!" I smiled thank you and we both walked faster, searching out a quiet corner. My girl used to bartend in this complex and knew every nook and cranny. She pulled me down a blind corridor that stopped with a single locked door and pushed me firmly against the wall. We were alone in the humid dark, the music from the next room muffled-loud and bass-y. I felt her breath on my neck, raising the tiny hairs in anticipation.

"You're all hot baby, why is that?" She touched my cheek. "You need to step outdoors?" She slid her hand over my clit and squeezed, just a little. Not enough. I let out a soft moan. "Or you need something else?" She squeezed again, dragging her fingers firmly back and forth over my aching cunt. I twitched, a spasm of pleasure running through my swollen clit.

"We don't have long, baby. What am I going to do with you in ten minutes?"

"Fuck me." I looked straight into her eyes, challenging her. "Fuck me!" I hissed, desperate for her cock. I hadn't felt her crotch but I was sure she was packing tonight. She had that raw air about her when she was harnessed up in public.

"Oh, that's what you'd like, isn't it? That's what you want. But you get a lot of what you want so maybe you'll just have to wait for it. Maybe tomorrow, baby."

She undid the faux mountaineering clip at the top of my trousers and unzipped me all the way down. She shoved her hand, roughly, inside my underwear and I was ready for her – hot, swollen and slick with juice. Her middle finger found my straining clit easily and stroked me right there, right on my hard little nub, over and over; rubbing, circling, pushing her finger back towards my cunt, teasing me. I was breathing hard, rasping, unconcerned that we might be discovered. That just made it hotter.

And then her finger slipped into my wet cunt. I caught my breath.

"Oh baby, you feel so good," she whispered in my ear. I clenched my muscles around her finger and she shuddered. "All right, baby, if that's what you want, that's what you get. You want me to fuck you? Huh? Is that what you want?"

I nodded, coyly. I wouldn't show triumph. She always gave me what I wanted but sometimes she made me wait if I was too presumptuous. It was a game we played, a game with a delicate balance. Her finger slid in and out of my pussy, causing the most delicious, desperate pleasure. But I wanted more of her. I wanted her cock. The cock she bought for me. The cock she knew would fit me good, just that little bit too big. The kind of cock I'd have to be dripping for.

She slid my tight nylon trousers down to my ankles. My oversized platform boots wouldn't allow me to remove them. I had no choice but to squat down a little, parting my legs from the knees, my feet firmly held together. I heard her zip coming down and watched with panting need as her jeans dropped to her ankles and her boxers quickly followed. I could have begged, could have broken my rule about begging, but she saw it in my eyes and that was enough for her. She pinned me to the wall and slammed her dick into me. Hard, up to the hilt. A deep cry escaped me as I felt the length of her desire filling me. She was never this quick, but I couldn't wait any longer and she knew it. She always read me with precision.

"Is this what you wanted, baby?" Her voice was gravelly in my ear. She thrust into me again, hard. "Is it? My stiff dick inside you? That's what you've been needing all day, isn't it baby?" She thrust into me again and again as she spoke, her cock slick with my juice as she plumbed my depths, driving it into and out of me with dizzying rhythmic perfection. Every time she thrust into me, the harness slammed into my clit, nudging upwards, rubbing it bottom up just the way I liked it. I could make only small movements to meet her thrusts; she had me pinned to the wall and I was trapped by my trousers, bunched and tight around my ankles. I felt a pinch in my back and slithered my hand around to smooth the back of my halter neck. I felt a wire, a long thin wire running the length of my back.

At that moment I realised that my radio mike was still on, attached to the back of my trousers on the floor around my ankles. The tiny microphone was still clipped to my bra and it was live. Through the fog of my cunt-driven brain I realised with a jolt that George could be listening. If any noise had been loud enough he would have heard it, even with his headphones around his neck. I couldn't stop us, though, couldn't bear to break the moment to reach down and find the off switch on the radio mike pack. As my girl's dick thrust into me again with force a delicious thought ran through my mind. Maybe he was getting off on this, too. That's kinda cool, spreading the fun around. I wasn't interested in touching him but the thought of him touching himself while me and my girl fucked made me hornier, wetter, hungrier. My cunt started to clutch and grab, milking my girl's cock.

I felt taken over by her, by my own desire and by the thought of a voyeur. I was panting like a dog, hard, fast and guttural. She was grunting from deep in her guts as she fucked me hard and it was this that finished me off. My orgasm rocketed out of my body like a Guy Fawkes display. I cried out as I bucked and twisted on her shaft. She collapsed against me for a moment to feel my spasms before slowly and gently pulling out of me. We looked at each other for a moment, with a mixture of love and satiety.

"Fuck, 20 minutes! I only had 20 minutes. I must be late!" I pulled my trousers up, zipped and clipped, and kissed her squarely on her hot mouth as she slipped her cock back inside her trousers.

"Come and find me when you're finished, baby, I'll be dancing." She turned to walk away, then turned back. "By the way, your mike's on." She smirked at me and began sauntering back towards the dance floor. She knew! She knew and she didn't say anything. It made me want her all over again. Our chemistry was explosive, but even if I'd been revelling rather than working there would have been no more, not just yet. She liked to build it up, she liked to tease herself. She'd take one slowly built up orgasm for every four of mine. That was the way she liked it. I watched her sexy arse moving as she walked away from me then I broke into a run to reach the end of the complex.

Half an hour had passed. I reached our meeting point and looked first at Dave. At least my panting could be attributed to the running.

"You're late," said Dave, slightly annoyed. "Ten minutes late. Time is money y'know, especially for camera crew."

"I'm sorry, Dave. There was a long queue at the bar."

"Well, I'll let it go this time. I got time for an extra beer and George got a couple of smokes. You look a little flushed, you ought to have rested."

"Nah, I had a quick dance, Dave, it keeps me hyped."

"All right, let's get set up for vox pops."

I looked at George. For someone who'd spent half an hour smoking by a gate on a cool evening, he was looking pretty warm and relaxed. His hair also seemed a little sweaty on the ends, like he'd recently been in a hot enclosed space. I looked at his headphones. They were around his neck as before, but I could see beads of sweat on the earpieces, glistening in the lights from the event complex. I smiled at the thought, hoping he'd had a good time on me.

Cecily and the Boy
Winsome Lindsay

Everyone knew that Cecily BonEnfant had the most gorgeous legs in the state of New York. Everyone, including Cecily. She was a self-aware, carefree girl with a shining laugh and a taste for the unusual and gay. She had several friends in the circus and adored Zora Neal Hurston, Gertrude Stein and countless others who were considered unfashionable in her set. This was 1923 and, like most girls her age, Cecily loved to have fun, drink and party until the sun rose, and even after.

Her parents were happy, equally carefree people. Her father was always traveling abroad, especially in France where he could be with those like himself, other Black intellectuals who liked to drink and discuss politics and art into the late night hours. He left his white wife, whom he still loved very much, and his pale-skinned daughter to the trials and treasures of America.

Cecily loved the arrangement and her mother, Madelyn, must have too, because she partied as much as Cecily did, staying out late with her friends, having as much fun, if not more, than girls half her age. Cecily loved her mother, but it was a distant kind of love, the sort that most reserved for their god on Sundays or for sorbet on a hot summer afternoon.

One day, Cecily went to yet another party. She thought it would be a party much like the others. The music was good and fast, just like she liked it. Unlike most Flapper girls, she still wore her dresses long. Sometimes they even brushed the floor, hiding the toes of her dancing shoes. It was always more of a surprise when the boys realized what good legs she had under all that lace or silk. When the music started, she would shake her shoulders and her hips like the rest of the girls, but keep her muscled brown legs covered. As the night wore on and her skin glowed with sweat, Cecily would throw up her skirts, flash their glory, and then cover them up again before the night was through. She never drank so much that she forgot to put her skirts back down.

On this particular night, the boys watched and waited for her to flash those darling legs of hers. Those who were new to Cecily were crowded out—they didn't know about the splendor about to be revealed. The usual round of girls and boys had already staked out their place next to her earlier in the evening on the dance floor.

One boy was new to the New York scene and so was also new to the phenomenon that was Cecily; but he had already seen her sleek cap of wavy dark hair with its diamond clips. Something about her drew him. It might have been that full mouth of hers or those brown eyes, all sparkling and wicked. Whatever it was, the boy was already enchanted, though for reasons of his own, he kept a good distance from the cocoa and cream beauty.

The evening grew later and the music got wilder and faster. Buttons and ribbons loosened, but the boy noticed that more suitors crowded around the scintillating Cecily even though hers—buttons and ribbons, that is—stayed right where they had been at the beginning of the night. He decided that even with his secrets he had to be near her. Then Cecily began to passionately dance the Charleston and those luscious legs of hers were revealed again and again. That decided it.

Eight or nine dances later, Cecily left the dance floor to find some refreshment. Some determined boys, despite being given firm "no's" many times before, tried to get the fair Cecily a drink and whisk her off to some quiet corner. She talked with them, took their drinks, and even laughed at their jokes, throwing her head back to reveal a delectable throat. Cecily invited some to come to her house for a party one day soon, but she didn't go off to anybody's quiet corner. Her girl friends were more interesting or at least were more *interested* in what Cecily had to say about the current state of Prohibition and the gangsters in Harlem.

The very interested boy drank while Cecily drank, watching her from the corners of the ballroom. When she was finally alone, he took his chance.

"You have a beautiful laugh."

Cecily looked up, surprised. Boys never complimented her on her laugh. Her legs, certainly. Her eyes, once in a while. One boy had even had the audacity to comment on the curve of her bosom. But her laugh? She smiled.

"Thank you, sir."

"Not 'sir', please. My name is Maria."

Cecily blinked and looked again. The boy was a splendid vision. Masculine and slim in top hat and tails, a blinding white tuxedo shirt and black pants that flowed over long legs like water. His soft mouth seemed to be made for laughter.

"Well…" Cecily said.

They drank together until the party was over, sharing laughs and the unusual details of each other's lives. Then Cecily invited Maria to her house for a swim. The boys at the party gaped in amazement. The girls stared with jealousy too, some at Maria, others at the boy.

The house was dark when they arrived in Cecily's car, a brand new Model T. They drove past the main building, past the immediate back yard and grounds to a patch of forest land. Back there was a hot spring that her mama's family had discovered long ago. When the weather was chilly the waters were more popular, but now that they were in the sweltering heat of summer, nobody wanted any part of it. That's why Cecily liked it. She could be alone here and imagine herself on some far off island as she floated naked under the stars. She always swam naked here.

Tonight Cecily had drunk much more than usual. The charming boy had taken her off guard. They laughed so much that no one bothered to count the drinks. Those drinks were many. Now, Cecily, at the ripe old age of nineteen, was a girl who knew how to hold her liquor. She could be ten sheets to the wind and would still carry herself like a queen, crown and all. The boy had similar skills. However, the unusual amount of drink loosened their tongues and inhibitions.

"I have never met a woman quite like you, Cecily," the boy said. His gaze said how very much he would like to see Cecily naked, but he was too well mannered to mention it. Even with two gallons of gin in him.

"I could say the same to you." Cecily took off his hat to reveal shining blond hair. She put the hat on the grass. The boy watched her bend down, watched the water's reflection shimmer on her skin. There were kerosene lamps surrounding the pool. They lit two of them with Cecily's matches and watched each other with eyes that burned just as brightly as the flames. She loosened his bow tie.

"Come swimming with me." Her gaze was a tease. Laughter hovered on the edge of her voice.

They became naked together, buttons loosened on her dress, then on his pants. The silk shirt floated to the grass, then it was shoes, socks, small bits of underwear, and gloves. Up close, Cecily's legs were indeed beautiful, strong and graceful like those of a peak-career racehorse; but it was all of her, this perfect, glowing girl, that captivated Maria.

Cecily wasn't a girl to show her body lightly. She was a tease, she'd be the first to admit, but to shed her clothes, all of them, as if she wanted the eyes of someone else on her, well that was an entirely different matter. The boy had issues of his own, like the thatch of pale pubic hair with the pair of lips and clitoris that immediately made themselves known. And there were those two breasts that rose from his chest like miniature half moons, small and shapely. Cecily immediately wanted to know their taste, to feel them against her own, but that wasn't something she would say out loud.

"May I touch you?" she asked anyway.

"Yes."

But shyness overtook Cecily and she plunged into the warm water instead. The boy followed, wanting to feel those brown limbs wrapped around him, to feel the wetness that he knew she would have for him. They played like dolphins, diving into the deep water and circling each other, brushing against legs, backs, breasts until they were both a little hotter than before. Eventually, they had to get out of the water. The boy rose, dripping, first. His body was betraying him in the old ways, tightening and moistening. Cecily followed, breathless and slick with water.

"Use my underwear to dry off," she commanded. "I have plenty back at the house."

The boy did, consciously searching for the scent that was Cecily, musky and womanly. He found it and buried his face in it. Cecily led him to the dress that she had spread out in the grass.

"Let's lay here."

Tonight's dress was simple, a long cotton number that was white with vertical forest-green stripes. Not many women would have been able to make that look good, but Cecily did. The dress was big enough to protect both their bodies from the prickling of the grass.

"Touch me," the boy said.

Cecily did, learning the geography of that pale skin that was different from her own, the slender shoulders with their sprinkling of tiny brown freckles, the throat that was slim yet strong, pale breasts that shone in the light and their strawberry hard nipples. Cecily's tongue tested their flavor and found them sweet, gasping low in her throat with pleasure even as the boy trembled under her, grasping Cecily's head to him, whispering things that neither of them had thought to speak before. When the girl parted the boy's legs it was out of curiosity. There was that beguiling moisture, the woman's body that unfurled under her fingertips like rose petals.

"Please," the boy begged.

Nervousness overcame Cecily despite the many glasses of gin and she withdrew, although her fingers did keep sneaking up to her nose. The boy could only look at Cecily, awed by the simple beauty of her body, the supple waist and legs, that powerful back and buttocks that he longed to bite and tease apart. His fingers wanted to touch her thighs and the breasts that were like the exotic pomegranates he'd eaten in Mexico years before. His nose captured her scent and held it.

They stared at each other, beauty beholding beauty, before Cecily finally reached out. She surprised him. They boy thought that she would like the others, would play with him but only to a certain point, withholding her woman's treasure from him even after he begged prettily with his skilled tongue. Cecily touched the boy's skin, tracing the softness between his legs, diving in where she had hesitated before. He smelled like summers on the Vineyard, warm and salt and wet. Her boy fell back on the improvised blanket with a sigh of wonder. Cecily pleasured herself by pleasuring him, curiosity compelling her to suck and lick at the weeping pink flesh, to drink the cream seeping from inside. She remembered how she liked to touch herself and took the sensitive button of flesh between her tongue and teeth, agitating it until the boy's hand clenched in her hair. Above her, he breathed her name and gasped. His thighs trembled like butterfly wings under her palms.

Through slitted eyes, the boy watched the graceful rise of her back and buttocks toward the night sky, their restless snakelike movements as she licked him wet, pulling pleasure from him in a long golden string of gasps and breaths and sighs. He longed to come up behind her, to plunge his tongue into her wetness to fuck her pretty pussy until she felt what he was feeling now, ecstasy blown on top of ecstasy with her clever finger buried to the hilt inside his woman's body. He came apart under her.

Cecily lifted her head, smiling. Dark waves of her hair fell in mink waves around her face and shoulders. Her mouth was wet with Maria. The boy pulled himself from his lassitude to tug Cecily down to the grass scented dress and borrow into her throat.

"I think," he said, licking the taste of himself from her face, "that you're going to make me fall in love with you."

The girl spread her legs for him when he sought entrance. Still kissing her, he stroked her eager young pussy, sliding his fingers over the thick tumescent pearl of her clit, over the dewy lips, then teased the shy opening. She wriggled under him, breathless and anticipating. He was her music. Cecily could feel it building inside her like the opening notes of the Charleston, faint yet compelling. His mouth tasted soft and fresh against hers, like a peach she wanted to devour, but her quickening body needed it elsewhere. She tugged at his hair until he settled that hot mouth on her nipples and sent the music tearing through her. The boy was inside. Her eyes fluttered at the sky, stared hard at the remnants of blue in the darkness, the brilliance of stars that felt like they had fallen inside her and were shooting back into the sky with each agitated moan, each push of the boy's fingers inside her. It was like dancing, really, sweat washing between her breasts, breath coming fast and uncontrolled, legs trembling as he pushed her past the point of exhaustion.

She was perfection. Breasts shuddering and heaving under him as her orgasm neared, legs splayed wide past the boundaries of the dress, her toes digging into the grass. Her hungry pussy swallowed his fingers, eager, creamy, and hot. He tugged her nipple hard with his teeth and she mewled his name and came, jerking against his hand. Her hair clung to her face in damp strands, dark against the wide, gasping mouth. After all her stars had floated away, she stared at her boy in amazement. He had done this thing to her. Cecily filled her arms with him, kissed his soft hair and flushed skin. She fit her legs neatly around him.

"Again, please."

He laughed.

Hours later, they fell asleep on Cecily's dress, wrapped together face to face until the morning sun found them.

The boy woke first and dressed himself. Experience had taught him that it was best to do so. When Cecily awoke she felt like it was Christmas, that there was something wonderful waiting for her when she opened her eyes. The boy sat inches from her, watching her. He was beautiful in the sunlight with his top hat on, his pale eyes and face shaded, the mouth vulnerable and soft.

"Good morning."

"I still want you," the boy said. "If you don't want me anymore, you'll never see me again."

Cecily slid up into the boy's arms. "Don't be silly." Then she put on her clothes, set her hair to rights, and drove Maria home.

At the house, Cecily tried to sneak past her mother's room, but Madelyn heard her. "Are you just now getting in, Cec?"

"Yes." She paused at her mother's door as if expecting something, but there was no speech.

"Okay, my darling," her mother said. "Wash up and come to breakfast."

Cecily giggled and dashed away to her room. In from of her long, gilt-edged mirror, she undressed her body, remembering her night with the boy. Next time, Cecily thought, touching herself, she would know even better how to please him. Her fingers stroked her belly, the rough curls beneath, then the responsive pearl between her thighs. It was like the boy was with her now, breathing deeply in her room, filling her with softness and tight anticipation. Cecily had to see him again.

The young, gay girl approached partying with a new abandon. What if the boy was at the next party? Would things continue as before? She hoped so. She needed it to be so.

At the next party there was nothing. Only the usual boys who tried to drink her under the table and touch her legs like they were trophies. When the music was fast enough for the Charleston or the Shimmy, Cecily danced like a girl inspired, flashing her legs and shaking her shoulders like she was in one of her father's churches and taken over by a spirit. The boy never materialized from the crowd. At the end of the night, Cecily went home with a group of girl friends and lay awake with them, talking about politics and the allure of girls who wore pants and top hats.

Weeks passed in an agony of slowness.

Soon, it was Cecily's turn to have an extravagant party. Her large house was draped in silks and velvets. Gin flowed from clever fountains set atop tables in every room and the house sparkled like it was lit with a million diamonds. Her mother had already abandoned the quiet upstairs of the house, where none of the revelers were allowed, for the shining gaiety of the party in full swing. Madelyn BonEnfant laughed as she danced by her daughter on the arm of a long-haired Spaniard. Cecily wasn't laughing. She hadn't seen the boy in weeks and she was beginning to get even more offers than usual from the other boys. It was all wearing on her nerves. She was even considering writing to her father so he could send a steamer to whisk her to Paris with him. Perhaps the boy was there. Cecily pouted and swept back upstairs to change her clothes. Everything disappointed her tonight.

In the empty hallway just outside her bedroom, Cecily stood before a long mirror with a cigarette in hand, its smoke bleeding from the gold ciggie holder that had been a gift from her mother last year.

"Is there no one in this blasted place to help me with my dress?" The dress in question gaped at the side from an open set of pearl buttons that ran from the curve of her breasts to her hip. Cecily didn't really need help, she just felt like whining. She hadn't seen her boy in forever and her mood was turning foul.

"I'll help." The soft soprano said from the end of the hall. Cecily looked up in pleasure. She didn't even bother to ask how he got into the house. It didn't matter. He was back.

"Okay." She turned her side to the charming young man, hiding her smile.

The dress was made of a deep chocolate lace stitched over an under-dress of the same luscious shade as her skin. The long, draping skirt caressed her hips and legs as it made its way to the floor. Her back was completely bare, except for six tiny silver chains that formed swaying bridges from one edge of the dress to the other.

The boy's hands slowly fastened the buttons while his greedy eyes devoured the sight of Cecily's soft shadowed skin that held the light like an amber-shaded Tiffany lamp.

"Would you like anything else?" the boy asked, wealthy and slim looking in a tuxedo shirt and tails, black pants and again that top hat. Both their eyes burned.

"Of course." Cecily put out her cigarette and embraced the boy. "Tell me where you've been. Tell me that you'll stay the night with me again."

She wasn't shy about expressing her need for the boy now. In all her nineteen years she'd never felt such freedom to do what she wanted with another person.

"I'll do whatever you want, whenever you want," the boy breathed against her.

Cecily laughed. "Come downstairs and dance with me at my party. I've been waiting to do that with you since July. After that…"

The boy danced with her, graceful and somber in his grey. "I was running away from you."

"Really? Why?"

"I was actually away on family business but I knew that I could've written. Please don't hate me."

"Never." Cecily grasped the boy closer. "I think I love you."

The boy laughed, giddy. "Really? Because I think I feel something similar for you too, but I didn't know if it was right or acceptable. Won't your family mind?"

"Perhaps." Cecily pressed herself against the boy. "But you're *my* boy, not theirs."

The boy blushed to the roots of his blond hair, charmed and charming all at once. "I'm very rich. I could take you to places where no one would mind or care how you lived your life, our life."

"We live in such a place now."

The boy laughed and held his girl closer.

As the two danced, people stared. Who was this boy who insisted on keeping up with her during the dances, especially the Charleston that was supposed to be for the audience of fawning suitors alone? The boy was lovely and graceful, true, but he wasn't one of them. He had come out of nowhere while they had been trying for months or years to grab her attention. Envy boiled in the room, but the young couple was immune to it, trapped in their own world of sweat and attraction, of possibilities and pleasure. After the dances, they parted. Cecily was loathed to leave her friends and the boy wanted to distance himself from her a bit, to see her fire from afar and see what he was being burned by. Like the first night, he stood in corners of the ballroom and watched her, catching Cecily's flame from every conceivable angle. When he had gotten enough of staring, he could tell that Cecily had too, she glanced over her shoulder often just to be sure that the boy was watching. Now, she looked to see if he was ready, because she was.

The boy gave her a signal, appearing at her side to snatch up a champagne glass before she could. "I'm sorry," he said, not smiling. "Did you want this?"

Cecily nodded, suddenly very thirsty and said parting words to her friends who stared at her with envy in their eyes.

Cecily led the boy to her room and locked the door. Before she could breathe, his flavor was on her tongue, bubbling along her taste buds like fine champagne, making her feel lightheaded and good.

"Kiss me like you mean it," the boy demanded.

Cecily devoured her boy, making him a part of her own skin, easily slipping off the shirt and jacket like she'd been practicing this moment for weeks.

This was why the boy had come back, to feel this rightness again. No one else had made him feel so good in his own skin, like they enjoyed the feel of him inside and out.

"Cecily...." The boy's fingers slid over her moist flesh, playing her like a sweet, responsive instrument and finding all the right notes that made her sigh and squirm against the bed. Cecily laughed, covering her mouth with her lace-gloved hands, at the honest pleasure of their game. The boy was earnest, determined, first touching her, sliding inside her (a gasp reared up high in her throat) and she widened her legs to feel a fuller contact, then he slid his fingers free and pushed her more firmly on the bed, nose searching between her legs. Cecily uttered one high scream. "We can't. Not here."

The boy found his destination, licking at the triangle of flesh. "We can," he insisted. She relented with a soft little moan and clutched his head to her. There was a noise at the door.

"Cecily?"

"Um," she breathed with difficulty because the boy had found the place that was making it hard to concentrate on anything but him. She pushed his head away. "Yes?" Cecily answered the voice outside the door.

"Are you ready?"

"Yes, oh yes, I am." Then, quieter, "Darn, I have to get back." She raised her voice again. "Give me a minute, I'll be right there."

The boy rolled away, pouting, but pleased by the taste he'd been granted.

"When can I see you again?" They both asked at the same time, and then laughed.

"Send a note, or come over. You know where I live," Cecily said.

"Okay."

They both fixed her dress, and then she slipped out the door. "I'll wait for you," she whispered before closing it behind her.

"What the devil were you doing in there so long, Cec? Do you have a man in there?"

The boy ducked under the bed at the sound of the inquisitive voice. Good thing too, because the body belonging to that voice popped around the door to look around the room. The boy held his breath. The sweet smell of Cecily's cunt was still in the air. Surely he wasn't the only one who could smell it? But the nosy girl wandered away at the sound of Cecily's laughing voice, "Come on, Viola. You have better things to do that find any imaginary lover man of mine."

The house was still overflowing with people, all who by now knew and disapproved of him, so the young man decided to fall asleep under the bed. It was rather comfortable. Maria made a pallet of the dresses and underwear he found nearby. He'd fallen asleep on more dresses this past month than he had ever when he was a baby. He snuggled into the silks and cottons to spend an uneventful night. Tomorrow when he awoke, his new life would begin.

Anonymous
Bethia Rayne

The morning of Brig's first modelling session she'd been awake since seven, plagued with alternate waves of excitement and apprehension. Even the woman she boarded with, Mrs Ertz, had noticed her nervous tension at breakfast and commented on her lack of appetite – Brig had only managed to stuff down two butteries.

The woods were still damp with the rain of the night before but, even treading with care over the wet, moss-covered branches that lay strewn over the woodland path to Miller's Last, the trail still brought her to the old mill in fifteen minutes. Brig leaned against an old oak and studied the mill: it was surrounded by a broken-down stone wall. The gardens hadn't been cared for in years and, for the most part, were overgrown with thorny, rambling roses and ground elder. The mill itself also needed renovation.

She wondered where Nadia Frost kept her studio. The round tower to the left looked as if it would be a good place, but the windows seemed to be darkened with some sort of curtain material not conducive to light. She could hear the river coursing along at the back of the house and wondered if the mill wheel was still there. It had been rather broken down even when she was a child. She walked up the uneven steps to the front door that opened before she could reach it.

Nadia Frost smiled at her. 'You made it, then – come in.'

Brig followed Nadia down the narrow hall to a large kitchen that was lit with warm mid-morning sunshine.

'Sit down in the rocker. Would you like some breakfast before we start? I'm afraid I can't eat too early. Around ten is perfect for me.' The long wooden table was decorated with a large jug of freesias, which scented the air with a delicate sweetness. Nadia moved around with a slow grace, putting a pot of tea on the table, a jug of milk, warm butteries, pots of jam, honey and marmalade. Brig was glad she hadn't been able to eat much earlier. Now that she was with Nadia, she felt shy but not so nervous. She had the odd sensation that, if Nadia brushed against her, she would crackle with electric tension.

Nadia sat opposite her smiling. 'Did you say you'd given up your flat in Glasgow?'

Brig hesitated. When she had spoken to Nadia in Albee's, she had kept the subjects to neutral ground: about her job, about Glasgow, what was on at the theatre and in the cinema, what type of books she read. This was different; it was more personal. 'Yes, I couldn't afford it, not without Mum's contributions. The original lease expired last year and the landlord was able to reset the terms. The rent virtually trebled over night.'

'Do you intend to go back?'

'I don't really know what I'm going to do.' Brig shrugged. 'I've given up my job as well. It just doesn't interest me any more. I used to think I would like to do a PhD, but now I'm not so sure it's what I want. Hell, I haven't got the money anyway. Totally broke, that's the reason I'm here.' She laughed and Nadia joined her.

'Well, one thing I can tell you – you'll never make a fortune as an artist's model. But it can be a lot of fun and – well – sexy.'

Brig felt a jolt in her stomach. Yes, she thought, modelling for Nadia Frost would be sexy.

Nadia's studio was an open airy room with three large windows right to the floor that faced the river. It was a bit different from what Brig expected – it was cluttered with all sorts of odd bits and pieces. A huge Victorian dresser stood in the corner of the back wall; a large, rectangular coffee-table was covered with magazines on art and plaster casts of hands and feet; the left wall was taken up with bookshelves that, like the windows, also ran from the floor to the ceiling, laden with books in no particular order and covering a wide range of subjects with an emphasis on the Middle East. Beside the coffee table was a single bed, covered in tatty cushions and a faded Egyptian-style throw, and an old fridge hummed in the corner weighed down with a heavily carved, wooden wine-rack packed with red and white. An Edwardian-style hat-stand stood just beside the door hung with coats, scarves and jackets in every colour and fabric.

The remaining walls were lined with finished and half-finished canvases of women in every possible guise. Brig did notice that one woman in particular seemed to feature in many of them. She was tall and muscular, and had short, cropped blond hair and hard amber eyes. She wasn't what you would've called pretty, but there was an intensity about her that made you want to look at her. Brig noted with satisfaction that the blonde's nipples were rather small and the fluff between her legs sparse. Somehow, she was kind of sexless. To the right of the room, directly in front of the last window, was a small raised platform, covered by a dustsheet. On it stood a single backless chair with iron legs. Nadia's easel and paints stood in the centre of the room.

The whole space smelled of paint, dust and stale wine. Nadia left Brig to wander around while she fixed the primed canvas onto the easel and put a selection of small samples of oil paint onto a palette she then attached to her left arm. Nadia's manner had changed. It was businesslike and brusque. 'Brig, take all your clothes off, apart from your bra, and put your hair up in a coil at the back of your head. There are hair grips and such over there on top of the dresser. Keep your Doc Martens on. And see that green, leather jacket on the hat-stand? Put that on.

'You're good at putting on makeup. Sometimes I have to ask models to take it off entirely or redo it. But could you make it a little heavier? More colour, not so subtle. More punk rocker, less natural.' She smiled. 'Don't be nervous, you'll be fine. Look, I'll put on some music. That sometimes helps people relax.'

Brig knew she was delaying taking off her clothes. She put on more makeup from her bag, making her lips an even deeper cherry, the heavy purple on her eyelids darkening the irises of her eyes to a richer hazel. Using grips from her own makeup bag, she put up her long dark hair. She was used to that; she wore it up at work. She took a deep breath and began to undress quickly, folding her clothes with unnecessary care onto the bed. The music was soothing; she'd heard it somewhere before – it was the music that went along with some film she'd watched, a kind of modern jazz with a lot of background piano. She felt strange. It was odd to have her feet and her breasts covered but nothing else. She was glad to put on the jacket, and even more glad she'd bought a new bra, balconette style in deep claret silk, covered with a fine net of pink lace, It glowed against the warm cream of her skin. She thought for a moment about holding in her stomach and then decided she would never be able to keep it up. Anyway, it would be too humiliating if she passed out from lack of oxygen. She turned around so that Nadia could look at her.

Nadia, for her part, grinned with appreciation – she was only sorry that Brig had undressed so quickly. With her figure, she'd have made a great stripper. 'Right, I want you to sit on the stool on the platform there. Look directly ahead at me, sit up straight with your hands on your knees, part your legs – come on, sugar, wider than that. Tell me if you get tired.' Nadia walked behind Brig, placing a large cheval mirror at an angle that showed a clear reflection of Brig's back. She could see Brig breathing deeply, trying to get herself to calm down; Brig pushed her hands heavily against her knees in an attempt to stop her legs trembling. Nadia talked to her in a light amusing way as she painted and gradually Brig relaxed.

Brig mentioned that she had always somehow imagined that artists could only concentrate on their work if they weren't speaking, a bit like writers. She hadn't realised it would be so hard to keep still for longer than a couple of minutes and her muscles started to ache. Nadia could see Brig playing that familiar game of trying to lose her awareness of how the passage of time seemed to have slowed from normal pace to a crawl. Brig commented that it was a lot more difficult than she had thought – how on earth did people manage to stay still for any length of time?

The initial rush of sexual excitement Nadia had felt when she saw the succulence of Brig's fully exposed cunt and the way her breasts hung low as if they were pulled down by the ripeness of her over-large, dark red nipples was relegated to the back of her mind. Now Brig was a subject, made up of numerous parts and contrasts: the different tones of her skin, the shadings and textures of the fabrics she wore, her muscles moving against the inside of her face as she answered Nadia's questions, the emotions flitting across her eyes, how the sun shining on the back of her head bringing out russet highlights in her dark hair; the tiny, scarcely discernible pulse of life in her neck; the rise of her ribs as she breathed.

Brig suddenly stretched. 'Sorry, I just can't stay still any longer, it seems hours.'

Nadia couldn't help giving a faint jerk of frustration, 'It's not even been five minutes – okay, take a two-minute break.' Nadia removed the palette from her arm and moved over to the window. She would've loved a drag, but it was one of her own rules that she didn't smoke in her studio as it damaged the canvases. She flipped the CD back into its wallet and reached for another. She liked to have the background music to films she'd enjoyed; it brought back the stories more vividly. She had wanted to be a musician when she was a child, but then painting became her one and only taskmaster. Brig was asking her about her family. She didn't want to answer – all these questions for her ultimately lead down one particular path.

It was a path she tried to tread as little as possible, but could never really escape from. She should've been grateful to her father for the money he had given her all those years ago to start a new life. The money had allowed her to pursue her life in Scotland, to do what she had thought she wanted. Now in her forties, she had this old house. She could afford to take a few years out, after fifteen years of teaching art history and selling line drawings of the postures of sex to many well-known-but-not-talked-of manuals on how to improve your love life. But the main condition of gaining her father's help had been that she didn't return to Cairo while he was alive. She missed Cairo: the intense heat dazzling on the white buildings, the smell of the okra leaves drying on market stalls, the old men smoking and drinking Turkish coffee in the numerous scruffy street cafes. She missed watching a craftsman carving intricate designs on an old-style brass coffee pot to sell to the tourists that thronged Khan al-Khalili, the voices of the faithful raised in prayer as the first light of the day caught the waters of the Nile and shimmered on its surface like fine lace; the heaviness of the air forewarning a Khamseen rolling towards the city from the huge, golden entity of the desert. Nadia mentally shrugged off the memories, all that was gone, belonged to another time, was it not her father who had said only fools want to go back to relive disappointment. It was so much simpler to say to Brig that she had seen nothing of her family in over twenty years, her tone alone preventing further exploration of the subject.

Brig was learning as the morning passed to stretch her muscles in the minute movements that prevented cramp. She'd begun to enjoy having time just to sit and let her mind wander, and the ten pounds Nadia was paying her per hour was more than she'd earned as a librarian run off her feet in the main university library.

They broke for lunch at twelve and Nadia suggested sitting out on the old stone back wall to have lunch, wrapped up tight against the damp and the slight chill wind coming off the river. Everything tasted better eaten outside: the frothy coffee made with an American machine that seemed to cater for every taste in coffee preparation; the cheese and pickle sandwiches in soft-grain, brown bread; the fruit pie made with spiced apples and sultanas.

As the day moved on into late afternoon, time became a liquid thing, hours could be slow and meandering or rushing and racing like white rapids. Eventually, Nadia said that the light was no good for continuing work. Why didn't they give up for the day and have some wine? The white wine that had been chilling in the fridge was from a Scottish winery, elderflower; it reminded Brig of summer days. Nadia had asked her not to dress yet and Brig began to feel the old nervousness coming back. She was finding it increasingly difficult to deal with Nadia's sudden mood swings, one moment distant and involved in her own thoughts as if Brig wasn't there, and the next studying and questioning her with an unnerving intensity.

'Do you have a girlfriend just now?'

Brig was on one level aghast that she'd been seen through with such ease and at another glad she wouldn't have to invent some imaginary love life dominated by men. She wondered with some embarrassment if Nadia had noticed how moist her pussy had become as she'd watched Nadia's hands manipulate the paintbrush and had swapped the canvas in her mind for her own cunt.

Nadia topped up her wine. 'Don't look so worried. You're talking to an old dyke here of some years' experience.' Brig wanted to laugh – maybe with age she'd get better at telling who was and who wasn't, but she doubted it. She should've realised that the absence of canvases of men was something of a giveaway. She felt suddenly irritable with herself – she wondered if Nadia was as aware as she was of her lack of experience. 'No, I don't have a partner just now. I'm glad to be on my own actually. I need some space to think.'

'How about fucking – have you put that off limits, too?' Nadia smiled at Brig's confusion. Taking the wine glass from her hand, she drew Brig up from the bed that acted as a sofa and towards the stool Brig had vacated just fifteen minutes before. Nadia's voice had taken on a husky quality. 'Sit for me like you did when you posed.'

Brig did as she was told, much as she seemed to do in a mindless way at work but now intensely aware that her cunt had begun to fatten and ache. Taking up a black silk scarf which had been lying on the floor, Nadia sat astride Brig, looking into her face, and Brig breathed fast in shock as Nadia grasped both of her wrists and, even before she could respond, began to tie them firmly behind her back. Brig had a feeling of being helpless, drawn by a stronger will than her own to somewhere she only half remembered, but longed to be.

Nadia leaned towards her, cupping her face with her hands. She kissed her mouth gently, sucking on Brig's lower lip, then drew back and again studied Brig's face. She licked her lips slowly. 'Would you like me to suck your clit like that?'

Brig felt a tightening, almost painful sensation drawing over her lower stomach. Nadia's denims scraped against the top of her legs; the red of her jumper seemed too bright for Brig's eyes. 'Yes.'

'It's all right, Brig, no need to whisper. There's no one here but me. Do you trust me?' Brig found she could only nod, she felt transfixed. 'I would like to blindfold you, is that all right?' Brig found having the blindfold on made her feel strange, as if she were floating, but it wasn't unpleasant. She could feel and hear things more intensely. For what seemed a long time, Nadia wasn't near her, and then her hands were on her thighs, forcing them wide apart. 'I'm going to enjoy this, sweetheart, you're so ready: moist and flushed like an overripe fig.'

Nadia's tongue trailed slowly up from Brig's knee to her inner thigh – every so often she held the soft sensitive skin between her teeth, giving tiny nips. Brig jerked like a puppet, her pussy started to contract, and she felt the first droplets of dew begin to drip down towards her anus. Her anticipation at feeling Nadia's mouth was turning to slow agony. Nadia blew gentle puffs of breath onto her fluff and then tugged it gently. Like honey in winter, she moved her tongue slowly down the inner lips of Brig's cunt, flicking her tongue into the tight, pouting core, tasting its salty moistness, before dragging it up to the tip of Brig's swollen clit.

Nadia licked it hard then, drawing back its protective hood. She started to suck slowly, every so often flicking the tip of her tongue expertly.

Brig's breath rasped in her throat as if she was being held under water. The first waves of orgasm, started to ripple through her belly and then there was the shock of sudden pain. The sensation stopped. Nadia had viciously nipped her clitoris between her fingers. 'Not yet, love – don't you find having to wait for things makes them sweeter?'

And Brig gasped as she felt the small, velvet-encased, metal clamp being slowly screwing onto her clitoris. Nadia was standing over her; she could feel her inner thighs rubbing against her naked flesh. Nadia lifted up her jumper, so that Brig could feel the clamps on each of her nipples, she drew herself upwards and Brig felt the first firm tug on her clitoris, only then did she realise that the clamp there was joined by threadlike chains to the other two which adorned Nadia's tits.

Nadia leaned forward, gently licked her ear, whispering, 'Suck my nipples.' Nadia moved slightly and Brig felt her nipples rubbing against her mouth, the slender chains of the clamps rasped against her chin. Brig tried to imagine the colour of Nadia's nipples against the espresso of her skin. Were they purple or red? She opened her mouth and, taking the right nipple as fully in as the clamp would allow, she sucked gently, every so often darting her tongue against the hardened tip.

'That's it, suck harder. How does that feel? Do you like it, or do you want to stop?' Nadia laughed. Brig couldn't stop the groans dragged up from her throat. She couldn't stand any more, and yet she did, her clitoris was burning. Every so often Nadia would reach down and stroke the tip of Brig's clit exposed above the clamp with her fingers. Brig found herself teetering on the brink of orgasm but never falling over.

Then two of Nadia's fingers were thrusting deep into cunt, she moved them in a twisting motion against the small, extra sensitive mound just inside the top of the entrance. Brig felt every part of her screaming for release. Nadia removed the clamp as suddenly and expertly as she'd put it on. She drew Brig's knees together and sat on her lap, supporting Brig's back with her arms, twisting her fingers around Brig's hands. Brig couldn't seem to stop the compulsive jerking of her body even minutes later. Tears soaked the blindfold, and Nadia was kissing her deeply; her tongue seemed to explore every centimetre of Brig's mouth; she drew Brig's tongue into her mouth and sucked it between luscious lips that tasted of Brig's cunt. Finally, she unfastened Brig's hands before sliding off the blindfold.

'I think what you need, sweetie, is a long, hot bath.'

Brig let Nadia remove the rest of her clothes and lead her up to the kind of bathroom that Brig only remembered seeing in magazines.

'You like it? I copied it from a television advert for chocolate.' The walls were painted a rich cream, the drapes a green gauze decorated with gold sequins and layered to give complete privacy. An unusual, brass-shaded light gave out a warm pink glow, but it was the bath raised on a dais, an oval tub with dragon's feet, that

Brig found enchanting. Nadia poured a heavily scented oil under the jet of steaming water. 'I'll leave you now, come down when you're ready.'

Brig looked at Nadia, disappointed. 'You don't want to come in with me?'

Nadia hesitated at the door, 'All good things come in time.' Her parting smile was mysterious and tantalising.

Brig walked back through the woods alone. She couldn't believe what had happened to her, how she'd behaved. The sensation of Nadia's last passionate, tender kiss lingered on her mouth, the ghosts of her fingers still twisted in her pussy. Nadia would be back from Glasgow on Tuesday; three whole days away, and then she promised they'd work again on the painting, her smile hinting at other things.

A Slice of Melon

V.G. Lee

When Kelly said, "Fancy a shag?", Laura replied, "Don't mind if I do", which seemed to satisfy Kelly, although Laura wasn't too happy with her own choice of words. "Don't mind if I do" was what Norma Next Door said to offers of tea, cake, Pringles and Bacardi & Coke. Fortunately, Kelly didn't know Norma Next Door.

When Laura was sixteen she'd had… well, she couldn't call it sex or a shag, she'd had "something" with Norma Next Door, who was eighteen and recently engaged to Rick, a deliverer of organic potatoes.

"I want to show you this thing Rick does to me. It drives me wild," Norma said, "it's instead of going the whole way. Rick wants to wait till we're married. Rick says holding back will increase our levels of sexual pleasure."

"But I'm not a man," Laura protested.

"You don't have to be, stupid. You've got the same hair as Rick, short and stubbly."

She took Laura behind a wooden clotheshorse, hung with her dad's vests and impressive Y-fronts. "Just sit on the floor."

Laura sat and watched Norma take off her knickers. Through the wall she heard the theme tune for *The Archers*. Her mum would be laying the table and looking at the clock to see if it was indeed five past seven.

"I want you to put your head between my legs," Norma said, standing with her legs wide apart.

"I don't know that I want to."

"But I want you to."

"I want to know what's going to happen first?"

"I'm going to come on the top of your head," Norma said.

"You are not." Laura rubbed the top of her head vigorously.

"Don't worry. I'll do something back to you".

"What?"

"Something. A surprise. Wait and see."

It hadn't been as straightforward as Norma coming on Laura's head. Laura had to advance the top of her head slowly up Norma's short skirt, so that her spiky hair only brushed Norma's vaginal lips, then retreat, then advance again. Retreat. Then advance again.

"Ugh, ugh," Norma kept repeating, "Your little head. Your little, little head."

It was quite exciting, tantalizing Norma until the moment when Norma locked Laura's head in the vice of her thighs and began to bear down hard, then to the right, then to the left, then a circular movement. At one point Laura saw stars. Imagined herself with a broken neck. Would it be considered murder, manslaughter or a crime of passion? Would it only come under the heading of 'an accident in the home'?

"Oh ye-es," Norma said, ingesting Laura's head almost to her eyebrows.

"My turn now," Laura said.

"Sit down."

"I am sitting down."

"Like this." And she pushed Laura back till her head and shoulders leant against the seat of an armchair. Then she positioned the clothes horse so that the struts fell each side of Laura's neck. Three pairs of Y-fronts hung between them.

"You part your legs like this."

"Shouldn't I take my jeans off?"

"Better not. Dad might walk in at any minute. I'll just undo your zip and ease them down." Laura felt the cool air caress her bare thighs.

"Ready?"

"Yes."

"Ok." Norma's fingers began to trace circles on Laura's skin. Laura shivered with expectation.

"Round and round the garden like a teddy bear; one step, two step, and a tickly under there," Norma recited then scrabbled on the outside of Laura's knickers.

Three times she did this before stopping. Laura heard her stand up, then Norma's hand appeared scrunching a pair of underpants. "These are dry," she'd said.

Now Laura was nearly eighteen, and everyone agreed, including Laura, that she was young for her age. Laura blamed her lack of cash and a widowed mother who was interested in every facet of her daughter's life as long as it was a facet similar to her own facets. Dreary facets, problematic facets. Sexual diversity facets had to be concealed, could not be discussed. If a television programme came on that could in any way further Laura's limited sexual knowledge, her mother turned the sound right down and began talking loudly.

Laura felt she had the general idea of what a shag with Kelly involved, but wasn't absolutely clear on the fine detail. Had she been able to order the *The Bumper Book of Lesbian Erotica, a photographic manual*, from the Libertas website, she'd have felt more confident, but it seemed bumper books were for wage earners rather than sixth-formers, as it was seventeen pounds nineteen pence plus postage and packing.

And then there was the difficulty of intercepting the postman and getting the package past her mother who always hung about the hall in the morning in expectation of a letter to say she'd won the Premium Bonds, which happened surprisingly often.

"Only the *Works of Shakespeare*, Mum."

"Really, darling, how fascinating. Does it include the Sonnets? Let's see if I can find, 'Those lips that Love's own hand did make'. Your dad used to quote that whenever we had an argument..."

"Just the New English Bible, Mum."

"I haven't seen a copy of the Bible in years. I bet they've made a hash of the Sermon on the Mount".

Kelly had been in the year above Laura, but was now taking a gap year before going to Brighton University. She wore black jeans and black tee shirts always. She was wiry with short light brown hair. Had long hands and feet. Laura had watched her in the school gym doing hand stands and cartwheels at a slow and thoughtful pace.

With such hands and feet it seemed possible that Kelly was capable of being a world famous pianist, a surgeon, or at least an Olympic athlete. Laura particularly admired her ability to never smile.

Kelly lived with her mum and older sister in a flat in Islington.

"They'll be at work," she said. "Place to ourselves."

Laura liked words but Kelly used only those necessary to make herself understood which Laura again found admirable and a goal worth aspiring to in her own life.

She wondered why Kelly had chosen her. Where Kelly's confidence came from.

They arranged to meet on Tuesday during her school lunch hour, which was actually one hour and three quarters now she was in the sixth form.

A date. My first date. She'd have liked to tell somebody but at school she'd already told everyone she'd been dating for years. She'd said boys as well as girls. Actually she'd said, "Male and female", which she'd thought sounded more sophisticated. She'd told Mum, there was plenty of time for boys when she finished her 'A' levels.

"Good girl," Mum said, "you've got your whole life ahead of you."

Laura walked through Ridley Road Market looking at the stalls wondering if a melon would be a cool thing to take or rubbish. It was the most sensual fruit she could see; taut creamy skin, some of them sliced open to reveal a glisteningly moist, pink inside. She and Kelly could slice theirs open. Well, Kelly could slice it open as it was her flat and Laura didn't want to seem presumptuous foraging for a sharp knife and a large plate. Carry several of the slices to Kelly's bedroom. Later, on the bed, the juice dripping from their chins making snail trails over their bare breasts and hanging like tear drops from their nipples. Now why had she come up with snail trails? That wasn't an erotic image at all. But the path of the juice would look like that – or slug trails. Better to stick to snails. Snails could be considered cute if one wasn't a gardener. She couldn't imagine Kelly gardening. What could she imagine Kelly doing? She bought the melon.

Nobody gardened, that was obvious. Laura stepped over two bikes sprawling on the path. Instead of garden there was a square of cracked concrete and three black dustbins with twenty-seven A, B and C daubed on the lids in white paint. Kelly opened the front door as she put her foot on the first step of five. Good sign. She must have been watching from a window.

"Hi," Laura said.

"What's that?"

"A melon. I thought it was a sexy fruit."

"Sexy?"

Laura reddened. "Well, erotic."

"Erotic?" Kelly stepped sideways to let Laura into the hall, "Go right to the top", she said.

Right to the top was up three flights. The stair carpet disappeared.

"Floor sanded," Kelly said.

"That's great."

"Yeah? How great? Pink door."

The brass door-knob came off in Laura's hand.

"Push, not pull," Kelly said taking it from her.

Laura went in, Kelly came in fast behind her and kicked the door shut. At first all Laura could see was shrouded shapes. The blind was pulled down shutting out the light.

Laura fumbled for a light switch.

"Don't," Kelly said, "don't move."

She lit a candle, then another. There were no shrouded shapes, just a double bed, a rail of clothes, a tailor's dummy wearing a dinner jacket and silk scarf, plus a narrow book case crammed with paper backs. The bed was covered in velvet patchwork of wine, green, blue, and black. On the floor next to the bed was a white, long-haired rug.

"Argos," Kelly said, seeing Laura looking at it.

Above the bed hung a drawing of a nude woman lying against a patchwork background.

"That's brilliant," Laura said.

"Sit. Lie. Don't stand." Kelly threw herself on the bed.

Laura sat. "Did you draw that?"

"Yes."

"Did she go to our school?"

"She's a mate of Mum's."

"Did you sleep with her?"

"Yes."

Laura put the melon down between them. On a television programme she'd seen, women were advised to sensuously draw attention to their face. ... *she touched her cheek then traced her top lip with her index finger...'* Those lips that Love's own hand did make... go away Shakespeare's sonnet, ... which reminded her of mum and on to dad when he was really ill, still wolf whistling at mum. Concentrate. *She moistened her index finger on her moist bottom lip, caressed the line of jaw, her hand gliding down her neck to the vee of whatever she was wearing...* only in this instance there was no vee, just the round neck of Laura's bottle-green school sweatshirt.

"Drink?"

"Like what?"

"Wine?"

In 75 minutes, English Literature. "Better not," Laura said. "We could have a slice of this. It's very refreshing."

By the flickering light of the candles Laura couldn't swear that Kelly smiled, certainly some lighter expression passed across her face.

"Back in a minute. Get undressed."

Quickly Laura took off her clothes, draping them neatly over the rail. There was no mirror, which was a pity. She'd have liked to reassure herself that her figure was ok, her breasts were her best feature and that her face looked attractive by candle light. She considered lounging back on the bed to imitate the pose of the woman in the picture, but the woman's hair was black and long enough to coil around one breast while Laura's hair was cropped and a silky blonde. Self-consciously, she sat on the velvet bed spread. How to sit seductively without inspiring derision. Tried one leg stretched out, the other bent, both hands holding the bent leg's ankle, too much like a yoga position which was fine if Kelly knew as little about yoga as she did, but not fine if Kelly knew a lot about yoga and thought Laura was pretending to be... a yogi? Where was Kelly?

Glanced at Kelly's book case – *Prozac Highway, Stone Butch Blues, Fingersmith, Ruby Fruit...* – so many books that Laura had heard of but never read. Did Kelly lend her books? Where was Kelly? Better lie down and look... seductive, voluptuous. Her breasts were definitely voluptuous.

Turned down the bedspread. Put a pillow behind her head. Stretched out her legs and crossed them at the ankles. Perfectly relaxed. Looked down between her voluptuous breasts and saw tufts of her darker pubic hair like the crowns of distant trees showing above a gentle hillside. Tiny distant trees above a gentle sand dune would be more accurate. Should she fluff the trees up a little or were they better sleeked down? Up? Or down? She brushed her pubic hair with the side of her hand.

"What are you doing?" Kelly asked, quite pleasantly, standing in the doorway. She wore a black silk kimono and carried a plate of on which two slices of melon lay.

"Waiting for you," Laura said. Realising that staring down through her breasts gave her at least three chins she rolled on her side and patted the bed invitingly.

Kelly sat down on the bed. The front of the kimono fell open. There was the curved shadow of her breast. *Like a scimitar*, Laura thought. Automatically she clenched the top of her thighs. *Make this not be a disappointment.*

They each took a slice of melon. It was almost exactly how Laura had imagined it. The juice spurted into her mouth, up her nostrils, ran down her chin, made snail trails over her breasts and hung like tear drops from her nipples. Kelly put her own slice back on the plate and caught each tear drops in her mouth. Her tongue flicked over Laura's nipple, her hand squeezed Laura's other breast. Laura stroked Kelly's hair, the back of Kelly's neck, over the silk cloth covering her shoulder and down towards the opening of the kimono.

She thought she imagined it, an involuntary intake of breath from Kelly. Kelly took Laura's hands and eased her back against the pillows, parted her legs and knelt between them. The thought left Laura's head. For the first time in her life she was focused. Shagging – wrong word. Fucking – wrong word. Softer, harder. Kelly kissing her breasts, her stomach, sliding in her fingers; two, three, four. Laura squirming, desperate. Face wet. Hair roots steaming. Kelly watching her face intently. *Something not right… not right… not right.* The voice fading as her excitement built.

She reached out to Kelly. "Let me touch you," she gasped, pulling at the kimono sash.

"Leave it." Kelly's voice sharp, almost… what was the note? Fear?

"Please." Laura eased herself up on one elbow and reached for the soft weight of Kelly's breast beneath the cloth.

Kelly took her hand firmly and laid it on the bed next to the plate.

"No," she said, "don't spoil it."

Which spoilt it. Laura's excitement didn't die. It became secondary. She turned her inner eye on herself, lying with her legs open, her skin flushed and damp, sweat gathered in the hollow of her neck and beneath her eyes, and then out towards Kelly, her body almost completely concealed, her portion of melon untouched.

"Why?" she asked, her legs closing like a flower as the sun disappears.

"I get my excitement from watching you," Kelly said. For her a comparatively long sentence.

"But that's not… the whole of it."

"What do you know?" Kelly slipped from between her legs and stood up.

"I know that's not enough for me," Laura said, "I feel like your victim."

"I withdraw," Kelly said, tying her sash more securely.

"Pardon? What?" Laura said, startled. "You withdraw? What does that mean?"

"I'm withdrawing from the shag," she said, picking up the plate with its one whole slice of melon, one smiling segment of rind. "I'll let you get dressed."

"Is that it?"

"Seems to be." And she left the bedroom.

Laura put on her clothes painfully; cramps in her stomach, ache in her heart, her mind... confused, hurt, embarrassed, angry. For a moment she looked at the picture above the bed. Had Kelly been enough for her? She thought of Norma Next Door. Was this to be her sexual portion; women always doing what they wanted and never mind about what she wanted?

Kelly sat at the kitchen table. She'd cut the flesh from her slice of melon and was eating it with a fork. She didn't look up.

Laura said, "I really liked you. I thought you were special. In a way I still think you're special."

Then Kelly looked up. *She looks much more than a year older than me, Laura thought, and not happy. Or confident.*

"You'll know what to expect next time," Kelly said.

"What do you mean?"

"The next time I ask you if you fancy a shag?"

"So there will be a next time?"

"If you want."

"If *you* want."

"Whatever. Thanks for this." She speared another chunk of melon.

Laura sat through English Literature thinking. What would she say if Kelly asked her again?

"You must be joking." "In your dreams!"

No, she would say "yes". Probably say, "Don't mind if I do", and spend the next hour regretting it. Follow it through to the end next time, because... ? Kelly could do cartwheels and hand stands, owned books she'd like to read, could draw, had a mother whose friends posed nude and had sex with their friend's daughters. Because Kelly was - not a million times, that would be ridiculous - but at least a hundred times more interesting and... complex than she'd expected her to be. Vulnerable as well. She'd certainly detected vulnerability.

Laura felt better. As her father used to say, admittedly about Arsenal, "It was a result." She felt a light tap on her shoulder. Miss Mayhew, the English teacher stood over her, making passes in the air with a clear plastic ruler.

"Are you with us, Laura?"

Laura resisted replying "I'm with the Woolwich", which would have got a cheap laugh but was a very old joke and one she'd rather not be associated with.

Instead she said, "I'm sorry, I was daydreaming."

"Fair enough," Miss Mayhew said, "I don't blame you."

Miss Mayhew was an attractive woman in her early twenties who wore knotted string ties. The other students reckoned Laura was her favourite. They were right.

E:volution
Sunny Dermott

I'm waiting for the bus into the city centre, hyped up for the night ahead. E:volution is in Leeds. I've been following E:volution for a couple of years now, but it's the first time it's come to my home town and it's going to be a special night. I'm leaning against the cold glass of the bus shelter, watching a lad, late teens, early twenties, smoking. I'm feeling sharp as the cold night, and cocksure.

Another lad comes over to the bus stop and his mate shouts "You been working?"

"Naah," he replies, "I've been to the gym." I look over, 'coz I've just come from the gym and I wonder if it's anyone I recognise from there. I always try to work out just before I go clubbing, that way I can walk in looking as pumped as I feel inside.

"The gym! You're a lost cause, faggot!" He mimes a punch at the other man's stomach. "So why you doing that, then? Waste of money."

"For strength. I've been going on the step machine..."

"With all the women! You poof! What do you want strength for?"

"You should try it for twenty minutes. You can hardly walk when you get off..."

I feel sorry for gym-lad, his mate is an arsehole. At least he's trying to look after himself, more than can be said for smoking-lad, who could really do with a workout.

Another lad arrives at the bus stop, who they know, and smoking-lad immediately shouts, "Kelsey's been going to the gym! Going to the step class with all the women!"

"No! Not the step class, not that," Kelsey protests, running on the spot and mimicking the on-and-off motion of step aerobics.

"The step machine!" Now he's wildly waving his arms up and down. His mates just don't get the difference, they've probably never seen the inside of a gym, and all he's doing is making them ridicule him more. Arseholes. The bus is always full of arseholes and I always find someone to scorn and someone to side with – usually many more of them to scorn, though.

The bus comes into the city centre, and it's only a short walk to the Union. I strut through the double doors and scan the room – it's typical E:volution décor. I love it. The walls are hung with billowing sheets painted with surreal, psychedelic scenes. The longer you stare at the monsters and angels, the more eyes they have – hidden faces emerge from what were previously breasts, buttocks, wings... the pumping shock of acidic techno that throbs from the speakers echoes the lurid wallhangings and pulsates in the ultraviolet light. DJ Tsunami's on tonight – it should be storming.

I catch Dan's eye, over by the bar. He's my best mate. Vix and Matthew and the whole crew are there, obviously. But there's no way I can be arsed with the queue at the bar, so I decide to check out who's in first.

Around the perimeter of the converted refectory, small groups of people sit on the floor in encampments of coats and assorted bags, trying to skin up discreetly, limbering up for the adventure ahead. They're all a little edgy, glancing around like I am, sipping water and bottled beer. Some of them are uncomfortable with the open space of the relatively empty club; they want to cling to the walls, but they can't lean against them as the sheets hang at least a metre from the walls, giving no support. It doesn't really matter, though; in an hour the place will be full, everyone will be coming up and they'll all be too busy dancing to lean on the walls.

Dan comes over with a beer for me – cheers – and a couple of Mitzis in his hand.

"You're Catholic, aren't you, Kirsty?" he asks. I am – but very lapsed. But he knows, 'coz I went to St Carmel's with his cousins.

"Yeah."

"Body of Christ," he says, with a blissed-out smile and an evil look in his eye, as he gently places the pill on my tongue.

"Amen," I reply wryly, chasing the bitter pill down with a swig of Miller – I love pills, but I wish they didn't have to make them taste so fucking disgusting.

In half an hour, I'll be loved-up, buzzing, but I'm already happy and horny tonight. Sleek, predatory, like a jaguar. Fast, dangerous and expensive. I'm confident enough even without the drugs, with my shiny and gelled black crop and my new Lambretta vest. E:volution is mine for the taking – lock up your daughters – and your sons.

An hour later and I'm dancing like a bastard. My whole posse are around me, Dan and Vix larging it – the hardest, best dancers in the place. And everyone's eyes are on us. We're the bollocks. We follow E:volution from city to city; it's our club. We're professionals, we show the rest how to do it, we've been at it for years. But for me, for now, it's time for some water.

The toilets are always a good place to meet people. You can always chat someone up there or in the corridors. The light makes it easier to see if the fox you had your eye on is really a monster. Although it's also true that the strange electric yellowness of the toilet light can make the drug-fucked face of your potential shag look positively eerie. And mirrors are always a bad idea when you're high.

I see this girl, kind of plain but compelling-looking, over by the sinks. She doesn't look too well; she's splashing water into her face and she looks panicky. I mosey over and ask if she's okay.

"I've taken my first pill," she replies, dazed, drips of water in her eyelashes making her mascara run. "I feel pretty weird."

"You'll be ok. Just get some water and some air. Calm down. In ten minutes, you'll be loving it."

I'm still the Jaguar, of course. Merciless, don't get me wrong. But it must be the Ecstasy, 'coz I feel compassionate about this girl. Something about her reminds me of myself ten or fifteen years ago when I was a nervous, naïve little baby-clubber. "Come here for a hug." I grin. It's the done thing. As I hug her, I notice her thick maroon jumper – no wonder she's hot – these amateurs! It's none too stylish, either.

"You want to take that jumper off. Too much heat can make you feel shitty when you're coming up."

She takes the jumper off and underneath she's got on this really retro tight green shirt with short sleeves and big lapels, and this repetitive white pattern all over. Repetitive beats. It's not my style at all, but still, it looks pretty cool on her. Then I notice her body – pale arms, small but defined biceps that pop out as she wrestles with the jumper over her head. Her breasts are high and large for her skinny frame, somewhere between grapefruit and honeydew melons. Tasty.

I tip her the wink as I leave the toilet – play it cool. I'm the Jaguar again. "See you later," I say, with the slightest twist of a sexy smile, as the door swings shut behind me.

I see her later on the dance floor. She's up now, and right into it. We all are. The faintest traces of Eat Static's "The Brain" are low in the mix, and I know how DJ Tsunami works. I hear it creep in before anyone else and I know what he's going to do to the crowd. He's so sly. I know that in a few minutes' time he's going to be blasting our brains and bodies with an erupting climax, an orgasm of trance. I anticipate the headrush and feel the tingle in my extremities. Mad fingers, helium feet. The girl from the toilets has launched into a wacky dance, pulling all these mad-bastard moves, some kind of eccentric parody offspring of rock 'n' roll and ballroom dancing with gesticulating arms. It seems to go with her 70s shirt, and she looks fucking cool. I watch her as the wave hits and we get taken under, see her low-slung hipsters and the slight curve of her belly between her jutting hip bones. The midriff is the new cleavage! I dance over to her, slowly, as the wave subsides.

"Want some gum?"

"No, thanks. Got some. Thanks, though." Big grins, big eyes. We smile at each other and hug again.

"Told you you'd love it!" Smile again. The kill is in sight. I take her hand, lead her to the toilets; she knows the time has come.

I was bored, then. I say then, but only a few weeks have passed. My life was so static. I wanted something fresh, something new to play with. I kept thinking about plasticine – the way it smells of potential when you first open the packet, the way the thin plastic sheet clings to the fleshy substance before you peel it off; the way you can never quite create anything as pretty as the pictures on the packaging. Plasticine – childish, fresh, full of potential. And you can always control what happens.

I used to be so different then. For a start, I was a virgin, which has got to be a rarity for a twenty-year-old. I was so shy, so terrified to approach people in case I was rejected. Truth be told, I was scared I would make a fool of myself through inexperience, and do it wrong… I never had any confidence about that kind of thing. I used to hate dance music, too. I was strictly an indie kid back then, complete with de-rigueur misery. Smiths and Pixies, Cure and Manics. The lines were clearly drawn in my mind. It was almost – no, totally – political. Us against them – the Trendies – because our music was about thoughts and feelings, and theirs seemed so devoid of creativity and talent. I was suspicious at first when my best friend Sam started going to that travelling dance night, E:volution – I thought she was joining Them – but, one night, when I was bored, I decided to go along with her and see what it was all about. That's when things started changing for me.

The transformation happened, or rather it began, in a pub in Leeds. In the cubicle, after I took the pills out of my shoe, I could still feel them under the arch of my foot, like the feelings amputees get in their phantom limbs. I slunk back into the corridor to meet Sam, scared and excited with my glass of bitter lemon in one hand and the surreptitious California Sunrise stashed in the other. Down it went, sacramental, with reverence and fear – I was a regular disciple of LSD but, until that night, I had been too afraid to take Ecstasy. Acid can maybe fry your psyche, but it'll never do your body any harm.

We finished the drinks and walked to the students' union and into the refectory, which was hosting E:volution. Sam had told me I'd need to take plenty of chewing gum, 'coz E'll make your jaw wobble and, besides, sharing it is a good way of breaking the ice. On the way in, the security people found all the gum in my bag and made knowing jokes about it; I got a little paranoid about being found out, but their smiles told me they didn't really care. The refectory was still pretty empty and quite cold, and we sat on the polished wooden floor looking around for some guy Sam knew – Bardsley – and checking out the big drapes decorated with UV reactive paintings. It wasn't long before I could see more vivid variations in the shades of brown in the wooden floor; the grain seemed more alive. This was a familiar experience from acid and I knew the pill was starting to work. I'm happy – I can handle this, I thought, it's not too bizarre.

Half an hour later and I wasn't so sure. My face began to sting and it was unbearably hot, like nothing I'd ever felt before. I got it into my head that I'd had battery acid thrown into my face. The stinging just wouldn't stop. I was paralysed, too scared to even say anything to Sam. All the fears I'd had about trying E came crashing back into my skull – tabloid stories of Ecstasy deaths, eyeballs exploding with blood, internal organs obsessing me.

"I... feel really weird," I managed to choke out viscerally in a sudden and uncontrollable wave of nausea. I lurched for the toilets. Everything looked green and dirty under the dull fluorescents, and my vision flickered as though strobe lights had been implanted under my eyelids. Pull yourself together, I tried to tell myself. Have a piss. Sit down. Calm down. I stumbled through the alien bathroom to the sink, everyone looking at me. I could feel their gaze and see their expressions – like I was in the zoo. I was freaking out. I hated this drug. I swore I'd never take it again.

I splashed water into my face repeatedly to get the battery acid off. Maybe I could neutralise it before any damage was done. I started to feel a little better, though still dizzy. When I lifted my face from the bowl, there was a trendy girl by my side. Her manner was gentle and she helped me get my jumper off. I noticed her eyes were amazingly large, and hazel. When I left the toilets, I felt a billion times better, though the cloud must've lifted so suddenly that I didn't notice that it had gone until I got back to where Sam was sitting.

"We have to dance," she said. "It doesn't just make you dance, like speed. You've got to work with it, Robin. If you don't start dancing when you're coming up, you won't dance all night."

The dancefloor was still quiet, although a few people had started to dance now – quite a few happy-looking freaks danced alone, in their own crazy worlds. I shuffled slightly opposite Sam, who seemed to know what she was doing. I was feeling quite mellow, but I had no idea how to dance to this music. I didn't know how to do all that hands-in-the-air stuff, and

I didn't know what was expected of me. I told Sam, and she said it didn't matter, just go with the feeling. In the end I just started doing the cheesy, over-the-top, old-fashioned dancing I do at indie clubs, thinking, if I can't fit in, I might as well make a big deal of standing out. After a while, I noticed people smiling at me approvingly, and I realised that I looked cool. I realised too that I was really enjoying myself, more than ever, and that I actually liked the music! It was nothing like the commercial rubbish I'd heard on the radio, or the stuff the bitchy, trendy girls at college liked.

I felt completely welcome. It wasn't at all how I'd imagined. There were Freaks, Indie kids and Goths as well as Trendies. Tribes mixed together, but there was no trouble. Everyone was there – gay and straight, young and old, every race, and a whole new race of smiling aliens dressed in ultraviolet theatrical costumes. Everyone was so hedonistic and happy and generous; people would offer you their water and treat you with genuine concern. And I trusted and loved them all – I made friends with a dozen gentle strangers; we hugged and stroked each other and it was perfectly platonic.

I thought about the girl in the toilets, her manner and her eyes. I kept seeing glimpses of her through the bodies on the floor – too often for it to really be her every time. She shifted and changed, like a mirage, and suddenly there'd be someone else in her place. My feelings towards her were different from my feelings for the smiling new friends. Those people were innocuous, but she made me catch my breath. I feared her somehow, but I found her compelling. It dawned on me that this feeling had something to do with sex and my virginity, the vicious circle that bound me. But with every minute the drug took more control of me, I became slowly more confident and more outgoing. And I liked the person I was becoming.

She's so loved-up, all affectionate, and needs to stroke my hands and my hair, the sharp black spikes resisting her fumbling. I just need meat, flesh. I bundle her into a cubicle and slide the door shut, slam her against the wall. I kiss her ferociously and she responds. Our hands are on each other, urgent; she grasps at my waist and pulls at the muscly curves, but as she moves up to cup my breast there's a reticence about her. I need to overcome her resistance. I kiss the cords of her neck, biting, going for the jugular. She moans, and I sink my fingers into the firm flesh of her tiny arse. I'm going to devour her. I manoeuvre her, get my thigh in between hers, and press upwards, insistently. I must be getting her nice and wet, 'coz she's squirming against me now.

Suddenly I hear the door of the toilets fly open. "Robin, you in here? You've got to come quick. We need to see Bardsley and sort out about getting a lift and staying at his, or we'll be stuck in Leeds. He said he'll go without us, and he's being really arsey."

My prey stops moving, and drops her hands. She's all up-tight now, and she whispers, "That's my friend Sam. Sorry. I've got to go. I've got to get this sorted out. She doesn't know... can we maybe... later?"

Okay, I think. I can do clandestine if she wants. She's got my interest now, so I want to see it through. So I tell her to go and make sure her friend is all right, and to spin her a tale about how she's been sick from the pill and how this older woman was looking after her. I say to tell her that I've insisted she come back to my house where I can keep an eye on her, give her a lift home tomorrow, 'coz I'm worried in case she's going to do a Leah Betts. Then, at the end of the night, I'll meet her in the taxi queue, and she can come home with me. She agrees and leaves.

Come two-thirty, I'm starting to fade. I'm finding it harder to go on all night now I'm pushing thirty. I've been hanging around at the back of the room near the stall that sells glow-sticks and body-piercing jewellery, with my trusty bottle of Miller – I always go back on the booze at the end of the night when my pill's wearing off, 'coz I know it'll help me sleep. It's a fucker but, unless I get a few beers inside at the end of the night, I always seem to end up lying awake, still frenetic inside my head, long after my body's tired and my object of lust is lying unconscious at my side. The rest of the crew are still dancing like bastards, but I've lost my buzz for now, and the time for chatting has passed – I'm in that silent, contented, reflective stage. I'm still looking sleek, keeping my cool, as I watch the whole of E:volution losing it to the overpowering vibe.

Still, when he wants to, DJ Poison can always wring the last traces of energy and life from me. He's on last, and his set's just reaching its peak. He cranks up the 303 and he's the puppetmaster, directing the crowd, manipulating our emotions. Before I know it I'm gone again, my hands in the air, pulse racing, back to life like a techno Lazarus and wishing that 3am was some far distant time. Then, just as quickly, I long for it. The adrenaline and the remainder of the MDMA in my veins has reawakened my lust, and I remember that I'm on a promise tonight. I'm really up for some sex, and that little eccentric girl with the witty clothes is just what I'm after, something with a different flavour, a bit of a change. At least I'm not going to just end up shagging Dan again like we sometimes do when neither of us has pulled and we're too full of drugs to go to sleep. We're just mates, but neither of us can really stand to be alone, and we do each other favours that way.

For the remaining half hour, Poison winds us up and drops us down again, with increasing frequency. He knows when we need to breathe and when we need to explode. He wants to take every bit of buzzing energy from the crowd and guide us to the very edge, leave us exhausted yet electric, satisfied yet wanting more. And then it's time, the lights go up and everyone looks around, dazed, smiling. We've all shared something wonderful. Groups reconvene, people promise to follow E:volution on; the next one's in Birmingham in six weeks. But I can't go, and I'm so pissed off! Vix and Dan are stumbling towards me through the remainder of the drifting club smoke, and it's time to get Matthew, drag him away from some floozy and remind him he's promised to give us a lift home. At least we don't have to wait in the cold for a taxi now. Vix and Dan look for Matthew, and I scan the room for the girl in the green shirt. I don't see her – no doubt she's already outside in the queue, waiting for me.

She was the Pied Piper, and I followed her away from the dance floor and off towards the toilets. It would be a lie to say I didn't know why she was taking me, but not an outright one. I was confused. The enlightened, affectionate new being that I'd become and the shy child I'd always been were doing battle for my soul and, as I stroked her and smiled benevolently, I felt a slight ripple of my previous queasiness return; I was uneasy and there was something dangerous about her.

When she steered me into a cubicle and started to kiss me, I was at once surprised and not; excited and terrified. I realised consciously what I'd always known on some deeper level, why I'd never been bothered about boyfriends and why the couple of blokes I'd dated back at school were so boring. The sap was rising at last, and after my initial shock I returned her kisses and groped at her body. She was so lithe and fit, and she had such an air of confidence; I was submissive as she pinned me to the wall and I felt like I was going to faint. All at once, the swoon was too much for me, and I pulled back. I had to buy time. I had no idea how to please this woman; I was about to make an enormous fool of myself. I wanted to be with her, but I was certain she didn't expect someone of my age to have absolutely no experience, and I was ashamed to tell her or to ask her to slow down.

I heard Sam come in to the toilets and start shouting for me, and I felt like I was saved by the bell. Somehow I managed get out of there without Sam realising what I'd been up to, and persuaded the girl in the cubicle, Kirsty, to postpone our assignation to the end of the night, giving myself a couple of hours to get used to the idea.

I didn't meet her. Maybe that was stupid, maybe I missed an opportunity, but I don't feel bad about it. At the time I told myself it would be unfair to leave Sam alone with Bardsley and his mates – he was in such a foul mood and, after all, she didn't really know him all that well. It turned out that he'd lost over 100 pills some time during the night, the little bag he'd intimately safety-pinned to his boxers (as he always did, to foil any frisking by the bouncers) had somehow come loose and when he'd gone to get something out for a customer he discovered it was missing. He'd wanted to leave then and there but his mates had insisted they all stay. He wouldn't stop scowling for the rest of the night, staring at the floor in the vain hope he'd spot his little bag, and I couldn't really let Sam go back with him in that situation.

But really, I know there was more to it than that. Exciting as it was, I felt out of my depth, and it was totally out of control. It was too much for me. The truth was, despite the first ever stirrings of confidence, I was too scared. I'd made enough voyages into the unknown for one evening.

Still, since then I've come a long way. I've been going out most weekends, seeing my old friends but broadening my horizons too, in a lot of ways. I've been going to other dance clubs too with Sam and her friends, and I've already noticed that you see some of the same faces around on the scene, wherever it is. People don't seem to mind travelling for a couple of hours when the atmosphere's that good.

I told Sam I think I'm gay, which she wasn't too surprised about really, and I joined a gay youth group – I'm really making strides. Some of us have been into the Village a few times – I still hate the cheesy type of dance music they play in the clubs there but, if I'm with a good crowd and I'm drunk enough, it doesn't seem to matter as much that the music's terrible. I even pulled a couple of weeks ago – I finally got deflowered by a really gorgeous nurse called Michelle.

I'm looking forward to going to E:volution again, because I loved it last time – I'll definitely be joining the trail! Sam and I are planning to go down to Birmingham on the train and just see what happens. We'll either end up at an after-party or just wander around 'til the trains start again in the morning. Secretly, though, I'm hoping I'll see Kirsty.

Blushing
Kate Wildblood

Filthy dirty daydreams. The kind that keep you awake at night.

I couldn't picture the venue, I could only picture her. I couldn't explain the reasons, I could only see the result. A flirtation I'm not suppose to have with a girl who supposedly means nothing by it. A possible shag I'm not supposed to touch. A circle of lust heading in the wrong direction that I should let lie. A cute girl, a nice arse, a grin that pulls you in. Drunken threats, mislaid plans. Then one day she calls my blush.

It'd been a few months since our original giggle-filled confessions, so I felt safe in the knowledge, her knowledge, that we were just mates. Coffees had been ordered, dinners cooked, meetings made. Matehood had arrived and we were getting close to full membership and all the privileges that affords. Sex and friends. It didn't mix. At least not with this one. Another afternoon, another decaf, another dredge through bits of the weekend we could actually remember. A walk along the beach. It seemed right, the sun had that setting thing going on and its pull was unforgiving. So we walked and talked. And talked some more. Life. Wife. And all the bits in between. Till we came to a natural stop, a moment we couldn't fill, a gap we minded. I blushed. She stuttered. We looked away. The heat of my blush traveled further down than it should have and I couldn't look her in the eye anymore. The daydreams were back and, with one look, she'd read my dishonorable intentions. And mates don't think that way.

I felt a confession welling up inside and looked to the sun for escape. As the words in my head began to leave my body, she got close. She put herself where the thoughts were and I asked her to stay. Head to head, the sun behind us, we leaned against some seaside wall as we leaned into each other. And the kiss I'd daydreamed about soon became the filthy fantasy I'd fought so hard to forget. And so began the ride. Consequences dismissed as I dug in. Boots against shingle, thighs against denim, lips against her. The sun coming down on a passion we could take nowhere. I just kissed her. It was all I could think of. I'd finally got to test those waters. The months of build-up, the endless anticipation finally seeing the light of day in the setting sun. Tasting the salt of her as the seaside soundtrack cracked on regardless. Buttons tackled, the skin I could actually get to doing to me what I'd dreamed doing to her.

And it continued. This clichéd kiss. This much needed embrace, this frustrated fumble. The waves crashing, the sun setting and the screaming queens. The sudden realization that sex outside in full-on, full-view wasn't quite what my filthy daydreams were made of. I caught her thought as she caught mine and we legged it up the shingle. And so a horn got us through the traffic. A horn that led us to a door somewhere, which led to a bed, which led to a blush. A monumental fucking "I can't do this" kind of blush you really don't need at a moment of impulse. But I survived. I shut my eyes and lived the daydream.

Which was a little grittier than I would have wished for. A touch too realistic as we eyed establishments more used to dirty weekend abusers. Our feet picked the steps that led us to a part-time receptionist on the end of a rung-too-often bell. No questions asked, just a bill presented. We scrabbled for change, for cards, for a means to an end away. I paid without thinking; the notice would come with consequences, later. A glance, a towel and complimentary drinks tray were offered and then we were gone. Stuffed in a lift, suddenly shy, too many moments, perhaps, as we thought what was ahead. I couldn't help but grin. It wasn't to be the only grin that day.

Further fumbles as keys were dropped, then found again. My relief was palpable, as the thought of facing that cold reception again not one I relished. The lock turned, the door closed behind us and then we were alone. If only the room was as big as the pause between us. I blushed. Again. She giggled. We looked. I couldn't keep my eyes off her. The wallpaper may have been peeling in our presence, but we couldn't see it. One of those moments was coming. I'd not seen till it had hit me, but now it was here. I was fucked if a few seedy surrounding were going to stop me.

"Pull me in, " I said. And she did. Perfectly. The kiss that sorely tested my stone foundations earlier on the beach took no prisoners in the privacy of this pillow-heavy room. I was lost. Every moment against her lips encouraged a heat I couldn't get enough of. My head, my body and my cunt screamed "more". So she just kept on keeping on. Kissing and kissing and kissing and kissing me. The lightest of teases followed by the strongest of intentions. Brushes with intimacy that barely rubbed the surface of me, and snogs that felt as if they could steal my very soul. My heart was in my pants, my chest, my boots; I couldn't stop the pound as this so-called mate of mine snogged me to within a bare breath.

I had a moment to think about it. We weren't naked yet, I mean. The anticipation was killing me and the ache, the need to touch her so great it began to eat away at me. Whereas moments before all I could think about was the kiss, now all I could do was imagine heat. Wet, hot heat. My fingers began to hurt. As did my cunt, the tip of my tongue, my clit. Which meant more courage was required, and probably another blush. I had to touch her. So I asked. And dutifully went cerise. In two places. She said something about wondering when I was gonna ever ask. I pictured a meter in my head. And got to work...

The jeans were Diesel. The pants black, butch and very cute in that boy-dyke-label kind of way. I made my way through the security – the belt, the chain, the buttons. And with eyes still firmly fixed on *her* now blushing face my middle finger found the place it was gonna become way too fond of. We both grabbed what air there was in the room with sharp intakes, the shake caused by my action taking both of us by surprise.

"God, you feel good," was my clichéd response to a clit so hot the heat was making my toes burn. This softhearted girl was feeling pretty perfect to me. The tops of my lucky fingers continued their stroke, definitely finding her burn to their taste. So I worked her and she worked me. Taking what she wanted as my hands wrapped themselves round an arse I'd only ever admired from afar and a cunt I never dreamt I'd lay a hand on. I cradled her as she stood there beside me; I came good on my flirtatious promises and she went with my flow. Sexy soundtracks filled my head as I leant into her, hand down her pants and having the time of my life. Monday afternoons weren't meant to be like this, were they?

Soon my bod got as jealous as it could cope with and the cop-off had to be had.

"Let's see what you're made of, sunshine," were the cocksure words I found leaving my lips and a spark in a blue eye was the only preview I was gonna get this p.m.

And so it continued. Hands warmed further on salty bodies, jackets peeled, jumpers lost, grins made. Girls coming together in a not-so-girly kinda way. Stripped down as fast as we could, the desperation to touch and to feel, to be part of each other evident in our every move. As our clothes scattered about us, I found it hard to focus. Her kiss had left my lips and was working me good. Down my neck, my throat, my chest, my breast, my nipples. Every moment of me taken care of. Caressed, checked, dealt with. Oh-so-efficient. Oh, so fucking horny. Better than any daytime distraction I'd been delighting myself with lately. So I bathed in the filthy glory of her. Feasted on the vision above me as she leant in, determined to break as many boundaries as possible.

There was no time for lines, promises or even words. I guess we'd been there. Now we were here to fuck. I didn't know what to grab first, where to go, how to handle it. As it was, I'd never thought this far ahead. She ran hands all over me as her kisses played with my soul. She placed her skin against my skin and I found the friction hard to take. Although the weight of her – I could feel *that* all night long. And when she finally placed those precious digits inside of me I saw red. My thoughts became as crimson as my cunt, as my blushing cheeks. I saw colours. Reds and pinks. Every hot colour I knew of and some I didn't. So I held on tight to my real daydream. Her back, her arse, her thighs, her sides. Some parts of the daydream fell off as the sweat generated between us, some parts I drew away from as the heat shifted from soul to skin to me to her and back again. She shagged me. We made love. I fucked her. We kept grinning. Hell, we enjoyed the view as we engaged in the jump.

I felt her fingers explore. She had led in with the one, but now she was having me with a handful. Her thumb took good care of my clit, gentle yet persuasive in its presence as her four fingers dug in, looking for that spot – parking up where she was more than welcome. "Come again," I wanted to shout, as I did what only a girl could do in this situation. Longer, harder, faster as the gentle explorations became a fuck I wanted to ride. Her eyes looking straight at me, her lips just a touch too far away from mine, one hand on the top of me, holding my admiring head in place, the other delivering a soul-shifting sensation I was gonna find hard to better. Well, at least for today. And as the tension converted to orgasm, as the strokes hit their mark, this mate of mine drew her fingers from within and replaced them with a clit that for a moment I thought she'd toyed with. My hands made for her arse, the grasp tight as her clit slid next to mine. And the frantic fucking became a labour of love as we watched each other's face light up, each other's grin become a giggle, each other's mouth open slightly with the "ooh" that accompanies the chuffed thought of "so good, baby". The rub, the fit, the two bodies primed perfectly, teased like hell yet knowing that an explosion is just around the corner. The worry kicking in that I was gonna come too soon, instantly replaced at the next stroke with the need to come right now. Working on the timing as I worked on the girl. Smiles replaced by looks of concentration. Getting off on her getting off on me.

And all that sweat paid off. We came good and proper. Laughing like lads as this shudder took hold of us. Like an ultimate connection our rocks got off in perfect synch. I felt that push as her clit dived deeper into me, I knew that melt inside as my come could wait no longer. We blew. And we loved it.

A breath or two later and that blue-eyed spark was back. "Shall we go again?" this buddy of mine asked and I think my brown-eyed gaze gave her the answer she wanted.

"Once more into the fuck, dear friend." I shagged my mate. I shouted louder than I did for my beloved Arsenal team; I held her more tenderly than any plant in my care and lost it further than I had on any local dance floor. I ignored consequence and care and held on tight as we fucked each other's brains out (in the nicest possible way). We let the dirty little daydream become the kind of sheet action we'd never imagined. As we came, we grinned and as we grinned we came. And I lost count and she lost count and I forgot to hold on and she spilt something and we flipped the bird and it got dark and we found the lights and then it hurt and then it didn't and then we slept and then she said something cute and then we did it all over again. And again. And again. And – again.

And we only did it the one day. Only engaged on an eiderdown just the one time, only had that particular post-fucking ache once. And the blush? I wish that too were just the once. But no. Every time I see her. Every coffee, every beer, every meet, I blush. Just the once. Subtle-like. But every time. Guess I'll have to get me another daydream.

Front-Page Girl
Tanya Dolan

Awakening slowly, Martina floated up to consciousness. Indistinct voices were riding on air heavy with the fragrance of the Chanel No.5 that she always dabbed on both the proper and improper places. She seemed to be in some kind of fantasyland – opening her eyes hadn't dispelled the dreams she'd been dreaming. Lingering dregs of alcohol befuddled her mind; sunshine glowed on the drawn blinds. It was morning. What had happened to yesterday?

The muffled voices were coming from her clock radio. Narrowing eyes that felt scraped, she focused on the square green digits that silently announced it was 8.45 am. Some cheery-voiced prick was giving the radio station's programmes for that Saturday. Saturday! Things were becoming clearer. The pieces floated back together like on a television news programme when the demolition of a tower block is run in reverse. Arnold Edwards' retirement party. Journalists from rival newspapers had joined the *Post* people to pack the Blue Oasis and give the able (if uninspired) old editor a good send-off. True to journalistic tradition, just about everyone had got as drunk as hiccuping hyenas. Though she could vaguely remember the early part of the evening, her memory had later gone into alcoholic meltdown.

That was worrying. She would have been volatile due to a sexual abstinence of seven weeks' duration (no celestial retreat, but an exercise to strengthen her character). It seemed as though for close to two months she had been living up inside of her own cunt. That was an oppressive dwelling. The tremendous power of sex, its terrific energy, had remained with her throughout those long weeks. The restlessness and the need to sip a dry Martini and a wet mouth may well have erupted with embarrassing consequences. It would be disastrous if she'd made an unreciprocated approach to one of the newspaper hierarchy.

What if she had seduced one of the tasty women in the office, some of whom were married? That would be frustrating. Much of the thrill of sex was retrospective. On numerous occasions she had thrilled again and again by running her last sexual excursion through her mind.

Exactly seven weeks ago yesterday, she had interviewed Chloe, a pretty, petite brunette, for one of those inane "Bride Made Her Own Dress" stories. Wearing a miniskirt and no panties, Martina had sat on the edge of a settee while the excited bride-to-be had knelt on the floor, laying out dress patterns and giving a commentary. Bored to bits, Martina had pseudo-carelessly opened her thighs. Staring goggle-eyed at the exposed hairy cavern wherein dwelt the soul, Chloe had leaned impulsively forwards to kiss Martina's inner thigh, halfway between the knee and the crotch. Certain that she had a convert, Martina had lain back, pulled up her skirt, spread her legs and put a hand down to open her swollen lips. She had come seconds after Chloe's totally inexperienced hot mouth and novice's lapping tongue had found their target. When Chloe had eaten her fill, Martina had introduced the bewildered but eager girl to the delights of having her cunt sucked. Chloe, a genuine *blushing*, but probably very *confused* bride, had married two days later.

Now the telephone purred. She was unable to summon either the interest or energy to reach for it. She heard the precise tones of her doppelganger, who answered: 'This is Martina Amorosa. Please leave your name and number and I will get back to you.'

'Pick up the phone, Marti,' Judy Marn ordered, adding a half-joke. 'Don't forget I'm the new editor. I could make or break you.'

Martina picked up the phone. 'This had better be important.'

'I was worried about you after last night,' Judy said.

Since when had Judy Marn given a monkey's fuck about her? Judy, who possessed a delicious perspiration that no deodorant could subdue past 11 o'clock in the morning, had all the selfishness of the ambitious career woman. She was a smooth operator, always thinking, but covering the computer working of her mind with clever little moves. Up to a week ago, Judy had been Martina's rival in the contest for the editorship. There had been dread in Martina's veins while awaiting a decision. It had been toxic and deadening. She had lived through desolate days.

The *Post* board of directors had chosen the low-key but highly efficient chief reporter Judy over her. The directors, though aware that Martina had the skill and flair to exploit the full potential of the newspaper, had been put off by her radical attitude. In an age when the media had everyone thinking alike and functioning alike, Martina Amorosa frightened people. The *Post* was so tired that it would have neither kicked nor screamed had she been allowed to drag it into the twenty-first century. But, by opting for Judy, the board had ensured that the newspaper would continue to cater for the rubber-stamp mentality of the masses.

Martina was a bad loser, but didn't regard that as a character fault. Appointing the new chief reporter was Judy's responsibility. It was an ideal position from which to snipe at Judy and plan her eventual downfall, giving Martina another shot at the editorship. She had a back-up plan if Judy didn't promote her.

Having spent several weeks on an almost-completed sensational exposé of a famous television celebrity, Martina intended to leak the story to the *Herald*, the *Post*'s rival newspaper. She would do this through Kate, a former lover who was a sub-editor at the *Herald* – where the editor was Judy's long-term partner, Gavin Wainwright. Judy would get the blame, and the resulting explosion at the *Post* would blow her out of the editor's chair.

'I'm more than a bit vague about last night, Judy,' Martina said.

As patronising as ever, Judy sympathised. 'Drowning your sorrows, weren't you, poor darling. It did surprise me somewhat when you tried to snog me up against a wall in the car park.'

Fuck a priest! Martina exclaimed profanely inside her head. She had made a move on Judy Marn, who would by now have crossed her name off the chief reporter list. How far had it gone? Lying still, trance-like, she gave herself a head-to-toe mental scan. Being aware of the workings of her body and the sparking connections and short-circuiting of her emotions was something she was good at.

There was no mild pain of a hickey on her neck, the hallmark of sex at a drunken staff party. So far, so good. Her nipples were erect. Was that a good or a bad omen? You couldn't really tell with tits. They functioned independently from you a lot of the time. Apprehensively, she parted her legs. Knees raised in a solo missionary position, she ran the mind probe slowly up the inside of one thigh to her cunt. Taking the flesh directly in her fingers, she opened it to probe more deeply. The fact she was wet, warm, and slippery inside was as expected first thing in the morning. It was good news. There was no indication of recent sexual activity.

'I am so sorry, Judy,' Martina apologised. With the position of chief reporter vacant, it was humble pie time.

'I admit that I don't like that sort of thing. Had it been Jude Law and not you, then I would have looked upon it as a compliment.'

'I wouldn't let Gavin hear you say that,' a relieved Martina laughed.

Martina, whose lovers were ephemeral and therefore bearable, wasn't into long-term relationships. She agreed with writer Erica Jong's description of monogamy as fucking the one you don't want to fuck while pretending he or she is the one you do.

'He's not here,' Judy admitted with a little giggle. 'Gavin's away at a conference this weekend. Which is my second reason for ringing you, Marti, to ask you out to dinner tonight. I can get us a table at Reno's.'

Martina could think of better ways of spending a Saturday evening other than in the company of the prudishly boring Judy Marn. The unexpected invitation had made her cautious. 'What, even after my behaviour of last night?'

'That's forgotten. Anyway, we were all pretty well smashed. Having dinner together will give us the opportunity to discuss the chief reporter vacancy.'

Did that mean that Judy had decided to promote her? An excited Martina could actually feel the tiny hairs rise on her forearms, and an icy-cold prickle ran down her spine. Then the reality of the situation, the mini-Cold War between Judy and her, hit Martina. Though not wishing to blow her chances, this was

Saturday, and she could afford the luxury of slipping into her cynical and anti-social mode. She said, frankly, 'You know that I'd have been likely to fuck-up arrangements in the Garden of Eden. Pardon my French.'

'I must admit that, talented though you are, you do tend to be rebellious at times.'

'Which means I'd most likely make life intolerable for you as editor.'

'I think that I know you better than that, Marti,' Judy assured her.

'I've known me a whole lot longer than you have, Judy, and I'm still not sure about myself.'

'Hopefully an evening together will make things clearer for both of us. Shall I pick you up at eight?'

Martina hesitated. An acceptance would smack of sleeping with the enemy. None of this would be necessary if she put her back-up plan into action. After a brief mental debate, she decided to give diplomacy a chance first.

'That will be fine, Judy. I look forward to our evening together.'

'So do I.'

Replacing the receiver, Martina lay back in her bed and relaxed. It didn't matter to her that she would be Judy Marn's dinner guest while planning her demise, one way or another, as editor. She kept her conscience at bay by reminding herself that people are like pet dogs. They might enjoy your companionship and obey you for any number of reasons, but true friendship and unconditional loyalty are out of the question.

Spending the day lazily, she came to life in early evening when dressing for her dinner-date with Judy Marn. She looked at herself framed in the dressing table mirror. Black and white - a monochrome beauty - that was Martina Amorosa's legacy from her Spanish father. Her long hair was naturally jet-black, while her flesh was as white and smooth as alabaster. The lovely image stared back at her. Then the dark eyes dropped to take in the firm swelling breasts that required no support from brassieres. Compared to her, Judy Marn, though her legs were slender and shapely, her hips slim and her small round behind held high and tight, was close to titless. The quiet and always slightly remote Judy bore an uncanny resemblance to the late Audrey Hepburn that men found irresistible, but it did nothing for Martina.

Standing, she walked to a full-length mirror. Striking a catwalk pose with a hand at each hip sexually aroused her. There had to be something perverted in getting turned on by your own mirror image.

Her red satin dress broke the chiaroscuro contrast of her hair and complexion with stunning effect. Add to that a scintillating personality and she had it all. Three months short of her thirtieth birthday and she had it all – except the editor's chair.

'I feel almost sorry for Judy,' she remarked without any real understanding of what she meant.

The reflection in the mirror looked back without showing any response. Then, slowly, it smiled.

The doorbell rang, and she went out to meet the woman who, on Monday morning, would be sitting behind the large mahogany desk that she had coveted for so long. For five years, in fact, since arriving in London with a degree in journalism, £225 in her pocket, and a determination in her heart to be somebody.

The air was cool. Night normally unnerved her a little. When darkness thickened, bad memories that sunlight holds off would come rushing at her, winking and exploding, too swift for definition.

Martina battled through her gloomy thoughts. Filled with self-confidence and resolve, she walked confidently to meet Judy Marn and whatever the evening might bring.

At Reno's the *maitre d'* guided them to their table. Some of the other diners were eyeing them slyly. Martina knew there was more than a touch of elegance about the way she held herself and walked that complemented Judy's delicate loveliness and sky-blue, chiffon-and-silk evening dress, so that they appeared to be stars of some kind. It gave her self-esteem a mighty lift to realise that they stood out among people who all looked so wealthy and so celebrated.

With the last wisps of the fog of depression clearing from her mind, she sat across the table from Judy, happy for her to confidently choose the wine and the meal for them both. A pianist played a non-stop series of sentimental melodies. A waiter brought their meal and Martina was now feeling really good. How often it happened that after the most morbid moments of despair, you discovered suddenly how brilliant life could be.

Judy was very different from when she was in the office. In the pale yellow light, her face had a mature, unselfconscious kind of beauty. With an easy charm, she skilfully tapered a general conversation into a discussion about their work. The sheer silk of her gown clung to the slender shape of her body, the open front of it hovering somewhere between immodesty and indecency. At the start of the cleavage of her firm but small breasts, a huge heart-shaped diamond pendant hung on a gold chain, dazzling Martina with highlights of colour. Even the way Judy tasted her drink was a sheer sex act.

'Is this a kind of socialised interview, Judy?' Martina enquired.

Beckoning the waiter over and ordering coffee, Judy let a little smile twitch at the corners of her mouth. 'Away from the atmosphere of the *Post*, Marti, we have come to know each other better.'

'Will you be making big changes?'

The haunting melody of "As Time Goes By" was having an emotional effect on Judy and the other diners. Unmoved, Martina waited impatiently for the tune to end. As the last notes on the piano faded away, Judy shook her head slowly in puzzlement.

'*Casablanca*,' she sighed. 'That tune never fails to get to me.'

'I never fiddle-fuck with nostalgia,' Martina said bluntly. 'The present always colours the past, and you could find a future you don't want has sneaked up on you.'

'You're incorrigible, Marti. Don't you ever take a simple view of things?'

'Nothing is simple,' Martina replied. 'You haven't answered my question about how things will be at the *Post* from now on.'

Judy looked at her steadily over the rim of her raised coffee cup before speaking. 'It's obvious that things can't go on as they were before. I will be running a tight ship. All will be revealed on Monday morning.'

The relaxing meal had worked magic on Judy, Martina had to admit it. She had a way of slowly raising her limpid violet eyes to look at the person she was speaking to. There was a level of intimacy in the mannerism that had a stirring effect. Martina was as horny as hell. Her celibacy had to end tonight if she was to retain her sanity. Sexual urges, like gases under pressure, seek a vent, and Judy Marn, to Martina's surprise, had everything needed to release hers. 'That was a lovely meal,' she said. 'I have really enjoyed myself this evening, Judy.'

Slightly embarrassed, Judy confessed. 'I earlier feared that it would be a disaster. But you make excellent company, Marti.'

'At this stage of a normal dinner-date, I suppose one of us would be asking, "Your place or mine?" Martina remarked.

Judy frowned momentarily and teased her lower lip with her teeth. Then she warned. 'I have known, and still know, a number of lesbians, Marti. Though I have enjoyed the warmth of strong friendship with several of them, sex has never been an issue. I have everything a woman could wish for in my relationship with Gavin.'

'Why the uncalled-for explanation?' Martina suspected that the pleasant evening they had spent together was making it impossible for Judy to be sexually neutral. As she had on several occasions before, Martina deduced that Judy was not quite so sure of herself as she appeared to be. Now and again, a slight hesitation of movement betrayed that there was something wrong at the centre. That was encouraging. Getting into her panties could be the first move towards becoming chief reporter.

Judy hastened to explain. 'I just wanted to put the record straight, as it were. Have I offended you?'

'Of course not.'

'I am so glad,' Judy sighed. 'We have never been close, Marti, and we need to be friends, as we will be working together in the future.'

'We'll be friends,' Martina promised. During their meal the antipathy between them had mysteriously vanished, unnoticed until that moment.

'I am so glad,' a relieved Judy said. She checked her watch. 'Church in the morning.'

Martina managed to give a non-committal nod. Sex was her religion. Having two fingers or a tongue up a juicy pussy was her now, her past and her future,

'Now, shall we finish off this splendid evening with a night-cap at my place?'

'Suits me fine.'

Stepping out into the somehow-always-fraught night-time of London, Martina looked up to find a sky dotted with twinkling diamonds. She was momentarily in the grip of something intuitive that made her feel good about everything.

Judy's apartment was decorated in tones of mauve with small accents of old rose and touches of muted green; its wide window gave a panoramic view of Kensington Gardens. After a taxing evening in which they had sized each other up like boxers in the opening round, they were having trouble relaxing. Martina watched Judy narrowly as she poured two glasses of Bacardi. Conscious of Martina's searching look, Judy raised her head. Martina held her gaze, mesmerisingly.

This was the testing time. The kind of telepathic exchange in which Martina could usually accurately gauge what another woman's response to a direct – but nevertheless discreet – pass would be. It didn't work with Judy. She was no naïve kid like Chloe the virginal bride. Martina could sense that Judy had just realised that she had wandered innocently into an arena of sex that was alien to her.

She had real class as she walked to Martina holding two glasses. Each curve of her slender, wonderful body complemented the other, a study in perfect symmetry. All the breath wanted to go out of Martina and none wanted to come in.

'I envy you, Marti,' Judy remarked to start a safe conversation as they sipped their drinks.

'The compliment is appreciated, but it is misplaced. You were chosen to be editor, not me.' Martina said with a smile. She had difficulty concentrating on the conversation, because Judy looked so radiant.

'That doesn't stop me envying you. You have got what it takes. To be honest, I fear that I will not be up to the job.' Judy looked tearful and her bottom lip quivered.

'A little self-doubt isn't a bad thing,' Martina assured her. 'It means that with your natural ability you'll be a superb editor.'

What a load of bollocks! Just as there are no honest businessmen, neither was there ever an honest lover. It was the accepted thing to lie to a woman before you lay with her, and Martina knew she was in overdrive.

Placing her empty glass on a small table, Martina reached a hand behind herself. Slowly she eased down the zip of her red satin dress. Allowing it to slip from her shoulders, she showed that she was not wearing a bra. Judy, entranced, stood immobile. She could not help staring at a pair of massive, self-supporting breasts. The dark brown nipples were of magnificent circumference. Reaching out to take Judy's right hand, Martina placed it on the smooth, warm skin of her stomach.

Pouting, Martina said huskily, 'Earn yourself a kiss, Judy, and you'll learn what you've been missing.'

Neither co-operating nor resisting, Judy allowed her hand to be moved up past Martina's rib cage. Certainty that Judy had never before touched the breasts of another woman increased Martina's arousal. Manipulating Judy's fingers, Martina put an erect nipple between a forefinger and thumb. She squirmed involuntarily with pleasure.

Bringing her head forward she kissed Judy tenderly on the neck. Moving her slightly parted lips up to the sensitive skin behind the ears, she was rewarded by the sound of an ecstatic sigh escaping from Judy. Delighted by this, Martina was then shocked as Judy's whole body suddenly convulsed into a state of rigidity.

Fearing that she was to be denied what she now so desperately wanted, Martina took Judy's face in both hands and pulled her close. She kissed her on the mouth in a surge of passion. It was the kiss of an expert, employing modest suction to draw Judy's saliva to her lips, where Martina avidly but gently welcomed it with her tongue.

The mental anaesthesia showing in Judy's now sultry eyes convinced Martina that she was winning. Mouths a fraction of an inch apart, they breathed in each other's breath. It was as highly erotic as tongue kissing. Judy was responding when a ray of sanity seemed to break through to her mind. Pushing Martina away, she cried out, 'No, no, no, I can't. We mustn't.'

The electric spell of expectation had been broken. Aware that there was no point in attempting to continue, Martina stepped back. Shrugging back into her dress, she zipped it up, reached for her handbag and hurried from the apartment.

She scolded herself bitterly for breaking the golden rule of never mixing business with pleasure. Surrendering to lust had ruined both the evening and her chance of promotion. Also, the feelings she had developed for Judy that evening would never permit her to employ the dirty trick that would instantly end Judy's editorship.

Martina had reached the lift when she heard Judy's voice tearfully calling her name. Undecided, she paused as the lift arrived and the doors opened. Then she nodded agreement to a decision made in her head, turned and walked slowly back to the apartment.

A distressed Judy was standing in the doorway. She looked up as if Martina was a doctor on call who would have some magical panacea for what ailed her. Not knowing what was at the root of Judy's upset, Martina was determined to find out. Having burned all her career and sexual bridges behind her a short time ago, she told herself that she had fuck-all to lose.

With relief, she noticed that though Judy's eyes swirled in a film of tears, she did not look to be deeply distraught. Her Hepburn hairstyle was intact. That was a good sign. When women threw a serious wobbly their hair went crazy with them.

'Please, come in, Marti,' she invited in a choked-up voice. 'I am sorry for the way I acted just now. It was all so new to me. It's no excuse, but I've been terribly on edge since being appointed editor, and things aren't as they should be between Gavin and me.'

The last bit was music to Martina's ears. Judy had innocently revealed that the road to a wet and hairy, welcoming Utopia was wide open.

Stepping to back to allow Martina to enter the apartment, Judy held a hand nervously across the cleavage of her dress, as if a bunch of pervs had spent all evening trying to get a peep at her tits. It was a delicate hand; long slim fingers tipped with dark-purpled nails perfectly kept. There was a haunted look in her eyes that went with the tense way she held her shoulders. Inside the dress her cute little breasts were rising and falling with an allure that wasn't lost on Martina. Passing an armchair, Judy sat down heavily on a sofa. 'I'm sorry, Marti,' she said again.

'Don't be silly,' Martina protested. 'It's me who should be apologising. I should have known what a huge step it is for you becoming editor, and it was insensitive of me to behave as I did.'

Head down, Judy was crying now. Genuinely moved by her distress, Martina sat down beside her and slipped an arm round her shoulders. She was unable to understand the feelings she had for Judy since being with her that evening. In an unsuccessful try at getting back to her old cynicism, Martina told herself that all she was suffering from was lust, not love.

For a heady second, the bouquet of Judy's perfume filled Martina's nostrils. The scent that was woman! Reaching out, she ran her fingers through Judy's hair, bringing her face close. It perturbed her to witness the normally self-assured Judy in such a state. She pleaded, 'Don't cry, Judy.'

Tears ran down Judy's face as she turned it to Martina. 'I am so glad you came back. I couldn't bear to be alone tonight, and though it may sound stupid, this evening I've come to look upon you as a good friend.'

'I'm flattered,' Martina replied, surprised to discover that she had spoken the truth.

'Just give me a moment or two and I'll pull myself together,' Judy promised.

'Of course,' Martina said softly. 'Perhaps it will help, be some comfort, if I hold you for a while.' Her intentions were purely altruistic at that moment.

As a result of Martina's tightening of her one-arm embrace, the top of Judy's dress opened slightly. About a third of her well-shaped left breast was on show. The sight dragged Martina right to the edge of temptation. Every inch of her demanded that her hand go inside the dress and explore the weight and feel of the breast, then caress it.

As if able to read Martina's mind, Judy tensed her body momentarily. Then she relaxed. She gave a long sigh, and her warm, fragrant breath stirringly brushed Martina's cheek.

With an arm still round her shoulders, Martina tentatively slid her right hand inside Judy's dress. With the hand underneath the bare left breast, but not touching it, her palm tingled to the warmth of the other woman. Stopping, Martina watched Judy's face for a moment, waiting for a response, some kind of reaction to help her decide her next move. The silence between them was so intense that it was somehow painful. Judy's top lip lifted slightly as though she was in pain, showing her white and even teeth. From nervousness rather than design, she drew a red tongue over ripe lips so that they glistened wetly, pleading to be kissed.

It was too much for Martina. It was weak of her; maybe she was taking advantage, but what the fuck! Even a saint couldn't keep control this close to the lovely Judy. She cupped the breast, taking the weight of it. She felt the roughness of the outer circle of the nipple rings against the edge of her hand. Martina watched the colour of Judy's eyes swirl into a smoky grey.

There was a tremor in Judy's whisper as she begged, 'Just be nice to me, Marti… but not too nice.'

That plea was beyond Martina's understanding, and unanswerable with words. Cupping the breast in a firm caress, she moved her hand gently upwards until a hard nipple was thrusting into the palm. Running the fingers of her other hand in through Judy's hair, she gently pulled her head back to kiss her neck and shoulders.

Judy's fake innocence was betrayed then as her dress fell away and dropped to her waist with a hissing sound. She must have prepared for this when calling Martina back to her apartment. Her naked breasts were high and firm with all the vitality of a magically retained youth. Judy moaned softly, her body becoming a live, passionate thing that quivered under Martina's hands.

Martina sought her mouth. Judy said, 'Please...' perhaps in invitation, or possibly a half-hearted prayer to have Martina stop. As she found Judy's mouth, Martina thrilled at the fire in her lips that ran like a sparking fuse down Judy's body until she curved inward against her with a fierce undulation. Judy's body was supple and warm, like a fluid that was completely filling the gaps between them. The kiss was long, slow, and deep.

When Martina at last released her, Judy leaned back slightly. Her eyes had narrowed. Her lips, moist, slackly apart, invited more kissing. When their mouths met once again, Judy's tongue shyly but wetly insinuated itself between Martina's lips. The tip first explored Martina's teeth, and then became more daring to do a sensationally erotic tongue dance. Martina fondled the warm, soft-skinned breast, causing Judy to gasp hot, sweet breath into her mouth. It was a thrilling handful, the round smoothness of the flesh contrasting with the pointed hardness of the marvellous nipple.

When at last the kiss ended, Martina feasted her eyes on the dark-brown erect nipple. Bending her head, she sucked it into her mouth lightly, gently and slowly. An ecstatic Judy cried out. Her body was trembling in little convulsions as Martina fed at the nipple while using both hands to explore the naked top half of Judy's body. It was plain to her that Judy was oversexed. That attributed much of her upset to her confessed estrangement from Gavin Wainwright.

Their mouths smeared wetly together, and their breath was coarse and hot. Getting up from the sofa, holding both of Judy's hands, Martina looked around for the bedroom. Taking the initiative, Judy led the way. Standing by the double bed, Judy let her dress drop to the floor and stepped out of it. The tiny white panties she had on had admitted defeat in any attempt at containing the bush of dark hair that escaped from each side and from above the thin material.

Then Martina dropped her own dress and slipped down her red panties, to be gratified by little cry of awe from Judy. Each fresh sighting of Martina's mass of jet-black pubic hair was always a shock, even to her. Where the thick bush ended in a horizontal line, an inverted V of finer hair ran up to a point at her navel.

Easing Judy down onto the bed, Martina lay at her side. Reaching between Judy's hot thighs, Martina parted surprisingly long, already wet hair with her fingers as she felt for the furrow of cunt lips. Finding the slit, she used the middle finger to coax the slippery swollen lips apart. Entering Judy with her finger, and rewarded by a thrust of hips and a low groan of absolute pleasure, Martina brought the knuckle of her bent thumb against Judy's clit, manipulating it with consummate skill.

Now using two fingers, Martina thrust in and out, in and out, each inward thrust bringing her thumb into play against a gratefully responsive clitoris. She was above Judy now, thrilling as she looked down on her. Judy's mouth was full and rich, showing the shiny white edges of her teeth. Martina could hear the rhythmic sigh of her heavy breathing as she lowered her head to kiss her. Their mouths were fused and ravenous as Martina kept the stroke of her fingers going regularly inside of Judy, and Judy thrust her hips up to meet each thrilled-loaded, sliding invasion of her body.

Gauging Judy's mounting excitement, which could be no more than a few thrusts from orgasm, Martina eased off. She had other plans and didn't want her to come yet. Tenderly but firmly, she guided the body beneath her. Judy proved to be a willing, pliant partner. She permitted herself to be moved into a new position on her back on the bed. Martina squatted over her facing Judy's feet, a knee each side of her head.

Feeling Judy's hands caressing her buttocks, Martina lowered her cunt towards Judy's mouth, then raised up again just before Judy had time to lick her. As she repeated this teasing action, Martina bent forwards, head between Judy's spread legs. First examining

Judy's juice-oozing cunt, Martina then used the fingers of both hands to open the lips and look in more deeply. A warm, musky odour was released, causing arousal that set Martina's head spinning.

Releasing Judy's lips, Martina raised her hands to lick eagerly at the cream on her fingers. Then she lowered herself steadily towards Judy's face. Having examined herself many times by using a hand mirror, Martina got an egotistical thrill at the thought of the sight facing Judy as she reached up obligingly to part the cheeks of her bum. The inner sides of the valley of the buttocks were stained with the dark yellow hue of maturity. The puckered anus had a narrow circle of white skin between it and a ring of coarse dark hair. As Martina lowered herself further, Judy would have no need to open the thick, dark, hair-beset lips of the gaping, soaking, pink-lined cunt that approached her so tantalisingly slowly.

Judy didn't require any teaching. How quickly the newcomer to lesbian sex learns, Martina thought as she felt Judy's tongue connect with her protruding clitoris. Prolonging the action to milk every morsel of enjoyment from it, Judy began to lick Martina from just above her clit down to her anus. Moaning to herself, an abandoned Judy then slurped away at the fully exposed cunt. She lapped up Martina's juices, titillating her clit and probing her holes.

Lowering her head, Martina kissed and licked Judy's cunt. As Judy built to a climax, Martina held back her own orgasm.

When the last, gasping, groaning, moaning of a massive orgasm came from Judy, Martina lifted a leg and rolled to one side to stop straddling her and lie on the bed. Moving round and spread-eagling her legs so that Judy was looking directly up between them, Martina began to fondle her own cunt and flick her clit tantalisingly.

Recovering fast after having come so explosively, Judy turned onto her face so that her head was between Martina's knees. With Judy still in the grip of the clarity of thinking that comes immediately in the wake of orgasm, Martina was worried that this was the point when her conversion to girl-on-girl sex might falter. There was an awful, drawn-out moment in which Judy was unmoving. Then a startling sexuality seemed to suddenly burn through her like a fork of lightning. Moving upwards, her lips parted as she kissed the sweat-moistened skin of Martina's inner thighs, before pausing to inhale the glorious scents seeping from her hot, sweet cunt. Judy was saying something, mumbling and muttering inaudibly as her mouth travelled up over the fuzz on Martina's stomach.

Then Judy's head moved further up to suck a large nipple into her mouth. Martina moaned at the pleasure this gave her, but it wasn't enough. Desperate for Judy's kissing, she clasped her shoulders and eased upwards until Judy was lying full-length on top of her. Opening her legs, Martina arranged them into the missionary position, skin against skin. With a sultry expression flooding over her face as she used a quick wiggle of her shoulders to have her and Martina's erect nipples to brush together. The erotica of this simple movement had plunged Judy into a state of frantic arousal. Martina could tell that the intense feeling was a new experience for her – exhilarating and frightening at the same time.

Then they kissed, with Martina drinking at Judy's mouth, which tasted of something too exotic, too erotic – and too wonderful – to be described, as their bodies thrust rhythmically against each other. With their tongues entwining, Martina slid her hand down between their sweat-moistened stomachs. Using two fingers, she spread the lips of her cunt wide. Judy, a fast learner, reached a hand down to do the same to herself, and then they ground their open, creaming cunts together in synchronised thrusts.

Soaring up close to the point of no return, Martina broke the kissing, pleading with Judy to go down on her to make her come that way. Eager to oblige, Judy slid down Martina's writhing body. Feeling Judy's tongue opening her puffy lips; Martina reached down to clasp her head with both hands, the fingers entwining in her hair. From years of experience, Martina knew that as fast as Judy could lick away her cream-like substance, it would be replaced. The lovely odour of a woman always intensified as the outer lips of the opening curled back.

Thrusting her pelvis forward, Martina felt the morsel of flesh emerge from the folds at the top of her slit. Eyes closed, moaning in ecstasy, she felt Judy's head raise a little as she opened her mouth over Martina's projecting clitoris and clasped it between her lips. Martina began to make odd, strangulated half-screams as Judy sucked and chewed at her clit with lip-covered teeth.

For a first-timer, Judy was fantastic. Her top lip went over the clit, the softness of the lip and the hardness of her teeth against her clit driving Martina crazy even before Judy added the finishing touch by inserting her long tongue into her cunt.

Then Martina's hip thrusting changed into a frantic threshing, and she held Judy's face tight against her cunt. Head squeezed between two hot thighs, Judy continued to work her magic. Panting, mouth gaping wide, Martina then screamed loudly to mark the consummation of the most beautiful act in creation.

Afterwards, they lay side by side on the bed, bodies lightly touching, both of them lost in a vacuum of quieting emotions.

'I have a confession to make,' Judy said, breaking a long period of silence.

'This wasn't your first time with a woman?' Martina guessed.

'It was, cross my heart,' Judy replied earnestly. 'No, it concerns you, Marti. Yesterday I had the board agree to make you chief reporter.'

Pleased for two reasons – one being the promotion, the other that Judy had asked her out that evening under false pretences, Martina remained quiet for some time. Taking a deep breath, she said, 'Now it's my turn to confess, Marti. When I had the full story of the Vinnie Faulkner scandal, I was going to sabotage your position as editor by passing it to the *Herald*.'

Waiting for an angry response from Judy, which would end their brief relationship, Martina couldn't believe Judy's reaction.

'That would have upset everyone at the *Post*,' she giggled.

Believing that she hadn't grasped the full import of what she had said, and what it would have meant to her relationship with Gavin Wainwright, Martina added. 'It would have upset Gavin even more.'

'Gavin who?' Judy said with a laugh.

Both smiling, they turned to each other and embraced.

Low-cut
Clare Sudbery

I hardly even noticed her at first.

It's a new job, I've only been here a fortnight. I've been on my best behaviour, and she's only the accountant.

She seemed nice enough, but, all right, so I made assumptions about her. I expect accountants to be boring, I admit. And straight. And anyway, I was too busy trying to get my head around selling wigs for a living. Well, not just wigs. "Transvestite services" is how we described it privately, although never to the customer (most of them were heterosexual, and married). We sold a lot of padded bras, too. And extra-large women's shoes.

She was quite distant, and terribly businesslike. But not someone I paid attention to.

And then the first Friday, there was one of those after-work dos. Somebody's birthday, maybe. I can't even remember.

I'd had a couple of beers and I was at the bar, waiting for the barwoman to come back with my drink. It was very crowded, and I was leaning full forward with my elbows on the bar, my toes on the rail, trying to make myself taller.

She materialised silently behind me. I felt a little nudge at my elbow, so I turned, and...

How had I missed those eyes?

She was gazing right into me, with a wide-open smile and eyes for drowning in. Her whole face was opening up to me, and I could feel myself falling. It was like she was a different person. It was like love at first sight. Except, okay, so it wasn't first sight. Technically I'd seen her several times a day for the last week. But this was the first time I *saw* her. Because she chose to reveal herself to me. She knew exactly what she was doing.

I sank into those eyes, and didn't notice that she'd asked me a question.

"I said, can I get you anything to drink?"

"Oh, yes, sorry, er, pint of bitter, yes, that'd be lovely."

I struggled to remember her name as she waved a note in the face of the barwoman, who was turning round, a pint of bitter in her hand.

Sheila. Of course. Sheila. How could one pair of eyes have such devastating effect?

She was looking at me again, laughing, enquiring. She obviously knew what thoughts were in my head. She wanted to know if I would slip away somewhere with her, right now. She started to laugh.

The barwoman was saying something. "Two pounds fifty."

She was talking to me. The beer was for me.

"Do you always drink two pints at once?"

As Sheila spoke, she nudged her hand against my elbow, and I felt the hairs bristle along my arm.

Her mobile started ringing. She answered it, exchanged a few short words, hung up.

"Bugger," she said. "Got to go."

She started to leave, reached a hand out to wave goodbye.

"See you next week," she said.

I reached out and grasped the hand. She was already half out the door, but there was a throng of people and she was stuck in a bottleneck. There were people all around us, but that hand stayed in mine. She wasn't looking at me, she was half out the door, but her hand was in mine. Then one last squeeze, and she was gone.

I couldn't stop thinking about her all weekend. I swear I had felt the sex flow between those clasped hands. I couldn't wait for the following week. I fantasised about her, and masturbated constantly.

On Monday I couldn't take my eyes off her. Such a neat trim figure, such a carefully contained sexuality. She was measured and distant, just as she had been the previous week. She didn't make eye contact. I hadn't forgotten that look, but I was beginning to wonder whether I imagined the whole thing.

I was in the office that week. I spend a lot of time in the office. People think my job is glamorous, that I spend all my time in the company of zany transvestites. It isn't. I don't.

In the afternoon my phone rang, and it was her. She wanted to go over some of the figures for one of our bigger clients. She said she'd see me in the meeting room.

She was already there, standing with her back to me, writing on the whiteboard.

"Sit down," she said. I did. I prepared myself for some dull number-crunching, hunching my shoulders.

Once I was seated she turned and did it again. Wide eyes, big smile, and my heart fell through to my boots. I could feel myself grow wet. She turned back to the whiteboard, wiggled her bum and started to talk about sales projections for stockings and suspenders. All I could hear was my heart in my ears, and all I could see was the very discreet line of her knickers under the tight arse of her skirt. She stroked her hand along the line of her delicate neck. I could see the downy hairs. Without even thinking I raised my hand to my own neck, felt my own fur, shuddered at my own touch.

"Did you bring the report?" she asked.

I waved a pile of paper, wordlessly.

She came over to where I sat, stood close behind me and looked over my shoulder. She reached out to point at a chart.

"It's all about the figures," she said.

She leant forward with her hand on the table, her breasts brushing against my shoulder. I could feel her breath on my neck. I was soaking.

"Nice perfume," she said quietly.

"Thank you." My voice wasn't working. It came out as a feeble squeak. I cleared my throat and tried again. "It was a birthday present."

I was very aware of my office-white blouse, and the small percentage of cleavage that she must surely be able to see from her vantage point. As if reading my mind, she lifted her hand and reached down into my blouse. I stopped breathing.

She brushed her fingertips against the rounded swell at the top of my breast.

"You had a little something," she whispered in my ear.

But then she straightened and returned to the whiteboard, started talking about wigs. I wanted to scream at her, "Come back over here!" but I didn't.

After the meeting it took several wads of toilet paper before I was dry. I tried to have a wank in the cubicle, but it was no use, I was hypersensitive, I couldn't get a grip. I began to dream of her tongue.

The next day I wore a low-cut top and a push-up bra.

She suggested another meeting.

She was sitting down this time. I sat across at the other side of the broad table.

"Here," I said. "I brought you a copy this time."

I leant over the table with the sheaf of papers in my hand. Right over. She looked exactly where she was supposed to look, and let her eyes linger. I felt the come seep out onto my labia. She let her eyes lift and meet mine, smiled a lazy smile, then lowered her gaze back down to my breasts. I carried on leaning over. She carried on looking.

I had a sudden vision of her, behind me, lifting up my skirt.

She took the report from my hand. She reached into her pocket for a pair of glasses, and started to read. I sat back down again.

The following day, I wore a very short skirt. I called her through to the meeting room, making a detour to the toilet, where I removed my bra and undid another button.

I practised moving in front of the mirror. If I leant over in the right way, my nipple swung free. Oops.

I found her seated again.

"I just wanted to check these graphs with you," I said.

I placed a piece of paper on the table in front of her, leant over to point. My whole breast swung free and dangled by her right ear. The cool air on my nipple made it pucker. I wanted her to turn. My nipple was inches away from her mouth. All she had to do was turn…

She stood up, turning away from me. She spoke with her back to me. "Mr Frodsham asked me to talk to you about your clothing," she said. "He thought it might come better from a woman," she said.

I felt my heart double its speed, and my cheeks glowed red. I hastily tucked myself back into my clothing. I'd imagined the whole thing. She wasn't interested. She was probably straight. She was almost certainly embarrassed by my low-cut top. It was humiliating. I would have to leave my job, I couldn't possibly stay.

She turned to face me.

"You really are quite outrageous," she said. She looked directly at my breasts. I felt naked, and my cunt throbbed.

"Rather sexy actually," she said.

She moved towards me and raised her hands, as though she were going to do my buttons up for me. I wanted her to do it. Anything to have her hands on me, if only for a second.

"Well, I think we both know how inappropriate you've been," she said. "I hope you don't mind, but I volunteered to talk to you," she said. She lowered her hands and sat back down. "But anyway. About those false boobs."

As I leant back over the paper, she moved a pencil. It rolled over to the far side of the table. I reached out to retrieve it. I was stretched far across the desk, and almost certainly waving my carefully selected black G-string in her face. I felt a light touch on my thigh. Surely I was imagining it. No, there it was again. She was stroking the upper inside of my thigh, each stroke bringing her closer to my cunt.

I was spreadeagled across the desk, and suddenly I noticed a mirror on the opposite wall. Where the hell did that come from?

I could see her eyes in the mirror. I could also see my own breasts, straining against the opening of my blouse. I arched my back, and they fell free. A finger was tracing, closer and closer... until it found the edge of my labia. My nipples were hard. I moaned softly; I couldn't help myself.

She removed her hand and stood up. I didn't move.

She was behind me now, grinding her neat hips against my arse.

She wriggled my skirt up and over, and slipped her fingers under the waistband of my G string, pulling it slowly down. It was moistly welded to my cunt, and when she tugged softly to release it, I let out another moan. I leant into the desk and felt its cool surface against my nipples.

"This is really bad, you know," she said quietly as she slipped one finger against my clitoris. I gasped.

"I know," I said.

"You want it," she said.

"I do," I said.

Suddenly her voice changed. "Stand up!" she ordered.

My legs were weak. I stood up to face her. My skirt was around my waist. My breasts were adrift. I felt foolish. But her eyes were still mine. She came towards me.

"I think we'd better straighten you out," she said. She took a breast in each hand, and my body arched towards her. She tucked them back into my shirt, and buttoned me up. She pulled my skirt back down over my hips. She leaned down to the floor, picked up my knickers and tucked them into an envelope.

I couldn't move. I needed more. I couldn't even walk. I *needed* her touch.

"Come on then," she said, and gestured to the door.

I hobbled out, defeated.

"Leave the bra off, though," she said. "You'll drive Mr Frodsham wild."

I was in the toilet, fixing my make-up.

She slipped in behind me, stood behind me at the basin, her eyes pinpointing mine in the mirror. Her hand slipped up my skirt again. I was instantly wet.

"You little slut," she said. "No knickers," she said.

She brushed her lips against my neck. I had to hold onto the basin for support, it was such a shock to finally feel her mouth against my skin.

"There are other places it can go," said a voice.

Did *I* say that?

She reached around and slowly undid the top two buttons of my top. My head was pounding, and my blood was lapping my body with glee.

One hand snuck under, and cupped a breast. Just cupped it.

I wanted more. I wanted hands up cunts, tongues on nipples, hard, frantic sex.

There was a brief delicious squeeze on my nipple, and then suddenly she was kneeling down on the floor between my legs, and her tongue... oh, her tongue.

She circled me gently at first, until my moans reached a peak, and then she flickered back and forth over... oh yes, just there. Right there. In my mind my cunt swelled up and I could see it there, hovering, swelling, and all I could see, all I could feel was cunt cunt cunt but the best bit was that, yes that, the best bit of all with the pitiful scarcity of names.

I was worrying that somebody would come in and find us. I was thinking about how clitoris is wrong, all wrong, it's a *hub*, or a nub, it's the sweet concentrated centre of my being and it's hers, all hers and oh God I'm alive, with blood and sweat and electricity running along skin and through veins and round ears and don't stop yes *there*, like *that*, and with eyes on the mirror I see breasts, beautiful breasts, with nipples proud and alert, bobbing with our rhythm until there are stars behind my eyes and I can't see any more because *this – is – it*.

I couldn't keep my emotions to myself and I cried out loud, my lungs bursting to join with the climax and shout with the glory of it all.

I was leaning against the basin, panting, moaning, grinding, pulsing, basking in the afterglow.

She stood up, and I was bereft. I grabbed her hand and forced it hard against me, leaning the deep post-sex throbs into her arm.

She smiled at me in the mirror.

Then she pulled away, and started washing her hands.

At 4pm, a thunderstorm started. I was sitting at my desk, staring into space and sniffing my fingers.

The thunder was really extreme; the storm must have been right overhead. From the tenth floor we could see the sky flash, as the darkening clouds rolled across the city.

She came strutting past my desk, businesslike and brisk. "I need to ask you something," she said, and marched off through the office, not waiting for an answer.

I was out of my seat in an instant and rushing after her. I caught up with her at the fire escape. I held the door open for her and then she ran full tilt down the grey concrete stairs, which echoed with whoops and yells as we laughed our way down, emerging at the bottom flushed and breathless. I was a few steps behind and she grabbed me, pushing me hard against the wall where she forced soft lips onto mine and ate at me hungrily.

Her whole face smelt of my cunt.

She broke away and pushed down hard on the bar of the emergency exit. It led out into a small yard full of bins, cardboard boxes and rain.

It was pelting down, and the thunder was still rolling. She pushed me out into the yard, where I instinctively put my arms protectively over my head. It felt as though somebody was throwing buckets of water down over us. I cowered there for a moment, and then she came close and pulled my arms down. She placed hers around my waist and pulled my mouth deep into hers. The rain trickled down around my ears and onto my neck, and it felt like a caress.

Then her hands were under my blouse, searching and urgent. I still wasn't wearing a bra. She giggled as she struggled with buttons and then suddenly the rain was running down over my breasts. I felt a hunger for flesh. I needed to see her flesh.

She had on a wrap-over top, it was easy, too easy. Her breasts were small and cute, with gorgeous large brown aureoles and button-pert nipples. We held hands up high, our nipples touching, our eyes locked, and then she pushed me hard against a wall.

The thunder rolled as she pushed her hand hard into my cunt, biting my shoulders and neck. We were wet all over, glistening and loud. Everything boomed and I felt drunk on the front and the madness of it all.

She wore trousers, and my hand found her cunt but then she was pushing me down onto the ground, and my face was thrust close to her smell, and her deep wet warmth. With rain and thunder and tongues and shrieks the whole thing melted into one, until suddenly it was over and we were quivering together, cold and wet and laughing in each other's arms.

We stayed there, arms wrapped around each other, chuckling in the rain.

"Do you come here often?" I said.

She laughed and nibbled my nipple, and I relished the earthy primal creature that nestled in my arms, shedding its prissy skin.

"I've never been here before. But none of my colleagues oozed sex all over my books before."

"You're not bad for an accountant," I said.

"It's all about the figures," she said.

"That's what I figured," I said.

"Shut up," she said.

So I did.

Contributors

Ginger Allen is from New York City and currently lives in the Lower East Side of Manhattan. The founder and lead singer of the band Sister Sez, her music can be heard in the lesbian short film *Risk*, now playing at LGBT film festivals worldwide. Ginger wrote and produced the short polyamorous lesbian film *Open*, due to hit the LGBT film circuit in 2005/6.

Rachel Kramer Bussel (who can be reached on both www.rachelkramerbussel.com and lustylady.blogspot.com) serves as Senior Editor at *Penthouse Variations*. Her books include *The Lesbian Sex Book* (2nd edition), *Up All Night: Adventures in Lesbian Sex*, *Naughty Spanking Stories from A to Z*, and the forthcoming *Cheeky: Essays on Spanking and Being Spanked* and *Glamour Girls: Femme/Femme Erotica*. Her writing has been published in over 40 anthologies including *Best American Erotica 2004*, *Best Lesbian Erotica 2001, 2004*, and *2005*, and *Ultimate Lesbian Erotica* 2005, as well as in *AVN*, *Bust*, *Cleansheets*, *Curve*, *Diva*, *Girlfriends*, *New York Blade*, *On Our Backs*, *Oxygen.com*, *Penthouse*, *Rockrgrl*, *The San Francisco Chronicle*, *Velvetpark* and *The Village Voice*.

Louise Carolin is *Diva* magazine's deputy editor. She was born in 1966 and lives in London. Louise likes journalism, for which she gets paid, but has recently discovered a new enthusiasm for fiction, in which one gets to play fast and loose with the facts while still telling the truth. "Calendar Girls" is for everyone who's loved and lost and lived to tell the tale, and particularly L.W. who always laughs in the right place.

Crin Claxton is a writer and lighting designer. Her butch-femme vampire novel *Scarlet Thirst* was published by Red Hot Diva. She is currently working on the second book in the series.

Charlotte Cooper is a writerjournalistauthor who lives in the East End of London. She's also a zine-monkey and part-time corporate whore who will do anything for money. Charlotte is an associate editor of *Cheap Date* magazine and boss bitch of The Chubsters, a vicious girl gang. She wrote *Fat and Proud: The Politics of Size* and her first novel, *Cherry*, got busted by Canada Customs for obscenity. Her writing is all over the internet and in a bunch of books and magazines as well. She loves the smell of burnin' nitro down at the drag racing track. Everything is explained at www.CharlotteCooper.net.

Fiona Cooper is the author of a collection of short stories and eight novels, including *Rotary Spokes*, *Jay loves Lucy* and, most recently, the erotic novel *As You Desire Me*, published by Red Hot Diva. She has worked in journalism and performance and therapeutic education. She is fascinated by past lives, the meaning of the universe and jazz piano. She is a star-gazing chaser of rainbows with a serious champagne habit. Addicted to black and white movies, she has a weakness for Pingu and the Roadrunner. She draws inspiration from all of the above, and lives by the sea. Modern technology has finally reached Ms Cooper and her website can be found at fionacooperbiz.biz.

Yvonne Dale is 38 and lives in Dorset. She has a stroppy 20-year-old daughter (and can't think where she gets it from), two pussy cats and two degrees. She is presently writing a book and working at a credit union – that is, when she's not gossiping or buying shoes that are impossible to walk in.

Rita Das was born in Glasgow to Punjabi Bengali parents. She studied Medicine in Edinburgh before moving to London to study Medical Sociology and research lesbian health issues. Her passions include creative writing, food, yoga, cycling and humanism. She currently works in Emergency Medicine at a London NHS hospital where she also teaches yoga. She had her first public poetry reading this year at the Kiss (Asian & Middle Eastern Lesbian and Bisexual Support Group) Fifth Birthday Event.

Sunny Dermott lives in Wigton, Cumbria, with her partner and their three cats, five doors down from the pub where Melvyn Bragg was brought up. She loves cooking and dressing up in silly costumes. In her spare time, she is a civil servant.

Tanya Dolan is the author of two erotic novels, *High Art* and *Starburst*. She lives on the south coast and is currently researching a factual book on three prominent sexologists of the past.

Eli Donald just turned 30 – and survived with a vow to enjoy life to the full. She lives with her partner in her hometown of Glasgow and is working towards her dream of becoming a web designer.

Astrid Fox has assimilated. She now receives huge kickbacks from right-wing Christian organizations for her lectures on the dangers of queer erotica. From time to time she cracks and writes furtive pornographic books and stories, amongst them the novels *Rika's Jewel, Cheap Trick, Primal Skin, Snow Blonde* and *The Fox Tales* (a finalist for the Best Writer Erotic Oscar Award 2003) as well as stories published in *Sugar & Spice* 2, *Wicked Words, Wicked Words 4, Wicked Words 5, Wicked Words 10: The Best of Wicked Words, The Mammoth Book of Lesbian Erotica, Viscera: An Anthology of Bizarre Erotica, Best Bisexual Women's Erotica, Libida, The Best of Black Lace* and *The Best of Black Lace 2*. This is one of those times. Then she repents and goes on a private retreat at a little-known order with her very close friend Sister Wilgefortis.

Scarlett French feels very lucky. Originally from beautiful Aotearoa (New Zealand), she has chosen to settle in London for now, where she works a job she actually likes, lives with her partner and an irascible marmalade cat, and indulges her love of increasingly ridiculous shoes. She has written poetry for 17 years but recently discovered the joy of writing erotica. She is a rabid feminist, a social theorist and a chocolate connoisseur.

Frances Gapper probably ought not to have used her real name, especially as her girlfriend Sue objects to any kind of erotic writing. But it's too late now. Her first name is Jane, a fact that often confuses people, except other ex-Catholics.

Linda Innes was born in Liverpool and now lives on the North East coast, with her partner and teenaged daughter. She has been a teacher, creative writing tutor, performance poet, silver polish demonstrator, stand-up comedian and arts administrator. She currently works for a Local Education Authority. Her first writing accolade was winning a red-and-white plastic handbag for her seminal work, "Letter to Father Christmas". Since then she's had poetry published and short stories have appeared in Diva magazine and *The Diva Book of Short Stories*. *Smother* is her first novel, published by Diva in November 2001. A darkly comedic psychological thriller, it explores a relationship between two women. She is currently working on screenwriting and her second novel, *Bedtime*. "Tongue Deep" is her first foray into eroticism outside her own bed.

Shameem Kabir has worked in television and is the author of *Daughters of Desire: Lesbian Representation in Film*. Her short story "Switch" was published in the *Necrologue* collection and the story found in *Va-Va-Voom*, "In and Out of Time", was the title story in the anthology edited by Patricia Duncker and published by Onlywomen Press in 1990. Part I, "In Time", is reproduced here by the kind permission of Lilian Mohin (in the original, two additional sections follow: "Out of Time" and "Time"). Shameem can reached on the following email: ShameemKb@aol.com.

Kathi Kosmider's short stories have been published in *Wicked Words 5* and in *Necrologue: The Diva Book of the Dead and the Undead*. She is working on a novel called *Coat* about her father's experiences in a German P.O.W. camp from 1939 to 1945.

Isabelle Lazar is a scathingly sexual scribe whose sultry writings have traversed the globe through dozens of publications including: *Philogyny: Girls Who Kiss and Tell*, *Early Embraces II*, *Skin Deep: Real-Life Lesbian Sex Stories*, *The Lesbian News*, *The Harrington Lesbian Fiction Quarterly*, *Unlimited Desires: An International Anthology of Bisexual Erotica* (BiPress), *Set in Stone: Butch On Butch Erotica*, *The Mammoth Book of Lesbian Erotica*, *Wet: True Lesbian Sex Stories*, and electronically on www.butch-femme.com.

V.G. Lee has written two novels – *The Comedienne* and *The Woman in Beige*. She is also a poet and short story writer. At present she is completing a collection of linked short stories. Working title: *The Visiting Hour*. You can find her on www.vglee.co.uk.

Winsome Lindsay is a repatriated Jamaican, happily relocated to her birth country after a thirteen-year sojourn through the United States. These days she spends the bulk of her days writing and watching the wind move through the leaves of the tamarind tree in her front yard. She can be reached at winsome_lindsay@yahoo.com.

Rosie Lugosi (www.rosielugosi.co.uk) has an eclectic writing and performance history, ranging from singing in 80s Goth band The March Violets to her current incarnation as Rosie Lugosi the Vampire Queen, electrifying performer, compere and singer. She is also Organisatrix of the infamous fetish event, Club Lash. She has won both the Erotic Oscar for Performance Artist of the Year and was runner up for the Diva Award for Solo Performer. As well as three collections of poetry and numerous short stories, her first single "Death and Destruction" was released on Switchflicker Records in 2004.

Ape McCabe grew up a child of the 60s/70s in a commune, where her main chores were feeding the chickens, mucking out the pigs, and learning all she wanted to know about sex by listening at doors and retrieving sticky sex mags from under the single guys' beds. As a teenager, she found out about real life when she hung with the gay guys out the back of the local drama club. She owes her exquisite taste in accessories to those rough, raw days. Ape is currently working on a piece about the horrific, life-shattering effects of cheese addiction, entitled *Tyrophilia, Mon Amour*.

Sophie Neon-Blanc was born in 1974 in Corsica, but moved to London as a teenager, where she studied at stage school, until being expelled for reading lewd poetry at the end-of-year recital. She has worked as a writer for underground and socialist presses and has had several stories rejected by lots of book publishers. She lives in a squat in Hoxton with her pet iguana, Amber. She has never kicked a football, but has enjoyed lots of casual sex.

Elena Moya Pereira was born in the Mediterranean town of Tarragona, Spain. After graduating in Journalism at the Universidad de Navarra, in Pamplona, she worked for *El Periodico de Catalunya* in Barcelona. In 1994, she won a Fulbright scholarship to study an MA in financial journalism at the University of Nevada, Reno, Nevada, in the US. She now works as a reporter for a financial news agency in London.

Bethia Rayne has worked as an English teacher and as a project co-ordinator and researcher of poverty, social exclusion and women's health issues in Glasgow and London, as well as abroad in Borneo, Egypt, Finland and the USA. Although also a volunteer for numerous organisations supporting gay men and women in the UK and abroad, and an aid worker in the City of the Dead in Cairo and Kampong Ayer in Brunei, when she's broke (which is frequently) she works as an artist's model and as a kept woman – ladies only! Currently, she is managing a small library and working on her Master's degree in librarianship. She wrote her first erotic short story as part of a workshop for would-be writers organised by the Glasgay festival, and ended up reading the story aloud in Borders bookshop. Needless to say, the small audience had swelled considerably by the end of the reading.

Helen Sandler was writing for gay men's skin mags under the name Jim Hardacre by the time she turned 21. After a ten-year apprenticeship she was ready to face the picky lesbian public with a rude and fleetingly infamous book called *Big Deal* (Sapphire/Virgin, 1999). Her second novel, *The Touch Typist* (Diva Books, 2001), is less rude – apart from a steamy transatlantic cyber affair. Helen has edited three anthologies of (non-erotic) short stories, two of which have won Lambda Literary Awards – *The Diva Book of Short Stories, Groundswell*, and *Necrologue: The Diva Book of the Dead and the Undead*. Visit www.helensandler.co.uk if you believe authors' websites are a rewarding source of further reading.

Cherry Smyth is Irish and lives in London. Her collection of poetry, *When the Lights Go Up* was published by Lagan Press in 2001. *Damn Fine Art by New Lesbian Artists* appeared in 1996, Cassell. She is also the author of *Queer Notions,* Scarlet Press, 1992. Other adventures of "Androula and I" appear in previous Diva anthologies and short fiction is published in *Chroma: The Queer Literary Journal* and in the *Anchor Book of Irish Short Stories*, 2001.

During **Clare Sudbery**'s 35 years on this planet she has been a lesbian, a bisexual, a Scrabble fanatic, a revolutionary socialist, a vegetarian women-only workers' co-op member and a meat-eating heterosexual computer programmer. She loves to talk and write about sex, but she can't be bothered doing it. She lives in inner city Manchester, in a decrepit house with bits of old ship in the cellar, a dismembered shop dummy in the garden, a toddler in the cot and a journalist in the bed. People hardly ever spell Clare's name right. It's Clare, like bare. And it's Sudbery, like surgery or carvery. Think sharp, think knives. Clare's first novel, *The Dying of Delight*, was published by Diva Books in May 2004. Her website is regularly updated: www.claresudbery.co.uk

Helen Taylor has written poems since a kid, and has had a few published. She's done hundreds of different jobs, and has lived in London, Australia, Thailand and Indonesia. She finally landed six years ago in Yorkshire, where she seems to have absorbed the landscape and processed it back out as *Black Moor* – a full-length novel based on the character of Chris Lyon, which hopefully will be finished by Christmas. "The Path" was of the first ventures into exploring Chris Lyon's character. Helen lives on her own, in a big house in Yorkshire with two cats, and a nice view of the moors. Oh, and she does a lot of scuba diving...

Monica Trasandes writes fiction, screenplays and plays. She recently completed her first novel, *Born Ugly: How I Accidentally Became a Trophy Wife*. Her short stories have been published in several literary anthologies including *The Sun*, *The Green Mountains Review* and the *VIVA* anthologies of 1999 and 2000. Several of her plays have been produced in Los Angeles, including "Vacation," about a lesbian and a straight couple grappling with "love, sex and other problems." Born in Uruguay, South America, she moved to the United States as a child and grew up in Southern California. She earned a B.A. in International Relations from U.C. Santa Barbara and a Master of Fine Arts degree in Creative Writing from Emerson College in Boston. Professionally, she has served as the editor-in-chief of Frontiers Newsmagazine since 1996. She is a founding member of the theatre group Playwrights 6, and a member of several professional organizations, including the National Lesbian and Gay Journalists Association.

Julie Travis, 37, has her horror fiction widely published in the British science fiction and slipstream small press, including *The Third Alternative*'s award-winning anthology *Last Rites and Resurrections* and the Lambda award-winning Diva collection *Necrologue*. Born and raised in London, she now lives in West Cornwall, where she recently held her first exhibition of black-and-white photography. She is seeking a publisher for her novel, a dark fantasy involving magick, genderfucking and the end of the world. Find her at www.darkworlds.chaosmagic.com.

Larry Tritten is a veteran freelance writer (*Scriptor horribilis*) whose work has been published in *The New Yorker, Harper's, Vanity Fair, Playboy, Travel & Leisure, National Geographic Traveler* and *Cosmopolitan*, amongst other periodicals. He has been called, at one time or another, a science fiction writer, a writer of erotica, a humor writer and a travel writer. He's done it all.

Wynona B. Verr has poured the experiences of an inquisitive teenage and louche quarter-age into erotic writing. A number of her stories have appeared on the country's leading lesbian and gay webzine, *Rainbow Network*, for which she was a channel editor, and a more sober piece (long-listed in the Spectrum Awards 2004) appeared recently in the award-winning *Necrologue*. She has been an occasional contributor to *Diva* magazine since October 2002.

Robyn Vinten came to England from New Zealand in the mid-80s and forgot to leave. She lives in an unfashionable part of north London with the neediest cat in the world. She plays football, tennis and, despite her advancing years, has taken to doing triathlons. She has three stories in various Women's Press anthologies and three previous stories in Diva anthologies.

Having enjoyed a dirty bassline for years thanks to her dj-ing career, **Kate Wildblood** stumbled into writing dirty words in 2003. Until now, nothing made it past the eyes of her closest mates, although she has managed to squeeze out the words all journalist-like for *Dj Magazine, Diva magazine, Queercompany.com, Rainbow Network* and *G-scene* since 2000. A Brighton import, Kate loves the joy the mix of dj-ing and writing brings to her life. Like the house music she plays, she intends to keep her fiction filthy from now on. If her missus doesn't mind!

Fiona Zedde is a transplanted Jamaican lesbian currently living and working in Atlanta, Georgia. She spends half her days as a starving artist in the city's fabulous feminist bookstore (Charis Books and More) and the other half chained to her computer working on her second novel and on an endless collection of bent and dirty stories that she hopes to get published some day. If you see her, please don't make jokes about her getting a life. She might bite. Those starving artist types tend to do that. Fiona can be reached at blue_knightshade@yahoo.com.